I0699706

Hollow Roots

J.J. Jensen

Mind Punk Publishers

To Grandpa J, for whom nature cured all ailments.

Book I: Needle & Bottle

Mind Punk Publishers

Gaze no more in the bitter glass
The demons, with their subtle guile,
Lift up before us when they pass,
Or only gaze a little while;
For there a fatal image grows
That the stormy night receives,
Roots half hidden under snows,
Broken boughs and blackened leaves.

W. B. Yeats, "The Two Trees"

I

— · —

Under Again

REDDING IS A FATTY growth, a pimple ready to burst over the pristine ridgelines and forestland surrounding Mount Shasta. Redding greases up, and Em, who prefers a leaner diet, tapers back down.

Not that the town didn't try to fatten her up. Two months serving at an Applebee's advanced a small claim over her body. She retched at first at the overburdened plates she served, the half-eaten plates she returned, but as her body relearned to absorb minerals and cell-building aminos, she tucked it all in—the plates no longer seemed so heavy. Her hips flared and spilled over the sides of her jeans, and an old friend returned: her pot belly, born in a flourish at thirteen but raised in captivity shortly after, where it withered and died. Her new pot was still very small, but it stuck out perfectly round against her shirt like she had swallowed a coconut whole. Staring down at it, wondering if it would grow anymore, left her warm and glowing.

Then Andre arrived and lit a cooktop under her. A cooktop set low to let the fat slowly render and dribble away.

Her old diet resumes in the Applebee's parking lot on a warm April night, around the back of the dumpsters, sheltered in shadow. A message of family—a sad message, of families bound with rubber bands—tries to shine from the restaurant, but it can't reach them where they stand. It must be the sadness that drew Andre here. He thought the restaurant would provide clientele.

Em's rarely drawn to the rougher sex, as she likes to think of them, but for Andre—skin like velvet upholstery, eyes a muscle relaxer—she'll make an exception. I'll happily recline into your chaise-longue skin, she thinks. She does, for a long night or two. No wildness—not even any clothes removed—just a steadfast, warm embrace. One prick from the needle and you don't need any more than that: the whole world embraces you.

When she's under, the sun-bleach of the streets feels like gentle watercolor; sober, she can see the caustic radiation rising from the pavement to scramble her brain. She quits Applebee's but still goes to Group and lies about quitting Applebee's. She sees Andre again; she stops going to Group. The days are long now. One late afternoon she rolls over in bed and drums her fingers over her ribcage. She reaches down and finds a cavity: her pot belly is gone. Somewhere in the intervening months, the needle killed it again.

This cannot continue, of course. Redding's dead in the water, Andre tells her. All the stimulus money is gone; the dealers have started dealing to each other. It's going to get violent soon. We need to go where the market is scarce, where pockets of cash are few but deep.

The "we" strikes her. It is a comfort except for times like now when she is sober and thoughts of change are blowing about. It is an infectious disease, change. She always catches it quickly and then just as quickly spreads it around against all will. "Hit the coast," she blurts out, hoping it will shut him up. "All those little towns between Eureka and Newport, prime real estate... yeah, I know no one's buying homes. But some of the homeowners had to already be there, to have a little wealth squirreled away. Others will follow them. You'll have no trouble finding something they want to buy, and you can get in early."

She is cutthroat on the come down; the edge makes her tactical, guarded, like she has doubled her age. Two months of true sobriety left her shuffling and fuzzy like she was fourteen again. Why had she left?

Andre, meanwhile: quiet, thoughtful, respectful: always, always. Dangerously so. He takes her seriously. He researches coastal towns online; he plots a course. She has spread the sickness deep into his lungs. Redding is a blight, but it moves slowly, and it is where she is. The ocean never stops moving. If she gets too close it might pick her up and carry her back to Glendale, where she won't get to choose whether she acts forty or fourteen.

There are few takers in Newport. Coos Bay has the tight collar of the law clasped over it. Klamath is a radar blip. Helped by their last big sale to a budding dorm dealer in Bend, Andre trades in his beat-up Corolla for an old camper van. Em, in a moment of masochism, names her Fiona. Who is Fiona? Andre asks. Em lies and tells him she named the van after her favorite aunt. To speak the truth would only cause them both to suffer.

They park Fiona in RV campgrounds and draw the curtains of her rear windows; inside, they prick and prick and span light years over the course of an afternoon. Or, depending on which side you look at it from, they churn afternoons into a few bleak minutes.

Fiona is a comfort as the days start to shorten again, and coastal winds send a chill through their bones; the winds cut through holes in Fiona's carriage, but they have heaps of blankets, a gift left in storage from the previous owner. When they are under, they pay the cold no mind. Christmas comes and goes without them noticing. They go under more often. The supply, unsold, starts to dwindle.

They try wintering illegally on national forest land. They will live off the land, Andre says. One problem: Andre cannot tell a juniper from a jade fern; Em knows even less. After a month, she sprouts little white hairs up and down her arms. The supply is now so low that if she were to take all of it, as small and emaciated as she is, she would still not overdose. "We need to eat," she says to Andre, cornering him against Fiona's back. "We're better off driving to some town and foraging a dumpster."

They drive to some town. Andre is still warm and patient, but he is diminished somehow. His muscle-relaxer eyes droop and lose focus; they have become so soft that they are in danger of dribbling out of his head.

A few miles from their destination—a small coastal town neither of them has heard of—Fiona sputters, rolls to a stop, and dies. Another one gone, Em thinks. Andre says he will walk into town to find a tow truck, but Em grabs him by the shirt and whispers, "Let her go, beau. She's old. I think she's more worn down than us."

They gather what they can from the old girl and walk down a service road that appears to lead nowhere: a thick wall of fog obscures their path. They walk through the fog for almost an hour. They nearly give up and turn around. Then Andre spots a wooden sign on the other side of the road, one so weather-worn that half the slats are missing. The sign faces the side of the street leading to the highway, back from where they just came. The faded letters lack enthusiasm, but the still intact message is friendly enough.

"We hope you enjoyed your stay in Rabbit Warren Cove!" the sign says. "Don't be a stranger," it pleads.

"You talk to her."

"Why do I have to talk to her?"

"Because you're... I don't know. Because you're nicer than I am. I'm too hungry and strung out to be nice. I'll probably try to rip her head off and drink her blood."

They approached the diner because it was the only spot they'd seen in town showing signs of life. Not the front entrance, at first; Em was serious about the dumpster diving, and a hulking vessel in the shadows of the adjacent alley offered promise. It will be like when we first met, she tried to joke, but the delivery was off. Andre chuckled regardless. The chuckle was dry and raspy, not imbued with his usual baritone. It was more like a clearing of the throat.

The dumpster in the alley must have just been cleared for the day: it was empty; it did not even give off much of a smell. Now they stand inside the diner near the front entrance, making themselves small—an easy feat, in their current condition—as servers flit by in the crowded space. There's no host they can see, but there is a bar near the entrance, and behind it stands a woman surveying the cheerful, bubbling chaos. She is almost as tall as Andre, and her skin is like his, too, though a bit more worn, like tanned leather. Her hair is tied over one shoulder in a neat double braid. The braid shines with threads of silver.

That's the owner, Em told Andre when she first spotted her. She could not explain how she knew, but her confidence convinced him.

They walk up to the bar together, though Em hangs back a bit, gnawing on her cheek to simulate some sustenance. The woman behind the bar invites them to sit—the barstools are nearly filled with seats, but a few patrons shift down a seat so the couple can sit together. "What can we get you, sugar pie?" the woman asks Andre. He's still got it, even as worn down as he is. Reserves of charm; years of it, Em guesses. Older women, she has noticed, are especially drawn to him.

"We were wondering if we could grab a table if that's all right."

The owner wants to oblige him. She scans the diner for any tables being cleared. "I'll keep an eye out, but I don't know if anything will open up for another hour. You can eat at the bar if you want."

"Yeah, we could do that." He winces; a kick to the shins is the cause. Em gives him a look that says, "Sitting at the bar is too obvious. We'll be caught for sure."

The damage is already done. The owner passes them two menus and introduces herself as Selma. Selma, but you can call me Sel. Especially you, Em imagines Selma thinking, as an aside to Andre. You can call me Sel anytime.

They stare at their menus, feigning indecision, even though they could probably eat any item listed. Any item or all of them. At the same time, Em is terrified at the thought of eating. She wishes the needle was enough to sustain her, though she reminds herself soon that will no longer be an option, either.

Selma comes back to them after several minutes. She seems to sense their apprehension. "Been a while since you had so many options, I take it?"

They freeze, unsure of how to respond.

"You're a long way from the PCT," she continues. "Did you get lost?"

The PCT? After a moment, Em pieces it together: the heavy backpacks nestled between their knees, the blankets collected from Fiona rolled and tied over the top. No junkies here, just a couple of college students on an extended break who tried to find themselves on a long-haul trail, started too late, and got themselves stuck in deep. She decides to shift the strategy. "We did get lost around Redding," she says before Andre can speak up. She thinks, it's not technically a lie—and as the comedown creeps up behind her, it feels less and less like one. "We knew which way the coast was, at least, so we followed a few roads and found our way here."

Selma turns her head quickly to look at Em, as though she is seeing her for the first time. "I was beginning to think you were mute," she says.

Not mute, just starving. There is only so much strength for words. "I'll be honest, ma'am," Em says, "we ran out of food a while ago. We haven't eaten in days. And, well..." she feels sweat forming on her forehead, her cheeks, her upper lip; she hopes

Selma mistakes it for tears. "We don't have any way to pay for a meal."

Selma is silent for a moment as the diner murmurs around her. The straightforward approach failed, Em thinks: we're back out on the street to scrounge. But then, Selma seems to accept it. She nods.

"I don't give anything for free," Selma says. She barely opens her mouth when she speaks and clips her consonants short. Shorter, it seems, when she is talking to Em. "You'll eat, first. It looks like you need to. Order whatever you want. Then you can get some rest upstairs—I have an apartment above the restaurant. But when you feel up to it, I have work for you."

They order and they eat, though not as much as they think they will. Andre orders eggs and toast and a coffee. He nibbles the toast and sips the coffee to help it slide down his constricted throat. For Em, it's those first days at Applebee's all over again: she is like a vampire who can eat human food if she chooses, but she won't get far without her nightly infusion.

The apartment is a single room with one narrow bed and a sagging couch. A bathtub with a showerhead but no curtain, a radiator that pops and rattles against the chill and the fog outside. The couch is too short for Andre to stretch out on, but he insists Em take the bed. It makes her a little sick, the sweetness, the unnecessary sacrifice. She tries to sleep, but the bed is too soft, and the noisy radiator sets her on edge. Above her, a ceiling fan spins and creates a useless breeze. She wants to turn it off but lacks the will to reach for the chain or find a switch.

She thinks, Andre, make yourself useful, reach up with all that tallness and kill that fan. But Andre is worse off than she is. He has folded into himself on the couch, barely covering half of it. He shivers and drips with sweat. Em remembers, months and months ago, Andre telling her he did not use. You don't, she said, and you think it's okay to be my pusher and my lover? That settled it for Andre. And between then and now, there has been no comedown for him. No comedown, ever.

She did this. She did all of it; it does not matter who walked up to who; she, like the moon, set the tide to swell. She supposes that Fiona did the same to her, not the broken-down van but her namesake—who is also, Em imagines, breaking down right now, what is left of her feeding the worms and helping the sycamores of Glendale grow tall. But then she changes her mind: never the victim, not this girl; if not for her, Fiona might still be walking around. She erodes shorelines. She is steadfast, and all the coastal towns and the humans who occupy them will eventually succumb to her.

Why fear the ocean, then? Well, there is still the capacity to fear yourself.

Em kneels before Andre, places a gentle hand on his knee, and says, "You've got to use, Beau. It'll get worse before it gets better. If the owner sees you this way, she'll know we're not a couple of hippy hikers."

"Wh-what about you?" He sounds like a wounded animal, moaning his words out. He is thinking, there is not enough for them both for it to break through the symptoms of withdrawal. He is probably right.

"I'll be fine," Em says. "I'm a professional."

She finds the kit in her backpack and unravels the rubber tubing. Taps out the powder onto a silver soup spoon. There is just enough left to dose him properly, she thinks. The spoon is impractical for a single dose—it's impractical for soup, Em thinks, you can barely get your mouth around it—but it's all she has right now. It's all she has ever had. Fiona stole it from the rectory at St. Stephen's as a parting gift, a symbol of their escape from ecclesiastical bondage. From one bondage to another, Em thinks. The spoon has a priest or maybe a monk etched inside its bowl, a robed and bearded man raising a lamp to ward off the dark. The holy man has seen a lot of darkness since St. Stephen's: years of cooking have tarnished his surroundings. He stands in defiant relief, growing more distinct, more confident of his righteousness, every time the powder boils over him.

Andre senses what Em is doing. He reaches out an arm—to accept the dose, Em thinks at first, but when she goes to tie him off, he waves her away. "I can't," he says. "How do you deal with this? I can't let this happen again."

"I guess it hasn't been so bad for me." Withdrawal is Hell, but she and Hell have an agreement. It's familial turf, somehow. She may not like it, but sooner or later, it's the only place that will take her back.

"I need to get clean." There's an edge to Andre's voice. Maybe for the first time.

"Sure, Beau, we'll get there." Though she wants to say, you can't: you can't leave me here alone with my infernal relatives. "Right now, we need to function. So that we can figure out the next step."

"No, I need to get clean now." Harder this time, more tapped into that wounded animal. He launches from the couch, bent over, stumbling, reaching for the apartment door.

"And where are you going to get clean, huh? You think there are any clinics in this tiny-ass town? Any methadone?" She is shouting. She didn't think she would with him. "You think anyone around here knows how to deal with your junkie ass?"

"I'm not a junkie."

"Well, you sure look like one." There is that change again, finding new ways for you to catch it, mutating just enough to keep circulating the globe.

He paws at the door, howls at it. Eventually, the animal breaks free and runs down the stairs.

Just her and the needle, then. And the needle wants to give her a kiss.

2

The Humboldt County Yeti

A DARK PATCH STAINS the pavement where the old boy rolled to sleep last night, and he thinks: poor lad, he's probably wet himself from fear.

The oily patch is the only sign Ol' Blue Eyes was ever here: no scattered gems from a broken side window, no burnt rubber, just the leavings of a seeping oil pan. The old boy's been abducted without much fuss.

Jonathan's room is on the second floor of the motel. He can make out three other cars in the motel parking lot from the landing. If there are more, the early-morning fog obscures them. Did any of their owners hear the roar of an engine in the small hours of the morning? Did the cars notice anything? He listens. They speak to him sometimes, not with words but through their rust spots, their calcified tailpipes, their balding tires: the cars tell tales of abuse and neglect, of nights spent cold under a whirring overpass.

This morning, the cars have nothing to say. Instead, a gentle breeze carries a voice through the fog. It's a voice from his childhood, one that others couldn't hear. Patches of speech emerge from static, like a poorly tuned radio station. He can't quite piece together a message, but the familiar voice raises the hair on his neck.

Jonathan tries to shake it off; he stumbles back into the murk of his motel room, looking for missing pieces from the night before. The car keys—which he unconsciously places on the righthand bedside table of every motel room he stays in—are missing. Ten minutes of frantic upturning of furniture and bed linens don't produce them. A simple theft: a burglary, technically; no hotwiring required. There's no sign of forced entry, no broken windows. But the room appears ransacked: clothing is strewn about, including, mysteriously, a pair of lace thong panties wadded into a ball at the foot of the bed. The bathroom is worse: a dense film smears the mirror, and the counter is littered with empty miniatures. Someone has lifted the tank lid from the toilet and placed it over the sink. The lid is dusted with a fine white powder, with fingerprints stamped into it here and there. Slender prints from dainty hands. One skinny white line of powder remains and seems to point at him like an arrow. That'll clear out the cobwebs. He takes a straw from an empty glass, shakes it dry, and snorts the arrow up his nose.

Not a burglary, then. He welcomed the abductor into the room with open arms.

He picks his way through the clutter, rights furniture, scoops up discarded clothes. The touch of wood and fabric, with the help of the cocaine, conjures a memory. He sees the abductor, his nighttime companion: a pale woman built mostly of sinew but with some strategic fortifications of silicone and collagen; her mouth is pillowed, which does little to soften its cruelty. The cruel mouth mimes a cruel laugh. She's laughing at his nakedness, at his penis lying limp against the side of one leg. He can barely stay standing or keep his eyes open. She drove them here; he would have insisted. If not, Ol' Blue-Eyes would be wrapped around a redwood off the side of the road, and if he were lucky, he would not be alive to see it.

He wakes up some more and the room becomes crowded. Decades of motel guests and housekeeping staff mill about, layered like painted figures on a canvas reused many times. Behind the abductor, or more accurately, beneath her, he sees Mina. This must be a memory too, because she looks like he remembers her, like no time has passed. Hair like a woolly black sheep, faint freckles dusting her cheeks and nose. She also laughs, but not out of cruelty. He's probably said something foolish. There's a sadness in the laugh, too: a weariness.

Mina's ghostly appearance tells him he stayed here once before, long ago. In the same room, no less. He must have packed that memory in brine and sealed it tight for it to surface only now. The rush from the cocaine helps, but he thinks the memory would have stayed hidden, possibly forever, if he had not returned to the scene of the crime.

He'll do well to leave this room and get on with his day. Too many ghosts, living and dead. Just a few miles to the west, the redwoods part before a small cove, and around that cove, there's a town. He was on his way there for a job when distraction called for him. Flashing lights in the wooded dark: flashing lights, whirring alarms, clinking glasses. A roadside watering hole, maybe. That must have been where he met his thief.

It's no more than a fifteen-minute drive to the cove from here, but on foot along a dark and narrow, wooded county road, it will likely take hours. No chance of a taxi for miles. Best get moving. He's left many things in Ol' Blue-Eyes better kept in a hotel-room safe: earnings to see him through the week, a defaced Ruger he bought at a gun show in Modesto, a pre-paid cell phone. He suspects he'll have to pay for the room. He pulls one of his boots from its resting place under the bed and reaches into it, down to the toe. His emergency cache is still there; a tight roll of bills, no thicker than a cigar, is wedged where the tip and the sides of the boot meet.

He dislodges the roll, gathers the clothes into his rucksack, and does his best to wipe away the more incriminating remnants from the bathroom. (One more pinch off the tank lid while he's at it to make the walk bearable.) It's grown lighter outside by half a shade. He swears the congregation in his room waves goodbye to him as he shuts the door, but it must be a trick of the light. They are only impressions; they've never responded to him before.

The breeze catches him again as he walks downstairs to the motel office. The voice on the breeze is more distinct now; he can make out a phrase or two. Forget about the car, the voice says. That old metal slug has only slowed your passage. Static garbles the rest of the message, but a few orphaned words make their way through.

Patience.

A child.

Home.

Things he's given up on having.

The motel gives a log cabin impression from the outside, its siding built from long semicircles of redwood. The office interior, with its fake teak paneling and dim yellow light, reveals the lie of that impression. A desk clerk sits behind plexiglass, thumbing a magazine. He's stretched and ashen like a sequoia; if not for his long, greying beard and curly locks falling well past his shoulders, Jonathan would suspect he was looking in a mirror. And the nametag pinned to his chest distinguishes things, too: Roy, no last name, no position.

"Checking out," Jonathan says before trying to clear his throat. His voice sounds thin and alien.

Roy looks up from his magazine. His eyes are not Jonathan's eyes; they are kind and the color of a clear spring day. The kindness winks out when Roy recognizes who's come in.

"Your girlfriend left early," he says. "Said she had an appointment but would be back for you soon. Said you'd settle up."

"She's not my girlfriend, and I don't think she's coming back."

"That's a shame." Roy quickly moves on from the gesture; he's already turned to his computer, assessing how much last night's activities will cost. "That'll be $420," he says. "Did you want to pay with your card on file, Mr. Johnson?" Dry emphasis on the "mister," suggesting Jonathan does not deserve the title.

"Four hundred twenty dollars? For a shitty motel in the middle of the woods?" Jonathan hears himself shouting. The dope's kicking in now; with it, everything rises a decibel or two.

"Now, now," Roy says, "no need for name-calling." He's a placid sort, Roy the clerk, an aging hippy from the look of it: a true Humboldt County stalwart. Probably has a couple of stalks of cannabis hidden among reeds on an acre or two not far from here; maybe he owns this shitty motel. Either way, he's probably used to strung-out travelers trying to ruin his Zen. "You and your not-girlfriend cleared out the minibar," he explains. "Maybe you didn't notice the warning printed on the side? It's all managed by sensors: you pull a bottle out, it gets charged to your room right away."

"That hardly seems fair. What if I changed my mind and put the bottles back?"

Roy gives him a cold smile. "You didn't put them back."

"Fine. We had a party," he says. With enough refreshments for a crowd of fifteen, except no one else showed up. "I can't use a card," he says. "I have enough cash to cover it." The card—his only card—is a formality. He needs it to access places like this or hop on a flight—not that he goes anywhere a flight would require. He tries to minimize his paper trail.

Roy chuckles a low, dusty rumble. He says, "No can do, brother. Credit cards only. In case there is any damage to the room."

"There's got to be another way. I'm guessing you own this place?"

"I'm a partner. That's very astute of you."

"And a partner can call some shots, right? Make a few executive decisions? Let's assume there are damages. Let's assume the worst. What would it take?"

The old hippy strokes his beard and smiles. He seems amused by the prospect. "Seven hundred should cover it," he says. "Assuming you didn't burn the room down."

Jonathan pulls out his emergency stash and starts counting bills. The whole roll unfurls, lying flat in his hand. "Will you take $680?"

Roy nods. "Pleasure doing business with you," he says. The stack of bills slides through a slit in the plexiglass. As it leaves

Jonathan's grip, he feels a sudden release of pressure: no Blue Eyes, no cash: just a rucksack with four changes of clothing, a toothbrush, a deck of cards worn ragged around the edges; a flask, running on empty; and a fraying but still reliable pocket atlas of California. He feels he could float onto National Forest land and reappear only as a rumor, a Humboldt County yeti.

Still, he knows himself. The empty flask will need to be refilled. In the woods, sweaty and sick within a day, within an hour, he will not last. "How far to the coast?" He asks.

"About a 20-minute drive if the weather's good," Roy says. "In this fog, I'd say more like 30."

"How about on foot?"

Roy looks toward the door. Like he's waiting for an overdue guest to arrive. He is silent for so long that Jonathan thinks he doesn't hear the question. "I don't recommend it," Roy says, finally. "In the fog, you'll lose the road, then you'll get turned around and..." he looks away; he's calculating, it seems, the value of Jonathan's life. "Or do what you want. You could always hitch. But people don't pick you up like when I used to do it."

"Thanks," Jonathan says. "I'll take my chances."

He starts to walk. He doesn't see how he could lose the road; the trees hedge him against its shoulder. No break in the redwoods except the artificial line the road cuts through them. The road is quiet. A few minutes from the motel, he starts to breathe deeper. He has space to ponder. The places built from wood are the ones that carry the most ghosts: the lumber skeletons absorb them all, maybe as a kind of exchange: one mortal husk for another. He wonders if the trees, as they are felled and dissected into building materials, their return to the earth delayed by human hands—he wonders if these trees invite the dead to them to commiserate. We are both made from the pain of your kin, they say to the ghosts. Let's wait out our slow rot together.

The living trees will carry voices, too, like Jonathan's old childhood friend. The voices are not quite human, but he prefers them to the ghosts. The redwoods enjoy singing: a seven-part chorus follows him as he walks. He can't make out any words, but the message of the music is clear: it evokes calm, openness, and non-judgment. He starts to hum the tune. He closes his eyes and drifts into the road. When he opens his eyes again, a wall blocks his path. Set into the wall is an old fire door, the kind warehouses used to have. He knows this door but has never seen it closed. With some effort, he slides it open. He leaves the trees and fog and sees entire constellations above him.

She tells him it took six hours to get the stars just right after they leave the show. Lots of grunting up and down a ladder. During the show, she lets him believe it was effortless.

Two prodigies stand together in one room, the envy of seniors displaying work alongside theirs: they had to wait three more years than the prodigies for the opportunity. It's her third showcase at twenty years old, his first at eighteen. Eighteen, but feeling like twelve next to her: being born in Chicago and living in cities all her life has an aging effect, one that seventeen straight years in El Centro cannot match. Despite these differences and having known each other for only a semester, they have lately been whispering a secret shared language like a pair of twins. Margaret Grosvenor, their mutual practicum professor and the accidental cause of their meeting, has since been more deliberate in her matchmaking efforts. She hovers only a moment to one side of their adjacent displays, quickly glancing to ensure the fuse is properly set to ignite.

The stars are for her display, but because they are strung, at Ms. Grosvenor's insistence, from the rafters of the studio—the old support girders from when the studio was a warehouse—their glow bathes his display as well and draws the crowd in the studio around them like satellites surrounding Jupiter. The stars are a cherry on top of her model of a public observatory for Topanga State Park, as much a proposal for civic planning as an architectural design. They weren't meant for his display, but they fit: his village of modern nomadic bungalows is set in a desert nightscape; he even added a small glowing campfire at their center.

It has fit with her from day one. He doesn't consider Mina attractive or ugly, only someone who fits. Tonight, her hair is bundled high on her head to reveal her neck, her lips are stained a waxy red, and she wears a top and skirt that shows off her waist and the curve of her hips. She's worn denim every day he has known her; he started to doubt if she owned anything else.

It's a plot twist he did not see coming but one he enjoys. He imagines life with Mina would be a series of plot twists, all unpredictable, none dissatisfying.

Since the showcase is private, they are permissive with the open bar. The two prodigies don't drink, as a rule, because they are underage and law-abiding and because they have too many other things to do. That night, they drink; they can defend a one-time loophole.

After two glasses of champagne, he tells her what happened to his father. He has told very few people: not Ms. Grosvenor, not even his mother, not the full version. He was fourteen, a light toss from where he is now. They were camping, just the two of them, in an old rental cabin in the Sierra Nevadas. In the thick of the night, Jonathan woke to find himself alone. The darkness intimated danger. He grabbed a flashlight and wandered through the woods surrounding the cabin for over an hour. He feared a bear had hauled away his father, or he went out to look at the stars and got lost. He thought he might be lost himself. Then he heard his father's voice, not through the trees but in his head. His father's voice told him to follow the ridgeline down to where it met the river. He did as it said. Before he could reach the river, he saw his father through the trees. He seemed to be sleepwalking; he crashed through branches without trying to brush them aside. Jonathan ran to catch up to him. Through the trees, he heard a screech of tires and a sickening thump. They had wandered over to the service road they took to get up to the cabin. When he came out of the trees, Jonathan saw his father's body crumpled beside an old pickup truck. The truck had careened onto the shoulder. It chugged noxious fumes. Beside his father's body crouched the driver, his eyes red-rimmed and his mouth blubbering.

Who knows what the truck driver had been doing? He might have been distracted for only a second. Jonathan had never thought to blame him for what happened. The way he saw it, his father had been complicit in his death.

The night is winding down. The other booths are abandoned, allowing the twin prodigies to find a quiet corner to avoid questions and fawning praise. Mina says nothing for several minutes. She has taken off her heels, which means she stands at the height he's grown used to. She wraps her arms around him, rests her head against his heart. She says, "Do you know what my family name means? Aslanyan?"

"Aslan, that's like a lion, right?"

"There you go, someone's read *The Lion, the Witch, and the Wardrobe*. We're a family of lions. My dad likes to boast that his great-grandfather earned the title by fighting for the Ottomans because he had a lion's courage. It's probably not true—he boasts a lot—but the name suits my dad perfectly: he's lazy and a player, just like male lions are."

"Is this supposed to make me feel better?"

"I'm getting there. You see, it's the lioness that holds all the power. My mother is fiercely protective of me and my brother. Too fierce—that's why I ended up here in California. Here with you." She squeezes him tight. "Now that we have a couple thousand miles between us, I can be my own kind of fierce. I know I can't bring your dad back, John, but I can protect you." She looks up at him, eyes soft and wide; she has never looked at him quite this way.

Mina suggests they sneak out the back; she has something she wants to show him. At this point, the showcase crowd is half-drunk and paying little attention to the students it's supposed to be showcasing. It happens every year, she assures him. They slip out through a loading bay and wander down Skid Row, offering pilfered trays of hors d'oeuvres to the tent city's residents. Then they turn up a block and find a downtown main drag after a fashion: instead of the cold, shadow-slinging towers of the business district, this street is lit up with low-slung storefronts and restaurants, and on this hot June night, doors are propped open, and shop owners spill onto the sidewalk in lawn chairs; every free ledge holds a boom box blasting music—salsa, cumbia, reggaeton—or the Angels' game on the radio. A woman outside one of the shops who could pass for Jonathan's mother greets Mina by name and asks, *"Quein es este chico?* You haven't brought him around here before. *Que lindo."*

"Mi esposo futuro? I'm so glad you asked, Marta. I found him in a gutter a block away. He cleans up nice, doesn't he?"

"You know my mother is from Mexico," Jonathan says. "I can understand you."

Mina gives him a sheepish grin, pats him on the chest, and says, "All the more reason to love you, hubby."

"Are you taking him to your special place, *Helemina?* "Marta asks.

"I am! And don't worry, if he doesn't propose to me there, I'll dump his ass."

The "special place" is an alleyway midblock. Long ago, some ambitious store owner threw a wrought-iron archway over the alleyway's entrance to the main drag. At the archway's apex, an empty light socket fails to deliver a promise of light. Not much illumination down the alleyway, either.

"Are you sure it's safe?" Jonathan asks. There are few alleyways like this in El Centro, few places where shadows collect to harbor potential murderers.

"There's light farther down if that's what you're worried about." She smirks at him, but her eyes are playful. "Plus, did you see all this commotion behind us? No one's going to try anything around here."

She heard about the alleyway from the source of its fame—not the builder of the archway but a more recent constructor, a muralist who could often be found selling roses outside the gates of the USC campus. He handed her a Damask stem one morning and said, for a few extra dollars, he would tell her of the best place in L.A. to view the night's sky. Not many took him up on the offer, thinking for that price, it must be a scam. Mina believed him. She was young; no one had yet stolen her trust.

The alley broadens in the middle. Under the yellow glow of a sodium light, a violet and azure sky shines with thousands of stars.

"This is my inspiration for the public observatory," Mina says. "The neighborhood loves these stars. I do, too. I want to give them a chance to see more than just a painting." She turns to him; the streetlight reveals streaks of gold in the blue-black curls of her hair, like obsidian doused in sunshine.

"I saw him again today, the artist," Mina says. "He said something I found hard to believe. Come to the Night's Sky tonight, he told me. You'll meet someone who surprises you. Someone who opens you up. Bring them with you, he said."

"And you brought me. But we've known each other for months." For years. Since childhood, it feels like.

"We have. But tonight, it kind of felt like I was meeting you all over again. What you told me about your father..." She looks back toward the thousands of stars. She draws a deep breath, and her lips tremble as she exhales.

"I didn't mean to scare you." They are standing very close now. He wants to wrap her in his arms and dive into the wall of stars, to swoon into their vastness, as though the mural's detail and mastery of color have conjured a portal to the heavens. Before he can try it, though, she moves away from him; something has caught her eye near the wall. "Come look," she tells him. "He must have known I would come."

Two Damask rose stems glow a pale orange in the streetlight in a tin can at the mural's base. She plucks them both from the can and hands him one, inviting him to smell.

"It smells like a dream," Jonathan says.

"If this is a dream," Mina says, "I hope we don't wake up."

3

Family

It is dish duty, and she is grateful for it. They discouraged dish-duty jobs in Group because it left you more isolated. Or maybe she just imagined they did—it was not that severe, was it? But they encouraged any job that forced you to interact with others. Social bonding was essential. She bonded, all right. Look at her now.

The grease just slides away: she doesn't have to smell it; in fact, she can eliminate it, all those calories ruined, toxified by detergents.

She is less worried about the white hairs on her arms or the hair on her head falling out more than usual. She worries about very little. She is so much smaller than Andre, and well, fuck him, she took it all.

She was right, as she so often is. Still not enough to overdose.

It is not like anyone can tell, not like she is challenging the dishes to a staring contest. She is functional every time, since the first time. She would play guitar, and well, if a little slowly, at parties. Fiona socialized—often, she had the whole room turned to her. Fiona did not touch the needle. She preferred drugs that kept her mind jumping around.

Em's signature song was The Beatles' "Across the Universe." It was the closing song of the night. Every time she reached the chorus, every time she sang, barely above a whisper, "Nothing's going to change my world," you swore the seal holding her tears back would burst, that she would not be able to finish. But she always did, even if no one was listening.

Selma has hovered over her since she came up and found Andre gone, found Em limp on the couch in about the same space Andre had shivered and slowly come to his own sort of Jesus—with the kit neatly put back in its place, of course, and her arms fully covered. Selma told her to change and wash up and she found, in the bathroom cabinet, enough medical tape to cover the offending elbow—always the same one, absorbing all that offense—and she covered a bit above and below, just to be safe. See? Functional. Selma glances at the wrapping from time to time. Not in a way most people would notice, but Em thinks she and Sel might dance the same offbeat step when they scope out a room: one that sweeps the room without it shifting an inch. You only notice a set of eyes on you if you can catch their rhythm.

No one lives permanently in the tiny apartment above the Sleeping Black Dog. It's for out-of-towners like Em, Selma tells her, and Em could guess why: she sees why the elderly owner might pick a spot with a firmer bed and a little more space. Em is allowed to stay the night. The weekend blows in, dishes reaching her hands as fast as she can wash them. She stays the weekend, too. She is not offered an extension to stay and does not ask for one. She is just there, not moving again.

Mornings are for dry heaving, for wiping the sweat away before she accumulates more back-of-house. At night, crumpled on the couch in exhaustion, she stares at the untouched backpack propped against the wall. Her clothes start to smell terrible. She throws them in a pile by the bed, opens the untouched backpack, and tries on a shirt. The shirt reaches her knees. She looks ridiculous but smells so much better. She smells like him.

It is harder this time. She hates to admit that maybe Group served a function, that they were not just Jesus freaks or a rusty cog in the system. She wants Andre and she wants to use and the two are linked now; it is a new complication she wishes would just go away. When she has to face it, when she turns on the bathroom light to wash her face and sees only herself looking back, no kindness there, just judgment and deep black troughs running down the inner corners of her eyes, bruises that match the telltale mark on her arm—she wants to grab her useless kit and plunge the empty needle up through that soft, judging jelly—or maybe she will use the silver spoon, why make it easy? If she digs in far enough, if she reaches her brain, perhaps she will hit a reset button, and Andre, the needle, her judgmental self, will dissolve, and she will go downstairs the next morning and scrub dishes as though it is the only thing she has ever done.

Selma sees all. It has been over a week now, and though Em's work performance never lags, her demeanor has shifted a little each day. She is like porcelain: cracks in her glaze have started to show. It is Sunday, one of the Dog's busiest days. After the brunch rush ends, Selma invites her out for a meal of their own. Just us girls, she suggests, away from work. Em protests—the kitchen's a mess, they need her—but Selma reminds her they were getting by just fine before her dusty ass stumbled in.

It takes fifteen minutes on foot to get where they are going. Selma tells her you can walk the town's perimeter in less than an hour, except up to the lighthouse, though Selma thinks of it more like a satellite, a miniature suburb. She never drives this time of year, anyway, unless she's going to Hoopa. Not when the fog covers the streets for half the day and rain the other half.

"What's in Hoopa?" Em asks. Selma responds by stopping suddenly and turning toward a gate that leads onto an elevated walkway built from wooden planks. The walkway leads to a house cut halfway into a gentle slope, the front entrance floating on a landing above the ground. It feels like a treehouse without the tree, painted in redwood shades to make up for the absence.

Selma opens the gate, and they walk to the house.

There is, in fact, a tree. Or the wholly intact remains of one, a wide redwood trunk around which the house has been built. The trunk extends down into the floor below. On this floor, where they entered, a substantial wedge of the trunk has a massive fireplace set into it: a custom one, Em thinks, from how neatly it follows the trunk's curve. It seems bold and impetuous to fit a source of fire into something so flammable, even when the fireplace is one of the enclosed, natural gas types like this one. The architect must have found delight in stretching the limit of what is considered safe. If Em had to guess, she would say the architect was a man.

Selma invites Em to sit while she makes food. Em chooses a spot near the fire, a wide armchair covered in rawhides. The armchair is wide enough to fit two people, or at least two as shrunken as she is.

It is quiet in the house. The fireplace wooshes from time to time to replenish gas; after a moment, a sizzle comes from around the bend of the redwood where the kitchen must be. Otherwise, Em would think Selma vanished. It seems contrary to the chaos of the Sleeping Black Dog, but Sel is not the cause of that chaos, not from what Em has seen. Patrons bring that energy, as do some of the employees. Like the remains of the tree that Em sits by, Selma stands firm, and the noise surrounds her, seeking to dominate, to usurp attention. But quiet is patient. Quiet needs no attention, but often enough, when the shouting dies on its own, all eyes turn to it.

The warmth and glow of the fire make the fog outside less threatening. The armchair, covered in deerskins, feels like a friendly animal nuzzled into her. She takes off her shoes and tucks her feet under her knees. She rests her head on one of the chair's broad arms. A comforting smell fills the house: cedar and baking bread, spices like Christmas. It reminds her of when her Aunt Maral—her true favorite aunt—would come over and make tahdig for the holidays. Her eyelids droop. She wonders if someone has dosed her without her knowing it.

It is a short dream, more like an impression: a stroboscope in a continuous loop. Fiona spins in a swimsuit on a beach. Her hair is a wonder in any light; here, in the SoCal sun, it shines like copper. Her eyes cannot pick a color, so much so that the colors in one eye do not match the other. Her nose, chest, feet, and arms are lousy with freckles. She dances as she spins, wiggles her hips. Hips like a boy. Em loves to grab those hips.

They fit neatly between her own whenever she and Fiona dance together.

Em does not know how she knows, but Fiona is sober in the dream. She, watching her lover spin and beckon for her to dance on the sand, is sober, too. It might be a memory: a rare enough moment for her brain to hold onto it.

Fiona keeps looking back at Em as she spins. She reaches out a hand; Em takes it, but the hand is coarse. It is not a teenager's hand.

Selma is shaking her forearm. Not unkindly, just enough to wake her. It is time to eat.

On a round dining table, two plates are set with forks and knives beside them; under the forks and knives sit two cloth napkins neatly folded into triangles. At the center of the table, a whole roasted salmon sizzles on a cedar plank. Beside it sits a steaming disk in a cast iron skillet. The disk looks like cornbread but darker. It smells like the greatest offering the earth could provide.

"This is acorn bread," Selma says, putting a piece on her plate with some salmon. "I make a batch once a week or so. It's the food of my people. The salmon, too."

Em has not been hungry in months but thinks she could lick the cast iron dry. She takes a bite of the bread and knows she can.

"Why don't you serve this in the restaurant?" Em asks, her voice muffled from mouthfuls of bread. "It would sell so well." She swallows. Her face lifts in a half-forgotten way; it takes her a minute to recognize the smile. "And salmon? You don't have salmon on the menu. People *like* salmon." Em does not like salmon, but she would eat it if it had the bread to accompany it. She picks up her fork and starts to.

Selma says, "You have a point, I suppose. But I make this food for me. Or for family or people in need. Some of the people who come into the restaurant are family, but I can't separate them from the ones who are not. And almost none of them need my help."

"I guess I'm an exception. I'm one of your 'people in need.'"

Selma nods. "For now, that is what you are." The quiet that follows suggests she could be family, too, with enough time.

"Your people," Em asks, "Are they... Hoopa?" There is a flash of a sign in her head. She and Andre ended up in Hoopa land, or close enough to it when they were looking for a place to winter in the woods. She remembers the sign that told travelers of remote and narrow roads that they were entering the Hoopa Valley. And she said to Andre: turn around, we can't camp here. When he asked why, she was vague. We could, I guess. But first, we would have to ask permission. And I doubt they would give it.

"Hoopa: yes," Selma says. "That's what white folks call us. But also, yes and no. That they are my people. That's why I'm here and not up there, up with the river."

"Why? What do you mean?"

Selma makes a face like she has eaten something sour. It seems she does not like to talk about herself. But once she starts, she also cannot stop. "My mother is white," she says. "She raised me outside the reservation, but we went up there all the time. When I was fifteen, my father taught me the Jump Dance. Mostly, the men did that dance, but he didn't care. Then, I went away and got a degree in San Francisco. I tried to fit in with the white folks. It didn't work so well. So, I came back up here to what I knew and applied to be a member of the Hoopa Valley Tribe. My father was one, so why not me? But I didn't qualify. I'm half-white. Blood quantum, they call it. White folks created the idea to try to destroy tribal culture from within; then, tribes started using it to kick the mostly white folks out. It didn't make any sense. My mother thought of herself as part of the tribe, too, I think. We lived in Willow Creek, as close as we could without being on the reservation. My father had stuff there, and he stayed in Willow Creek for as long as he stayed anywhere else. I am part of that tribe. But they say I'm not, so here I am."

"Why didn't you go back to Willow Creek?" Em asks. "To be close, at least."

Selma sighs. She looks out the window toward the sea. "San Francisco bit me," Selma says. "Not the city—I hate the city, all those people climbing over each other—but the land around it. Me and the ocean are tied together, I think. It must come from my mother. She's from Eureka."

"Yeah, I know that pull," Em says, sliding another forkful of salmon into her mouth. The salmon reminds her of campfires on DOI land in Oregon. Not fishy at all.

"This is stolen Yurok land we're on now," Selma says. "Sometimes, I see tribal members come into town. There's a fishing beach not far up the coast, and they will come into town for supplies. Sometimes they eat at the restaurant. They are nice enough to me. They can't tell I'm half-white."

"Why do you keep going up to Hoopa after they snubbed you?"

Selma chuckles. "They rely on me! It's ironic, I suppose. I go up to see my mother in Willow Creek—she gets lonely now that my father has passed—otherwise, I would not go up as much. But I'm a hydrologist and a river ecologist; that's what I went to school for. They have their own ecologist but he's still green, still learning. I'm like a mentor. In exchange, I get to fish the river as much as I like. The salmon we're eating calls the Klamath watershed home. We help the salmon along its path down the Trinity River, through the Hoopa Valley. It needs our help after the federal government constricted our waterways."

"Damn feds, always causing trouble," Em says. Without realizing it, she has finished everything on her plate and reached for more. Her stomach churns, and she burps, loud and hard. "Wow! Sorry about that," she says.

"It's okay," Selma says. "I'm glad you're eating. People can't live just on drugs."

Em keeps eating but more slowly now, her eyes set on her food. She says nothing. There is nothing for her to say.

"My brother died of a heroin overdose," Selma says. "I know all the signs. You're pretty good at hiding it. He was, too."

Em still says nothing, but she looks up. She sees no judgment on Selma's face, only concern. Then, feeling like she is jumping off a cliff into murky waters, Em says: "I am someone that needs your help." This time, she pronounces each word like she is reading a proclamation. This time, she believes it.

"I think you do," Selma says. "If you want the help."

Em looks down again and nods: nods to the food, the earth's offering, the river's; to the table laid so neatly for its dinner guest; to her body, stripped of warmth: fed, until now, by an illusion.

"The boy you were with," Selma says. "Andre. Do you know where he is?"

"No. He was very strung out. He said he needed to get clean."

"He might have found his way to the clinic in town," Selma says. "It just opened a few months ago. It's small. I don't know what kind of resources it has. But they would take him in if he asked. They're a free clinic, I believe."

"That's good," Em says. "I hope he made it there."

"You can check if you want. I know the woman who runs the clinic. She might not be able to tell me much, but we could see if anyone has asked for you. If he wants to see you, that will make it easier."

"Sure, I guess. I kind of doubt he wants to see me, though. I'm the reason he's as bad off as he is."

"Do you love him?" Selma asks the question, as she seems to ask all questions, with no hint of judgment: there is no right or wrong answer. It allows Em to respond more honestly than all the times she has been asked something similar.

"I'm not sure if I love Andre or anybody," she says. "I'm not sure I know how. When I think about it, I feel cold all over. They say you should feel just the opposite. I feel like jumping off a tall building."

"I don't know who 'they' are," Selma says, "But they're wrong to say there is only one way to feel love. Sometimes, when I think about some of the people I have loved, I want to jump off a building, too." Selma stands and offers her hands to Em, palms up. Em stands as well. Uncertain what is going on, she rests her hands on Selma's. Selma grips them, closes her eyes, hums quietly for a minute or so, then opens her eyes and says:

"I think you might love Andre. You're bad at showing it because you give him a lot of grief, but you would not do that if you didn't care about him."

"What's the hand holding for? Some kind of shaman ritual?"

Selma lets go of Em's hands. "You're still healing, so I will forgive that ignorant comment. I was checking your pulse. I figured you would be thinking of him, and the blood flows in a particular rhythm when you think about someone you love. Or you could have a heart condition."

"I hope not. But my family history's a little muddy, so who knows?" Em sits back down and looks across the room to the fire. The blue tongues of flame, dancing silently behind the glass, elicit action. "What should I do?" She asks the flames. But it's Selma who answers.

"Only you can decide," Selma says, "but in my experience, having people you love around you makes a day worthwhile, if not always easy. The white folks I see every day at the restaurant: I love most of them, even if they sometimes make me angry. It's the same thing when I go up to Hoopa. Then I come back here to this house, to my tree, sometimes alone, sometimes not. That's a different kind of love. I have only one suggestion," she says. "If you do try to find Andre, wait until you know you're ready."

Em wants to ask *how* she will know she is ready. But then she thinks, I know I'm not ready now. Maybe it's as simple as that. Knowing and not knowing are two sides of a coin spinning in the air. One day—it could happen tomorrow or weeks from now—the coin will land on the knowing side.

Selma did not just invite Em over to feed her and peel back the veil of the lie between them; she wanted to see if Em might be more comfortable here, with a chance at some company and a little distance from the restaurant. Em takes very little time to decide that she would. The house has two bedrooms on the ground floor, both small, but the mattress in the spare is such an improvement that the bed back at the Dog might as well be a shelf of coral.

She moves in that night. The spare room appears to have been last decorated by a high schooler. Not Em's version of high school, perhaps: more like versions she saw as a kid on TV. There are apparent teenage signs—posters on the wall of indie bands filled with pretty boys, sadly few with pretty girls—but also less obvious ones, like forestry maps next to the band posters and a hulking box on a desk with a microphone next to it. There are dials on the front that suggest it is a radio, but not any kind of radio Em has ever seen.

A framed photo on a bedside table gives a clue to the owner of all these things: a blond girl, eyes bright and teeth gleaming, hooks a comfortable arm around Selma's shoulder. They are standing on a beach, and the day is clear and calm.

They are awash with color. Color is made for them.

At breakfast the following day, Em asks Selma who the blond girl is. "She is another girl who needed my help," Selma says. "She's also the closest thing I have to a daughter."

"You haven't really mentioned her," Em says. "Is she still around?"

Sel seems surprised by the question. "Oh yes, she lives in town. She comes to the restaurant all the time, but she's been away. I'm sure you will see her soon, maybe even tomorrow. I did not mention her because it wasn't important. You have enough to think about."

Comments like that, as so often happens, only make Em think about it more.

4

Boilermakers

THE TWO PRODIGIES ARE now locked in a conjoined orbit that only the most devastating force can break. Although Jonathan remembers this happening years later, in the dream, or whatever this is, it happens before they can round the night off with a kiss. The horizon bleeds a white-hot pulse of destruction. The Night Sky, Mina, Los Angeles, they're all obliterated; he's on the road before a pair of headlights, sweat dripping from his brow. The smell of diesel fumes and burnt rubber almost makes him retch over the thrumming hood that was mere inches away from cutting him down.

"You're lucky you're not dead." A woman's voice from behind the headlights. Frank, but not cruel. Almost playful. In a way, he hasn't changed positions all that much.

He can make out the silhouette of a pickup truck in front of him. The woman has craned her head out the driver's side window. He can't see eyes or a smile—she wears a ball cap, maybe has a ponytail tucked underneath it—but he senses no judgment from the peering head.

"How did I get here?" Jonathan asks.

"No idea!" She throws up an incredulous arm out the window. "Where are you going?"

"A town nearby. Or sort of nearby. I think I got lost. In the fog, not anywhere else." As soon as he says it, he realizes how ridiculous it sounds.

"You got more than lost if you wandered onto this back road without seeing it." He wonders, did the same thing happen to my father? Did the woods blind him with visions of his past?

Am I just a little bit luckier?

She gets out of the truck. The truck, an old chain smoker, a ten-gallon-a-day diesel addict, chugs in protest when she sets the brake. She shakes a dismissive hand at its grumbling.

She looks young. Not young enough to be a daughter of his, but close. He was right about the cap and ponytail: Giant's cap, long blond braid thrown over one shoulder. A white tank top and a pair of Dungarees. He still can't see her eyes.

"Come on, you old drifter. I'll give you a ride."

"I'm not that old. And you don't know where I'm going."

"You can tell me. At least, I hope you can."

"How do you know I won't...you know? Try something."

She spreads her legs in a "V" and rests a pair of fists on her hips, elbows jutting out. "I have a Taser in my back pocket and a .44 within easy reach in the cab. Plus, you're scrawny, and you look like shit. I'm pretty sure I could kick your ass."

"Now I feel like I should get a ride from you. You'll protect me from bears."

"With a .44? I'd probably just piss the bear off. But yes, you should ride with me."

They climb into the truck and set off. From the dome light in the cab, he is briefly offered a better look at the driver's face: pointy chin, high round cheekbones, and a mouth always on the verge of slinging some sass. The mouth says, don't let these other parts fool you: I'm not to be fucked with.

"Where to?" she asks.

"Just a town along the coast. Rabbit Den Cove, I think it's called."

"Rabbit *Warren* Cove," she corrects. "Foxes live in dens. Rabbits, warrens. Not that there are any rabbits in the Cove. Unless they're sea rabbits." The sass mouth cracks a smile. "That's where I'm headed, too, so you're in luck. Anywhere specific you need to be?"

"Yeah, I'm starting a job. I have the address here somewhere." He starts fumbling through his backpack, remembering after a moment that the job details, like too many things, are probably crammed into his glove compartment. "Or maybe I don't. I'm pretty sure I'm late, anyway. What time is it now?"

"Nine-thirty or so."

"Yeah, I'm late."

"It's a good thing I found you. It's probably another two hours on foot from here. You'd be out of a job, for sure. What made you think you would make it on time?"

"I didn't have much choice. My car was stolen."

"That's rough. What kind of car?"

"An old Cadillac," he says. Not just any old Cadillac, but he keeps that thought to himself. A 1967 convertible Coupe de Ville, Capri Agua, with a cream leather interior, in impeccable condition. He named it "Ol' Blue Eyes," not because of the color but because he dared to believe the old crooner might have driven one just like it.

She whistles, long and low. "Very rough," she says. "You, Mr. Drifter, are running up quite the tab of bad luck."

If only you knew.

"I'm Jonathan, by the way," he says. "In case you wanted to call me something other than 'Mr. Drifter.'"

"I was kind of having fun with it, but sure. Jonathan. Very formal. I'm Alexis." She drags the three syllables of her name through a muck of irony: Alexis is not one for formality. "Can I call you Johnny?" she asks.

"I suppose. May I call you Lexi?"

"You may not." But then, she smiles. "Unless you buy me a drink."

Rabbit Warren Cove, Humboldt County, CA, is nestled in a hook of space formed by a seaside lagoon to the south and Redwood National Forest to the east and north. A narrow strip of land between the lagoon and the Pacific forms the tip of the hook, which rises to a sheer bluff known as Morningstar Point; at the bluff's feet, the high tide covers a perilous reef and a few rock outcroppings that become islands when the tide drops. There was a working lighthouse here once, but the Coast Guard decommissioned it and shifted the beacon farther south as fisheries in the Cove shuttered, unable to compete with large-scale operations in Eureka. The derelict building still stands on Morningstar Point, a dark magnet that attracts bored teenagers and strung-out adults.

The town's small historic center is laid out in a grid of streets a few blocks wide in all directions, forming an almost perfect square. From this square, tendrils of roadways radiate outward along the banks of the lagoon and inland up into the foothills, where only nationally protected forestland can stop their encroachment. They are new additions, built in the last fifteen years, mainly to accommodate second homes for Bay Area residents seeking a quick escape. From above, the town looks like a virus rising from the ocean to infect the Northern California countryside.

As of the 2010 Census, the population is 976. The population has dropped precipitously since the 1960s, when it peaked at close to 3,000. The remaining stalwarts are aging fishermen and some of their children, though many leave after high school, thus the declining numbers. A small but steady contingent of Vietnamese immigrants, their children, and their grandchildren have suppressed the bleeding some since the 70's, but they can only do so much. With no fisheries and no more logging due to all that protected land, there is not much left to keep folks in town. There are still a few minor exports—a little Humboldt County green, a little Mexican brown—but these vices tend to cycle through the local economy, fueled by high school dropouts and, very often, their desperate mothers.

Jonathan has come here about the lighthouse and the economy, ostensibly. He does not remember an address, but he remembers this much, at least, plus his client's name, which is more like a moniker: The Sturgeon. He has wondered more than once if the job's a bad joke at his expense. But at the mention of the lighthouse and The Sturgeon, Lexi whoops in joyful surprise. "You are doubly in luck today, Johnny. I'm the Sturgeon's partner! And yes, you are already very late, but I think that's forgivable given the circumstances. The Sturgeon extends his heartfelt apology, but he can't meet with you until later tonight or tomorrow morning. Had a bit of an emergency come up. He tried calling, but I guess your phone is out of commission, too?"

It's the discovered connection that inspires a telling of the town's life story, though, from Lexi's enthusiasm in the telling, he suspects any small prompt would do. "It's not that there aren't any legitimate jobs," Lexi elaborates. "My dad worked for the Forest Service for years, and I've spent a few summers planting seedlings—I just finished another one. It kicks your ass every single day you're out there, but it's great being outside."

"What does your dad do now?"

"He's dead. A felled tree came down wrong, and he couldn't get out of the way in time."

"I'm sorry."

"Why? Do you make a habit of felling trees onto unsuspecting foresters? It was years ago, anyway. And I have Betsy here to remember him by." She pats the seat of the old truck. "She reeks of Marlboro's, and no matter how much air freshener I spray on her, I can't get the smell out. I always figured the cigarettes would kill my Pop."

"Here I thought you were the smoker."

"Not Marlboro's." She smiles. "Nothing as boring as that."

No dead fathers rise to greet him from the tobacco terpenes seeped into the truck's upholstery. The ghosts shirk from cars, even ones barely holding onto life. He suspects all the metal and movement throws them off.

By 10 am, they are in a booth at The Sleeping Black Dog, the town's preferred diner and whistle-wetter. There are other bars and restaurants in town, but nearly half the populace, a few hundred hungry souls, make a daily appearance at the Dog to fill up on eggs, whiskey, and gossip. They are lucky to get a booth right away—others mill by the door as servers slide by them in the tightly packed space, squeezing themselves thin to get between tables—but then, Lexi is friends with the owner: she has a standing reservation; few others do.

"Shouldn't we head over to the Sturgeon's office?" Jonathan asks. "He does have an office, right?"

"Never before breakfast," Lexi says. "And yes, we'll get there. I like to do a little business over breakfast anyway, don't you? It takes some of the starch out of it."

"'Takes the starch out,' what are you, 80?"

"It's something my pop used to say. He was old-fashioned like that. I guess I am too, a little."

The food arrives. Huevos rancheros with a steaming pile of tortillas on the side, and at Lexi's insistence, for Jonathan, the Dog Pile: two flapjacks flanked with bacon and sausage, and maple syrup in a small crystal jug. "You really look like shit," she says when he protests. "Like you haven't eaten in days."

Selma James, the proud owner of The Sleeping Black Dog, delivers the food herself. She does this for her friends with unfailing consistency, no matter how busy the restaurant gets. "Good to see you back in town, girl," Selma says. She reserves a gleaming white smile for Lexi; Jonathan gets a cool appraisal. "Are you entertaining drifters now?"

"Believe it or not, Sel, he's a contractor. For our friend on Crescent Street. I'm just helping out."

"All right, all right. Tell his frail white ass I say 'hi' when you see him. And you—" Selma turns to him, one eyebrow raised, her large brown eyes demanding a response.

"Jonathan, ma'am. Nice to meet you."

"Mmhmm. Don't try anything with this one." Selma nods to Lexi. "The whole town will come after you. I will come after you. Understand?"

"Wouldn't dream of it, ma'am." But, as she has demonstrated, Lexi can take care of herself.

"Good," Selma says. "The drifter has manners, at least. Welcome to town."

After Selma leaves, Jonathan says, "The town's very protective of you."

"Yeah, because of how awesome I am." The sass mouth strikes a pose. "But Selma's exaggerating. I did kind of become the town's adopted daughter after Pop died. I was twelve. But only Selma took it seriously. She's basically my mom."

"No real mom?"

"She is my real mom, even if I still call her 'Sel.' If you're talking about the one who pushed me out, well—she's probably in Tahiti right now chasing cabana boys. I never really knew her."

Another echo from his trip to the past in the forest. Except now the roles are switched, and this girl, this young woman, barely older than he was back then, is the one laying it bare: dead parents, childhood traumas, and all. He feels he should reciprocate as Mina did and share in that common bond of a parent lost too soon. He almost does. But where, in the dream, his goodwill extended across galaxies, here it withers; cold sobriety winked it out.

This conversation is too heavy for breakfast, so Lexi suggests they set it aside and eat. She piles a tortilla high with ingredients and finishes it in two quick bites. The smell of grease from Jonathan's plate makes him queasy, but he forces a wedge of pancake into his mouth. The sugar and butter activate his brain almost immediately. He considers the exchange between Lexi and Selma, the words used. Some pieces are out of alignment.

"You've been out of town?" He asks Lexi.

"Yep," she says with a full mouth. "Just getting back from a fishing trip up near Klamath."

"And the 'friend on Crescent Street,' I'm guessing that's the Sturgeon?"

"Correcto."

"You said I was his contractor. To Selma. And that you were helping him out. But I'm your contractor, too, right? Since the two of you are partners."

Lexi sets her fork down. She chews her food carefully and swallows hard. Then she says, "Of course you're my contractor. But it was the Sturgeon's idea to hire you; he's the one who procured you, so to speak. He handles most of the hiring. I handle books—and strategy. Speaking of, should we get started?"

"He never mentioned having a partner."

"I'm not surprised. It's a new arrangement; just started about a month ago. He's used to working alone, so it probably slipped his mind to mention me. You'll see when we get going—if you remember much more about the job description—you'll see I know what I'm talking about."

He must admit that his early-morning betrayal has left him wary of strangers, even young, pretty ones the rest of the town seems to trust. He looks out into the diner. The building is old—a brick-and-mortar establishment built from genuine bricks and mortar like many found on small-town Main Streets across the country—and remarkably well preserved. He scans the elaborate carvings in the wainscoting of mermaids and waterfowl dogs, of fishermen commanding skiffs through rough waves; the tin drop ceiling stamped with fleur-de-lis that, if you squint, look a little like anchors; the glass-backed, tin-topped bar near the entrance; the mosaic-tiled floor with barely a crack or a piece missing from it. He searches for fissures, for stories hidden in the material. He comes up with nothing. The cocaine high that revealed so much in his motel room is long gone, and there is too much chatter happening in the present to make out much of the past.

His concerns start to fade as Lexi presents the job details—for a while, at least.

As previously alluded, the Pfalzgraff Lighthouse was built in 1902 to allow safe passage to the increased volume of ships to Rabbit Warren Cove. For a time, trade between the Cove and Eureka was frequent and easier overseas than overland. A nearby tributary of the Klamath River spiked its own late, brief Gold Rush, far enough from existing supply lines to make the remote outpost the only other coastal passage in the region.

In boom times, Eureka traded shipments of gold for every possible luxury and, in turn, a luxurious culture. Elaborate Victorian homes cropped up in the Cove's downtown; Pfalzgraff

Lighthouse was the greatest and latest addition. The last, it would turn out.

"We've never been able to compete with Eureka's harbor," Lexi says. "The water's too shallow here. The big ships stayed away."

Trade in fishing helped—salmon was abundant enough—until the ships carrying the fish grew bigger. And bigger still.

"You said the lighthouse was decommissioned," Jonathan says. When was that?"

"January 5th, 1962," Lexi says, as though she is giving a report for school. "Two months shy of its sixtieth birthday. Like the worst graduation present." With a tortilla, she wipes and dabs at the egg yolk clinging to her plate.

"The family who ran the lighthouse was devastated, according to my pop," she says. "Three generations of McKinley's ran it: Thomas, Victor, then David, with Samantha prepped to replace her father—she would have been the first woman to keep a lighthouse in Humboldt County."

"Is Ms. McKinley still around?" Jonathan asks.

"Samantha? She is, but she's Mrs. Nguyen now. She married a Vietnam War refugee. Had four kids and six grandchildren. A lot of them are gone, too. Two of her boys died young. Boating accident; heart attack. Her only daughter lives in Missouri, I think. Most of the grandkids ran down the coast after college, or up it. Except for the ones in Missouri."

"And the remaining boy? The son?"

"A mama's boy, for sure. After she retired, he took over for Samantha at the Cove's only pharmacy. Now I think she spends her days fishing—there's a community fishing beach not far up the coast. Papa Nguyen's long gone."

"You know a lot about this town."

"I'm the town darling." She smiles, but not with her eyes. "It's expected of me." Lexi looks out from the booth onto the chattering breakfast crowd. Maybe searching for Selma: maybe scanning the room for someone else, someone Jonathan has not yet met. Any one or all of them could be setting expectations.

Anyway, they are veering off course. Time to turn the dinghy back toward home. "By all rights, the Pfalzgraff lighthouse should be on the National Register," Lexi says. "There was a push in the '90s, when city coffers were full, to designate several blocks downtown as a historic preservation zone, like Eureka did with their Old Town. We're right in the middle of where it would've been; most of it was centered around Aspen Avenue and Coulter Square just across the street. There was a separate push to preserve the lighthouse at the same time. It had to be separate because of jurisdictional concerns: the land the lighthouse sits on is within the town's boundaries, but the Coast Guard still controls it."

"That hardly seems fair," he says, "since they have no use for it anymore." Jonathan looks down at his plate. All but the sausage has disappeared, tucked away without him noticing. He is starting to feel the effect. His stomach churns. Grease seeps from his pores and mixes with the already impressive pools of sweat. "Can we order some coffee?" he says.

"Have at it, Johnny boy. I'm more of a tea girl."

Coffee arrives, this time from one of the servers. Jonathan wonders if, with his presence, the matriarch isn't giving her adopted daughter some space. He cups the coffee mug in both hands. The coffee is weak, but it helps with the shakes. And the oncoming headache, bound to be a mile long.

"Cold?" Lexi asks.

"Hungover." He's surprised he admits it.

"Well," she says, "you might have to buy that drink for me sooner than later, and one for yourself. A little hair of the dog at the Dog, am I right?"

It has more than crossed his mind.

"The preservation zone didn't pass, I take it," he says.

"Barely. That is, it barely failed. By the thinnest of margins. The deciding 'nay' vote came at the eleventh hour from our elder statesman, Drake Parsippany. He's been on the town council since before I was born, and he was a property owner well before that: he rents out three or four storefronts downtown. You'd think he would be all for keeping our downtown charming." She looks up to the ceiling, smiles to herself. "He's running for mayor this year. For only the third time."

Plates are cleared, and Lexi, eyeing Jonathan's steaming cup, orders a cup of Lady Grey. With a splash of whisky in it.

He asks, "Does that count as the drink I owe you?"

"It doesn't count as a drink if you add it to tea." Her look says, I'll bet you've used that line before yourself.

"What happened to the proposal for the lighthouse?" Jonathan says. "That fail, too?"

"Not exactly. It's been in limbo for the last 20 years. The Coast Guard hasn't heard a convincing proposal to restore it. They also haven't heard any convincing alternatives. According to them, the demolition costs aren't worth it, not if there isn't a plan to generate revenue. What they need is a zinger of an assessment, one that proves the lighthouse's value."

"That's where I come in."

"You got it, Johnny." Her tea arrives. She inhales the rising steam deeply and takes a long sip. He can taste the bite of the whisky from where he sits.

"What if I assess that the lighthouse isn't worth saving?"

"I doubt you will. The Sturgeon wouldn't have hired you otherwise."

"Why, because I'm malleable? Because I can be bought?" The sweating and shakes bring with them, often enough, a wash of paranoia.

"I hope not!" she says. "Your words, not mine. If the Sturgeon hired you, it's because you'll know value when you see it."

He leans back in his seat and takes in the girl before him. Her nose is small and sharp, like a checkmark. Long pale eyebrows almost meet, in a quick plummet, at the bridge. Her eyes are green, or maybe amber, and they don't stop moving; they skip at the prospect of mischief.

"You're unusually confident for your age," he says.

"Really? I thought this was how recent college graduates were supposed to act." Lexi sticks out her tongue at him. Not the typical behavior of the partner of a consultancy firm. Appropriate for a recent undergrad, though.

"Do you have any photos of the Pfalzgraff Lighthouse? And a sign-off from the Coast Guard? Something official?" All at once, he needs a guarantee.

"Sure do. Photos I can show you now. I think the Sturgeon has an email from their preservation officer—the Coast Guard's officer, which in this case goes through DHS—allowing property access to a private party. Normally, the officer would need to do any assessment themselves, or their deputy would, but I think they made an exception because of the blended jurisdiction. Also, I don't think they have a deputy right now. Recession cuts, and all that." A breezy, plausible answer. But then, she seems as capable of producing plausible answers as most people produce a sneeze.

"I'll want to see that email, of course," he says. "Just to make sure we're not breaking federal law."

"Of course. We can swing over to the office in a bit." She examines her mug of tea—reading the leaves, perhaps—then tips the rest into her mouth, swishing it a few times before swallowing it. "The photos... you would have seen them already," she says. "They were part of the job description online. Old pictures from the archive, nothing too revealing." She rests her elbows on the table, leaning in, back stretched like a cat's: this is how boring the photos are, her posture says, how unworthy of our time. "Why don't we go look at the lighthouse right now? It's a quick drive from here. Just a look: we won't be climbing any fences or anything."

"I suppose we could do that," he says. The alarm is up—a pulsing red beacon in the fog—but he is weak from his hangover, from wandering through the woods and taking an unexpected dip into his youth. There's fatalism in his resignation, too. Where else do I have to be but where I'm being led, from one day to another? If today I am led off a rocky cliff into the ocean, so it goes.

5

Maelstrom

IT IS A NEW day at the restaurant, and a new fire is lit under Em: a white-hot one designed to incinerate bone.

It starts when Selma makes a radical suggestion: that Em should take a hand at serving. "You can be a runner for today," Selma suggests. "You won't be responsible for any tables, but you will get a larger portion from the tip pool."

"Wait, are you going to start paying me now?"

"I think you have paid back your meal already. If I *don't* start paying you, the Department of Labor will sniff me out." Selma chuckles. She leans close to Em, drops her voice to a murmur. "Also, you're better at washing dishes than Victor. His mother begged me to get him a job. I don't know how the boy moves so slowly—and he is not on any drugs, from what I can tell. If I am paying Victor, I should be paying you."

So, Em straps on an apron, rolls her sleeves down low to cover her arms, and enters the chaos.

It starts well enough. She sets tables and delivers drinks. A coffee carafe becomes an extension of one of her arms. She brings the aroma and texture of the acorn bread to the front of her memory and mounts it there, like a slide in a projection. It makes the smile she offers patrons genuine, for the most part.

About halfway through the morning rush, there's an order at Table 12 for coffee: black, no sugar. A server named Tina, who is nice enough from Em's limited experience with her, took the order after being waved frantically down. Tina comes to Em with a look that spells trepidation; it is not a look she often wears. "The guy who ordered the coffee looks on edge," Tina tells her. "Keep an eye on him for me?"

Table 12 is a window booth along the back wall. Em equips her smile, sets the coffee next to the man who ordered it, and offers a greeting she hopes comes across as cheerful. Not too cheerful, though.

The man glances up at her and nods, mutters a thanks. A woman sits across from him, her back to the window. She looks at Em and smiles, but her smile has a question in it. Who are you? The smile asks. You must be new to town.

I know who *you* are, Em thinks. You're Selma's adopted daughter, whose likeness I fell asleep looking at last night. She has filled out some since the photo, not just her body but her confidence, which already shone plenty bright. Em feels a warmth descend her spine and spread into her legs. This usually means she is turned on, but today, she wants to smash her trusty carafe against the girl's face. The two feelings might be one and the same.

And the man, well. Tina said to keep an eye on him. Em finds she cannot do much else. His glance causes time to expand with explosive force. She is a fixed point, uncertain if she will ever move again. The universe grows outward from her.

The man is withdrawing from something. She can tell by how he fidgets and how he sweats. He twists his wrists in a particular way. She does the same, to the same uneven beat, when she has not used for a couple of days. Sweat pools on his upper lip and around the hollows of his eyes. She sweats there, too.

A coincidence, maybe. But then, he displays other features, rare ones that are hard to replicate. His skin is like firewood burnt down close to ash, with a few spots spared by the flames to give it some warmth. Em's skin is the inverse: like an ancient yew tree, threads of old grayish growth peeking through bands of ruddy brown. An uncle she only met twice—last she checked, he lived, mercifully, in Chicago—remarked on her unusual coloring once. He asked her, Are you sure you are a true Armenian? Whatever that meant. No one in the family had skin quite like hers. From Em's experience, it was a unique color across Los Angeles County; in Redding, she stood out like a car on fire.

But the skin, well, that's not similar enough: Em just has an intuition about it, like a string inside her has been pulled taut. The eyes are confirmation. The eyes set the kindling.

Her mother looks up at her from a memory. It has been so long since Em has seen her mother's face, even just recalling it, that she is not sure who is looking up at her at first. Em's mother looks up through a cutout in the wall, a window that lets her see the rest of the apartment from the kitchen. It's their old place in Glendale—a dim, yellow-tinged place—and Em wonders, Mom, are you there still? Are you moving even less than I have managed to do? In the memory, Em has asked her a different question. Her mother stares at her and says nothing. She sets down the spoon she has been using to stir the rice.

"Why do you want to know?" Mom finally says.

Em's not sure why she wants to know, but she knows she must give a reason to get anything. "Because I know nothing about him," she says. "Don't you think that's a little strange?" She is thirteen. Still very curious. Curiosity has not yet burned her.

"I told you," Mom says, "he was an architect like me. And an asshole. He ran off with another woman."

"But that doesn't *tell* me anything." She also thinks it is a lie, that is, why he left. It is too generic to be true. And her mother is no fool: she would have sniffed out a cheater and kicked him to the curb before any thought of marriage or children passed between them. She did it with a boyfriend or two after her father when Em was still very young. There stopped being boyfriends after that.

"Fine," Mom says. "I'll give you something: you have his eyes."

Em thought that, too, was a lie for the longest time. No one had eyes like her: no one, she had started to suspect, in the entire world. Fiona would sometimes stare at Em like she was hypnotized; then she would have to look away. This, just like the song, from a girl with her own kaleidoscope eyes. They are beautiful, Fiona told her, but they freak me out. They freaked Em out, too. Her eyes contained thousands of shades, all of them gray. That, on its own, might not be unsettling, but all that gray *moved*. It moved one way when she was happy or in love, another when she was angry. The movement was subtle: it required you to focus on the eyes for several minutes to see anything—unless you knew what to look for—and most people still came out thinking they imagined what they saw. Doctors would look at her, unsettled, but they would never broach the subject.

One day, Em decided she wanted proof that all that movement was not just a trick of the light. She filmed herself and pictured a time when her mother had set her off. She nearly gasped when she looked back at the video: her irises formed two hurricanes gathering strength, the pupils acting as the eyes of the storm.

She sees a slight shift when he glances up at her, a dowel drawn through the ink. She sees it immediately because she knows what to look for. The eyes register something he is probably too strung out to notice. The irises swirl, which suggests to Em that maybe, unconsciously, the man has recognized someone like him. Someone like him in a way that no one else is.

Em gives him no opportunity to take a second glance to reinforce that hidden notion. She walks away and distracts herself by refilling coffee and chatting idly, fielding questions to the new girl, the one half the town has already heard so much about, another young soul Selma James has taken in.

The tears come when they can, when she retreats to back-of-house and sits against the dishwashing station, her old friend, and no one, for a moment, is looking at her or for her. Her theory has been disproven, and something becomes so clear that it threatens to split her down the middle: that is why her mother hated her so much. You cannot hate something genuinely without loving it first—and her mother had loved him, she is sure. Then comes a reminder you had not bargained for, a daily admonition of your past, a copy of the strangest eyes you have ever encountered.

She finishes her shift. She says to Tina, please, take my tips: you deserve them. Tina shakes her head, but she accepts. She tells Selma that she's tired and is going to the house to lie down. She walks the lonely path to the house built around a tree. It has started to rain. The rain heightens senses that the fog fails to do.

Em does not blame Selma. Her part in it, if there is a part, is coincidental. And the blond, the little white girl who is not so little anymore—a woman, really— is not to blame either. Is it the man's fault, then? Or her mother's? Should her mother have lied to her about her father? It would not have mattered, though. She would still have spotted him on sight.

As she unlatches the gate to Selma's house, she concludes that it is no one's fault, not even hers. Maybe Dear Old Dad will leave as quickly as he came. She wants it to be true, but she doubts it is. He would not be sitting across from a local if he were just passing through. And anyway, Em gets the sense that folks do not just pass through this town.

With Selma's help the night before, Em transferred all the belongings from the upstairs apartment to here. Hers and Andre's. She gathers their clothes into a pile, washes them, dries them, and rolls them into compact cylinders. She gets all the clothes into her backpack and even one of the blankets from Fiona, but not everything they brought into this town will fit. She thinks about what stuff Andre might not want to part with, which Em knows is a short list: he does not give much thought to stuff. His sketchbook and charcoal, probably. And the dog tags that never came off his neck but that must have right before he ran off, maybe in a fit as he was coming down: he would want those for sure; they were his mother's. She slips the dog tags around her neck and tucks them under her shirt. It feels illicit, wearing his mother's tags. It also feels right.

Then, not quite knowing why—and there really is no room for it—she stuffs the photo of Selma and her adopted daughter into her backpack, too. In its place on the bedside table, she puts the kit, silver soup spoon and all. Em is not much of a writer, so she hopes this will act as a note: a thank-you and an apology.

6

Justice

THE DETAILS, AT FIRST an asset to Lexi's credibility, have started to pile on. Too many for a random con; that would take too much effort. But there is so much confidence being displayed, like he's being asked, as you would in a confidence scheme, for his in return.

Still, she knows too much. These are not random details; he starts to remember. The Coast Guard jurisdiction, that's accurate. And the architectural heritage, taking from Eureka's example, he remembers that, too. That's part of why he wanted to see photos, because the image of the place comes back to him: an elaborate Victorian display, like the Carson Mansion but longer, heftier; a moored ship with steepled roofs for sails, bay windows for portholes, a wraparound porch for a deck, filigreed gables draping the hull. And as a foremast: the light tower, grand and octagonal, jutting against the sheer cliff face, its crow's nest shining safe passage. If she shows him anything else, he will be at her mercy.

His memory matches what they pull up to in the old pickup, although a faded version: shingles rotted and falling off, graffiti spread across the porch, the light tower's windows a target for bored teenagers throwing stones. Lexi was right: a photo does nothing to prepare you for the task at hand.

A chain-link fence surrounds the property. From what Jonathan can tell, it has been there for a while. It is made from sturdier materials than the ones he sees nowadays, and it's as weather-worn and graffitied as everything else.

He looks back from where they have come. The crest of Morningstar Point lies above the fog, the cove hidden below. Not that any sunlight greets them: the skies above them are overcast, with darker clouds blowing in from the ocean. A chilling breeze carries sea spray and droplets of rain.

"You like your shades of grey around here," Jonathan says.

"It's much nicer in the summer," Lexi says. "It's a shame you couldn't come then."

"How do we get in?" By which he means, how do we get in legally?

"There's a section of the gate that swings open over there." Lexi points to an opening in the fence bound with a padlock and heavy chain. "We have a key back at the office."

"Why didn't we grab the key before coming here?"

"We don't need it yet," Lexi says. "The Sturgeon asked us to wait for him before we started the assessment."

"Paperwork and all that?"

"No. I can handle your paperwork. It's something important, but he won't give me any details." Lexi looks toward the ocean, her pale eyes reflecting the gloom.

"What do we do until then?"

Lexi seems not to hear him; she studies the lighthouse for answers to what she's not being told. Something on the roof has caught her attention.

"Strange graffiti up there," she says.

"Oh?"

"Yeah. It's new I think, from the last time I was up here. It has been a couple of months."

"Are you a graffiti aficionado?" he says.

"Kind of," she says. "I mean, I know what signs my former dropout classmates like to spray all over town. They think they're being original, but they are all copying somebody else. This is different. It's distinctive."

She points to a narrow crook in the roof, a steeply pitched section near the light tower, clean of any other tags; climbing up there would be risky, even with a ladder, but one tagger has deemed the risk worthwhile. The graffito is crude but evokes a clear image: a horned animal hangs from its legs, its long neck slashed and drooping downward, blood flowing into a wide basin.

He is surprised Lexi saw it first, that it did not pulse at him like a neon sign.

"What do you think it means?" Lexi says.

He has had a long time to think about what it might mean: a decade or two. A ritual sacrifice, maybe. Or trauma from his childhood—he remembers a time on a neighbor's farm when a calf's throat was opened in front of him, the gash smiling with toothless gums. Has he been here before? Scrambling up to the rooftop blackout drunk, stamping his supposed trademark after a successful conquest? It's unlikely. A copycat, perhaps. Or a warning, a message that says, I know what you are; I know what you did. Except even he's not sure what he is or what he might have done from one day to the next.

He deflects: "It means any restoration of this place is going to cost a small fortune, maybe more than your town can afford. Even with federal aid."

"You're no fun," Lexi says.

"I'm not paid to be fun."

He is visibly sick now. It could all be an incredible coincidence, her pointing out the mark that way, but there is already so much out of alignment. He could run, he supposes. But he'd be caught in a day or two without Ol' Blue Eyes. Better to draw out his aggressors and make them show their teeth. He will know where he can hide if he can tell friend from foe—or foe from disinterested party.

Lexi gives him an opportunity. "So, what to do now," she says. "We could start your paperwork. But the Sturgeon probably won't get to you until tomorrow anyway. You're kind of off the clock. And hungover. And my brain is telling me it's still on vacation."

"And I," he says, "still owe you that drink."

They arrive back at The Sleeping Black Dog around noon. No booth this time: none desired, none required. They sidle up to the bar. Jonathan runs his fingers over the grooves in the stamped tin tiles. It provides a small comfort where there are now few enough.

Lexi requests two usuals. What's in a usual, Jonathan asks. You will see, she says, and you'll enjoy.

And he does: it's whiskey, that much he can tell. But it smells like it's been plucked from a meadow and stirred in a cauldron. A witch's brew, dusky and wild.

"What is it?" he asks.

Lexi looks at him sideways. "It's a classic: a Sazerac. I pegged you for a hipster, Johnny boy. An old hipster, but still."

"It's lovely," he says. "Better than straight-up Jack and a Coors, for sure."

"A boilermaker," she says. "Very respectable. It's probably better that you're not a hipster."

Lunch is quieter than breakfast, by a hair. Jonathan starts to make out double exposures, reflections in the window with no solid counterpart. With whiskey on his lips, though, he is less concerned with ghosts and what they might reveal.

He asks if he can buy Lexi another Sazerac. Then Lexi offers a round. Then, a second. Soon, the afternoon sun pitches a cold light through the tall French windows lining the street. The dining room has cleared out. Steady rain drives a rhythm of calm.

A familiar halo surrounds him, one that spirits struggle to penetrate. If he is in danger, he is no longer bothered by it. Lexi is compromised, too: eyes narrowed, her mouth less wound up with sass. She turns in her stool and evaluates him like he's a portrait by an old Dutch Master. "You have unusual eyes," she says.

"Did I sprout a third one on my forehead?"

She laughs and swats his hand. "No, dumbass, I mean the color. I thought your eyes were just dark, but this light does strange things to them. Almost like they're made for this light. It's like a tempest in there, swirling around."

"My mom always said I had eyes like iron. Like father, like son, she said; I got them from him. Your description's better," he says. "It's poetic."

Lexi raises her glass in a toast: "Two semesters of creative writing at Chico State paid off!" She upends her drink. Jonathan raises his glass and mimes like he will do the same, but he sets the drink back down and watches Lexi. She has started to sway. She orders another drink for herself.

Right here, he might have a chance at some truth.

"Lexi, can you be honest with me about something?" he says.

"You'd better catch up with me there, mister, or... I'll win."

"Win what?"

"The drinking game, obviously," she says, scoffing. "What do you think we're doing here?" She laughs at a private joke. Or at him: he may have been the joke all this time.

"That graffiti we saw up at the lighthouse," he says. "Are you sure you've never seen it before? You saw it, like, right away. Like you knew where to look."

She's calculating, trying to recall something that seemed to happen years ago. "You mean the goat thing? The one that was like—?" she slashes a hand across her throat. "No, man, that was new. I told you. What are you trying to say? Are you saying I'm a liar?" Her voice rises at this last part, but it may just be an effect of the drinking. If there is indignation in her voice, it's part of the show.

Lexi continues, unconcerned, it seems, where her integrity lies. "The Sturgeon told me to look out for signs," she says. "Signs of trouble, he said. He said we'd need to start being more—what was the word he used? Contentious. No—conscientious." She approaches each syllable like a hairpin turn in the road. "We'd need to be more conscientious after you came."

There it is. Something he's not meant to hear, a sidebar between colleagues that only a tipple or two could shake out. Or it could be a blown cover: there could be no colleague, no Sturgeon, just a classic bait and switch. Either way, he has heard enough. There have been close calls in the last twenty years: a pullover outside of Corvallis in 2001, a bank in Chico freezing his funds for several days in 2008—he stopped putting money in banks after that. Was Lexi working at that bank then, maybe to help pay her way through school? Perhaps she was involved with the freeze. Maybe she got curious, started to investigate further on her own, and thought the situation warranted some vigilante justice. It all seems too personal, deliberate, and strange to be anything else.

So far, the tally: one foe identified, zero friends confirmed.

Jonathan stands up abruptly; he apologizes, says he needs to "break the seal." He strolls to the bathroom, trying to be casual.

The men's bathroom is empty, but its windows are high and narrow, no good for escape. Four ancient urinals line one wall. They are massive, their bowls sculpted from marble and built into the wall and floor, as though they are an extension of the tiling. Jonathan walks to the farthest urinal and unbuttons his jeans: he does need to break the seal.

As he finishes up, he notices that the urinal he stopped at differs slightly from the other three. A thin fissure runs across the bowl along the back, where the wall meets the floor. It's not a crack—the line is too clean and straight for that. He follows the line with his eyes and finds that it continues into the floor tile, following the curve of the urinal and meeting the wall on the other side. It looks like someone once tried to cut the bottom of the urinal and pluck it, drain and all, from the floor.

He has an absurd thought: what about through there? What if I lift out the bowl and escape under the floorboards? The bowl is large enough to stand in, so the hole it left behind would, in theory, accommodate him. The thought comes on the same swift breeze and in the same voice as the one he encountered in the woods that told him to linger, to abandon Ol' Blue Eyes and all worldly concerns. The breeze, with the thought, leaves as quickly as it comes.

Jonathan returns to the bar, conjuring excuses as he walks. He hovers over his bar stool. I think I'll turn in early for the night, he tells Lexi. I don't want to repeat how I feel now, tomorrow. A conceivable lie, he thinks, as though he has not felt this way every day for months.

"Did you book a room already?" she asks. "The Cove Country Inn on Aspen Road is the only game in town, and it hosts a lot of long-term guests in the winter. You might have trouble finding something."

"Thanks. I'll take my chances."

"All right. The Sturgeon has a Murphy bed in his office if you change your mind." He starts for the door. Lexi turns to her drink, but after a moment, she calls for him to return as though she has forgotten something important.

"What is it?" he asks. His hand is on the door.

"Cheers," she says, raising her glass. "To the future of the Pfalzgraff Lighthouse."

Jonathan's drink still lies on the bar, barely touched. An egregious sin. He may not see another for a while. He walks back, clinks his glass with Lexi's, and throws the drink back in one swallow.

A metallic taste lingers on his tongue, like granules of citric acid. Too late to spit it out. He tries to run toward the door, but the floor has turned into a bog. He turns around; it's nighttime now, the Sleeping Black Dog bathed in amber light and lively again, drinkers jostling tables to reach the bar, beer spilled on the floorboards. Along the back wall, a solo crooner sits on a platform with a steel guitar, piping blues standards through a small amplifier. Lexi has disappeared from her barstool. In her place sits Mina. She's clean, not covered in blood or bruises, but apart from that, she looks like she did the last time Jonathan saw her.

Mina approaches with a familiar look on her face. A sad, long-suffering look. "Let's get you home," she says.

Crescent Street is a short walk from here, Mina assures him. Only a few blocks. Meanwhile, Jonathan traverses mountain passes, basks in pristine alpine lakes, and communes with snails, hares, and raccoons.

As they approach their destination, he starts to make out street signs and buildings again. On a long pier sits a row of offices and storefronts fashioned from an old warehouse. The cove that is the town's namesake laps gentle waves against the pilings.

Two women flicker within the same physical space: Mina in one blink, Lexi in the next. They reach above the lintel of one of the office doors and produce a key. In the office, at the back in a separate room, there is a bed as promised. He is lowered into it. He shivers, wet from the rain. The two women leave the room and close the door behind them. Jonathan hears the click of a lock.

A window by the Murphy bed looks out on a row of parking. There's a rumble outside, then an arc of light passes over the room. He knows that rumble like it's the cry of his child. If he had a child, he thinks, and unbidden, an amalgamation of his and Mina's traits form into a person as real as he is: a girl, an adult by now, if barely one. Twin headlights slice into his daughter. Through the window, they shine over a toothy steel grill that juts out to a point, the hood extending like the snout of a stingray. In the twilight, he struggles to make out the color of the car, but if he had to stake his life on it, he would say the body is an unblemished Capri Agua; the top is up, but he is sure the interior is lined with exquisite cream leather cushions.

This is it, then. Revenge at the hands of two strange women: two strange women and a wife, if he counts his hallucinations. It is better than prison, he supposes. Cleaner, less paperwork. And ultimately, he figures, more just.

Jonathan wishes he could focus solely on his fate, whether it be torture or a merciful, quick death. However, as the headlights wink out, other concerns rise from the shadows. The room he's been dumped in is filling fast with ghosts. He stares at them as they start to form a queue; they stare back. They seem to know he can hear them because they begin to talk.

He gets little sleep that night. The dead have much to say.

7

Going Sideways

"Solomon, Solomon.... I'm sorry, no one by that name has asked for you."

"And you're sure you can't let me know he's here now? Or that he was here and left?"

"Not unless you're law enforcement." The receptionist offers her a sympathetic smile. She looks like she has had a lot of time to perfect the smile she gives to worried loved ones. "Do you have his number? Maybe you could try calling him."

Yes, I have his number, Em thinks. I also have his phone. But revealing that will eventually lead to a conversation about missing persons and filing a police report. Not what she wants, and a futile effort anyway.

Em tries a bolder approach. Two birds and all that, she figures. She asks to see a doctor. She explains that she is in recovery and that it is not going as well as she hoped. The receptionist hands her a form attached to a clipboard. She sits and stares at the form, pen in hand, uncertain what to disclose, what to keep hidden. If Andre is here, she wants to give him a clue. She knows her Social Security number, but stamping that indelible mark in a database will send her flying back home for sure. No insurance to back it against, anyway. She gives her actual birthday, dialing it back a year as always—Andre doesn't know the correct year, either. The name is perhaps the trickiest. Her first name is no problem, but the surname is: it is too distinctive up north, so far from Glendale. Em remembers that before she had it legally reverted, her mother had taken her father's name. Junk mail still addressed her by the name for years afterward. It's a surname that does not usually warrant a second glance. It's masochistic to use it now, considering who drove her to flee to this clinic, but she cannot think of anything better. She writes the name down and is careful to replicate it on the signature line; a capital "D," she realizes, at least in cursive, is not all that different from a capital "A."

Emma Davies. Reading it makes her sick to her stomach. It feels like she has written her mother out of existence.

She hands the clipboard back to the receptionist and the receptionist takes the clipboard to a back room and Em is sure there will be resistance, that she will have to lie some more, but less than five minutes later, the receptionist says the doctor will see her now. She has been in enough clinics and hospitals to know they always ask more questions. But Andre is here or is nearby: his smell wafts through the vents in the waiting room. Other acrid smells that do not belong in a clinic mix with Andre's. She is wary of those smells and that she can suddenly smell so much. What triggered this ability? The acorn bread, maybe. It seemed to have magical properties. Either way, she has tapped into the animal Andre discovered in himself as he came down for the first time. She senses his fear. She must find him soon.

In a windowless examination room, a nurse asks Em what she is recovering from, and when she tells the nurse, he asks if she needs any methadone to help with withdrawal symptoms. She is so surprised to hear they have any in this tiny, remote town that she says yes, even though she doesn't need it. Once she has found Andre, she figures, a little to help cope with today's revelations would not hurt, and it may make it easier for the two of them—assuming he will take her back—to get down the road to somewhere better, somewhere the needle or her father cannot touch them.

The nurse says the doctor will be in soon to administer the methadone. He closes the door, and Em flies into a panic: they do not "administer" methadone in her experience, not if someone can take it themselves. She is about to run out the door and down the hallway—maybe if she is quick, she can find the room they are holding Andre in and get the fuck out of dodge—but then there is a knock on the door, and in walks the doctor with a box of vials.

"Emma? I'm Dr. Niequist," she says, offering a hand. Like she is greeting a colleague. Em accepts the doctor's hand. When she is asked to sit on the examination bench, she does.

Dr. Niequist reminds Em of the girl in the photo she stole, or more accurately, the grown-up version that left her so jealous and flustered. There are a few differences. The doctor is older and has less of a sheen: her hair is dark red and tied in a bun; her eyes are dark, too, almost black. The dark hair and dark eyes match a coolness that spreads through the room and gives Em goose pimples. But the doctor's confidence—that she shares with the smiling blond back at the diner.

"I'm sorry about the injection," Dr. Niequist says, gesturing to the vials. "We ran out of oral medication over the weekend. You'd be surprised how in need we are of methadone around here."

Would I be, though, dear doctor? Em only nods.

Dr. Niequist asks what arm she prefers, and Em rolls up her sleeve and unwraps her trusty vein. The doctor remarks on how clean her arm looks. There is a bruise, but Em has managed to keep it small. And track marks? It must be a miracle that she has kept them at bay. Casually, like she is complimenting Em on a style choice, she says: "As far as heroin addicts go, Emma, you are a professional."

She is tied off above the forearm; she is asked to flex; in slips the needle. Her infernal family wears different clothing but still moves with the same swagger. The smell of Selma's cooking hits her. She thinks, I'm not ready; I made a mistake. But it is only methadone. It will help with the nausea, sweating, and shakes. At worst, she will go under for an hour; when her head is clear again, she can focus on finding Andre.

She does not go under. She goes sideways. And the fresh hell she steps into nearly kills her.

Book II: Roots

Mind Punk Publishers

8

— · —

The Flayed Lamb

"...Yeah, he seems to be okay. He's sleeping now.... I don't know, I went home. Maybe? But I doubt it.... No, he was—he could walk just fine. He kept calling me Mina.... No idea.... Compliant? That's kind of a strange word choice.... Okay, okay. Yeah, I mean, he didn't fight me. He seemed to be off in some other world. Why is that important? ...Okay, I will.... I said I will, Triddy. Look, I've got to go. The boss just pulled up.... Triddy—what did I give him?"

It is Lexi's voice, but it sounds like an imposter is using it. The woman speaking is afraid of whoever is on the other end of the line. Afraid of "the boss," too, it seems. He did not think Lexi was capable of fear.

The room is dark because the blinds are now drawn shut, but slivers of grey sunlight manage to peek through. The door to the room is now unlocked and open a couple of inches; a warm light reaches for the bed and almost touches him. The ghosts are gone, for now, shrinking from the daylight.

It's not clear if Lexi's question is answered. She asks, and at the same time, the office door swings open—the percussion of rain against the aluminum awning picks up in volume for a moment—and he hears a great deal of shifting: drawers opening and closing, papers rustled, Lexi nervously clearing her throat.

"How's our boy?" A deep and flinty voice. The voice drowns out other frequencies. Not loud, but there is no reason for it to be. Jonathan imagines that the voice's owner may have been an orator once.

Lexi says, "He's still sleeping, I think. I didn't want to wake him."

No one speaks for a while. Or even moves, it seems. The rain speaks for them.

"I think it's time to wake him," the orator says. "I'll leave that to you—if you think you can handle it."

No response from Lexi, but wooden chair legs scrape slowly against the floor, and the door to the room swings open. "Oh good, you're awake," Lexi says. Her face is in shadow, but Jonathan thinks he sees a smirk. The timid girl on the phone has been tucked away. "Time to punch in," she says.

Jonathan swings his legs off the Murphy bed and hops out of it. He feels like he is made of elastic—though, as he walks into the main room of the office and light hits his face, the elastic becomes brittle. He craves water and asks for it. Lexi hands him a glass.

The office is equipped like a ship's cabin. Like an old ship that would have traversed the Atlantic to convey pilgrims or rum or slaves. Dark teak wainscotting lines the walls. The floor is made of strips of ash that creak and moan with every step. False portholes, ship's wheels, old and whimsical maps, and hundreds of framed photographs, most of them in black and white, hang everywhere. There are two desks. One, near the door, is a simple writing desk of Scandinavian, mid-century design. It feels out of place here, so it is appropriate that Lexi, who also feels out of place, sits down behind it. The other desk, in a nook in a corner against the far wall, looks like it has been built from the prow of a skiff. Beside the prow stands a tall, bearded man in a fisherman's cap, red flannel, and faded dungarees. He may be in his sixties, but he may also be older: he is gaunt, withered, and pale, with dark patches around his eyes and the hollows of his cheeks. This does not stop him from standing upright and proud. He grips the prow like he is about to jump in the boat and take it out for a morning fish.

Jonathan is perplexed by this man before him but grateful to be alive. He expected to wake up tied to the bed if he woke up at all. He expected a sinewy woman, his thief from Sunday night, to stand over him, to mock him and laugh at him, maybe even torture him, for his crimes against women. He would not have been surprised if Mina hung around to see the morning.

This old man, though—who must be the Sturgeon—makes the prospect of being tied up and tortured sound like a beach vacation when he offers a hand and says, "Good Morning, Mr. Davies. It's a pleasure to finally meet you."

Jonathan stares at the outstretched hand, convinced it will grow teeth and bite him. He stammers, "I think you've made a mistake. My name is Johnson. Jonathan Johnson."

"Oh? Is that so?" The man's eyes light up with mischief. "Yes, Johnson, Johnson. After Philip Johnson, am I right? Your favorite architect? It's a clever pseudonym; I'll give you that. Subtle. You could have been showy and gone for Koenig—he's better known, after all. I admire your integrity."

Jonathan's gratitude for being alive is quickly dissolving. The elastic in his limbs breaks, and he nearly topples over; he grabs the edge of the skiff for balance. He's now very close to the Sturgeon. Something in the man's eyes causes his pulse to quicken. At the same time, an inky blackness rises from the top of the Sturgeon's head and spreads down his sides. The blackness wants to consume the Sturgeon, but something keeps it from advancing over his face and limbs.

"You're wrong," Jonathan manages to say. He finds that the blackness gives him some strength to resist. "It's after James Johnson," he says. "Not that I would expect anyone to know who that is." He did think of calling himself Koenig, who was a personal hero and, if he had to pick, his favorite architect. But he agrees that would have been too on the nose: he studied under the man for one glorious semester at USC before he retired. Thunder rumbles through the office with a quick follow of lightning, close enough to outshine the dim, warm light inside. In the flash, he sees Pierre Koenig's face where the Sturgeon's should be, just as he remembered the man: wizened but still sharp, fierce blue eyes cutting into him. He lurches backward, hands poised for a fight.

"Look, I don't want any trouble," he says. "Whatever this is, whatever you want from me, we can work something out. I won't even press charges for the drugging and kidnapping. Just let me leave, and we can forget about the whole thing."

"Yes, the drugging," the Sturgeon says. No more Koenig in his face, though Jonathan must admit that the two would look very similar if Koenig had worn a beard. "That was an unfortunate turn of events," he says. He looks over Jonathan's shoulder, which causes Jonathan to spin around. Lexi has moved from behind the desk and stands a few feet before him, blocking the office door. She stares at him, not unkindly, and opens her mouth like she is about to say something to him—an apology, he thinks, would be an excellent start—but she looks past his shoulder, her expression pained. "He was going to run, Pete!" she whines, like a child defending herself from being scolded. "I panicked, okay? You said he was important. I couldn't let him get away."

"If he got away, he got away," the Sturgeon grumbles. "It's not our place to detain people. I was *hoping* you could use your charm to convince him to stay. That's why I hired you."

"Pete, huh?" Jonathan says. "So, you have a real name? And you, Alexis, just some lowly employee?" He swivels his head between the two of them, not sure where to look. His stance is wide, and he keeps his arms raised, palms open, fingers together, like an imitation of a kung fu master. Not that he is anything close to one. He has started many fights—mostly because his mouth ran ahead of his brain—and he has lost every time. He asks, "What other fun secrets would you like to reveal in this variety hour?"

As a reply, the Sturgeon—or Pete, or whatever his name is—gestures to an armchair across from his desk. The inky blackness still wavers around him like a corona. There's leverage in it, Jonathan thinks. He lowers his hands. He walks to the armchair and slumps into it. Wary eyes dart back and forth between Lexi and the Sturgeon. Something in Jonathan has caught the Sturgeon's interest: he sits behind his desk and scoots his chair close, leaning forward, like he is examining Jonathan under a microscope. Barely above a whisper, he says, "Just as I thought."

"What's 'just as you thought'?" Jonathan asks. But the Sturgeon waves a dismissive hand. "We'll get to that, I promise," he says. "First: the basics. One question at a time. I'm not sure what Alexis has told you, but she is my intern. She expressed interest in my work, and I thought she would be perfect for our special project."

"Well, that's pretty far off," Jonathan says. "She said you and her were partners."

"And I am, kind of," Lexi says, shuffling over to the skiff desk. "Right, Pete? You said you couldn't do this without me."

Pete says, "At the moment, Ms. Niequist, I'd say your internship is on probation. You're lucky to be here right now."

For once, Lexi has nothing to say.

"As for my own subterfuge," the Sturgeon continues, "I kept certain things hidden so as not to scare you away. I'm hoping now to gain your trust. Perhaps the easiest way to tell you who I am, in a way you're likely to believe, is through a story."

The story takes place on the shores of the Salton Sea during a heady summer, one that will shape the lives of two boys on the cusp of adulthood. Most summers before this, the two boys had spent picking watermelons in the Imperial Valley, but that year the melons were meager and few: they needed no small hands to help gather them. They rode their bikes up from El Centro most days—other days, they hitched—and wound their way through the empty streets of Salton City, kicking up miniature sandstorms in the undeveloped lots, then heading to the water to get relief from the summer sun. There was still a marina back then, but doom was on its doorstep: the waterline, rising year after year, had already come to the top of the marina's piles.

Boats rarely make their way to the pier, but that day, there is one so massive it has two stories. The boys have seen few enough boats to imagine any would require more than one level: those are called ships, and they don't belong on the Salton Sea.

The boat is too large to fit in the harbor; it bobs just beyond it, hesitant, wary of this half-abandoned town. On the aft deck, a girl lounges in a polka-dot bikini. She is close enough to the pier to see the two boys dangling their feet in the water and staring awkwardly at her. She sits up and waves. They wave back. A mixture of curiosity and boredom compels her to stand, jump into the water—with barely a splash, like an Olympic diver—and swim over to them.

The girl hops up on the pier, and the boys scramble to make room for her. She is older than they are, but not too much: sixteen if they had to guess. Her straight blond hair flows down her back—despite the swim, there is barely a tangle. Her skin is tanned a shimmery bronze. Bikini or no, to the boys, she is a sight to behold.

"I'm Candace Singleton," she says, offering a hand. Full name, needlessly, like a movie star, as though Elizabeth Taylor had walked up to you and felt the need to introduce herself by anything other than "Liz."

The boys introduce themselves, too. Roland, who sits closest to Candace, offers only his first name like the plebeian he is; Pete follows, giving a feeble wave, not daring to look into Candace's eyes for too long. Roland is thirteen, Pete twelve. Though only a year separates them, lately Roland seems to have reached a mountain pass where Pete does not yet have the strength to join. Roland is thirteen but already spoken for: back in El Centro there's a girl he met while working the fields—about the same age as Candace, he guesses—a girl named Rosi from Mexicali who stole his heart when she toppled him over for picking too slowly. Roland did not know it then, but Rosi had already fallen for him, too; the shove was her way of showing affection.

Roland is thirteen and already spoken for, but then, Roland is thirteen. (Pete, meanwhile, is smitten but hopeless.) Candace is a siren, skinny-legged and smooth as soft-serve. Her parents brought the boat down from Palm Springs for a spin. They're staying on the North Shore, near the yacht club. "What's a yacht club?" Roland asks. Candace says, "A club for yachts, of course."

Roland leans over to Candace and murmurs something Pete cannot hear, which makes Candace laugh. He is doing that a lot these days, Roland, saying private things that make girls laugh. He is tall, making him look old enough for high school girls to give him their ear. He is pale eight months out of the year—drawn of color, almost like he's dead—but he bakes a golden brown in the summer sun. That seems to make it easier, too. And those eyes. Those eyes draw a crowd if you don't look at them for too long.

Pete lives with a perpetual foot in his mouth. Thousands of words collide inside his head, trying to make inroads to his mouth. Standstill traffic just behind his tongue. He is ginger, which means he is pale eight months out of the year, red and blistery the rest. No matter how much sunscreen Ma Davies slathers on him. He hopes the burn across his cheeks and nose hides the quiet fury and shame he feels rise as he is ignored again.

He had selfish motives for what came next but can only admit that many years later. It's a split-second decision, but as it happens, as he and Roland go tumbling into the water, his brain justifies the act as one of salvation. Salvation of Roland, salvation of the life he is meant to have with Rosi. It works—Jonathan is living proof of that—but Pete only meant to embarrass his friend, not to maim him. He did not count on a hidden barb, a discarded anchor wedged in one of the piles. Roland manages to wriggle from Pete's grasp and swim back up to the dock after that, screaming in pain—not just from the wound but from the saltwater mixing in with it. Blood gushes from his back, just below his ribcage. Candace screams almost as loudly as Roland does and immediately jumps off the pier, swimming back to the safety of her parent's yacht. A short while after that, the yacht departs for the North Shore. The boys do not see the boat, or Candace, again.

The wound from the anchor leaves a scar that looks a little like a fishhook. It is a scar that demands its story be told, especially to boys the same age as Roland when he first got it. Roland tells the story, or a version of it, to his fourteen-year-old son as a cautionary tale. It's the last piece of advice a father gives to his son.

The Sturgeon waits for a sign of recognition. Jonathan says, after a long silence: "I guess that makes you crazy Uncle Pete." Pete was not, as far as Jonathan knew, an actual uncle. Rosi told tales of an old college buddy of Roland's, who Ma and Pa Davies unofficially adopted because his parents frequently lost track of him and did not seem to care where he had gone.

"'Crazy Uncle Pete,' huh?" The Sturgeon says. "Is that how Roland referred to me?" He scratches his beard, thinking the nickname over. "I guess that's warranted. I've always had my eccentricities."

"And you really go by the Sturgeon?" Jonathan asks. "Or is that another cover?"

"Think of it as a trade name," the old man replies. "Sturgeons are ancient fish; there's even some evidence that they're as old as the dinosaurs. Tough buggers, too, and a little ugly. Kind of like me."

"Aw, Pete, you're not ugly!" Lexi says.

"Are you trying to butter me up, Ms. Niequist?"

"Maybe a little," she says quietly.

"But I did also use it as a cover in this case," Pete continues. "These days, legally, I go by Peter Davies—yes, I took your parents' name—and considering how paranoid you tend to be, even though the name Davies is as common as mud around here, I didn't want to spook you."

"I guess you think you know everything about me?" Jonathan says. "Clearly you don't, since you got my favorite architect wrong."

"Phillip Johnson was a Nazi, by the way," Lexi says. "What? He was! I learned it in school."

"Alexis is an excellent researcher," Pete says. "She won't uncover everything perfectly, but she did all the legwork to track you down and make a convincing enough profile for you to want to come here in the first place. Not that you didn't throw us plenty of curveballs. We almost lost you outside of Willow Creek—"

"—But then I had the thought: oh, he's probably gone up to the casino to have one last fling," Lexi says, "before he dives back into work."

"Wait, you two were tailing me?"

"Just me," Lexi says. "This old man can't spend hours on end in a car."

"I could do it just fine, if not—"

"—For his arthritis. Pete's got terrible arthritis," Lexi says. Pink plumes rise above her head and wiggle their way to the Sturgeon. They are like a mantle, these plumes, a protective aura—but not for Lexi. Two smoky auras—one black, one pink—express something abstract, something Jonathan is meant to understand. For now, all he understands is that his perception has changed and whatever drug he was given is likely the cause. He lets the auras be for now.

"Okay, you went looking for me at the casino," Jonathan says. "Then what?" He's curious, too, about what happened up there.

"I didn't, actually," Lexi says. "Go looking, I mean. I figured that would be too obvious. I knew you would either stay up at the casino overnight or just take a quick trip and then maybe make your way to town. I didn't expect you to stop at a roadside motel."

"But we're fortunate to have many friends in the area," Pete says. "Roy knew to look out for a man in his late thirties driving a baby-blue Cadillac. No one was counting on a woman stealing said Cadillac in the dead of the night—least of all you, I'm sure. Roy called me as soon as you wandered off on your own yesterday morning, and I called Lexi."

"But you got the Cadillac back," Jonathan says. "Unless I dreamed that. I saw it roll in last night."

"We did," Pete says. "Not on a scratch on it, either. I saw the Caddy parked outside Sam's—"

"—That's the pharmacy I told you about," Lexi says, "the one Samantha Nguyen owns—"

"—I knew right away it was yours," Pete says. "Plus, we have the license plate on record to verify. It looked like it had been abandoned. The hood was down, and the seats were covered in rain. I found the keys in the ignition. It was pure luck that someone else didn't steal the car."

"Wait," Jonathan says, sitting upright, "you're telling me my baby got his insides wet?"

"Geez," Lexi says, "a woman disappears without a trace, and he's only concerned about his car getting soggy."

"Need I remind you that the woman committed grand theft auto?"

"She's still a person, Johnny!"

"That's enough!" The Sturgeon stands—with concentrated effort, Jonathan thinks—arms extended, knuckles firm on the desk, like a silverback striking a menacing pose. "I know tensions are high right now. This is not how I hoped to start. Let's be grateful that we found the car and hope the missing woman is okay. It's why we're here, anyway, if you'll allow me to explain."

He sits down carefully. Lexi pulls the chair around from her desk and sits as well. She glances at Jonathan with a quizzical look: whatever Pete is about to say is news to her as well.

"My trade name is not the only cover for this job," Pete says. "And Lex, my sincere apologies, but I had to keep the details from you, too, until now. In retrospect, perhaps I shouldn't have; maybe last night's hoopla wouldn't have happened."

"That's okay, Pete," Lexi says. "You're telling me now." She sounds relieved—because the pressure is momentarily off her, Jonathan imagines—but she also sounds nervous.

"You came here about a lighthouse," Pete says. "There's real work to be done there, don't get me wrong. If she can be saved, she's worth saving. If not, well... we have more pressing matters."

The fate of the Pfalzgraff Lighthouse is one battle—a lynchpin battle, perhaps—in a war that's been quietly waged in boardrooms and council meetings for decades. In the last six months, the war appears to have escalated and taken a darker turn. "I believe," Pete says, "Alexis filled you in on our local real estate tycoon and amateur politician? Drake Parsippany? Most folks in the Cove don't know how much property he owns because he takes great pains to keep it hidden. It's all in a holding company with no obvious ties to him, and his holdings don't just include properties in Rabbit Warren Cove: Drake holds plots from Crescent City to Arcata. There's a rumor he owns a rowhouse in Ferndale, where he possibly winters, and that he has designs on buying up that town, too, once he's done with the Cove."

"That's why we brought you on now," Lexi says. "We know he goes *somewhere* in the winter. Better chance of us being able to snoop around, ask questions of his tenants."

"Oh, did 'we' bring him on, Ms. Niequist?" Like a furry caterpillar, one of the Sturgeon's eyebrows stretches into a sardonic arch.

"You know what I mean, Pete."

"Okay," Jonathan says, "So, some guy flush with cash is buying up property while the market is still low. Last I checked, that wasn't a crime."

"Maybe not," Lexi says, "but it should be."

"Politics aside," Pete says, "I've been gathering clues and have reason to suspect that there's more to it than that—that yes, potentially, my boy, all this land acquisition has a criminal element to it."

The Sturgeon started to have his suspicions last July when Lemuria Holdings, the clandestine company Drake uses to conduct his real estate deals, bought the old cannery on the west side of Rabbit Warren Cove. "That on its own wasn't suspicious," he says. "The cannery has just sat there for decades—with a bit of elbow grease, I'm sure the old warehouses could be put to all sorts of good use. That's what I thought Drake was going to do—maybe turn it into a shopping center with some restaurants, something the hipsters down south would eat up—and I went over to investigate because I'm nosy, and I don't trust that greasy politician. But I found no sign of renovation several months in."

"Maybe there were construction delays?" Jonathan suggests. "Also, he doesn't have to do anything with the property. No crime there, either."

Pete nods. "All valid points, Mr. Davies. Though, there's one thing I know about Drake Parsippany: when he buys a property, he wastes no time putting his mark on it. The cannery was no different. He had workers doing something to the site, all right, but it was something I had never seen him do: the workers were drilling. Deep drilling, like they were reaching for oil. What's more, they always did it in the dead of night when they thought no one would be awake to hear or see them. Joke's on them—the Sturgeon hardly ever sleeps."

"I wish you would sleep," Lexi says. "You look tired, Pete."

"I'm fine," he says, waving a dismissive hand. "I'll sleep when I'm dead."

Jonathan agrees that the Sturgeon looks tired; his clothes hang a little large on him. But then, maybe it's the effect of the black cloud hovering around him.

"That's kind of suspicious, but I'm still not convinced," Jonathan says. "I also don't see what this has to do with the lighthouse, or me."

"I'm getting there," Pete says. "It's a lot of little things adding up, a confluence of mysteries. After a few months, the drilling at the cannery stopped, and the workers presumably had some downtime. Just after Thanksgiving, I saw an old friend down at the Sleeping Black Dog, someone I hadn't seen since the summer: Raymond Skinner."

The Sturgeon explains how surprising Raymond's summer disappearance was. The son of a fisherman and a decent one himself, he was one of few children born into the Cove's post-industrial state who never once thought to leave. He started drinking at the Dog at eighteen and kept at it, like a convocation, for over a decade; all that kept him from the bar these days were his daughter's weekend soccer matches and the occasional errand run or getaway with his wife to Eureka. Or, for weeks at a time, a contract job, but lately, jobs had been scarce.

Raymond told no one at the Dog what kept him away until the holidays because he had signed a confidentiality agreement, and he did not trust himself not to spill the beans over a couple of pale ales. Now, with the Sturgeon, he is finally spilling; he overturns the barrel and douses the bar with confidential information.

Much of what Raymond says the Sturgeon already knew from his late-night stakeouts, but after his fourth beer, Raymond happily discloses more about what's going on with all that drilling. "We found a cave, Pete," Raymond says. "They wouldn't tell the excavation crew what we were supposed to find, but we had a seismologist, a geologist, and a botanist on-site poring over schematics, so it was something serious. I'm still not sure why the botanist was there. Anyway, we were drilling through solid bedrock for several weeks—until we weren't. We had cut into this long tunnel. I didn't get much chance to explore, but it looked like the tunnel went on for miles—hard to tell, but the light from our headlamps didn't hit anything when we looked north or south. The tunnel was really wide where we were, too: you could have built a house in there."

The excavators only went down into the tunnel once to verify it was safe; after that, the geologist and botanist went down to take samples from the rock. The following day, Raymond got a call saying that his contract had met its natural end. A week later, he received his last paycheck, which included a payout for the rest of the contract period, plus a little more, an unexpected bonus. "Hush money," Raymond says. "But I can't keep this to myself, Pete. I'm not sure what their plans are for that tunnel, but it can't be good for our town."

In a gesture to his newfound riches, Raymond pays for the Sturgeon's drinks that night. In a way, it feels like no time has passed, and though he is hesitant, part of Pete looks forward to chatting with his old friend tomorrow night—maybe about the tunnel, maybe about nothing: fish tales and kids growing up too fast. But Raymond does not show up at the Dog the next day or the day after. On Monday, his wife comes to the bar, first angry, then distraught. Raymond has not been home all weekend.

Two months later, county police, having no leads, closed the missing person case of Raymond Skinner.

"Raymond's disappearance was the first one I knew about," Pete says, "but it wasn't the first to follow the pattern. A Yurok woman went missing last April from a roadside stand she managed a little farther up 101. Rumor had it that she had set up the stand on contested ground—there was a natural spring near the highway that the Yurok consider sacred, and the woman set up the stand as a form of protest—lately, Lemuria Holdings had its eye on the parcel surrounding the spring. The parcel is on unincorporated county land, but for generations, no one has tried to develop it, maybe out of deference to the Yurok, maybe because no one thought the land was worth developing. Two weeks after Drake's company put in a bid for the parcel, the woman and her stand vanished. Some claimed they were swept out to sea by a tsunami, though I think we would have heard about that."

"Lots more have disappeared since then," Lexi says. "Selma told me about it. Yurok women make their way down from the valley to the coast and never make their way back up. Apparently, it happens all the time—few know or seem to care except the Yurok or the Hoopa—but in the past two months, they say, the women have been disappearing more frequently." She stares at the Sturgeon apprehensively. "Pete, why didn't you tell me we were looking into this?"

Pete sits up with a mouth full of cotton. "I—I didn't want to worry you," he manages, finally.

"I was already fucking worried," Lexi says. "What if they went after Johnny's mystery car thief? What if they come after me next?"

Pete nods, looking down at the piles of paper on his desk as if he has forgotten something there. He says, "You're right, of course, of course. I should have told you from the start." His black cloud shrinks a little.

Jonathan has moved to the edge of the armchair without realizing it. Ready to leap up and act or run, whichever the situation calls for. "What's happening is very alarming," he says. "Horrible. And someone should do something about it. But I don't know what you think I can do," he says. "I'm no detective. I'm an architect, and not much of one the past few years. There are better assessors in this state, ones who have expertise in lighthouses. I've done one lighthouse job that involved nowhere near the work you would need for what Lexi showed me yesterday. I know even less about caves or tunnels. Throw missing women and fishermen in there and I'm lost."

The Sturgeon eyes Lexi and nods. Lexi pulls a photo from the stack of files she is holding. There, blown up in sharp relief, is the graffito they saw yesterday, the flayed lamb hung to bleed.

"Do you recognize this symbol?" Pete asks.

Jonathan nods. "Lexi and I saw it yesterday," he says, "when we went up to check out the lighthouse."

Pete shakes his head. "Don't fuck with me, boy," he says. "I know too much about your past. You know this symbol from somewhere else. From much earlier."

Jonathan glances at the doorway; he wonders if he has the strength to bolt out of it. The Sturgeon reads the glance perfectly. He raises a hand like you might with a wild, unpredictable animal and crouches a few inches above his seat. "Mr. Davies," he says, "we mean you no harm. Whoever you think is after you—"

"—I don't think anyone's after me," Jonathan says. "I *know* no one is after me."

"What is it, then?" Pete asks. "What are you afraid of?"

"I'm afraid of myself!" Jonathan grips the photo with one hand, jabbing at the symbol with a shaking finger. "This is my symbol," he says. "I did this. I don't remember doing it, but I must have."

"If you don't remember drawing the symbol, how can you be sure you did?"

"Because there's no other explanation," Jonathan says. "I saw myself drawing it. Not in a memory, but in one of my visions. And I was there. I was there the first time."

9

The Seed

SHE RISES FROM THE examination bench and stumbles out the door without anyone trying to stop her. It's as though the good doctor knows what will happen. It is black on the other side of the door, black as the space between galaxies. She steps into the blackness and falls. Not the cosmos, then; gravity is pulling her somewhere.

She falls, and no wind flows over her, no sound of rushing air. She knows she is falling only from the lurch in her stomach and the helpless flailing of her limbs. Then, she thinks of spreading her arms and legs wide. Her stomach calms. As Sister Hortense from Physics would explain, she has reached terminal velocity.

Unfortunately for Em, there is no rest for tortured souls. She floats peacefully for only a moment, thinking this must be what death is—a feeling of inky floating before no feeling at all—until she lands on a hard and unforgiving surface.

She has landed, sitting upright, on a bench in Echo Park. Before her, on the park's lake, paddle boats generate ripples of opal and gold; beyond that, the downtown LA skyline shimmers in the heat. Em thinks she must not have fallen anywhere after all, that she has merely been startled awake, as so often happens when a fall in a dream meets its natural end.

Not that Em would not know anything about that. She never dreams, not once that she can remember. A cue from her body—a lightness in the bones, the skin of her arms blemish-free—reminds her that she is only thirteen years old, that she's been waiting, holding an illicit latte in a paper cup from the bookstore café up the street, for her Aunt Maral, and she wonders if it has finally happened: a childhood of not dreaming and she has dozed off on this bench and caught up all at once, her brain fabricating a love affair to scandalize the habit off of her Theology teacher, Sister Roberta; a clandestine flight from school; a tragic death; and a year on the lam, flirting with redemption in a small coastal town before meeting—too conveniently, she must admit—her famed deadbeat dad, who sends her to fulfill her destiny as another statistic, another loss on the drug-war battlefield.

The lack of dreaming, up until now, has worn on her, and the increasing hormones have not helped. Grace Bellamy told her something unsettling on the knoll between the rectory and Garner Hall—Garner is where the biology nerds linger with the lab rats and turtles long after the vesper bell rings. Grace said that if someone doesn't dream, that means they are a psychopath: she learned it in Intro to Psychology, so it must be true. Em does not believe Grace Bellamy heard any such thing in a psychology class or that St. Stephen's has psychology classes, but she does not rebuke Grace with her usual, carefully honed barbs. Em is one of Garner's biology nerds; she does not let Grace Bellamy know this. She wants there to be no deterrents for Grace as she draws Em from her path to help Sister Beatrice embalm baby pigs: a task Em does not relish, one she is happy to detain, especially for someone like Grace. The girl is fifteen, an otherworldly age. In the dorms long after lights-out, she has caught Grace wandering in the halls with her friends, strutting around in nothing but panties and a scrunchy top. Scrunchy tops are for bimbos—a crinkly package to wrap around someone who thinks of themselves only as a gift to be offered. But Grace fills out the scrunchy top exceptionally well. Em would never wear one, but she can't stop staring when someone like Grace Bellamy does.

Like any idea told by someone with the power to pull you into their orbit, Grace's pop psychology finds a niche in Em's brain. That it goes unsubstantiated but not disproved only burrows the idea further in. Em's singular logic starts to dissolve. She posits to herself that psychosis is not normal: psychosis is the sharp drop on one end of the bell curve. Ergo: I am not normal: the girls of St. Stephen's check out the boys of St. Andrews at a coed event, and I witness it all because I'm checking out the girls. I'm not normal; I'm on the sharp drop of the bell curve. And what's more, I don't dream. I must be a psychopath.

Knowing now that she can dream provides Em no relief, not when dreaming, for her, is so vivid that she still feels the years of experience swollen inside her, influencing how she fidgets—more with her bottom half than with her top— informing how she looks toward the skyline, not with a cosmopolitan thrill but with disdain. How the contents of the cup in her hand no longer feel dangerous — coffee is small potatoes. Maral finally arrives and sits on the bench next to Em. They exchange

Aslanyan family drama and complain about the August heat. Maral asks how the new school is going. That brings Em to discuss her newfound psychological identity.

She means, at first, to only discuss the events of the day: her realization that having no interest in boys and letting pretty girls scramble her brain means she is "other," and because she is "other," she is mentally unstable, possibly dangerous. She bears the realization out in a vomit of words, as she always does with Maral, and because that is what she does with Maral, she keeps going: she describes the imagined future years of her life and how they cling on, how her first remembered dream refuses to let go.

Maral looks at her niece in a way she never has before. Is it fascination Em sees? And maybe wariness? Em looks away, suddenly ashamed to have shared so much and convinced she has finally alienated her aunt, the last person she thought she would. Then she feels her aunt's arm around her shoulder. The strange look has gone; Maral has rearranged her face. Almost like she was wearing a mask—or is she wearing one now? But unlike her face, her words are straightforward.

"Emma, *sireli*," Maral says, "what would cause you to call yourself that?" As though Em has declared she is a potted plant. "Do you know what it means to be a psychopath? I do. You forget that I'm a criminal prosecutor; we see it all. And when you spend enough time dissecting the mind of a criminal, you can't help but start to think like them, just a little. The difference between me and those criminals—not everyday criminals but the truly heinous ones who carry no remorse—is that I can separate having the thought from acting on it. If psychopaths want something, the only barriers they encounter are physical ones. No concern for other people enters their minds. Now, when you're looking at these girls at St. Stephen's, what do you think about? What do you hope will happen?"

Maral never talks down to Em or makes her feel like her concerns are invalid, even though she is only thirteen. But Maral has never spoken to Em like this. Her aunt is lean and sharp; her hair falls in a quick pointy bob just above her jawline, and she wears bespoke suits that run tight down her boxy shoulders and around her narrow waist to put all that sharpness on display. So dressed, according to Em's mother, she has laid waste to white-collar criminals in the courtroom; then, after hours, the clothes and the woman behind them have taken down more "traditional" members of the court—most of them White men—who were foolish enough to take a cursory glance at her short stature, her compact frame, and assume she was no threat. Em has never seen this side of her aunt until today. Maral's tone is light and jocular, conspiratorial—as if she were talking to a colleague in the DA's office.

Why the change? Only last week, Maral held a gentle watch over Em for their entire visit as though she feared her niece might shatter from a gust of wind. Did the effects of the dream, or even just talking about it, make Em seem less vulnerable and childish? She does feel more adult, though not quite at the criminal prosecutor level. Maybe just enough to face difficult questions head-on.

"Mostly," Em tells her, "I don't hope for anything. I'm kind of just afraid."

"What are you afraid of?"

"I'm afraid of what will happen if they catch me looking at them. Any of them. What will they think if they notice I've been checking them out?"

"And Grace?" Em's lips form a tight, thin band at the mention of her crush. "What do you want from her?"

"I guess I want her to like me. Like, she doesn't even have to be into me, you know? Just like me."

"Nothing sinister about that," Maral says. "Why do you want her to like you?"

"I don't know; she's just.... Grace is gorgeous and put together, and people just flock to her. If someone like that likes me, maybe there's hope for me. Maybe I'm not so weird."

Maral smiles and gently squeezes her niece's shoulder. "It is safe to say, Emma, that you are unequivocally not a psychopath." The word "unequivocally" is new to Em. She is flattered when she looks up its meaning later but unsure it applies to her: a girl caught in a holding pattern of ambiguity. "You want to be liked," Maral continues, "not to further an agenda, but because you think Grace liking you reflects your character. That's natural; that's how most people think. If anything, I'm more worried about Grace's mental state. Sounds to me like she's stringing you along and planting falsehoods in your brain. If anyone is a psychopath, it's Grace."

Em giggles at the thought or tries to: it comes out more like a dry, weary chuckle. *Just like Andre's laugh right before he fled from you.* She sees the boy screaming and tearing at the door to a rundown apartment in a town many miles away (if the town even exists). She thinks, put the dream away; you're awake now. But in the dream, at least one person liked me for a while. And

Fiona—Em still remembers moments when saying "I like you" to her, and her saying it back, felt more revolutionary than the three similar words their peers preloaded with so much weight and trepidation because, for them, the butterflies and stomach lurches, the gasps and shaky knees, the make-out sessions in the woods behind the cemetery—all that gave way to a quiet afternoon on the beach listening to the tide roll out, saying very little, hardly moving, just enjoying each other's company. Dream or no dream, the memory allows Em to put Grace Bellamy on a high shelf and not reach for her again.

There must be more to the dream than that—more than morsels of wisdom to chase away self-involved teenagers. Em asks for Maral's honest opinion, and her aunt sits a little higher on the bench at the request, removing her arm from Em's shoulder and clasping her hands in her lap. Poised, like she is about to give difficult but crucial advice.

"I think the dream is what you make of it," Maral says slowly. "That may sound trite, but it's the best advice I can give. You can assume you're destined for that future or take it as a warning of what to avoid. Maybe this will help." Maral opens her palms. Like a magician, she reveals something Em swears was not in her hands a moment ago: a necklace with a small brass chain and a locket shaped like a teardrop, no bigger than the tip of a finger. There is a seed inside the locket, Maral explains. "Not just any seed," she says. "It's a lemon seed from a tree as far from LA as you can imagine. *Tatik* Lucine, your great-grandmother, gave it to me before we left Crimea. She had a small grove of lemons in her yard, so I assumed it must have come from there, but she claims it came from the homeland, from an ancient palace grove in Yerevan that her great uncle had the privilege to tend. She gave me the necklace and told me something very strange. *Tatik* said: 'From the seventh daughter of Aslan, this seed shall bear eternal fruit.' One day, I would have a daughter and give her the seed, and her daughter, in turn, would plant the seed and fulfill the prophecy. At least, that's what *tatik* hoped for. Now, I'm a woman of reason, but I think certain traditions have value. I've given up on having children—not because I don't think I could; there's just no room in my life for them—but you, Emma, are as much a daughter to me as anyone."

Maral fastens the locket around Em's neck. The metal feels warm on her skin, and the touch of it reminds her that this is how it all started. The dream, the seed, and a future foreseen in exacting detail until this moment. Em tried at first to resist the flow of events, but after a while, her memory of what was to come, the certainty of it, made any other path seem daunting—even if following the path led her to flee Glendale and all she knew out of willfulness and fear. She must have forgotten the dream as time passed: why hold onto it when waking life starts to play it out for you? But she forgot the dream at her peril, she realizes now. Had she remembered, she would not have mistaken this moment for anything more than a distant memory.

"Hold onto that doubt," Maral says. Her voice floats above her, back toward the exam room door hanging high in the sky. It still sounds like Maral—the cadence is the same, the way she pauses to choose the right words—but now each word is a song. A song no human could sing. Em wonders if this is how angels would speak. "We are deep in the roots now," Maral says. "You are special, *sireli*, but the roots do not discriminate. They will try to keep you here. They will make a convincing case that what you see has not already happened, or worse, that it does not matter that it has. Pay attention, and whatever you see or think, hold onto that doubt. Doubt is what will get you out of here alive."

Maral stands. A heavy breeze sweeps over the pond and carries Maral with it as though she is no more than a pillar of dust.

10

━ • ━

The Bloody Girl in the Bathtub

IT STARTED WITH A boy pinned to a telephone pole. It ended with a girl bruised and bloody in a bathtub.

The boy pinned to the pole made no sense. He was pinned by an old Ford stake truck from the 1930s. To match the era of the truck, the boy wore suspenders; his short hair, combed and pomaded, looked like a polished bowling ball. It was as though someone had staged a traffic fatality from a different time. The scene would make any driver pull over or call for help, even if they were confused about what they saw. Jonathan tries to get the person driving him to stop, but the driver pays no attention; he does not seem to see what Jonathan sees. No one else on the busy road pulls over, either.

The boy makes less and less sense as the weeks wear on and Jonathan keeps coming up this road. Every time he passes the corner of Sunset and Beverly, there they are, the boy and the truck, a single entity now. The boy does not decay; the truck does not rust. They are forgotten, except by Jonathan, who knows nothing of their history, only their demise.

Jonathan is 21 years old. USC is freshly behind him, and fast on its heels comes a stampede of job offers, so many that Jonathan has trouble deciding what to pick. He is weary of the grind of downtown—tent cities overtaking whole blocks of Skid Row, despite the booming economy; the smell of piss and motor oil permeating Pershing Square—weary of the daily struggles he sees in South Los Angeles, too. He opts for a position with a high-end housing firm to keep him and Mina comfortable. Mina does not object. She grew up poor in Chicago, sharing a room with three other siblings and, for a few years, a mattress with one of them. She figures that room to breathe and move about will help her keep the observatory efforts on track. When Jonathan's salary allows them to build a home in the Pacific Palisades, she squeals in delight—the house is just a short drive from where the observatory crew has started to break ground.

He first sees the boy pinned to the truck the day he gets his first client, a client who insists they meet at the site in Beverly Hills where their new villa, in Jonathan's expert hands, will soon stand tall. Maybe it's the pressure of his first big gig that causes him to see things. He pumps his client's hands and effortlessly absorbs the baroque, sometimes contradictory vision for the villa; running on overdrive and away from his thoughts, he returns to the firm's Santa Monica office and makes the design his own, drafting it on paper. The other architects, most of whom have switched to computer-aided design and which Jonathan learned to do as well, find his antiquated approach charming—the way you might look on, with a mixture of disdain and pity, at an architect coming up fast on retirement: watching him work with one eye, scouting his corner office with the other.

That night, though his engine runs on fumes, he sits down with Mina in their temporary Palisades apartment to lay out the designs for their dream home. On his way home, he picks up a bottle of wine to celebrate his first big client. (At least, that's the reason he gives Mina.) They work their way through the bottle as they sketch rough plans, fashioning themselves a millennial Ray and Charles Eames—fitting since the lot they have purchased is just a few scant blocks from the iconic home the Eames's designed and lived in for so many years. The wine and their hopes and dreams, conceived on paper, help him forget the boy pinned to the pole.

The next day, the boy is back on his mind. After work, he drives back to Sunset and Beverly, the opposite direction of home. There they sit, the boy and the truck, throngs of Rodeo Drive shoppers paying them no mind. They are not of this Gucci and Balenciaga world. They are trying to tell Jonathan something he forgot. They fail to remind him, day after day. He keeps coming back.

He moves on from his first big client, and as though a switch is set, he stops visiting the corner of Sunset and Beverly. Sets that trauma on a high shelf. But he has subsumed the trauma as his own: it follows him, it mutates and meets him farther down the road, huddled in alleyways, ones darker than the Night's Sky mural in the Arts District downtown. He goes out for lunch with colleagues in Santa Monica and passes a midblock service road that dead-ends into a loading bay and a cluster of slumbering dumpsters. On the loading bay, a pair of eyes grabs him and makes him turn his head. He wishes he hadn't.

Some of Jonathan's colleagues have come around to accept his quirks—and he, in turn, has stopped drafting everything on paper. Lunch that day is a "boy's lunch," a concept that makes him cringe but that he must oblige to make friends at the firm. Fellow architect friends, at least. Women work at the firm—he befriended Haley, a senior partner's executive assistant, on day one—but if there are any women architects, they must keep them on another floor. Food is optional at boy's lunch, but there is a two-drink minimum. Hard liquor is encouraged. In other circumstances, Jonathan may object to drinking on the job, but the sight in the alleyway makes it more palatable. He orders a Tom Collins. When he gets flack for ordering a "bitch drink" for his second round, he orders, and to his surprise thoroughly enjoys, a bourbon on the rocks.

After lunch, he breaks free from the overloud crew of architects, who have grown obnoxious, claiming he needs to run an errand for his wife. He returns to the dead-end service road. The eyes are waiting for him. The eyes have not moved. They continue not to move, just stare forward, unblinking, as he walks toward them. Around the eyes, a girl materializes. A White girl with stringy black hair covering half her face, a canvas satchel slung around one shoulder on which several slogans, by way of pinned buttons, demand several things, including A Reunified Germany, Abolishing Apartheid, and Release of the Central Park Five. She sits slumped over on the loading bay, arms outstretched, palms up. Two gashes in her wrists ooze a slow trickle of blood down the loading bay and into the street. Jonathan thinks she must be dead, but when he steps closer, she says, still not looking at him, "This wasn't me. I didn't do this." He asks, "What didn't you do," though he looks at her wrists and knows the answer. He reaches for her shoulder to shake it and try to rouse her; he falls forward, catching himself on the loading bay's edge. There is no girl, no pool of blood in the street.

Jonathan returns to the office to gather his things. He leaves early and heads to the library. The buttons help him sketch a rough timeline. He searches the internet for twenty frustrating minutes, then heads to the microfilm; there, he pores through months of articles in the Times and the Santa Monica Sun, from January 1990 onwards, for mention of a young girl found in the street dead and suspected of suicide. He gives up when the Times confirms that the German Democratic Republic has been integrated into a new, Western, Federal Republic of Germany. There is no mention of a young girl committing suicide. There are no mentions of suicide at all. It's not newsworthy if someone believes death came at your own hand.

The stars reveal themselves as he pulls away from downtown Santa Monica and into the low-lit foothills of the Palisades. He tells Mina that a new client kept him burning the midnight oil. She sets him down and gives him a back rub. She has no reason not to trust him, not yet.

Jonathan avoids the dead-end service road, looks away if he must pass it, and in return, the dead make more conspicuous appearances. When he goes for a swim near home, a body washes up on the beach right next to where two children build a sand moat—oblivious, they form the moat around the body, burying the evidence. He avoids the beach after that. Months later, when he and Mina go out to dinner to celebrate the groundbreaking of their new home, a puffed-up middle-aged White man in wide lapels and a ruffled dress shirt clutches his chest, then clutches Jonathan's sleeve before falling face-forward next to their table.

Jonathan leaps up with a shout and draws looks across the restaurant, though the only look he cares about is Mina's: large round eyes wide but calm, lips slightly parted, studying him, wondering what could have given her even-keeled husband such a fright. He says it's nothing, a darting shadow he thought was a rat. He orders another bottle of wine.

The wine steadies his increasingly agitated nerves—until that won't cut it, and he resorts to keeping a cheap bottle of bourbon locked in his desk. Eventually, he finds, with the benefit of alcohol, the dead come around less, too. That's when his slow descent pitches to a sudden, quick drop.

He does not lose clients right away. Jonathan finds he is a functional alcoholic, and many of his clients—and colleagues—appear to be, too. When the house is complete—a modest but powerful place, filled with natural light and nestled in a grove of persimmons, the ripe fruit reflecting warm and cheerful tones in Mina's study that reminds her of autumn in Chicago—Jonathan brings his new ersatz friends to call, first for the occasional after-hours business meeting, then, as the drinking gets worse, several times a week. Mina, still not much of a drinker, retreats to her study. Construction on the observatory is ramping up; she needs to focus and pull her own long hours. He sees what is happening but in a dull way, as though viewing it on the small black-and-white TV screen Ma and Pa Davies used to keep, and hardly ever use, in their front room.

It all comes to bear one morning when Jonathan claims—not for the first time after staying up late with a freewheeling client—that he is wretchedly sick and cannot work. Mina looks at him levelly: she has errands to run, she tells him; she will be out all morning, possibly longer; she hopes that gives him ample time to rest undisturbed. Cool but accommodating, not geared to make a fuss or lash out about his third late night in a row—how do you expect to feel, he imagines her saying, when you've had so much to drink that you can't get off the couch and come to bed? He wants her to lash out. He needs a trigger as outlandish and irrational as what he still sees in the height of his drunkenness—the dead nudge him gently, like concerned friends, to make sure he has not become one of them—he needs that push, or believes he does, to tell Mina what the hell is wrong with him.

Noon comes, and he is still sober, a manageable state when he stays home, where the ghosts can't seem to find him. But in place of the dead, long-ignored thoughts lurk and haunt. He feels Mina slipping away. When he's in deep and bellowing nonsense, she pretends to listen, then goes to another room. Or she takes her car out, that is how she describes it—I'm taking the car out, won't be long—as though it's a pet in need of exercise. He's not sure how long she is gone because she does it when time, for him, has stopped playing by the usual rules. Today, she gave a timeline; he can track the hours, and his body refuses to sleep and truncate all that wait and worry. He doubts Mina would have an affair, but that only means, when the circumstances call for it, that she would not hesitate to leave him.

At 5 pm, his brain decides that the onslaught of thinking must end. That the dead, with some liquid assistance, are preferable. Like a marionette, his body dangles from a tether tied to his pounding skull and shuffles the short trip down the hill to Patrick's Roadhouse. Patrick's has become Jonathan's favorite haunt in the short time they have lived in their new home for obvious reasons: he can easily walk there, load up on cheap beers and greasy diner food, say hi to Bill, the owner, then drift back home on a thoughtless cloud. He tries that today, but his thoughts, heavier than usual, still weigh him down when he steps out of the roadhouse. A gentle winter rain starts as he walks to make sure he stays grounded; the rain picks up and soaks his clothes within a block. He ducks into a bar, an old, breezy place that caters to beach bums. He encounters a few, including a surfer who sits at the end of the bar with a bloody stump for a leg and a ragged gash in his side, intestines slipping out and looking like the sausage links he just ate at Patrick's. Jonathan orders a double bourbon on the rocks and tosses it back, which dims the mutilated surfer a shade or two; two more doubles and he's gone, or at least not visible. Jonathan thinks he can hear the surfer wailing in the background, like a cry for help in the night several houses down that you know you should not ignore, but you too often do.

Jonathan orders a fourth double bourbon to try to shut out the wailing. He tries for a fifth, but the bartender cuts him off. He gets up, stumbles, and kindly but firmly is asked to leave the bar. Luckily, there is a liquor store just two doors down where he gets his usual desk cabinet fix. He sips from the fresh bottle of Jim Beam, clad in a paper bag, as he walks back up the hill. It's dark out now. No surfers crying for help, no fears that Mina will leave, no thoughts of work the next day or the mortgage or whether he will ever build the nomadic bungalows he designed that Mina's shining stars illuminated at that first architect's showcase, the bungalows he hoped would replace the tent cities of Skid Row, which only seemed to grow the farther he moved from them. Even the rain, which flattens his hair and drips into his eyes, is no longer of concern. There is so little of Jonathan walking up that hill that if someone were to ask his name, he would say no one ever gave him one.

The rest of the night—except for the impending vision—returns to him only much later and only in patches. Mina's hair, high and wild, shining like veins of onyx from the light in the doorway. Lots of shouting, mostly from him. A feeble attempt, from him, at reconciliation: he thinks he may have tried to make a pass at her. In response, he remembers being shoved onto the living room couch. From there, it is a short, sharp drop to unconsciousness.

Blistering from the worst hangover of his life the next morning, he gets up from the couch where he must have slept and notices, with some alarm, that the front door is wide open, and a suitcase mysteriously sits not far from it. He goes to the kitchen for water and hears a gentle moaning down the hallway. Down where their bedroom lies. He takes slow steps toward it, his heart in his throat with each step. The bedroom is a shambles: drawers thrown open, clothes piled on the bed—some neatly laid out; others, many of them his, wadded in heaps—all of which tells a tale he already knows of a wife desperate to leave his rapidly deteriorating husband. What's been scrawled on Mina's vanity mirror, however, presents a mystery more profound than the open door and the suitcase beside it, a mystery Jonathan finds, after nearly two decades, he cannot run from or shake off.

In lipstick—the same shade Mina wore that fateful night at the showcase—a hurried and wavering hand has drawn a rune, a symbol to ward off demons—or perhaps, to invite them in. Jonathan is not sure at first what the rune is supposed to represent. However, when he gets closer to examine the scrawl and runs a hand down one of the posts supporting the mirror, the room goes dark. He sees the rune being drawn through the eyes of the artist and feels the intent manifest in a fractured mind. Wherever it is drawn, this symbol shall mark where the lamb, skin peeled back to reveal its true and unblemished nature, will slowly bleed to appease the gods.

The eyes he looks through, which his guilt-stricken imagination proposes must be his own, drift from the mirror to the ensuite bathroom door. A heavy boot kicks the door open, causing the jamb to splinter. Sitting on the toilet in tears, Mina is shocked by the sudden intrusion but quick to respond: she lifts the toilet tank lid and sends it crashing down on the intruder's head, causing shards of porcelain to scatter across the room. The intruder stumbles but is not brought down, fueled, it seems, by the will of a violent and vengeful god. The intruder drives Mina against the back of the bathtub. She hits her head against the tub's lip; stunned, she moans out Jonathan's name, barely above a whisper. The intruder bends Mina over the tub, pulls down her pants, and enters her roughly from behind.

When a knife comes out, when the flaying is about to begin, Mina pleads, not this way. I know what you want, she says. I'll give you what you want, but I need to watch you do it. I want to watch you do it. The mind behind the eyes thinks this one is worthy: none of the others were so willing. The knife drops, and Mina takes her opening, lifting the long, jagged shard of porcelain that slid within reach under the tub and plunging it deep into the intruder's upper thigh.

Jonathan hears a howl inside his head. The intruder staggers back, running from the bathroom and beyond the bounds of Jonathan's vision. Morning light creeps into the bedroom. He hears the moaning again. It's coming from just beyond the bathroom door, which lies slightly open, the jamb torn half off the wall.

He does not dare go in. She is alive and, from what he saw, not too severely injured, though she may have a concussion. He shoves the wads of his clothes stacked on the bed into an old backpacker's pack, the one he took the night his father wandered blind onto a country road and had his life cut short. He drives Ol' Blue Eyes as far as Malibu, where he stops at a payphone to report, as a concerned neighbor, a possible breaking-and-entering the night before at the new house at 330 East Rustic Road. I heard shouting, he says. Calls for help. You might want to send an ambulance as well as police.

II

— • —

The Roots

THE WIND SPEEDS UP and swirls around Em, bringing dark clouds that blot out the sun. The clouds twist upward in narrow bands to form a bulbous cone, the open exam room door shining from the cone's tip like a distant planet.

The clouds are like the base of an old yew, Em thinks. If she were looking at the yew from inside of it.

St. Stephen's has an old yew in one corner of the quad, a fat and meandering tree that the nuns claim predates the school by over 300 years. When Em saw the grand sequoias just before the school year started—part of her thirteenth birthday party, and she imagines, a feeble apology from her mother—they left her with the impression that old trees have no other way of showing their age than growing improbably high. The yew defies this notion. Its age is apparent from its whorls and numerous stu-dent-imposed scars, yet it does not tower over Garner Hall like Em would expect. During its multiple centuries, it has primarily thickened, the base suggesting deep bands burrowing into the earth that the branches could only hope to emulate. The tree spellbinds Em. It seems impossible to have survived as long as the nuns claim, so she asks Sister Beatrice for proof. The sister provides, using evidence she collected herself. "This is a Pacific Yew," Sister Beatrice explains. "They don't live quite as long as some of the genera in the Yew family, but they hold their own." Em reads the results and feels transformed: a living thing, she finds out, tells time with greater accuracy than any historical record written by humans ever could.

She falls in love immediately with biology. She signs up for as many of Sister Beatrice's classes as she can for the next semester and spends afternoons under the yew, drawn to it unlike any tree—when Em lies under its canopy and reads Darwin, she swears that a three-part chorus hums her a calming tune.

It is her reading spot, hers alone, and she keeps it that way by telling everyone who passes that the tree is poisonous. Not a lie, but she does not correct her classmates' assumptions that sitting under the tree is enough to slowly kill them, as though her willingness to sit under it does not contradict that idea. She sometimes wonders if they have reasoned that out and chosen to leave the strange new girl alone; when she reads, however, those thoughts do not bother her as much; with a book in her hand, she does not need or want any other companions.

When the girl with the copper hair approaches the yew one day, and Em, catching the briefest glance of her over her book, gives the usual missive, she acts as though Em has said no more than a welcome greeting. The girl sits against the tree, far enough away from Em that her back is turned but close enough that Em can still see her. She is, at first, an unwelcome distraction: the copper hair, burnished by afternoon sunlight, draws Em's eyes away from *The Origin of the Species*—a hard enough book to absorb without such novelties on display. Em has never seen hair quite this color except in movies and thinks it must be a bottle job, but after looking at it a little longer, studying the girl's roots and the fair hair on her arms, Em changes her mind. The girl pulls out a book, too, and Em finds she can no longer read Darwin, that whatever the girl is reading is far more interesting. With Em's impeccable vision—a trade-off, she supposes, for the swirling horror show of her irises—she can make out passages of the book without any trouble from where she sits. The book describes a land covered in snow, a scene Em would have difficulty picturing were it not for the vivid description:

> He watched sleepily the flakes, silver and dark,
> falling obliquely against the lamplight.

The girl turns the page, and Em spots a title: *The Dubliners*. Em imagines the land these Dubliners occupy as an endless stretch of cold and darkness.

The dream part of Em steps back and wonders what would happen if she shifted the timeline; contrary to what the dream dictated, what if she introduced herself to Fiona here? What impact would it have if they bonded over books before they bonded over other, less literary drugs? It is a thought she would have had that day. Still, another part of her—the future part, she realizes—has draped another layer over her consciousness. This layer asks the question primarily out of curiosity, not because it thinks any behavioral change would have an impact. The future self interjects only briefly, but for the roots, it is enough: at the first sign of self-awareness, the day dissolves, and Em is catapulted forward.

She is in a bathroom stall, crying. Crying and bleeding, thinking she is about to die alone on the toilet. She has had, up to this point, an academic understanding of menstruation; she knows now that no book or bored middle-school teacher could prepare her for the feeling that she has internally ruptured her femoral artery, that the walls of her cervix have become porous, and that without immediate medical attention, she will soon bleed out. What's more, she is paralyzed by embarrassment: why should it happen at 2 am and force her to wake up one of the sisters (or worse, one of her bunkmates) to ask if they have a tampon, a pad, an ACE bandage, or, better, a tourniquet? She would rather die than reveal her burgeoning womanhood.

A head pops over the stall to her left. A head she recognizes, the copper hair a little less distracting under the dim lights of the dormitory bathroom. The girl who reads Joyce for fun and does not fear poisonous trees quickly assesses the situation. "Heavy flow?" she asks. Em nods, realizing then that it must be only that, strangely disappointed that she is not about to die. "I get them all the time," the girl says, "so I'm always prepared." She ducks her head back down briefly, then reappears with a tampon. To Em, it looks like a contraband cigar wrapped in a frilly package to conceal its identity.

Em reaches up and takes the tampon. She unwraps the tampon and studies it, and she hopes that the girl, having fulfilled her nightly duty to alleviate unexpected periods, has ducked back into her stall. But the girl remains perched above her, watching, expectant. She has a small nose that looks like a thumb hitching a ride; the nose twitches when she suspects things are not entirely aligned. It twitches now. "Something wrong?" she asks, noticing Em's blank stare. Then the girl's eyes go wide. "Oh, sweetie, is it—is this your first time? Fucking hell, what a place to have it. I'll be right down. Can you—?" She points down to Em's stall door. Em wants to protest but finds that her hand unlatches the door without her having much say. The girl steps in. She smells like strawberry shortcake and diesel fuel, and Em gets a good look at her eyes, eyes like hers, in a sense. Where someone might study the girl's eyes like a painting, they would study Em's like an approaching storm.

The girl takes the tampon from Em. She displays the applicator and runs her hand down one side as a perfume-counter girl might with the latest fragrance. Then, uncharacteristic of a perfume-counter girl, she squats and mimes the tampon's insertion. Em laughs, no longer worried about the bleeding, but laughing makes her wince. "Bad cramps, too?" the girl asks. Em nods. The girl reaches into her back pocket and produces a tin of mints. The mints are long gone from the tin; rows of little cylinders wrapped in paper lie in their place. They look somewhat like tampons, too, only much smaller.

"If you must know," the girl says, as though Em had looked at her with accusation, "these are what brought me to the bathroom at this hour. I don't just hang around the bathroom at night like some menstrual good Samaritan. I have a hookup down in Venice: my buddy Pedro. He only deals the best shit. A drag off one of these, and you'll forget all about your periods. Two drags, and you might forget your name."

Em knows intuitively what the little cylinders are from her favorite TV crime dramas, and because the dream has laid it all out for her, it displaces any fears about the drug's effect. She inserts the tampon, washes her hands, and in the far dark corner of the freshman-floor bathrooms of Laurie Hall, she smokes her first joint with a Junior, with the future love of her life. Properly acquainted, the girl finally offers her name—hearing it feels like reaching a satisfying plot twist in a book, one Em saw coming many pages ago. When the girl suggests they kiss—another first for Em that night—Em thinks she can taste the girl's name on her lips. Fiona: the essence of strawberries and diesel fuel; the same taste the marijuana provides. I must taste that way now, too, Em thinks.

She wants to linger in this darkened corner longer than history would dictate. For a while, she does. Many years pass. Not years in the sense Em has come to know them, not the span of events that led her here, not anything she can trace in time. She feels older, though, the more she lingers. As she ages, she also expands; she feels her toes creep into the grout between the floor tiles; her fingers, pressed against the wooden siding as Fiona embraces her, find purchase between the slats and climb, climb, climb through the rafters and into the night's sky. It is almost too late by the time she recognizes her expansion. She recalls Maral's warning: you are special, Emma, but the roots do not discriminate. That much is clear—they mean to take her as one of their own.

As though rising from a deep sleep, she opens her eyes. Sunlight shines through a distant window at the end of a long hallway. The hallway smells of antiseptic. (And of Andre—very faintly, she can make out his animal scent.) She sits in the hallway in an uncomfortable chair. No one is coming to find her. No one comes to give her any news. She has spent the night in this chair, in and out of sleep. Picking her way through *The Structure of Evolutionary Theory* for the third time, despairing that she will never fully understand it.

Anywhere but here. Even the cold camper van where a too-familiar body lies drawn of its color would be preferable. Em thinks, I'm aware! I know what this is, damn it! But at this moment, awareness does not seem to be enough.

A door near her opens; a nurse steps out. She approaches Em slowly. Her mother is awake, the nurse tells her. She wants to see her. Em enters the room, and the nurse walks down the hallway, leaving them alone.

The hospital room is nice enough, Em supposes. Unshared, with a bathroom in the corner. It is dark here, though; the curtains are drawn at her mother's request. There should be flowers, but there are none. Maral would have sent flowers. That she has not sent any flowers confirms to Em that she has vanished from the earth or has at least gone to such a far reach of it that no one can contact her.

Her mother sits upright in the bed, staring. Her lips parted like she was about to say something. Her eyes move quickly across Em and suggest that she is considering a hundred different ways to start the conversation. To explain. She swallows them all.

"How are you?" Em asks. A stupid question, but she must start somewhere.

"The doctors say I'll pull through," her mother says. "They were concerned about liver damage, but I guess I'm still young enough to fully recover."

"That's good to hear," Em says. "Not really what I meant, though."

Her mother huffs and looks down at her upturned wrists, which still bear scars but have improved in the last two years. A stranger would hardly glance at them.

"What are you reading?" her mother asks, gesturing toward the book Em cradles in her arms. "Something for school?"

"If only," Em says. "This is probably a little advanced for high school. It's advanced for me, but I'm trying."

"Can I take a look?" Em hands the book to her mother. "It's hefty," she says. "*The Structure of Evolutionary Theory*. I had no idea you were interested in evolution."

"It's kind of a new interest." Em wants to say that by "new," she means "in the last two years," but she keeps this to herself.

"What's the big takeaway?" her mother asks. "That is if you've gotten that far in the book."

"Well, there's a lot to unpack," Em says. "Probably the most interesting thing is the theory of punctuated equilibrium. The idea is that evolution happens in short spurts followed by long periods of stasis. At least, I think that's the idea. It's kind of complicated."

"Short, as in years?"

"Short, as in tens of thousands of years. Short from a geological perspective."

"And here, I just design buildings," her mother says. "My daughter is trying to unravel the mysteries of life itself. You sound so grown up. When did that happen?"

I don't feel grown up, Em thinks. But instead, she says: "I guess it happened while you weren't looking." There is genuine despair in her mother's eyes, more profound than any futility Em feels at understanding evolutionary biology. Her mother clears her throat and swallows the despair.

"Do you like it at St. Stephens?" her mother asks.

"It's fine," Em says casually. "It was hard at first, but I've gotten used to it. I like some of the classes, at least." She does not dare mention Fiona or that the two of them skip the classes they deem unimportant, like Catechism, to pursue a turf-side practicum on Pharmacology instead. She would have told Mar-al, but her mother, she imagines, would not be so receptive. Not even at her lowest and humblest.

"I never meant to send you there," her mother says. "As you know, I haven't gone to church and never forced you to. And your grandmother still hasn't forgiven me because the place isn't Orthodox. Sometimes, I think she was angrier at me for that than these lovely souvenirs I gave myself." She raises her wrists, waving around the slit marks—the stigmata, the nuns might say—like they are a pair of chic new bracelets.

Her mother means it as a joke, but it falls flat. In the quiet that follows, Em tracks the irregular rhythm coming from the hallway: the syncopated chimes of the monitors in other rooms, the swift shuffle of footsteps when one of those chimes decides to break into a solo. "According to the doctors," Em says, "you weren't so committed this time. I mean, you didn't even take the whole bottle."

"Emma, I—"

"—Don't, Mom. Just... don't. I know what you're going to say."

"I know I've failed you, Em. I've failed a lot of people, but you are the only one I really care about failing. I'll bet the nuns would have a lot to say about what I've done."

"Or grandma," Em says. "You've done this twice to her now." And to me: to me. "It's not like the Roman Catholics are the only ones who think killing yourself is a sin."

"Don't put it that way," her mother says. "It sounds so harsh, 'killing yourself.'"

"What else am I supposed to call it? I'm calling a spade, a spade."

"But I didn't —"

"—No," Em says bitterly, "you phoned it in this time. What, I guess you were just lonely? I could have been there for you. Instead, you had me carted away at the first sign of trouble like I couldn't handle it. But you taught me how to handle it. You taught me to 'fight the world,' remember? 'Don't let the bastards grind you down,' you told me. What happened to all that?"

"You don't know what I've been through." Her mother's voice is small and petulant, like a child's.

"I don't know because you won't tell me! You won't tell me what you've been through; you won't tell me about my dad; you won't tell me anything!" Em tries not to think about it too much, but everything she had known and trusted in her life came tumbling down shortly after she asked what her father was like. Her mother, harsh but fair, reticent, yes, but endlessly supportive of the two-woman crew she had established with her daughter—two scrappy Armenian bitches against the world—seemed to crumple when forced to think about her erstwhile husband. Something else must have happened, but it is not for Em to know. She wants to know, but whenever she beats the odds and gets her mother to open up, it comes at a cost not worth the knowledge.

"What's important," her mother says, "is that I'm finally getting help. Real help. So that I can be there for you. That's what I wanted to talk to you about." Em knows what is coming, but that does not stop the fear from bubbling up inside her; like trauma, revisiting its source does not make it hurt any less. "I'm going away for a while," she says. "A recovery clinic in Pasadena will take me next week. It's expensive, but I have a little saved up, and I can refinance the house if I need to."

"Next week?" Em says. "But I get off for summer break at the end of the month."

"Yes, I know. It's morbid to think about, but if I had been, well, 'successful' this time, it wouldn't have been much different." Her mother hands Em back the book. With its heft gone from her lap, she seems impossibly small and light, as though only the book was giving her substance. "I wish my sister was still here," she says. "She would have known what to do. She would have taken care of you where I can't. But she's not, so that's that. That's why I think it's best that you go live with your uncle in Chicago." She says this last part slowly, giving each word space to disperse through the still hospital air.

"For the summer, you mean." Em says it like she is reciting a line—not because she believes it, but because her role requires it. It makes sense now why her mother is putting St. Stephens down—a school she touted two years ago as a "great opportunity."

"Maybe we could work something out," Em says. "I've made some friends at school. Maybe I could go live with their parents for the summer."

"It's not just about the summer, dear," her mother says, her voice now flat. She stares down at the bed, unable to look her daughter in the eye. "Will they take you for Christmas? For Easter? And more than once? I can't ask you to impose yourself on another family. Not when you have family who can care for you while I'm healing."

"Wait, what you mean, 'more than once?'"

"It's going to take a while to heal. The program at the clinic is a minimum of six months. It's a little more intensive than your usual rehab. After that, they suggest you take another nine months to ease back into daily life."

"But I barely know my uncle," Em is trembling now, her voice squeaking like she is thirteen again. "He gives me the creeps, and his wife—who, are you forgetting, is only eight years older than me?—she's a fucking gun lobbyist! In Chicago!"

"Emma, language."

"Give me a fucking break, Mom. You used to drop F-bombs around me all the time. What happened? What have you done with my mother?"

"Emma, I just can't. I..." her mother raises her arms in front of her face, tears rolling down her cheeks. "Please, Emma, do this for me. I need to know you're OK. Your uncle is flying down right before I go into the clinic. He's already booked his flight. Emma, please." Her mother reaches out, grasping for the invisible cord she hopes will draw her daughter back.

"You can't have it both ways, Mom," Em says. She puts the book in her pack and heads toward the door. Before she leaves, she turns around and says: "Maybe I should start calling you 'Mina' since you've abandoned the idea of being a mother."

She walks out, her mother calling after her weakly at first, then louder, her screams reverberating down the hallway, nurses rushing to calm her down.

And I ran and ran and ended up in the same place. Half-dead in a hospital. Before she pitches forward again, a vital thought pops into Em's head: perhaps the start of a way out. The book had not played a role before now. She kept it in her sack, and perhaps as a result, perhaps not, the conversation devolved much quicker and became much uglier: no eloquent exit, more vulgarity. Then, she recalls where this alternate version of reality came from. She had wanted her mother to see the book, but at the last moment, she had tucked it into her sack. After she busted out of St. Stephen's two days later, riding with Fiona in her brother's camper van up the coast, freshly stocked by Pedro, she thought about what would have been different if she had kept the book in her arms. It would have ended the same, her fifteen-year-old self reasoned, but perhaps there would have been more art to it. Two years later, her current self, spinning out of control like her mother, sees a different value in the fantasy. Maybe she could have shown her mother something good in her life—just a piece of it. Perhaps, from that, things could still have turned another way.

She starts to understand that the roots do not mean to project her life like a continuous reel devoid of interpretation. They curate her memories; some moments lived in the current reality, some imagined: a branching path.

The roots are telling her a story. They are telling her that things could be different. That her journey is not destined for despair.

12

Acceptance

As Jonathan recounts parts of his life that he has told no one about, parts that have remained secrets so long they have started to take on the character of myth, Lexi sits tall in her chair and takes notes. She is all angles when he finishes: back arched, shoulders and knees tucked in tight, pen pinched between index finger and thumb over a fresh page, so rigid and forceful a grip that Jonathan fears the pen will snap.

The Sturgeon, leaning back in his chair with a cruel shine in his eye, is more pacific. "Tell me something, Mr. Davies," he says. "Did you have a seeping wound in your upper thigh when you woke up that morning?"

Jonathan is incredulous that he would ask such an obvious question, but when he sits up with his knee-jerk response—of course, I did!—it catches in his throat. It would have been difficult to drive to Malibu, then up the coast to wherever he deemed a safe distance, without needing to rush to a hospital first. He has avoided hospitals for the same reason he avoids prisons: too much chatter from the angry or anguished dead. "I guess I didn't have one," he concedes.

"Here's another thing to consider: did you notice muddy boot tracks throughout your house?" When Jonathan shakes his head, the Sturgeon adds, "Police identified the tread of what they think was a size-13 Carhartt working boot. Do you wear a size 13, Mr. Davies?" Head shake. "Did you, at the time, own Carhartt boots?" Head shake. "Through some... resourceful sleuthing on Alexis's part, we were able to access police records surrounding the alleged assault of one Mina Davies the night of November 15, 1994. Mina had the foresight to request a rape kit when police arrived at your old place. The results ruled out, without question, the possibility that you raped or even had consensual sex with your wife that night. But Jonathan—" here he wheels his desk chair closer to where Jonathan sits, leans forward, almost touching him— "I think it's important you know, according to the report, that Mina didn't need a rape kit to know you weren't the one who attacked her. She maintained your innocence, even though, for a short while, you were the prime suspect; leaving town didn't do you any favors."

It's as though Crazy Uncle Pete is retelling the plot of a crime drama on TV, one loosely based on true events but with a twist near the end to give viewers a sliver of false hope. He sits there listening to the rain and Lexi scribbling notes. For the first time, Jonathan acknowledges the gaps in his retelling and how the facts the Sturgeon has presented help fill them in. These facts are too new to him to carry the weight of truth, but they drift into the porous reaches of his mind all the same, like windswept seeds that settle on promising soil.

"You said you found a report related to an 'alleged' assault," Jonathan says. "They didn't find who did it?"

"I'm afraid not, son. The police entertained a few suspects besides you, but none they could pin down. The case has been cold for years. Now, if we can navigate this old trawler back to the moment at hand—"

"—Right. The graffiti on the lighthouse. The flayed lamb."

Lexi pulls another photograph from her file and bolts it, in a left hook, to the Sturgeon, who passes it to Jonathan. The photo brings his past to sharp relief: Mina's vanity is just as it was over 18 years ago, smeared with the wax of the blood-red lipstick. "We already knew the graffiti bore a striking resemblance," the Sturgeon says. "But it's good to see your reaction to it all the same. It could be a copycat, of course. It could be that someone had access to the same evidence we did and has been using this symbol to wreak a different kind of havoc. But then, of course, there's another possibility." He lets that possibility sit unspoken in the room; by letting Jonathan voice it quietly inside his head, he gives it more power.

Perhaps there is room for redemption.

The Sturgeon continues: "You said you're only an architect, but you've already demonstrated that you have other talents, even if you choose to deny them. It seems that it runs in the family. Your father told me, not long before he passed, that he started seeing things after you were born. He told me Pa Davies would visit you at night and look over your crib. But as you know, your grandpa died years before that. Roland didn't sleep much after Pa Davies started making night calls. His insomnia just gave the ghosts more opportunities. For over a decade, he just ignored it, muddled through somehow. It wore away at him, and I suspected something was wrong when I came to visit, but he would just dismiss it, say it was the daily grind. When he finally admitted to me what was going on—which he never did with Rosi, another behavior you picked up from him—I told him he should see a specialist. He told me I could go to hell. That's the last conversation we had, and I regret every day since that I couldn't—or didn't—do more to help him. Maybe I'll do better with you." There is genuine hope in Pete Davies' gruff, tired voice, a hope that seems to diminish the black cloud threatening to envelop him.

"What do you think you can do?" Jonathan asks. "To do better by me?"

"With any luck," the Sturgeon says, "I'll put your affliction to good use. Someone in this town, in Humboldt County, is abducting women at an alarming rate and seems to be turning men against their better nature. You've already shown us you have a knack for uncovering events that others would prefer to keep hidden—I have no doubt if you had kept digging, you could have unearthed the secret of that girl in Santa Monica everyone dismissed as a suicide. You've been given a gift, my boy, if you choose to look at it that way. Maybe at the end of all this, you'll find who assaulted Mina all those years ago. I know you may still feel guilty—"

"—As you should," Lexi mutters to herself.

The Sturgeon darts a warning glance at her, which she ignores, her eyes still set on her notebook. "Guilt has done you no favors," he says. "If you'd spent some time in the last 18 years trying to own your problems, maybe you could have come to terms with what you were culpable for." He looks at Lexi again, with more kindness this time; she catches his glance and slowly, painfully looks up from her notebook. She jots down a quick note on a fresh page and tears it out, handing it to the Sturgeon without a word.

"Ms. Niequist wants you to know," the Sturgeon says to Jonathan, reading Lexi's message, "that you are a coward, possibly an irredeemable one. Even if you choose to join our little investigation, she may never speak to you again. If you choose to leave, she will make it as hard as possible for you to be on your way."

"What does she plan to do?" Jonathan asks. "Slash my tires?"

The Sturgeon clears his throat in a half-chuckle. He says, "I imagine that would just be the start."

Jonathan looks at Lexi, who finally looks at him. The pink protective aura has shriveled back inside her; without it, her detached appraisal chills him more than the winter rain outside ever could. They stare at each other for several minutes. After a while, Lexi registers a change in Jonathan's resolve, a lifting of the shoulders, a straightening of the back. She affords herself a small, grim smile.

With a smile just as grim, Jonathan says, "I'll bet the lighthouse is full of ghosts itching to tell a story or two."

13

The Floor

Don't despair, the roots say. Unless....

Darkness again. She can make out the distant shining planet of the exam room door but nothing else. It smells of dampness here, of peat and rich earth. And something else. A fresh offering for the soil, the excess of life bursting from its carapace and warding off most living things, leaving a feast for the insects and microbes, then finally for the trees.

She was wrong. The hospital room with her mother was more bearable than this.

Their last words to each other were perfunctory. A hasty goodbye from her, a nod from Fiona, no eye contact. No "I love you." They operated under the casual assurance that they would see each other again.

Em went out for—what, a magazine? A stick of gum? Something non-essential. She wishes there had been more weight to her departure. She hoped the roots would show her something like that, an alternate path where she and Fiona had collided, where a pleasant morning turned sour because one of them misspoke or revealed an irredeemable secret. Em envisioned it happening daily in the brief period when she was sober, a period that grew briefer as the months marched toward winter. Fiona would turn against her nature in a fit of Catholic guilt. Or maybe Em would accuse her of doing so out of spite, not because she believed it. The roots show none of these paths, perhaps because they recognize no merit in them; they know, as Em does, that these possible outcomes stem from baseless fear.

She may not remember why she went out, but she does remember why it took her many hours to return.

The beach babies have decided to learn more about their state's majestic mountains. There is no easy path along the Sierra Nevada range like there would be if they clung to the coastline, but the meandering roads suit their mood and make it harder to predict where they are going. That day, the trees embrace them from all sides. Early snow has slowed their passage but not their spirits. They rest in an RV park in a mountain village, waiting for the snow to stop. Em goes out. She walks to a nearby market and buys the anonymous, trivial thing. Then she steps off the road and into the woods.

These trees do not sing quite as beautifully as the grand old yew at St. Stephen's, but the words they sing ring true—though if she were asked, Em could not articulate what those words are. An unmarked path winds uphill, a fondant of snow hiding any trace of past travelers. The trees suggest that she should christen the virgin snow with her footsteps. She obliges.

She dusts snow off a log and sits. She looks at the thing she bought, struggling to understand it. It feels alien in these woods, and because she is in the woods, it feels alien to her, as though the trees have stripped her of human knowledge.

The sun is already low in the sky when she emerges from the trees and steps back onto the road. She goes back into the market to warm up a bit. Unzipping her coat, she quickly realizes something is wrong. The locket is gone, the one with the lemon seed Maral gave her that day in Echo Park. The cause, she likes to think, of everything that has followed. And so it continues to do, as it keeps her from Fiona while she asks the staff at the market if they found a missing necklace and again after they all say no, prompting Em to return to the woods, now convinced that the necklace must have slipped off there: that the jealous trees must have taken it.

She walks into the woods in the quickening dark; then, realizing how easily she could get lost or abducted or maimed, she returns to the market and buys a flashlight and a can of bear spray. The girl who checks her out—who looks physically the same age as Em, if in no other fashion—stares at the purchase, then at her, with a worried look. "It's fine, hon," Em tells her. "I know what I'm doing."

She does not know what she is doing. The stars come out as she walks. Already, the snowfall has covered the tracks she made. The path does not, at least, diverge, but she cannot tell how far she came the first time, and she has no clue when the necklace would have slipped off. When she sat on the log, maybe? And where was the log? The trees no longer sing; they dance instead, their branches swinging, trunks swaying to the rhythm of the wind. She fails to interpret the dance.

Not dressed for the dropping temperature on the mountain, not imagining California could get this cold, she starts to shake before finding the locket. If it is out here, she reasons, it will probably still be here in the morning, buried in snow but still here. If she does not turn back now, she will freeze.

An unwelcome thought greets her when she returns to the camper van and sees the cold body on the bed in the back, lips drawn of color. I must have frozen after all, she thinks. That poor teenage checkout clerk found me the next day, and eventually, Fiona got word, the police asked around, and she came down to the county morgue to identify me. Now, my ghost is examining my body, enthralled by its frigidity.

The thought is absurd—for starters, the body is not in a morgue—but after realizing the absurdity, Em recognizes the thought's purpose: it is a deflection. Her brain, incapable of accepting who the body in the van belongs to, is trying to protect her.

Fiona's body is frighteningly cold. On the bed beside her body, Em's kit sits open; the needle and the rubber tie-off lie a short distance away, near an upturned palm. Em makes out the smallest hole in one of the arm veins, a droplet of blood on the bed sheet. An excellent first-time jab. But it is hard to know how much will be too much, even with experience. Watching Em do it, night after night, would not be a good gauge for Fiona. She was just a little smaller than Em—enough to make a difference.

Around Fiona's neck hangs the locket. It must have come off in here, somehow, when Em shuffled off the bed to run her pointless errand.

As she sits in the dark, the smell of decomposition hanging around her, she recognizes that this level—for that is how she has come to understand the shifts, like if a forest canopy had levels that descended into the earth—this level is different from the rest. She is at the bottom. And it seems that at the bottom, you feel more than you hear or see. Returning to the worst day of her life, from here on the floor, was a tactile experience: not once did she step out from the darkness into a waking vision as she had before.

Recognition of this idea is essential. It is how she differs from the others. What others does she mean? She feels them all around her: the ones who have made it this far. When you make it to the canopy floor, more often than not, you do not rise again.

Fiona is here. What is left of her travels, by feel, through the dark, seeking the others, looking for an opportunity to climb. There was no smell of decomposition in the van that night, not when she dropped the body outside an emergency room in Modesto, either. This would be the smell Fiona gave off after they interned her, against her wishes, at Forest Lawn.

From Glendale to the mysterious town of the north. It is as though, through living earth, an expressway passed between them. It is challenging for the dead to punch from the bottom through that canopy. Em knows this intrinsically; it runs, like a chill, through her uneasy limbs. Simpler to meet Fiona here.

But is that all she means to tell her? That I saw you as I left my body and descended into the earth? That maybe I forgave you? Even that is an interpretation. All of it is. By feel, by sight, or through sound, that is all language is. There is no single truth to it. There are only signs.

Em chooses to believe that Fiona forgives her now. She reaches for other signs and runs her fingers back along the path until she finds the critical moment again: the irony that the necklace should be here, where she waited too long to look, from the start.

There is more to it than irony, though. Em could not have recognized it at 16 because the irony provided flair, and at the time—had it been only a year?—she softened the edge of the world with flair. She has no taste for irony now. Not at the bottom; no room for it: irony is an expulsion of gas, and down here, gas is trapped in soil and stone.

She feels the grooves of the locket with Fiona's cold neck resting below it. The skin around the locket feels colder than other parts, almost frozen. An effect of the locket and its metal chain, perhaps? But it would not have been this cold. If it had, they would have frozen to death at night.

Em allows a horrifying thought: did the locket kill Fiona? Was it ludicrous to think so? From what she had experienced, a transcontinental seed sat at the apex of her prediction of over four years of her life. Because the seed, of course, would be to blame, not the locket holding it. As though it knew, somehow, that Fiona must be stricken down to perpetuate the timeline, the one that was meant to be: there was no other way. It slipped off her neck and Fiona found it and the seed knew she could not resist wearing the locket, and once around her neck, all that was needed was a push, a subtle shift of mood, a simple transfer of chemical compounds through the metal to convince her to act more recklessly than she usually would. Could a seed cause all that?

Of course, it could. That is why Em ended up here.

It does not matter what caused Fiona to shoot up. What this moment offers is an alternative. A different explanation than

Em's default litany she has returned to every morning since it happened—I am the only cause. Before this moment on the floor, her reasoning went something like this: no heroin user, no heroin, no source that could so quietly, casually, stop Fiona's heart. Without Fiona, she no longer had, in theory, any reason to run. In Chicago, she would be chastened, rehabilitated, and given a second chance like her mother. The problem was she felt she deserved no second chance. If she had waited and done as her mother asked, her heartache over losing Fiona might have lasted only a year when she saw her again. Because she had not, her loss would last a lifetime and be at her hand. Em was irredeemable. She did not deserve her uncle's compassion or anyone's.

The seed as an accomplice allows space for the idea that no person or thing is at fault. A girl put on the necklace of her true love. She overdosed. Her true love, unaware, wandered through the woods.

Em can see why others may get lost here on the floor, why the dead can hardly rise. The floor strips away excess like a eucalyptus shedding its bark. Most lose any sense of self. But for Em, it clears away the clutter.

A killer seed is just an idea—an incomplete one at that. Complete or not, ideas cannot survive on the floor. Ideas, like a heated fluid, must rise.

Em starts to rise on the current of the idea. One level up, more ideas cause the current to swell. She has a sense of what all this is and how she ended up here. More importantly, she knows what she must do next. That's the crux of it, she realizes, as she surges upward, up past the twisted innards of the giant yew and through the exam room door: a sense of the future is the only way out.

She wakes up in darkness in a hospital bed, in a much larger room than she left. Tubes run down her arms, one for breathing in her nose. Her bed lies in a row with several others. On either side of her, women lie unconscious with tubes and wires running over their bodies. She can make out more rows of beds in front of her, and though she cannot see too far in the dark, a cue from the roots tells her that most of the beds are occupied: most of them with women.

Em knows she must leave but is not sure when. The impulse to leap out of bed immediately is strong, but that route, like water flowing down a mountain through an unseen seep in the rock, is likely to bend in many ways.

Out up from the roots, on the other side of a path so precisely laid out for her, the future is less certain. She thinks back to what Aunt Maral told her that day in Echo Park: you can assume you are destined for what you see or take it as a warning. It could also be a guide. Freed from the idea that what she sees before her is destiny, she now sees thousands of paths, some more likely than others, but each possible. The trick is to check for the right signs. She knows what to look for, but as waking thoughts collide with the certainty of purpose the roots provided, she wonders if she has the patience for the signs to appear.

Faced with what she knows might happen, what she wants to happen, giving it life in her mind also brings her loss to bear.

Sorrow wells up in her, and she cries quietly out of respect for those slumbering in the room, though she doubts a sob or a mournful wail could wake any of them now. In a lab refrigerator hidden deep in the bowels of the clinic sit rows of full specimen jars, a collection of tissue samples extracted in the name of the ghastly experiment unfolding here. In one of those jars—the one tagged, erroneously, under "Davies"—the body of her unborn daughter hangs in fluid, waiting to be picked apart and studied.

Before the injection pulled Em down, she could not have told anyone she was pregnant. Now, she does not know how she missed it: her ability to sniff out trouble and sniff out Andre, for one, should have been a clear sign. The injection that robbed Em of her daughter also allows Em to see her clearly, as though her sacrifice was necessary to clear the way forward. She wonders if that was the sign Fiona was trying to give her on the airless floor; perhaps she and the unborn child were the same. Without that blood spilled, would she have made it out? Or would she have seen her destiny in an endless cycle, as she imagines the others around her are now?

She knows that her daughter's body must meet Fiona's and return to the earth, even if she does not know why. She cannot leave the clinic without it. Many paths out of here leave her alive, but very few do so with that precious jar in her hands. She sees no sign of Andre in those paths and wonders if she will see him again. The thought saddens her, but her happiness can wait. For once, she must be patient, stay aware, and heed the signs. It could take days. It could take months. She now has trouble picturing things in days or months; time shows itself in turning shadows, in a twitch of an eyebrow, in the correct word said.

Em listens for the rustle and collective sigh of the captured souls surrounding her. She breathes. She abides.

Book III: Blood & Soil

Mind Punk Publishers

14

History

If you asked him, he would not have guessed that he would ever spend Valentine's Day interviewing the living memory of a self-professed murderer. Yet there he is in a ratty basement illuminated by a single floodlight, the ghost flitting in and out of view, pacing— which, he would later learn, is a typical behavior of Pfalzgraff's ghosts.

So: the living now would, from time to time, show a smoky aura—a secretion of awareness, a sense of self, the stuff that memories or dreams are made of, if you will—that would peek out and feel its way through the living person's surroundings whenever they tried to reach for something beyond their immediate perception. At least, this is how Jonathan has come to understand it. He concludes that the ghosts, once so material, like video superpositions on a landscape, are now little more than smoky auras detached from a body, which change color depending on their mood and may, through colossal will, occasionally form the outlines of a face. But boy, do they reach. Jonathan speaks, and they are happy to respond. Like many among the living, if he asks questions about their former lives, he can hold their attention for hours.

This Saint Valentine's Day is on track to be his worst, though oddly, he must admit, it resembles one of his best. Jonathan's first Valentine's Day with Mina was the first time they decided to have sex: for Jonathan, who had nearly zero sexual experience, it was a night of multiple firsts. After an overpriced dinner so fraught with expectations that neither of them ate much, they returned to Jonathan's apartment. Mina sat on the couch, and he paced in front of her, uncertain where to start or who should make a move on whom. Mina said, "If you don't stop pacing, I'm going to call this off and head home." In so many words, he gives that same demand of the ghost.

The ethereal remains of Thomas McKinley stop in front of the floodlight. The smoke descends to Jonathan's level as though also trying to sit.

"Alright, so," Jonathan says. "Why did you kill your daughter?"

The smoke starts to spiral and glow red; then, appearing to consider that Jonathan may threaten to leave again, it calms. A thin tendril reaches for Jonathan's hand and swirls around his wrist.

The ghosts do not communicate in words so much anymore. Young ones still speak, like the teenage girl he met in the alley when Jonathan himself was just past that age, and by "young," he does not mean those who died young but those who have recently passed. The boy pinned to the telephone pole by the stake truck did not speak and had been dead for over sixty years. But then, he was also more substantial: after Jonathan's pharmacological rewiring, anyone that long dead no longer has a body to pin to a truck. With nearly a century of death weighing him down, Thomas McKinley is a wordless cyclone. To communicate, the impression of the man passes his misty tendrils over Jonathan's skin—it feels like a chilled custard running up his wrist—and feeds him memories through osmosis. The experience consumes Jonathan's consciousness as it did when he entered the wall of fog surrounding Rabbit Warren Cove and dipped his toe into happier times from his past.

The winter day in 1930 was not so different from Valentine's Day, 2013: similarly drenched in a cold, persistent rain, the coastal winds buffeting the cliffs of Pfalzgraff Lighthouse and sending the shutters flying nearly every hour; Thomas eventually sent his eldest son Victor out that day to nail the shutters down, where they would remain, parts of the lighthouse needlessly shrouded in darkness, even in summer, for almost twenty years. The land-side end of the maritime house had a covered deck on the second floor—the aft deck, if you will—that connected to Thomas's bedroom. He lingered on the deck increasingly in recent years after the untimely passing of his wife, Nancy, who had run out into a busy street in town to rescue a dog from an oncoming produce truck, only to be struck by it herself. The bedroom carried the effects and smell of Nancy long after her death, and Thomas could no more fumigate the room or sell the furniture she had picked out for them, or her perfumes, her ivory hair picks and combs, than he could stand to be around them. He sat in a rocker on the deck, often sleeping there, a bottle of moonshine his only companion, staring out onto the winding path leading down the bluff from the house and to Rabbit Warren Cove beyond, wondering as his mind started to slip away thanks to drink and torpor if he might one day see Nancy walk up the path and wave to him as she climbed, as she always used to do.

A fence divided the land reserved for the lighthouse from the county road, just as it does today. It was a more modest affair then, a simple row of unpainted pickets tied with chicken wire that Thomas had built after he and Nancy arrived at the strange, gleaming new structure, a marvel of Victorian industriousness with a Californian twist. Thomas had tried, at least, to match the house's grandeur by attaching an old ship's wheel he found on the beach to the fence's gate. Nearly 30 years on, the wheel had been stolen, and the gate hung limply on its hinges, its repair one of Victor's tasks that the boy—a soft lad, frequently sick, not built for this life the way his father was—continued to neglect.

Thomas had not wanted children. He was one of eleven himself, part of the second batch after his mother, who wed at fifteen and had her first child quickly after, took a five-year break—some might call it a protest—to get an education and briefly join the suffrage movement. The five youngest McKinleys grew up in a household built on nervous tension. He felt no desire to recreate such an environment.

Nancy, a suffragette herself, insisted. She asked, "Who will tend the light tower when you can no longer climb the stairs?" And though his limbs worked just fine as he sat in his rocker and brooded, Victor now climbed those stairs. A brilliant job he did of it, too: the boy rushed polishing the lens, the light beaming in patches as a result, and he often forgot to fill the kerosene so that in the middle of the night—a critical hour, as many ships set off then to arrive at San Fransisco by sunrise—the light would flicker and sometimes fade entirely. The sudden dousing of the calming sway of light always woke Thomas up; rarely did it wake Victor. Thomas would scramble to the tower, refill and light the kerosene, and because he was still drunk at that hour more often than not, little stopped him from thundering into Victor's room and giving the boy a sound hiding, even though he was now eighteen.

The seeker who has stumbled quite inexpertly into Thomas's realm starts to nudge against his vapors, saying, "This is fascinating stuff, and it tells me a lot about your character. But I still have several people to interview and very little time. If we could get to your daughter...." This seeker must be truly green: no patience, no understanding that you cannot possess time any more than you can calm the roaring surf. But Thomas relents; he was approaching the subject of his daughter regardless.

That blustery day, Thomas sits in his rocker, deeper in the drink at this hour than usual. He blames the weather, but the house has lately been offering him strange intimations: tales of hidden treasure beneath its foundation, promises of a life with Nancy again if he can unlock the secret of the land. These fables come in whispers, as though someone stands behind him, bent toward his ear. Not daring to hope what the house speaks is true, Thomas tries to drown out the whispers with moonshine. It affects what he sees. A woman in a long brown frock stands at the gate at the path's edge. It has finally happened: Nancy has returned. Then he blinks, rubs his eyes, and sees that though this woman wears one of Nancy's dresses, she cannot be his wife: tufts of blond hair peek out from the woman's hat. Nancy's hair is chestnut brown.

It is only Agatha, his daughter, whose hair is the same limp blond as his. He half-remembers Agatha telling him she was going to town to see if there were any leftover crusts at the bakers that they could add to that day's soup. Agatha, now 16, has started wearing her mother's dresses because it is too expensive to buy new ones or even fabric to make her own—besides, no one ever taught her to sew. Agatha fills out Nancy's dress a little too well.

Standing beside Agatha is a man in an ivy cap and a long navy coat. Thomas has never seen this man before. (Come to think of it, he does not remember when a visitor last came to the lighthouse.) He stands too close to Agatha for Thomas's liking. What's more, Thomas thinks he notices the man lean forward—for a kiss, perhaps? More importantly, Thomas sees the man reach into one of his coat pockets and slip something unseen by Agatha into the basket she carries.

How can Thomas have seen so much, being so far away? He mistook his daughter for his wife at first glance, after all. There is still doubt in him, the doubt that warned him of the merit of Nancy going so frequently to town—and what Hell hath that wrought?—but the doubt is giving way at the insistence of the whispers floating through the house, seemingly through the earth itself. The whispers recite him a mantra:

There is no truth in the way you have come to know it. Doubt reveals the multitude of possible events. The more you can predict what will happen, the wiser you will become.

Thomas does feel sager in his middling years; it is a consolation, a direct exchange for his stolen joy. The conviction of his wisdom carries him off the aft deck and down to the ground floor to meet Agatha as she walks through the front door. "Good evening, papa," Agatha says, startled to see him at the foot of the stairs but careful to maintain a beatific smile. "There were very few scraps at the bakers today. I should have gone earlier." She has taken off her hat: even in the dim light of the front room, Thomas does not know how he could have mistaken the dull, coarse strands of her hair—which she recently cropped at the jawline in response to lascivious fashion—or her sallow cheeks, the insipid looks she gave him, for his precious Nancy.

"Perhaps you should not have gone at all." Thomas is not tall, and lately, because of the drink and torpor, he has developed a belly, but he holds the stair railing to help him stretch to his full height and sticks his gut out to display his rising conviction. "I saw you with that man," Thomas says. "At the end of the path. He means you ill. He means to poison you." The words come less from him than from the whispers, as though he is being fed lines from a radio program.

"Who, George?" Agatha says. "You needn't worry about him. He offered to walk me up the path, is all. He's the pastor's son. He has no designs on me if that is what you are worried about."

"I am not worried," Thomas says, "by so unlikely an outcome." Thomas sees he has hurt her—she steps back from him as though she has been struck—and though his doubt peeks up for a moment, the whispers quickly crop it like a scythe cutting tall grass. "I believe that he literally means to poison you. I saw him slip something into your basket."

"How could you possibly—?"

"Give me the basket."

"I won't." She has taken another step away from him into the hallway. One leg behind her, like she means, if needed, to turn and run. "It's only leftover rusks, papa, and not that many. I would have seen if he put something in there, even something small."

Thomas walks down the hallway toward her; she maintains her distance with every step. "Give me the basket, girl, or I'll take those rusks and throw them into the ocean, and we'll eat stone soup tonight."

"Mother wouldn't stand for this." Her hand is on the door to the cellar, where the kitchen is. She could thrust it open and close it in his face, which Thomas is sure she means to do, and by the time he got to her, she would have taken the poison and fulfilled her part of the suicide pact she has entered with George, an evident anarchist—for how could she not? How could she live any longer in this house of perpetual misery? The thoughts flood Thomas and deprive him of reason. The drink, the drink, it must be the drink, a tiny part of him says. But the whispers respond: who cares if alcohol brought you here? You have almost unlocked the secret. To back away now would damn you to loneliness. It comes together then; the poison is meant for him! The anarchist means to take down the keeper, to wreak havoc along the cove's shore. Little does he know that Thomas welcomes this abrupt end. This must be the secret that the whispers intimate. By poison of another's hand, he will rejoin Nancy and rid himself of torment.

His resolve to take the basket doubles, just as Agatha has opened the cellar door, taking advantage of the brief distraction his revelations allowed. He lunges for the basket, ignoring her pleas for him to stop—"you frighten me, papa," he remembers her saying, the phrasing a small torture, suggesting that he has frightened her for most of her young life—and in the struggle, as she manages to wrench the basket free from him, the back of her head collides with the iron finial protruding from the sconce on the cellar stair landing. The finial, shaped like an orca with its mouth open and teeth exposed, has a smear of blood, as though the orca relished in its first kill.

Perhaps Agatha would have survived the blow to the head alone, but the ensuing topple down the cellar stairs did her in.

Only then does Thomas hear Victor's footsteps rushing downstairs—Victor, who is always too late. He does not intend to involve the boy in what comes next. Victor closes the cellar door behind him and barricades it with a sideboard set on the landing. Reaching Agatha at the foot of the stairs and finding her no longer breathing causes him some dismay, though not near as much as what he feels when he searches among the scattered rusks, along the cellar walls and under cabinets and shelves, and finds no sign of the poison he desperately requires.

There is ample rope in the cellar, and as a former navy man, Thomas remembers a fair knot or two. The cellar walls are not very high, but neither is he. As Victor starts to rattle the door at the top of the stairs, pounding on it, feebly asking what's going on, Thomas finds the beam running along the ceiling and sets a stool under it. This will do just fine.

15

— • —

The Council

Lexi rolls her eyes. "So, you're saying voices in his head told him to do it? How original."

It is the first thing Lexi has spoken aloud to Jonathan in nearly two weeks. He wants to draw attention to this milestone but fears she will escape to her notebook if he does—like causing a deer you have been observing to flee once you make eye contact with it. He says instead: "Sadly, I think it's a common affliction among men. Among alcoholics, especially."

Lexi sighs—a sigh of resignation, Jonathan thinks, though not one that also comes mixed with resentment, as many sighs in the preceding weeks have done. The warm green corona that rises from her reassures him. "I guess you would be an authority there," Lexi says. "How's recovery going, by the way?"

The Cove, limited in many resources, at least has a local Alcoholics Anonymous chapter—or, more accurately, a hybrid crew that meets weekly at the old rec center and welcomes people dealing with the abuse of many substances, the majority recovering from heroin. Jonathan has attended three consecutive meetings and plans to attend a fourth tomorrow. The coffee is undrinkable, the rec center floor smells permanently of sweaty feet, and he cannot relate to his fellow substance abusers as much as he would like—he dares not reveal the light show they display as they confess their transgressions. Still, it is good to talk to the living for once, plus it gives him some insight into this often morose, shuffling town.

To Lexi, all he offers is: "It hurts. But the steady work helps distract me."

"Steady" is an overstatement of what he has been doing for three weeks. First was the physical labor: the Pfalzgraff Lighthouse is a shambles, a sinking ship with rotted floorboards, impassable stairs, and moldy furniture toppled over in the hallways, creating every possible barrier to its deeper reaches. They had to find an alternate path to the cellar than down the stairs where Agatha McKinley met her untimely end. Jonathan knew nothing of Agatha's or Thomas's deaths at the time, but intuition drew him to the cellar. He assured his colleagues they would find answers there if nowhere else in the house.

And so they did: after locating a service entrance around the side of the house where the land sloped downward before reaching the cliff face and clearing away several layers of debris someone had piled against the door, they came to the cellar. The threshold bared the same mark of the flayed lamb they had spotted on the roof, simplified in its smaller scale but likely by the same hand.

In the cellar, he was inundated by the dead, as though they were drawn to the closer proximity to the earth. The young ones were eager and seemed to run on a stronger signal than the rest, so he worked backward through time. He first addressed the cook the McKinleys had briefly hired when David tended the lighthouse, an elderly Black woman who lasted two months before she was found on the kitchen floor with a knife in her chest. The local newspaper covering the incident neglected to give the McKinley's cook a name, as though the sea had birthed her to feed the lightkeeper and his family. The cook offered her name to Jonathan immediately; she was still young enough to speak after a fashion, her face still appearing around the billows of her form, which pulsated with electric, purple veins. "My name is Rebecca Kensington," she said. "I was 78 years old and still had most of my wits about me when I died. Until the last few days, at least." She then kissed Jonathan lightly on the forehead to help him see what caused her mind to turn in those last days.

It started as she prepped Sunday dinner: the wall clock presented a problem. It had a modern design fluted with chrome and ringed in enamel the color of a robin's egg. It was an anachronism in the kitchen, which had not been renovated, the cracked Delft tiles and sooty potbelly stove seething quiet resentment against the shiny addition. There was more prep to be done than usual that day because David had invited a Very Important Assessor over for dinner, and they must make sure he had plenty to eat so as not to cloud his assessment of the lighthouse. After Rebecca nicked herself peeling potatoes for the third time, the kitchen insisted that she tear the clock off the wall. The kitchen had never spoken to her before, but then, she had never nicked herself so much, either, so the usual rules seemed to be breaking down. She tore the clock off the wall, and because she did, dinner was not served at exactly 5:30, which brought David's wrath down on her a few hours later. David's daughter Susan tried to console Rebecca, saying her father was not usually like this, that the assessment had left him nervy. But Rebecca said she wanted to be alone and returned to the kitchen, which had much to tell her.

The kitchen assured her that her time had come. She had served many families well over several decades, but this family could not be helped: this family was a tumor. Like a surgeon sent by God, she must excise the tumor from the good Christians of Rabbit Warren Cove. But she could not, even as the week progressed and the kitchen grew more insistent, bullying her into taking a knife to David and Susan's throats. She was raised never to hate but had grown to hate David McKinley all the same, a fact the kitchen exploited; still, for Susan's sake, who was only ten and innocent in Rebecca's eyes, she could not act on this rancor, even as the kitchen reinforced the idea that it was the last, best purpose of her life. On Wednesday, her hand slipped while breaking down a side of pork with a cleaver, and she sliced her thumb nearly in half. She swooned as the blood came gushing out; grisly visions filled her head; the hand that held the knife demanded more blood be spilled. Though surprised, the kitchen did not seem displeased when she cut through the rest of her thumb and continued with each finger, seeing how effortless it was with the heavy cleaver. The kitchen quickly shifted tactics: this is not the sacrifice we hoped for, it told her, but any life given ultimately serves the Lord.

After Jonathan recanted Rebecca's story to the Sturgeon and Lexi—who had watched him stand in the center of the kitchen, barely moving, refusing to respond to their shakes and snapping fingers, for over two hours—they finally told him about the lighthouse's reputation for gruesome deaths. The authorities knew of five who died in the six decades the lighthouse remained active, Agatha and Thomas being the first, and none died from disease or natural causes. Victor held on to establish a sullen brood of his own, just long enough to see his first-born son weaned; his son being the last of five, four girls giving him a sideways glance even as Josephine, the oldest, scooped him up and pretended he was God's favorite cherub. The next morning, Victor was gone. A few days later, they discovered his shoes cast aside not far from the cliff face, the assumption quickly mounting that he had succumbed to the pressures of family life and jumped onto the surf-swept rocks below. That was the version investigators knew and maintained like liturgy. But more on that later.

After Rebecca, Jonathan met Natalie. Just Natalie: if she ever had a family name, the roots had absorbed it long ago. (Meanwhile, the Humboldt County sheriff's office knew her as Natalie Rosenbloom.) "What roots are you talking about?" Jonathan asked. Natalie, who no longer had a face but who could still faintly speak, laughed a high trill that, to the unobservant, might be mistaken for glee. The newly sober Jonathan had grown much more observant and heard only nervousness.

Natalie readily gave what was left of herself to Jonathan, so much that the tourmaline layers of her form, which glittered in the dim kitchen, encircled Jonathan and bathed him in prismatic light.

Unlike Rebecca, who let him view her experience from a neutral distance, Natalie surrounded him with it: the gentle chill of a spring evening, breath sweetened by bubble gum, a wandering, impulse-driven mind. It is difficult to handle at first, the sensation not unlike when Mina carried him from the Sleeping Black Dog across a psychedelic landscape, but worse because now he occupies the lingering memories of a sixteen-year-old.

Natalie never thought she would be a mother, let alone at sixteen. Her birth mother left her on the doorstep of the Calgary Institute for Girls before she could crawl—that's what her caretakers told her, at least. Bringing another baby into this world made no sense, not when babies might end up where Natalie did. The Calgary Institute closed when she was ten, and Natalie and four other girls went to live with the couple who ran the hardware store in a little coastal town the girls had not heard of. The couple, who gave Natalie the family name she was known by and had already forgotten, taught her that parents served a function beyond creating life; the other girls, who quickly became sisters in more than just a name, also taught her that parents could be kind. The oldest girl, Jane, lost her parents when she was ten and remembered them fondly seven years after their deaths. All these positive stories of mothers gave Natalie some hope, but not enough to want to be a mother herself. She had not lost her mother or father to death, not that she knew. What if she was just as capable of abandoning a helpless child?

Natalie started high school and dared to think about going to college. Meanwhile, her body filed a formal complaint against her avoidance of motherhood and any activities that may lead to it. David, the light keeper's son—or his nephew, but no one called him that—was younger than Natalie by about a year. He was sullen and brooding at school, leaning against the perimeter fence in his leather jacket and boots; you would think he was trying to be James Dean, except that he had no interest in the perfect coif: he wore a fisherman's cap all day. David only took it off every once in a while at a teacher's insistence. He was an orphan, too—not like Natalie, but close enough. He left her gooey and distracted.

They got to know each other as chemistry partners. David did not try to command the test tubes like Natalie's previous partners, who she noticed, possibly for the first time, had all been snot-nosed boys. David was smart enough not to pretend to know anything: he asked Natalie open questions; he asked for her permission. Because she found him dreamy, Natalie returned the favor and opened up for David much more than her budding sense of self felt comfortable with. When she started throwing up in the girl's locker room before gym class, when she began to show and was asked by the school if she might need, for the sake of the baby, to take leave for the rest of the year, the sense of self stopped resisting.

Natalie is a cyclone of thoughts: one arm of the storm fomenting all the missteps that led to motherhood; another trying to grasp the world decaying around her decades after her death; and at the eye, sitting on a bench in the Pfalzgraff lighthouse yard in the final hour of her life, she ponders anew the impermanence of all things. Her foster parents did not ask her to leave after Baby Samantha came. Still, Natalie noticed the strain on the household, the subtle toll little Sam exacted from the other girls, and decided it was best that the family who helped conceive her also helped raise her. But from the sweltering, messy hearth of the Rosenbloom household, she entered a cold and unpopulated place: a vast house occupied by two sad men who were, at best, indifferent when she showed up at the door with Samantha on her hip.

Natalie is at first confused by David's change in demeanor—how could he be so willing to rub her aching back at school and pick out baby names when he could now barely look at her? Then, the coldness enters her, too, and she wonders if the ocean is to blame. The sound of the waves is ever present in the reticent house; without a family to guide her, they start offering instructions. When she puts baby Samantha down one night and goes to her own cold bed, the waves insist that she smother the newborn. She refuses, which only seems to anger them: their insistence becomes a command, one so loud that Natalie cannot sleep. Five nights later, shuffling through a haze to put the child down, Natalie startles awake and finds a pillow clutched in her hands, her baby writhing underneath. She leaps back and runs out to the bench in the yard, convinced now that she is worse than her mother, that the waves have nothing to do with it; she is a godless heathen, not fit for motherhood or college or deserving of kindness, and feels consumed by the pursuit of pleasure, that it is all she is made for, clearly, since it brought her to this. She will abandon her child as her mother did her and seek out a life, likely a brief one, of anonymous thrill.

Natalie stands and means to act on her newfound purpose. It's true that she does not believe in God, not like her foster parents do. Still, before she left school, she read Sophocles' Antigone and agreed with its general premise that a life beholden to fate seems unavoidable. The Fates have no desire to make her journey simple. Moonlight shines in diffuse patches behind heavy clouds, making each step down the bluff to the road and the wild world beyond an act of faith. The pitch is steep, the path running in switchbacks to make it easier to climb and descend. At one point, Natalie loses her way in the dark. She steps on what she thinks is a tree stump and hears a low groan and a gentle crackling, like ice on a frozen lake about to collapse. Then, Natalie falls, not down the bluff but through the earth, through endless darkness. When she finally lands, she finds she is back on the bench in the yard, once again plotting her escape. Natalie is not dead; she is only stuck in time. This unusual man from the future caught an early strain of her in the kitchen like someone might catch a cold; with any luck, he will carry her away from this damnable house where she will mutate, proliferate in others, and thrive.

Jonathan wonders how to tell the girl that her body is gone, that she has become a part of the soil, and that only an earthquake could move what's left of her. He does not attempt to explain the living world to a dead teenager. However, after Jonathan pulls back, with some difficulty, from her shimmering form, he wonders if Natalie may be onto something. The girl's thoughts linger in the following days like symptoms from a nasty infection; they mingle with his own thoughts, raising the notion that he should abandon AA and the investigation and succumb as she did. Curiosity is his inoculation. He wishes he could say that the value of the cause alone keeps him going, that finding these women and exacting some justice for them makes sobriety and the assault of the dead bearable, but he is unsure he would have stayed if only for that. He wants to know what drove Natalie to almost murder and abandon her child, what caused Rebecca to cut out her heart, or Thomas to believe that he must poison himself to return to his Nancy. Then, of course, there is Victor, no impression of him yet deigning to rise from the floorboards. Despite a rising dread that all this ghost interviewing is a waste of time, the simple joy of uncovering a mystery keeps him from running.

"I just don't get it, Johnny," Lexi says, reading his thoughts. "I don't get what any of it means."

"With Thomas, you mean?"

"With Thomas, with Natalie Rosenbloom, any of it. Like, what are we supposed to see? What are the patterns?"

"There might not be any patterns." He feels he is deflecting—for Natalie's sake or perhaps his own.

"They all keep coming back to the ground," Lexi says. "The ghosts, I mean. That's a pattern, right? You keep finding them in the basement, as low as they can go, except for Natalie, who found a way to go lower. And Victor probably went lower than all of them if he jumped off a cliff like everyone says."

"Right. And the voices Thomas heard mentioned secrets 'below the foundation.' But no mention of tunnels, exactly. And no sign of that rotted stump Natalie supposedly fell through." That I fell through, Jonathan thinks; his stomach lurches, remembering the sensation.

"Voices: another pattern," Lexi says. "The house seems to bring out the worst in people. Could it be other ghosts?"

"I guess it could, but where would the ghosts have come from when the house was new? When Thomas heard his 'whispers?' His wife died far away from the lighthouse."

"Something outside the house, maybe," Lexi says. "Below the foundation, like you said. But then, what is the graffiti all about?

I mean, there's a lot of talk of sacrifice from the ghosts but no mention of lambs being slaughtered. And no sign from them of anyone else prowling around, right?"

"Not that I saw. They don't seem aware of the present except for noticing me." Or rather, what they know outside their personal history does not seem to follow the rules of the living. Why did Thomas call him a "seeker?" What "roots" was Natalie talking about? He has held back these details from Lexi and Pete, worried they would complicate an already tangled narrative.

"But, OK," Lexi says. "So, there are patterns. Patterns that don't lead us anywhere. It's just...." She flutters her lips like a horse might. They seem to have the same thought: it's fruitless. The ghosts cannot help them find the missing, not when they might still be alive. Jonathan can see the wear on Lexi: the green glow around her winks out, and there are other, less preternatural signs he has noticed in the last few days: dull eyes and hollow cheeks; she may not be sleeping or eating much.

"Do you have any Valentine's plans?" Jonathan asks her.

"Do I look like I have plans?" She gestures to her laptop, which she has already returned to, tapping away. While Jonathan has spent most nights talking to ghosts, Lexi has spent her days running reconnaissance, finding leads herself, and—along with the Sturgeon, when Old Pete is up for it—interviewing them. Lately, her focus has settled on Raymond Skinner. Of all the known disappearances, Raymond's raises the most questions: his most readily points to a motive for their prime suspect. Their only suspect, Lexi must admit. But the leads on Skinner have led primarily to consternation: tentative agreements to meet left unfulfilled, or when they are, as was the case yesterday, someone who claims to have known Raymond a week ago seems to forget why they are meeting or who the man is. Lexi, not a fan of despair, has responded by doubling down.

"I know we're running on borrowed time," Jonathan says, "but you look like you need a break for a night. How long have you worked today?" Or, he thinks, for the last ten? Have you taken a day off since we started?

"I don't really know," Lexi says. "I just get up and go." He is unsure, but Jonathan has seen signs—a duffel bag at the foot of her desk, a toothbrush in a cup in the bathroom—that she has been sleeping in the Murphy bed in the office most nights. "I was asked out on a date tonight," Lexi says, looking up at him sheepishly. "I said yes—kind of—but I wasn't really planning to go."

"Why not?"

"Why not? Why not, Johnny?" She pushes her chair back from her desk, arms gripping the chair rests tightly like she means to launch from it and body-check him. "Maybe because women are disappearing around here, and we're no closer to knowing why than when I dragged your ass into town. Kinda makes a girl skittish to go on a date."

"Do you know the guy?"

"Yeah. We went to high school together. Both played clarinet in the marching band. He's nice enough."

"Then why not take a break with someone who doesn't know about the case? With someone you trust enough to sort of say yes to a date? You've been hanging around with just Pete and me since January. I know it's hard to believe, but I was once a workaholic, too. I know what burnout looks like: look where it got me." Lexi evaluates him coolly, her lips drawn tight. Her look says, yes, you told me all about it, home wrecker. Wife abandoner. But then, she loosens her grip on the chair and shakes her head: it's a dismissal, but not of him.

"I hate it when you're right," Lexi says. "It's fucking freezing in this office most of the time, even with the space heaters. It would be nice to warm up at the Dog with a hot toddy. Oh, sorry."

"No need. Other people can drink and even discuss drinking in my presence. If witnessing grisly point-of-view deaths hasn't sent me back to the bottle, you mentioning a delicious winter beverage won't, either."

"I don't know. It looks like you're salivating as we speak." She smiles. A small gift after days of sullen looks.

The date is at 7 pm at the Sleeping Black Dog. Just enough time for Lexi to run home and pick out an outfit and appropriate lipstick color. She leaves Jonathan with a magnanimous bow. Or a mock of one, perhaps.

Jonathan heads to the Dog himself on foot. In an odd twist of fate—Sophocles was right, dear Natalie—he now lives in an apartment above a bar, the last bar he drank in, no less. The apartment has a street entrance, but if you have a key, you can just as easily walk up through the rear stairwell behind an innocuous door opposite the Dog's kitchen. While walking this way would seem to be a needless temptation, for the last eighteen days, he has preferred to pass by the tin-stamped, glass-backed beauty with its rows of illuminated bottles, giving Selma a curt but friendly nod as he walks to the rear stairs. It is a helpful warning, he reasons. You kicked the shitter last time, pal. The universe doesn't want you dead yet; instead, your shenanigans dump you into successive torments, leaving you talking to murderers and runaways—not even living ones—because they are the only ones who can stand you; no one else has the patience to hire you. He lies on a ledge in a deep pit, the bottom still far below. With another slip, he could reach it before death—and who knows what pain and degradation lie there? He is also no longer so eager to die: there are things to do now, mysteries to uncover.

They keep coming, the mysteries, the disappearances. Selma James is now Jonathan's landlord after a fashion, and instead of paying rent, with the Sturgeon's blessing, he has been updating her with details of the investigation. "She was the first to let me know about the increase in disappearances," Pete told him. "It's only natural to keep her in the loop." Selma has eyes on half the town. She tells Jonathan about the girl she took under her wing who stopped coming to work the day after he showed up and got sloppy at her bar. "She was troubled," Selma says, "but she was doing much better before she disappeared. I don't believe she just ran off. Please find her if you can."

Without a drink to distract him and no obligations this evening, all Jonathan cares to do is skip dinner and sleep. Sleep was hard in the first few days of his recovery, but now, even in the uncomfortable bed in the small and dingy room, he is unconscious before his brain can complain about his surroundings. The ghosts follow him into his dreams. He is Natalie again, driven by impulse and wandering through the dark before falling into the unknown, trying and failing to penetrate the secrets of the black box he has entered. Then, the earth around him shakes with rhythmic force; his eyes pop open; someone is at the door, knocking incessantly.

He half-expects that Selma has come to tell him that his rent check, so to speak, has bounced, that his services in the investigation are no longer needed, and that he must, therefore, pay up or ship out. But the Sturgeon is pounding on his door, with Selma hanging back a few steps by the stairwell. She looks less apologetic for this intrusion than Jonathan would prefer. "He insisted, said it was important," Selma says before walking back down the stairs.

The Sturgeon's eyes are wild: wild and worried. He says, "Did everyone just fuck off to Lake Tahoe?" He marches past Jonathan into the room. "Where have you been?" he demands. "I've been trying to call you for almost an hour. From you, I might have expected this, but not Alexis. Her cell never goes to the second ring. I think she might be dead."

"I'm sure she's not dead," Jonathan says. "She probably just turned her phone off for her date. And I silenced mine because I'm wiped out from six swing shifts in a row. What time is it, anyway?"

"Date?" The Sturgeon says, blinking stupidly. "What's she going on a date for on a Tuesday?"

"I don't know, Pete, maybe because it's Valentine's Day? Didn't you see all the red and white streamers on your way up here?"

Pete paces, muttering to himself, "That's why they did it tonight," before checking his watch, as though Jonathan's original question traveled through a bad connection, and he is only now hearing it. "7:45—shit, we've got to go. Put some pants on."

"Wait, go where?"

The Sturgeon groans. "If you'd picked up your damn phone, you would know. The town council called a special session tonight. On Valentine's Day, naturally, when folks are less likely to come."

"Wait, do they even have a quorum?" He doubts it, but he still pulls on a pair of jeans. "Half the council's still scattered across the state for winter break." Including Drake Parsippany, last they heard. Jonathan prays to the spirits who prowl through his dreams: please do not let him be one who came back early.

"They must," Pete says, "and we must be there. Come hell or high water. Did Ms. Niequist say how long her date was going to be? Or where she was going?"

"Not that I can remember." Pete must not have seen her sitting downstairs in the restaurant, assuming she is still there. Jonathan hopes he will be similarly unobservant as they head out.

The town council meets less than a hundred paces from the Dog at a square brick meeting house that has been alternatively used, over the years, as a grade school, library, and event space. Its multipurpose nature is on clear display as they enter just before 8 pm; the Sturgeon wonders if he read the date wrong. The main room is dimly lit and lurid with color, the walls projected with cones of red light more reminiscent of a horror film than Valentine's Day. Near the center of the room, an unlit mirror ball questions its purpose. Above the red lights, a banner reads, "Sadie Hawkins Dance 2013."

The room is sweltering; with the lighting, Jonathan feels like he has entered a kiln. He imagines how bread yeast must feel in a similar situation: a promising environment that, with a gradual increase in temperature, leads to destruction.

"Yes, come in; come in," says an amplified voice near the end of the hall. "We're just about to get started."

The hall is too large for the crowd huddled at its far end. There might be times when the room is packed with seats, but there are only two short rows tonight, enough to accommodate about a dozen citizens. On a small stage against the back wall—a shallow dais, really, just high enough to keep dancers from colliding with a live band—six council members sit in a fan of chairs, their faces lit by stage lights taped to the floorboards. The effect of the lights is jarring: the council members, lit from below, look like wax-figure movie monsters on display.

The council member who ushered them in tries to excuse what appears to be, at first glance, either performance art or an intimidation tactic. "Sorry for the mood lighting," he says. "The high school was gracious enough to cancel their Valentine's dance at the last minute, but some pioneering prankster thought it would be funny to seal the light switches with Super Glue. Good to see you here, *Monseigneur* Sturgeon. Please, take a seat." The speaker is a short, broad White man who appears to delight in eschewing Northern California codes of informality: his colleagues wear khakis and polos or a cotton blouse at best; he wears a navy pinstripe suit, a pink satin shirt, and a silk checked bow tie that gleams aggressively in the floor lighting. As they sit, the Sturgeon gives Jonathan a grave look. That's our prime suspect, the look says: Mr. Parsippany, flown home early to roost.

"We thank you all for attending this meeting at such short notice," Drake says. "Naturally, we'd prefer a greater representation from our body politic—most of you know how 'engaged' our council meetings can be—but we couldn't avoid meeting any later. You see, it's come to our attention—"

The double doors of the meeting hall swing wide with a crash. Through them comes thundering a curious trio: a withered man with a bushy white beard, as tall and spindly as quaking aspen; a teenage girl in a wheelchair, hair done up in a bouffant, lips beet-red, a sequined gown peeking beneath her winter coat; and pushing her along, a person of similar age dressed in coat and tails, platinum-blond hair tipped with green and rising above their head, like a dove with its wings outstretched.

"I couldn't imagine why the first high school dance I actually wanted to go to would be canceled without warning," the girl says, wheeling toward the stage at breakneck speed, "but seeing your face, dear chairman, it now all makes sense."

Drake's smile never wavers as the latecomers approach; Jonathan thinks the smile might be set with shellac. "Postponed, my dear, not canceled," Drake says. "And I don't believe I know to whom I owe the pleasure of this mild intrusion."

"Cut the crap, Drake," the girl says. "You and my mother-in-law are thick as thieves."

"Oh, yes, of course," Drake says, who, if genetics allowed him to grow one, would likely be twirling his handlebar mustache in mock contemplation. "Deidre, I hardly recognized you. You've grown into such a supple young woman." As she approaches and finds a place near Jonathan, her companions sitting beside her, Deidre looks like she has taken a bite of something unsavory—something she likely means to lob toward the stage, with any luck dislodging Drake's shit-eating grin.

A throat clears behind Jonathan: the tall, withered man also means to speak. "Council bylaws require a week's notice to all residents of Rabbit Warren Cove if a special session is to be held," he says. "You can't just come together and make decisions without allowing for public feedback."

"Oh, but we did," Drake says. "Right, Euphemia?" He looks to a woman two seats down from him dressed in a black turtleneck and matching pants. Small brown eyes peer nervously across the room over a long, sharp nose. "Yes," Euphemia offers quietly, her voice half-drowned by microphone feedback. "We sent out fliers last week."

"So, there you are," Drake says. "If your notice got lost in the mail, my sincere apologies, Mr.—sorry, remind me of your name?"

"Rolfe. David Rolfe. You know me: I never miss a meeting."

Jonathan whispers to Pete, "This seems very intense for a small-town council meeting. Who are these people?"

"I think you underestimate the furor of small-town residents," Pete whispers back, "though a handful of us are more fiery than most. That's Friends of Pfalzgraff House: a self-appointed committee seeking at all costs to preserve the lighthouse."

"That's the whole committee? Two teenagers and a senior citizen?"

"Seventy-five percent of the committee, yes," the Sturgeon says. "David's wife is on bed rest right now. I think the one pushing Deidre's wheelchair is her partner. Her—or maybe his?—name is Jax. They don't speak much at meetings. Some-times, I speak on the committee's behalf as a consultant."

Drake says, "Let's get to it then, shall we? It has come to the council's attention that a scourge has run through our town of late. A vice that threatens the very fabric of this precious seaside community. Perhaps some of you have already guessed what I'm talking about?"

"You?" Deidre says. The comment elicits snickers from the Friends of Pfalzgraff House and a couple of others in the room; some try to shush her.

"Very funny, Ms. Creed," Drake says. "I'm sure Beth would delight in you cracking jokes about such a grave subject."

"I don't know what Beth 'delights' in," Deidre says. "As far as I'm concerned, she's just a woman who hangs out with my dad."

"Anyway," Drake growls, a hairline fracture running down his plaster smile, "The scourge I speak of is drugs. Opioids, specifically. I know this scourge has run through cities across America, but I never thought it would touch our precious town. We're not like that; we don't stoop to such moral depravity."

Jonathan thinks back to what Lexi told him his first day here and can almost feel the collective eye-roll in the room. This is not news, dear chairman. Some likely feel the Cove is exactly depraved enough to succumb to opioid addiction; they may trade a bottle of pills or two if it helps them make rent on time or just get through another bleak day.

"Many of you may already be aware of this pernicious blight," Drake continues, and he makes eye contact with Jonathan as though reading his thoughts, "so you may wonder why we need a special council meeting to address it. Well, my friends, we may be closer to finding the source of the drug trade. Peter, if you would do the honors."

A small pale man stands and sets a poster pad on an easel. His face is as round and flat as a dinner plate; his eyes, soft and watery, are as placid as a cow's. Dressed in a checked shirt and cargo pants, you might suspect he would produce a series of home improvement videos online, maybe even host a public-access TV program, before concluding he cast votes to sway the Cove's fate.

The Sturgeon, in an aside to Jonathan: "That's Peter Nguyen. He chairs the local chamber of commerce and runs the hardware store in town."

"Susan Nguyen's son?"

"The same."

Peter flips the poster pad open to an image that jolts Jonathan. It is the same photo Lexi handed him the first day on the job, superimposed to fill the poster pad: the graffito of the flayed lamb, still haunting them all.

"This symbol," Peter says, producing a laser pointer from his shirt pocket and swirling its little red dot around the graffito, "has been identified by Humboldt County authorities in connection with a known crime ring the sheriff's office believes has recently made inroads into our area. As the chairman said, this crime ring has been known to deal drugs; they may even be involved in trafficking. Not just drug trafficking, mind you. We, the sheriff's office, and our Coast Guard representatives with the Department of Homeland Security have reason to suspect that this crime ring is trafficking human beings as well."

Jonathan and the Sturgeon exchange worried looks. Silently, they say to each other: the opposing team is running our play to their advantage—much better than we have been.

Another council member, a woman sitting at one end of the arc of chairs, leans into her microphone. "Councilman," she says, turning to Peter, "this is the first time some of the present members, myself included, are hearing about a possible drug ring. Why is DHS getting involved? Why not the FBI?" Never mind, Jonathan thinks, that authorities would not care much for a town council to air the details of a criminal investigation before the public. Jonathan knows Drake is bluffing; he did not expect someone within the chairman's ranks to call him on it.

The doubtful councilwoman looks to be in her fifties, roughly the same age as Drake. Where the chairman is composed of boxy forms and vertical lines, she is flowing and natural: a linen shirt under a cardigan that reaches her knees, all cream and earth tones; shoulder-length hair a gentle wave. "Sally Davis," Pete whispers to Jonathan. "A retired district attorney and journalist. Don't let her appearance fool you: she's tougher than an ironside."

Drake replies, "Mrs. Davis—"

"Ms." Pronounced with an ending "z" that Sally draws out.

"Yes. Ms." Another crack in Drake's veneer. "Councilwoman, you may well guess why DHS would be involved. This photo—" he points, accusingly, at the graffito—"was taken at the site of our beloved eyesore, the derelict and clearly crime-ridden Pfalzgraff Lighthouse." As though cued, Councilman Nguyen turns the page of the easel pad. The lighthouse appears in full view, as sad in the photo as Jonathan's nightly excursions have confirmed it to be. If you squint, you might make out the flayed lamb on the roof—but you would need to know what you were looking for.

"I knew it!" Deidre wheels herself to the edge of the stage, her bouffant quivering slightly and shining under the lights. She would leap onto the stage if she could. Jax, now standing, appears ready to do so on her behalf. "It's always about the lighthouse, isn't it, Mr. Chairman? The Friends of Pfalzgraff House don't believe your half-baked lies for a second. Looks like your own council doesn't, either."

Peter Nguyen says, "If I may—"

"Not now, Peter," Drake says. "It's true that we didn't have time to brief all council members before holding this hearing. Councilwoman Davis, my apologies; Billy, I extend the same." Drake nods to the tall, wiry man sitting near the easel and Peter. "That's fine," Billy says, fluttering his lips, then muttering, too close to the microphone, "No one tells me anything half the time anyway."

"My council," Drake continues, "has or shortly will be provided—as will you, my lovely citizenry—with substantial evidence to make an emergency decision regarding the lighthouse's fate. Councilwoman Parowan, will you please relieve Councilman Nguyen at the easel and present your findings?" From the Sturgeon's running dossier: Linda Parowan, former city planner, geologist, and forestry expert, a woman who gives exacting, technical instructions on the best places to fish and promises to bore the staunchest fishermen in the telling. She walks to Councilman Nguyen, barely acknowledging his presence as she slides into the space between him and the microphone he was just speaking into. Peter sits, looking chastened.

Councilwoman Parowan dons a thick pair of pink reading glasses, pulls out her notebook, and begins. "Construction of the Pfalzgraff light tower was completed shortly before construction of the surrounding house began, on November 14, 1901. The light tower has a third-order Fresnel lens that was still intact as of the last assessment on April 23, 2011. The light tower and surrounding house sit on a bedrock of Jurassic sandstone, shale, limestone, and composite, part of the Franciscan Complex, which stretches...."

Linda Parowan's voice drones with little inflection, causing Jonathan's attention to drift across the room. Even in the dimly lit space, the council and the small crowd watching them shimmer with color. Plumes of magenta. Mossy greens. Slivers of goldenrod. Diaphanous ruby. Then, he notices something unusual. A room illuminated by souls: by unspoken desires, private failings, unchecked fury, some lights brighter than others, but every person giving host to prickly, self-defacing awareness. All except one. Jonathan does not always see auras around the living, but in a room where emotions run universally high, not showing even a peek of one is suspect. Council Chairman Parsippany now sits and listens, unmoving, to Linda's presentation. His likely deceit, the barely suppressed rage he must feel at those who dare question his authority, gives off no light. He is a candle winked out: a body moving without deference to a soul.

A murmur runs through the council. A shifting of tone, a damper pedal pressed to soften the mood. They are about to deliberate. The citizenry has had the opportunity to provide feedback, which they must have done—Deidre's aura, like an ocean trawler's net woven with diamonds, briefly casts over the crowd and blinds him with light—but he makes out no details of the conversation or what Linda Parowan has said that could be so convincing or so damning. The lighthouse is doomed; he can tell by the murmur that enough council members agree it holds little value compared to the land it occupies. Jonathan has also been inching toward this conclusion for the last few weeks, but his reasoning differs.

He stands, looks the room over, and gives a gentle wave. "Sorry to delay the night anymore," he says. "Can I a call a point of order?" Everyone stares at him, including the Sturgeon. Later, he will ask Jonathan what compelled him to stand up when he did—an action that will throw their efforts widely off balance—and Jonathan will not be able to give a reasonable explanation.

"You may not," Councilwoman Davis says, "but I'm happy to call one on your behalf. Euphemia, please note the point of order. You have the floor, Mr....?"

Uncertain that subterfuge will help him in this setting, Jonathan gives his real name. Drake says, "Mr. Davies has been conducting an independent feasibility study of the lighthouse's restoration. Our own Pete Davies brought him to town—you're his nephew, isn't that right, Mr. Davies?"

"That is right," Jonathan says slowly, thrown by Drake's depth of knowledge but not so thrown to correct his slight misunderstanding.

"Very well, Mr. Davies," Sally says. "You have the floor."

Jonathan is handed a microphone. He feels awkward using it in front of such a small crowd but feels he must follow decorum to get his point across. "Forgive me for not knowing your procedures front-to-back," he says. "But I know the state's requirements, and those generally need to be considered as part of any land-use decision, even an emergency one. I don't believe we've heard the results of an environmental impact analysis for the proposed development. Has one been conducted?"

"That was the purpose of Councilwoman Parowan's report," Drake says, "to highlight the ecological importance of the site and the need to preserve it from further degradation by criminals. Not to mention the public safety concerns."

"All valid points, Chairman," Jonathan says. "But that doesn't answer my question. My restoration assessments always involve some level of impact analysis. I've found some concerning evidence that would preclude, at least for now, effective restoration of the lighthouse or what the council is proposing is the highest and best use of the land."

"And what is that?" Drake asks, his voice cracking. No smoke or glimmer rises from him, but Jonathan can tell Drake's patience has worn to the barest nub.

"A burial site," he says. "Or a cache. Possibly several, scattered near or underneath the lighthouse. Based on the artifacts, the sites are native, likely predating Western settlement in the area." The crowd talks all at once: shouts of disbelief and shock, nervous laughter, and a demand for order from the council members. Jonathan is also surprised by what he said, as though he read the words in the auras surrounding him before understanding their meaning.

Drake stands and shouts, all pretense evaporated: "Mr. Davies, I demand you present your evidence immediately! This is highly—"

"—Chairman." Sally has risen as well, slow and stately. Her calm, clear voice cuts the chairman's tirade short. "I agree that the way Mr. Davies has presented his case is irregular—but so is this meeting. The point of order still stands. We did not complete an impact analysis; clearly, we should have. I motion we postpone the land-use vote until Homeland Security has had a chance to complete its criminal investigation. Or at least until the next scheduled council meeting."

"Seconded," Billy says. He sighs the word, relieved he does not yet have to vote on such a heated topic.

"All in favor?" Sally, Billy, Euphemia; then slowly, warily, Linda. Drake and Peter keep their hands down.

"The motion has passed," Sally says. "The council will reconvene on April 13. Deidre, Jax: I'm sorry your dance had to be canceled for this waste of time." As the crowd disperses, Sally adds, "Mr. Davies, one more thing. I'm also sorry you've been led to believe that the Pfalzgraff Lighthouse is open to contractors. With an ongoing criminal investigation, I strongly suggest you suspend your assessment until further notice."

The council starts to drift off the stage. Chairman Parsippany lingers: he is a monument cast in pitch, still and inscrutable.

The Sturgeon is fuming as they leave the meeting house. He asks Jonathan, "Is it in your nature to sabotage everything you touch? Alexis should have been here; she knows how to keep you in line."

16

— · —

The Date

ALEXIS WOULD NOT HAVE wanted to be there—not when a Valentine's date commands her attention more than the liveliest council meeting ever could.

Charlie Buford—who now prefers to go by "Charles"—has matured significantly since high school. That alone may have kept Lexi from capping the date at an hour, but Charlie has exciting news. He has been working for the San Francisco Chronicle for the last year. He started as a fact checker and quickly rose through the ranks, becoming a features reporter in just six months. Proving to be no slouch as a journalist—Lexi fondly remembers his writing from school—the Chronicle has assigned Charlie what promises to be the highest-profile scoop of the year: an undercover investigation of Lemuria Holdings.

"So, you work there now?" Lexi asks. "At Lemuria?"

Charlie nods. "That's part of why I go by 'Charles' now. Charles Rasmussen, as they know me there. I also never really liked to be called 'Charlie.' It sounds kinda like a joke name."

Lexi disagrees, but she keeps this to herself. Charlie and Lexi: the two names go together without sounding too cute. But she might be getting ahead of herself.

"What have you found out so far?" she asks. "If it won't jeopardize your investigation, of course."

"You're not a corporate spy, are you?" Charlie chuckles. "What are you up to these days, anyway? I feel like I've been talking your ear off."

"Oh no, your life is way more interesting than mine," she says. "Just some temp jobs, clerical work. It's hard to find much else." Lexi wants desperately to reveal the hidden bond they share but thinks it is too soon: Pete would likely not approve, not with the strangeness they have dealt with the last month or so.

"I guess I've been luckier than most," Charlie says. "A little dishing probably won't hurt."

The investigation is in its early days. Charles Rasmussen, hired as a procurement specialist at the beginning of the year, has seen the real estate investment firm field some odd requests. Some items, like an eight-foot diameter rock auger, make sense based on the evidence the Sturgeon and his scrappy team have already collected. Other items raise more questions than they answer. Three hundred sterile lab vials. Forty hospital beds. Two hundred fifty cases of salicylic acid powder. A thousand rounds of .30 Carbine ammunition.

"What do you think it all means?" Lexi asks. "It almost sounds like the company is preparing for war."

"That's what I thought as well. But who would a company go to war against? I was sent to investigate rumors of misappropriation of funds. Looks like I found it—but it's not like the CEO is taking the corporate jet to Tahiti with his mistress. Something bigger is going on." Charlie requests another drink. Lexi has not been drinking as much lately; the investigation has demanded her sobriety. It appears, however, with Charlie's unknowing complicity, that the investigation is about to break wide open, which loosens her resolve enough to follow his lead: she orders a boilermaker with a double bourbon on the rocks; what the hell.

"Do you know the meaning behind the name 'Lemuria?'" Charlie asks.

"It has something to do with lemurs, right?" Lexi knows much more than this: uncovering the name's origins was a natural first step in her early reconnaissance. Still, she knows better than to show enthusiasm for such a niche topic. Not yet.

"That's part of it, yeah," Charlie says. "Lemuria is a mythical lost city, a whole lost continent, really, like Atlantis. There are differing opinions on what happened to the continent or where it was supposed to be—not surprising for a myth. But one weird offshoot of the myth suggests that the survivors of Lemuria's fall founded a new, underground city, the city of Telos, beneath Mount Shasta. I hate to entertain conspiracy theories," and here Charlie leans closer to Lexi, the drink and the intrigue having loosened him as well, "but when nothing else adds up, it some-times pays to think like a conspiracy theorist. I think someone near the top at Lemuria Holdings believes that Telos exists and is trying to dig a tunnel to it without anyone noticing."

"'Near the top,' like the CEO?"

"Sure, maybe. Or the board chairman, someone like that." Charlie pauses. He appears uncertain whether to continue. Did Lexi say too much? It was a natural extension of Charlie's suppo-sitions to call out the chief executive, so Lexi is unsure how she could have. She wonders if he might be withholding information. All the more reason to press on. Gently. "If that's true," she says, "no matter who is pulling the strings—probably multiple people, right? You need at least two for a conspiracy—what would they gain from finding Telos?"

"Great question. Do they mean to send aid? Or wipe out the city and repopulate it? It's an out-there theory, I'll admit. But corporate executives have done stranger things. There is supposed to be untold wealth in Telos. Folks get a little nutty when there's a promise of buried treasure."

"Don't they," Lexi says. And a short while ago, that is how she would have described the notion: nutty. But Jonathan has relayed too many strange things to Lexi for her to discredit the idea entirely. Men seeking to repopulate the earth, to shape it in their image, is a trope as old as civilization itself. If you did it in secret, if you bypassed the onerous requirement of wiping out billions and focused on thousands instead, targeting an ancient race most people did not believe existed, and gathering, as spoils of war, enough resources to last through a nuclear winter or the devastation of climate change, to wait out civilization killing itself above ground—if you truly believed that and were self-absorbed enough to think society would be better for it, why not try? It would explain the disappearances. It would explain why none of the missing women has yet shown up dead. Strangely, it gives Lexi hope.

She wants to keep going and be swept up in a detour from her research until she reveals, in a romantic flourish, that she and Charlie were meant to cross paths. She almost does: Lexi waves Selma down, ordering another double bourbon to toast the impending occasion. The look Selma gives her changes her mind. Selma would have caught only snippets of what they said, but her adopted mother's intuition knows no limit. Something in Charles Buford does not add up. Lexi waits for a lull in their conversation, then politely thanks him for a lovely evening.

Lexi connects Selma's admonishing look to reason once she steps outside, the biting wind clearing her head. If Charlie works undercover for the Chronicle at Lemuria Holdings, what is he doing in the Cove on a weekday? Lemuria is headquartered in San Mateo, a short drive from San Francisco but a long drive to anywhere in Humboldt County. She supposes he could have flown into Eureka, but why would he? Lemuria has no satellite offices. Not unless you count the secret tunnel below the old cannery.

On all sides, the town is raising walls against her: walls of smoke and subterfuge. Her elation with Charlie deflates, allowing paranoia to settle in its place. She spots a bulky shadow in the alleyway next to the Sleeping Black Dog. The shadow shifts and lengthens and starts to follow her. She walks faster; Pa's old pickup is just around the corner, and if all else fails, she has her canister of mace. And the shotgun in the cab, if she has time to reach it.

Footsteps behind her, five to six paces back. The pickup comes into view. She pulls out her keys and laces them between the fingers of her right hand, the points of the keys, like talons, raised just below her knuckles; her left hand holds the mace. She thinks coming to a dead halt and swiveling around, taking her pursuer by surprise with the mace or a swing of her key-hand, might be more effective than running—if she can time it right. She gets no opportunity to try. From around a hedge not far from the pickup emerges another dark figure. The figure steps toward her and passes under a streetlight, and she makes out a face. A face from childhood. A face she has sought out for weeks. She nearly cries out in surprise and relief.

"Raymond!" She runs to him, no longer worried about the footsteps behind her. "Where have you been? We've all been so—"

"Stop." It is Raymond Skinner's voice, but it has more flint than Lexi is used to. He holds a revolver near his hip, the barrel pointed just below Lexi's chest. No more footsteps behind her. "Put the keys and the pepper spray on the ground," Raymond says. "Now."

Lexi does as she is told. She means to raise her hands above her head to show she is not a threat, but before she can, her arms are pulled behind her back and her wrists bound with a zip tie. Her screams for help are cut short when Raymond stuffs a sock in her mouth and secures it with duct tape. A heavy pillowcase comes down over her head. She is led, stumbling, to the pickup's passenger side, the smell of Pa's cigarettes in the upholstery offering little comfort.

A voice by the passenger window muffled behind the glass: "It's better this way, you'll see. We need to know how much you know." Charlie. He sounds more like he did in high school: simpering and making excuses.

How could she fool herself into thinking it would be any different?

17

— · —

Seekers

LIKE AN APPARITION REMATERIALIZED, Drake appears before everyone else at the foot of the stairs outside the meeting hall. He blocks Deidre's path down the accessibility ramp, causing her to shove past him, one wheel of her chair nearly running over his foot. He does not seem to notice. He beams, his smile like a gloat that he directs to Jonathan and the Sturgeon, who stand at the top of the stairs, uncertain how to proceed. The smile says: you will not get rid of me that easily.

"Mr. Davies!" Drake says to Jonathan. "Forgive my initial discomfort over your rather unexpected call to order. I sometimes act with undue haste, but it is all in the best interests of the town. Please—" he beckons Jonathan down the stairs with a twirling wrist—"let's discuss how you might continue your work without disrupting Homeland Security's investigation. Perhaps over a nightcap in my study? I have a place just across the square."

"I'm 20 days sober," Jonathan says, "but I appreciate the offer."

"A tea, then. I have an excellent jasmine in my cupboard." It is not a request.

Jonathan looks at the Sturgeon. He appears worried but resigned, his downturned eyes suggesting that the only way past this roadblock might be to push through it. He shields his face with one hand and mouths, "Be careful."

The inscrutable Mr. Parsippany lifts an upturned palm to Jonathan as he comes down the stairs, like a dancer poised to lead his partner in a waltz.

It's all flash and nonsense, a false monument of decorum. Halfway across Coulter Square, Drake's smile turns sour. His posture shifts from that of an inflated politician to a ranger scouting the woods at night. Or, perhaps, a wolf propped on its hindquarters. "I underestimated you," he says to Jonathan. "You're green, but you have a keen instinct. It is easy, with age, to dismiss the value of that. Tell me, do you know what they called this square in the past? Before it was Coulter Square?"

"No clue. But I have a feeling you're going to tell me."

"On the contrary." Drake stops before a statue at the center of the square. The statue depicts a man on a horse, the man's gaze sweeping over the town in wary appraisal. "What do you see in the statue?" Drake asks. "Take your time; we're in no rush now."

Jonathan looks at the man's square jaw, the veins in his hands as he grips the reins and the corded muscles of the horse, and, at first, sees little more than a romanticized depiction of masculine resolve. But then he thinks about the words Drake used: is there something *inside* the statue he is supposed to see? Stone is usually silent for him—but if something living lay beneath or between it....

He kneels and runs a hand over the tufts of grass peeking from the statue's base. The statue stands on fertile ground; in its place, long ago, a living monument unwittingly aided in countless atrocities.

"I see death," Jonathan says. "There was a massive tree here with a wide, gnarled trunk. The tree bore strange fruit, as the song goes. They hung from every branch until there was no more room, then men came with ladders to cut them down so that more could hang."

"What you see," Drake says, "happened over 150 years ago. Rabbit Warren Cove was a fledgling settlement then. We stumbled on Yurok land quite by accident, and the Yurok were not happy about it. The tree, an ancient yew, was sacred to them. By sacrificing them on it, we ensured the raiders who came to town a proper send-off to the afterlife."

"You're harboring a lot of guilt for something your town did long before you were born. It's not like you had any control over it."

"You mistake me, Mr. Davies. I bear no guilt for what happened: the town did what it must to survive. I do, however, acknowledge my part in the lynching because I was there. I was one of the men who cut the bodies down."

Jonathan stands and stares at the small, strange man. Moonlight shines across Drake's back and casts him in silhouette. Somewhere between the meeting hall and the statue, his politician's coif has become disheveled. His breathing is ragged, each exhalation ending in a low hum—almost a growl.

Drake says, "I know what you are, Mr. Davies. More than you do, it would seem. I had an inkling when you walked into the council meeting and did not give off the usual twinkle. I knew for sure when you started talking."

"You're like me," Jonathan says. "You see the dead."

"The dead are the dead," Drake says. "Flesh and bones, an offering to the soil. What we see is information. A recording captured in the earth that the trees absorb. We function as interpreters—that is, if anyone cares to believe us. But also, I am not like you. For one, my kind tends to live longer. If I were like you, I wouldn't need you."

"What are you, then?"

"A cousin. The word I hear most often thrown about by the remnants of the dead is 'emissary.' I see memories and pass them along. I can't, however, communicate with those memories. Not that one communicates with the memory or the person who had it—a memory has no self-awareness, and the mind behind it is long gone. But if you're able, you communicate with the trees through the memories. If I'm not mistaken, Mr. Davies, you are able. They call your lot 'seekers.'"

Seeker. That is how Thomas thought of him, if dubiously. And the roots poor Natalie clings to must be the conduits Drake speaks of; human memories that have lost their original hosts find new ones in the roots of the trees. But do the memories truly lack awareness, as Drake insists? Even now, he feels Natalie directing his thoughts as though a well-meaning parasite threatens to disrupt the progress he has made. She whispers to him, "Maybe this strange, ancient man will lead you to where I am buried. Then, we can be hedonists together, leaving all other cares behind."

"So, allegedly," Jonathan says, "I can communicate with trees, and you can't. Why is that important to you?"

Drake says, "I take it you have 'spoken,' as it were, with the past residents and unfortunate victims of the Pfalzgraff Lighthouse?"

See? Natalie says. He knows what we are all about. Jonathan does not respond. "I'm certain you have," Drake continues. "Otherwise, you would not know what lies beneath the house. We are going to find the tunnels, you and I. Tonight. There is no time to waste now that you have spread that nonsense about native burial grounds to the council. While we are at it, we might even solve a longstanding mystery or two."

"What if I don't feel much like spelunking tonight?"

Drake groans and shivers from head to foot like a dog shaking itself dry. "I understand your hesitation, Mr. Davies. There is a lot of information to take in at once. But are you sure you can trust your new friends? Friends who drugged you and tricked you into a job? They do not truly know who or what you are. They can't possibly understand the mighty empire that lies just beneath their feet."

"Why should I trust you over them?"

"You know I am what I say. I would not know what I do about you otherwise. If you still do not trust me, it matters very little. You will help me." Drake steps closer to Jonathan. Though he is forced, given his height, to look up at Jonathan from this distance, it does little to diminish the quiet authority radiating from him. "Do not cross me, Mr. Davies. I might not be able to talk to the trees, but through advances in science, which I could only dream of when I was young, I can harness their power. And for the good of mankind, I will harness that power against you if I must."

18

The Black Cloud

If Pete could sprint across the square, he would. Panic driving him to absurdity, he considers whether Deidre would be willing to relinquish her wheelchair. But this is no different than if the sea roiled underneath him and the motor on his skiff gave out. He would draw the oars and row to shore, no matter how long it took.

That is how dying works, right? It happens in stages and at different speeds. You carry on until it finishes.

He makes it back to the Dog just as the first droplets of the burgeoning storm sprinkle the pavement. The place looks obscene with all the lovely polished wood draped in candy colors. Even the mirrored bar back has hearts taped to it. Such a wasteful holiday. He knows that Selma cannot ignore the trappings, though. Hers is one of the few kitchens in town with food worth swooning over.

She is not at the front of the house, so he rounds the corner, past the stairs leading to the upstairs apartment. A shift of air pressure, a compression around his temples, tells him to turn back to the stairs and climb. He is out of breath when he reaches the upstairs landing. How much energy remains? He knocks on the apartment door with what's left.

The door opens, just a crack at first, then in a freewheeling arc. Selma has already turned away, pacing the room, but she gestures for him to enter.

"Jonathan's been taken."

"Who?" Selma sits on the edge of the bed. She looks through Pete as if she is addressing vapor.

"Jonathan. The young man who's been helping us with the investigation. The one who has been staying in this apartment for the last month."

"Oh, yes," Selma says. She looks at him now. "I forgot his first name. Don't need it when we see each other every day and don't say much. I suspected something was wrong. That's why I'm in here."

"Why are you suspicious?" Pete asks. "What happened?"

"It's raining. It always rains when there's conflict. It's like the earth is trying to cool us off. But also, Lexi."

"What happened to her?"

"There was a man. She was on a date with someone from out of town. No, that's not quite right. From here, but he left. Anyway, I wasn't sure what they were talking about, but I saw how Lexi was letting her guard down with him when she should have kept it up. I came over and reminded her with a look. The wind shifted after that. She got up and ended the date and looked at me like she understood, and I felt pressure in my head like I do when it's about to rain. Bad pressure. I couldn't see for a moment. When I could again, she had left." She stands and looks around the room with a sigh.

"When did this happen?" Pete asks.

"A few minutes ago." They stare at each other. Thinking the same thing. "Let's go find her," Selma says.

They move as quickly as they can, but Pete has fire running through his veins, and even descending the stairs, it feels like they are covered in broken glass. Selma puts a hand on his shoulder.

"Is it the chemo?" She asks.

He nods. He dares not speak its name—in case, by invoking it, the poison manifests into an immobilizing demon. "I had a round of treatment this morning."

Selma helps him down the stairs and orders him to sit in her office. "I will find her," she says, ushering him to her desk chair and handing him a plastic waste bin. "In case you need to hurl."

As soon as she leaves the room, he does. He has eaten very little today, so mostly, bile comes up. The acid burning his throat tastes almost sweet. Stupid. He needs to take better care of himself. He has no time to eat or rest, but there will be even less time if he does not. The doctors assured him of that. The whole town is disappearing; his kin, or the closest he has to any, are being held hostage, and he is less than useless, puking into a bucket.

A whole day seems to pass before Selma returns. Her hair is matted by the rain, but she does not care or notice. "No luck," she says. "Her truck was already gone. No surprise there. But I went to her apartment, and it was dark and quiet. I tried calling her cell, too. No answer."

"I should have tried calling her too," Pete says. "I tried earlier."

Selma pulls a chair across from him and sits. "You are doing what you need to right now," she says. "There are times for acting and times for stepping back. When you step back, sometimes you can see more."

"But they could be in danger!"

"Yes. But slapping your fist against your palm won't remove them from danger." She grasps his clenched hands and pries them gingerly open with her fingers. "What do we know already?" She says. "What do we know about the investigation? What do we know about Lexi? And Jonathan: why was he taken? Who took him?"

"Drake the Snake," Pete says. "He came back early from his winter roost."

Selma spits on the floor. "The abomination. The snake in the reeds that can't be caught. Why would he want Jonathan? He's from out of town. No one would think he is a threat."

Pete says, "Not unless he was foolish enough to open his mouth. At the council meeting, he spouted some nonsense about tribal burial grounds. The council was about to vote to demolish the lighthouse, and he threw in that wrench. That set Drake off. He cornered Jonathan and all but threatened him at gunpoint if he didn't come with Drake immediately."

"Where did they go?"

"Supposedly to one of the Snake's many houses in town. But I very much doubt that's where they are. I think they went up to the lighthouse."

"How do you know it's nonsense about the burial grounds? The whole town occupies ancestral Yurok land. It's more likely than not."

"It's nonsense because we would have come across it already, and he would have said something to me beforehand because ever since he got sober, the boy excels at keeping his mouth running. Plus, I can tell when he's trying to cover something up."

"And I know when you are." Selma leans close to him. She brushes his cheek with the back of her hand. Pete shudders—not from revulsion, but because it has been far too long since anyone has touched him this way.

Selma says, "You know I'm a sucker for folks who have lost their way. Even dumb-ass White folks. Wouldn't have let Jonathan stay here if that wasn't true. The girl who was here before him, the one who's missing, she was the same. Smart but troubled. What's the saying, 'Still waters run deep?' Well, it is only once the Chinook reach maturity and after facing many perils, swimming against raging currents, out-maneuvering the claws of their predators, that they finally return to the still waters where they were spawned. Your boy holds more in him than you know, and you know more than you're telling me."

"Yes," the Sturgeon relents. "I have kept things from you. And that's not fair. Not when you have been so critical to our efforts, helping us follow leads and pulling all the many strings you hold in town."

"Is that all you think of me as?" Selma says. "A string-puller?"

Pete grasps Selma's hand and squeezes it gently. "Oh, Sel. No. So much more. I feel like this cancer is stripping my humanity away."

"Far from it," she says, drawing his hands to her mouth and kissing them lightly on the wrists. "You are a stubborn seaman, though, and that's a hard shell to crack." She releases his hands with a look that says: later. When we are all safe again. "Now, what's going on with our boy?"

In a summary version, Pete reveals the secret anguish responsible for the death of his adoptive brother and how that led him to decades of long-distance monitoring—some may call it an obsession—of his brilliant but deeply troubled son. "After he left Los Angeles, I thought I had lost him. I figured he was dead or had left the state. Then he showed up in Eureka on a public intoxication charge. It felt like he had come too close to our little town for it to be a coincidence. Like he was searching for acceptance without knowing it. Roland died because he felt like he was losing his mind and that no one, not even Rosie, could stand to put up with a crazy person. I saw Jonathan following the same path, just much more slowly. So, I posted bail for him anonymously and, with the help of friends, broadcast job postings he couldn't resist across Humboldt and Shasta Counties, even a few in southern Oregon, so that I could keep him close. Then I found a reason for him to come here. I realized it wasn't enough to keep him afloat. If he couldn't rid himself of the torment his brain was causing him, he needed to put it to use."

"Now who's the string-puller?" Selma says. "It's good that you told me about Roland. Holding secrets like that can cause them to fester in your gut. You don't need any more festering. Does Lexi know about this?"

"Most of it. After it all kind of slipped out."

Someone knocks on the office door, and Selma calls for them to enter. A young woman dips her head across the threshold. Over jet-black hair tied in a bun, she wears a red headband with two glittery hearts dangling from springs, giving her the air of a lovestruck ladybug.

"Yes, Tina?" Selma says.

"Front-of-house is cleared out," Tina says. "We haven't seen anyone come in for a drink for over an hour. I think our regular drinkers got turned off by the VD getup again. Plus, anybody that did come in was pissed that there wasn't a bartender. Are you okay?"

"I'm fine," Selma says. "I had to deal with a small emergency. Helping a friend. You remember Mr. Davies, right?"

"Hey." Tina waves at Pete. "Should we close early? It's only 11, and my tips suck, but it'd be nice to hang with my boyfriend tonight before I pass out."

"Of course, dear," Selma says. "Yes, let's lock up. Can you let the kitchen know? I'll be by in a little while."

"Sure," Tina says. She steps into the room. In her hands is a black fleece jacket. "Someone left this at Table 7," she says. "Lost and Found?"

"Table 7? I'll take it." Selma tries to keep the emotion out of her voice but clearly fails because Tina asks her again if she is all right. "I'll be fine, dear. It has been a long night, is all. I'm sorry for the confusion. Good night." Tina leaves the office without another word, but the look she gives Selma shows she is not convinced—for one thing, Selma has never called her "dear" before.

"Is it Lexi's?" Pete asks about the fleece.

"No," Selma says. "I don't think so. But she and her date were at Table 7. It might be his." She examines the jacket. A company logo is embroidered across the breast. Two figures in long white robes hold up a shield. On the shield, two mountain peaks stand in relief, one flat-topped with striated slopes like a volcano. Beneath the shield is a motto:

In tutela nostra Limuria

"Strange logo," Selma says. "The mountains on the shield kind of look like Mount Shasta."

"I agree," Pete says. "And I recognize that phrase. It's Latin. They borrowed it from the British Indian Ocean Territory's coat of arms."

"How the hell do you know that?"

"You know me. It's maritime stuff. I eat that up."

"What does it mean?" Selma asks.

"'In Lemuria we hold our trust.' Or something like that. Ah, shit." Pete leans back, running his hands over his face in frustration. "This is the logo for Lemuria Holdings," he says. "Drake's company. Lexi was researching it to try to find evidence of suspicious activity, something to tie him to the disappearances. She must have found someone from the company willing to talk."

Selma asks, "Why would she sit down with the enemy? Do you think she was undercover?"

"Maybe," Pete says. "Or maybe her date was. Maybe he was acting as a double agent."

"She was letting her guard down a lot and drinking," Selma says. "I haven't seen her drink in weeks. She trusted him—until I reminded her to ease up—but she might have already said too much." Selma stands. "I'm calling the sheriff's office."

"Wait," Pete says. "She's been missing for less than two hours. The sheriff won't do anything, not until we have conclusive evidence that someone has a reason to threaten her. We need to know why Drake built that huge tunnel underneath the cannery. The burial-ground theory may or may not be hokum, a way to undermine Drake's efforts and slow him down, but these spirits, or whatever they are that talk to Jonathan, keep signaling that there's *something* underneath the Pfalzgraff Lighthouse. Like a secret cache or tunnel. And the way Drake reacted to Jonathan's statement at the meeting tells me that he knows that, too. Maybe he dug, didn't find what he wanted, and is using Jonathan to find another way into the earth."

"Telos!" Selma says.

"Pardon?"

"It's the name of a made-up city," Selma says. "Lexi's date mentioned it." She sits again. "When I was doing fieldwork for my PhD," she continues, "I helped the Quartz Valley Reservation assess the health of their waterways. I had this grad student working for me named Chad, a White guy who would not shut up about his theories about Mount Shasta. Terrible worker, too. Anyway, Chad kept talking about Telos, a city under the mountain that was supposed to be where the Lemurians went when their continent sank or whatever. The citizens of Telos were supposed to be almost like gods, and the city had untold wealth, like walls made of diamonds and other crap like that. I'll always remember that because of how mad it made me, because the Shasta people hold that mountain sacred, and he came in and pissed all over their heritage, to their faces, with his occult garbage."

Pete says, "That explains the depiction of Shasta on the logo. My god, could Drake really believe there's some supernatural city there? But why would he dig in the Cove? It's hundreds of miles away."

"I don't know," Selma says, "maybe he thinks there's some underground bullet train, too? White folks will believe anything when it comes to the occult. And that makes them dangerous."

"Now I'm really worried for Jonathan," Pete says. "Drake already found a large cave under the cannery when they dug. If there is truly a network of tunnels under this town, we need to find a way down there and see what he has been up to. The dig site is too risky. And if I go up to the lighthouse now, I'm likely to set Drake off and start a firefight. Jesus, this is impossible!"

Selma says nothing for several minutes. She stares at the office door with narrowed eyes, hesitant to speak her thoughts.

"What is it?" Pete says.

"Nothing," she mumbles. "It's crazy. But I don't know what else to do. You know the rumors. Folks have talked about tunnels under the town for decades. Weird things they hear. Wind whistling where there's no wind. And we have our own rumor right here at the Dog that even I played up to encourage business: the urinal."

"You can't be serious."

"If Jonathan can talk to ghosts," Selma says, "I don't see why someone can't build a secret underground chamber under a piss pot."

They drive Pete's truck back to his office on the pier to collect supplies. Unsure of what they need, they gather a small, peculiar arsenal: shovels, pickaxes, flashlights, Pete's shotgun and several rounds of ammunition, several feet of nylon rope, emergency rations, and a small block of C-4 that Selma scowls at. "Why do you have that?" she asks Pete.

"It's from my time in Vietnam," he says, looking sheepish. "I may have smuggled it back home. You know, for research." While they are packing the supplies into the truck, she slips the C-4 into the waist of her jeans to dispose of later.

As Pete approaches the cab of the truck to drive back to the Dog, Selma comes from behind and deftly plucks the keys from his hand.

"What are you doing?" he asks.

"It's past midnight," she says. "You need to rest. So do I. Even if you didn't have cancer, we're no spring chickens. If you keep going, you're going to make a mistake and injure, maybe even kill yourself. And then, you're of no use to your friend or my daughter."

"He's like a son to me, too, Sel. I've come to think of him that way."

"Good. Then you'll get some rest so you can help him properly."

She guides him by the hand, like a forlorn child, to the back room of the office with the Murphy bed. They lie on the bed facing each other, sharing their worry in silence through half-lidded eyes. "Just a few minutes," Pete says. "Then I'll be right as rain."

19

— • —

Blood Rites

It rains gently; the cloud cover quenches the moonlight. In the dark, the lighthouse looms like a hydra emerging from a bog.

"Lovely weather you have here," Jonathan says to Drake. "You should rebrand this place as a resort town."

The old wolf is not amused. "This is why you fail," he says. "How do you think I have survived all this time?"

"I don't know. You're being preserved by the petrified redwood stuck up your ass?"

"If you had focused instead of cracking jokes, you might have pulled off your brilliant investigation without me having a clue."

"Maybe. But history is full of humorless despots like you. You're a bore. No one wants to come to your party."

Drake grabs a fistful of Jonathan's shirt and yanks him down to eye level. "You do not know what I have done," he says. "What I have sacrificed. The women in my care would have—!" He stops himself and releases Jonathan.

"Would have, what?" Jonathan brushes himself off. "Lived harassment-free lives?"

"You will see," Drake says, "when we find our way down."

They pass through the gap in the fence Pete and the team made weeks ago, walking carefully up the rain-slicked path to the house. On the way, Jonathan's flashlight reveals a large stump he had not noticed before. The harsh light and the rain make the dripping, tangled mass of wood look like a cornered animal crouched in terror, teeth bared for a fight. The stump appears to be hollow, its top collapsed and splintered. If it were intact, it would be wide enough to stand on.

A whiff of Natalie's bubblegum breath rises from the darkness, intoxicating him. He turns away before the scent can drag him off the path.

They reach the back door to the kitchen. The flayed-lamb graffiti above the door taunts Jonathan. It was all he cared about for the longest time, and their investigation yielded no answers, no possible clue as to who Mina's assailant was or why his calling card might be here. Drake starts to chuckle behind him. The chuckle evolves into a grating, high-pitched laugh.

"Something funny?"

"Perhaps not to you," Drake says, still laughing. "Let's get out of this damp; then I'll tell you."

They go inside. Right away, Jonathan can tell that the dead clustered here are agitated more than usual. Maybe the rain contributes. Perhaps that's why he finally located Natalie's fateful stump, as though only the right conditions would reveal it. As Drake begins to explain his disturbing mirth, Jonathan finds it hard to focus. They surround him, their hazy tendrils coiling around his arms and torso like an anaconda.

"Your face!" Drake says, bent over, struggling to catch his breath. "Truly, it was priceless. I had hoped to see how you would react to the tag."

"Wait, that was you? So help me—" Jonathan lunges for Drake but stops himself when the old man raises a pistol to his chest.

"Not so fast, Mr. Davies. I abhor unnecessary violence. Let's ensure your behavior doesn't necessitate it, yes?" Jonathan backs away. "I assume, based on your reaction, that you believe me to be responsible for what happened to your wife. Her name is Mina, right? A beautiful name."

Jonathan says, "If you don't get to point real quick, I'm going to rip off your face before you have a chance to pull the trigger."

"Unlikely," Drake says, "but I will spare your feelings. I did nothing to Mina. I have been nowhere near her; I find Los Angeles distasteful. However, I, too, know how to investigate. Or, rather, my people do. You see, my boy, my team has been watching you for a long time. We needed a motivator, a reason to draw you here. A chance to reconcile your past demons seemed like a good reason as any. So, we conjured one."

The dead murmur around Jonathan. "He lies," they say. "He does not represent us." Jonathan feels the room darken and shakes his head clear. Not yet, he thinks. Let me hear him out.

"What do you mean?" Jonathan says. "Are you suggesting that my wife wasn't assaulted by some random intruder with a gruesome calling card?"

"I know as much as the police do," Drake says, "and only slightly more than the fellow investigators you consider friends. Maybe there is a roving maniac still out there attacking women and using that symbol, but I imagine you or your colleagues would have uncovered reports of it happening in the last 20 years. No, Mr. Davies: my team sprayed the graffiti on the lighthouse. I know the Sturgeon's connection to you, so it was only a matter of time before he convinced you to come to town."

Jonathan feels a heat spread up his neck and a desperate need to sit down. He stumbles to the folding chair and floodlights he left behind earlier that evening, switches the lights on, and slumps into the chair. The remnants of the dead sometimes shirk from the floodlights, but nothing can dissuade their embrace tonight. Their tendrils wrap around his neck and slither into his nostrils. Then, when he can no longer move, they speak to him in a chorus. He recognizes many of the voices, but some are new. It feels like every broken window and splintered beam speaks to him.

"It is almost done," they say.

"What is?" he asks.

"Your involvement. You have been very kind and patient with us. Soon, the emissary who accompanied you tonight will reap the fruits of his actions. You have been instrumental in that reaping."

"What if I don't want him to reap any fruit?"

The chorus is silent for a moment. The hazy tendrils shimmer as if they are thinking. "We had not considered that. But it is of no matter. It will happen, though it may take longer if you are not involved until the end."

Jonathan wants to be angry, but mostly, he feels deflated. "Do what you want, then. Fulfill your agenda."

"We do nothing, want nothing. We have no agenda. We are only stories."

"You mean, you tell stories."

"No, friend. Stories cannot tell themselves. You are the teller. If you tell us, you may find peace."

The tendrils loosen their grip and start to swirl, forming an eddy that surrounds him. Jonathan hears Drake shouting, but he is miles away now, across a deep canyon. The eddy intensifies, blotting out the floodlights. When Jonathan arises from the ensuing darkness, he is bathed in sunlight.

"Josie!" A young girl, no more than six years old, cries out across a windswept bluff. She sits in the grass, grabs tufts of it, yanks it free from the ground, and then sprinkles the blades over her dress skirt. She appears to be building a nest in her lap. Her blond ringlets shine in the sun. It is all too precious. All gone and shifted too soon.

The girl looks in his direction. The dark pockets under her eyes make her look older. Ancient. She is wary of what she sees.

An older girl, 14 or so, walks up to the girl in the grass and crouches beside her. "What is it, Amelia? Oh, dear, you'll ruin your dress that way. Come, let's get you into your play clothes." She picks Amelia up, swaying her back and forth to scatter the grass. She then spins her, causing Amelia to squeal. She whispers something into the older girl's ear. They both look in his direction. The teenager is beautiful: her nose is slender, her lips are full, and her long auburn hair falls down her back in a thick braid. An amalgam of her parents, she is fairer than either of them. Oh, Josephine! You are a ruiner of men.

Like the sister in her arms, Josephine's beauty bears an advanced patina for her age. Her gaze is similarly wary. The two girls have already witnessed more than their fair share of heartache, and they are staring at its source, a man for whom the earth whispers dark secrets that he must act upon.

The girls walk inside. On clear days like this, the lighthouse looks almost cheerful from the outside. If only its contents could reflect the same mood.

Victor finally has the son that society insists is his pride and joy. After only nine months of nursing, Little David has given up his mother's milk and devours tins of mashed carrots and peas instead. He is a thick-set boy, far fatter at this age than his four older sisters were. Perhaps he will start devouring the floorboards next.

He wants his children to be healthy, not insatiable; this house does not reward lusty appetites. That was the problem with his father. He sat in a torpor, letting his brain rot from hooch and the incessant voices. If he had disciplined his mind, maybe Amanda would still be alive. When they came for Victor, as it seems they must for the master of the house, he was better prepared. To bend unquestionably to their will is suicide. Diplomacy matters. No, he would not kill his wife and daughters in their sleep, no matter how many treasures their spilled blood might reveal. What would you offer us, then? A new life, perhaps? One not yet well defined? We know the act of making one, at least, aligns with your desires. The new ones are not as nourishing, but we can put them to other use. So, Victor offered his nextborn. Would that it were another girl. The more little David consumed, the more Victor felt the time was right to cast the baby into the ocean. Still, he could not do it. What if David was his only male heir? Who would run the lighthouse after he was gone?

Luckily, another child was on the way, an abomination that would make a far better sacrifice. This seemed to please the voices: for the past several months, they had remained silent even with David still alive.

"Papa! Breakfast!" A small bronze head peaks out from the house. Greta. With Mom tied up with David, Greta has taken on more chores: sweeping the landings, hanging the linens in the side yard to dry—and most importantly, learning how Papa takes his eggs. Josie is responsible for the smallest of her sisters who can't help themselves, but lately, that does not include Greta. Unlike Bea, who is two years older but still being told how to put one foot in front of the other, Greta does all this without prompting. She could not grow up fast enough—though maybe it's the growing that spoils them.

He walks inside, taking long strides under the inverted pram that serves as a canopy, the bow dipping demurely and nearly kissing the crown of his head. When Victor enters the house through here, he feels like a king. High ceilings and windows on three sides, overlooking the point, perhaps pull the most weight to ensure the Grand Dining Room lives up to its name, but his favorite spot is by the fireplace: a custom piece fashioned around the curve of the light tower's base, with an enameled iron cauldron set on a retractable arm, just like the one at the famous Fallingwater House. Victor was told his GI Bill funds were to be used only to purchase a home or educate himself. Well, the lighthouse was his home; it was not his fault that the government would not sell the place to its keeper. And he had learned everything he needed to know right here. What would college tell him about navigating the spirit world? Nothing. So, instead, he honored the ghosts of the house with an extension, a space to feast when times were high and ruminate when they were low.

The dining table is set, and his spot by the fireplace, at the head of the table, stands ready to fill. The girls have outdone themselves today: the china platter they typically reserve for guests teems with stacks of bacon and fried eggs; a disc of cornbread, still steaming, rests on a folded towel in a cast-iron skillet; and the coffee, all for him, glimmers next to his chair in a silver carafe. He is nearly brought to tears. All that's missing is the entirety of his brood to share this bounty. Greta ushers him to his chair and sets his napkin over his lap. Bea pours him a cup of coffee. Josie cuts the cornbread into wedges and serves him a piece on a china bread plate. No sign of Amelia or Mom or little David; no places are set for them. The girls sit, and Greta says a quick prayer before they fill their plates.

Victor sips his coffee. "Good," he says. "Sweet." He looks over his three eldest. Bea nods, staring at the bacon slab in her hand like it's made of porcelain. Greta prods her eggs. Josie raises a forkful of cornbread to her mouth, chewing carefully. They glance in his direction but not at his face. "Where are the others?" he asks. "Is Mother not feeling well?"

"She has a name, you know," Greta says in a small but defiant voice. She then winces and glares at Josephine, who sits between her and Victor.

"None of that, girls," Victor says. "Greta, I, of course, know your mother has a name. But you don't call her Sandra, do you? Why would I call her that to my girls?"

Forks scrape against china. All except Greta's: she holds hers upturned in a tight fist.

"David is colicky again," Josie mumbles. "Mother is taking care of him. I drew a bath for Amelia because she is filthy from playing in the yard. No food until she's clean."

"Who made up that rule?" he asks.

Josie looks at him, finally. Her face opening like she's had a quiet epiphany. "You did, Papa." Her voice is flat.

Breakfast proceeds with no more conversation than the crackle of the fire. Soon, the skillet of cornbread holds only crumbs, and Victor pours the last of the silver carafe into his cup. The coffee is so delightful that he has drunk it all in just half an hour. He feels expansive; it matters hardly at all that Amelia has not surfaced and a relief that David and Sandra keep each other occupied far from his view. He has all he could need right here. But they are especially sullen today.

"Bea, dear," he says, "You're awfully quiet. Cat got your tongue?" He laughs, surprising himself.

"I'm fine. I just have a headache."

"She has cramps," Greta says. "Ow! Josie!"

"So help me, Greta," Josie says, "if you can't shut up for one—"

"Girls!" Victor's voice is too loud. His head feels heavy and hot. He closes his eyes for a moment. The girls are whispering to each other. Their voices flow through a thin glass tube. When he opens his eyes, rainbow halos shine above their heads.

"I think it worked," Josephine says. At least, Victor thinks it is Josie. He is having trouble distinguishing one girl's face from another.

"What did you do?" Victor demands. He tries to lift himself from his chair, but the heaviness has spread to his limbs, making standing a herculean task.

Beatrice says, "Did you think we'd just let you keep getting away with this crap?"

Greta says, "You deserve this, buddy."

Josephine says, "I'm glad you enjoyed the coffee so well. See, we put antifreeze in it. Makes a great sweetener." She is standing over him. Her mother gifted her a pleasing height, if not much else. It is early yet, but he can sense an increased luster in her hair, a flush of the skin. He can practically smell the changes on her. Such a waste.

He has words for all of them: "I will hide you all! I'll take you downstairs and show you what obedience means." But all that comes out of his mouth is a warbled slur, a crude syllable of hate wrapped around swollen lips.

"What's the matter?" Beatrice says, mocking him. "Cat got your tongue?"

"They know what you did to me," Josephine says. "They know that I'm not a floozy. That you put this thing in me. And maybe I would have let you get away with it, too. But you had to get greedy. I wasn't enough for you. No one touches my sister and lives to brag about it."

Victor gurgles mute indignation. He stumbles out of his chair, flailing, reaching for the wall behind him, nearly falling head-first into the fire. He gropes for support against the lime-stone slabs of the fireplace and finds the top of the poker hanging from the retractable cauldron. It feels as heavy as an anvil as he pulls it from its hook, but he manages one unseeing heave of the weapon, one feeble attempt at self-defense. The edge of the poker finds purchase in something soft. A body hits the floor. The girls are screaming. Then, Victor's head explodes in pain, and there are no more terrorizing thoughts, no more predatory fury.

20

— · —

The Urinal

HE WAKES UP AT 4:30. Selma is no longer in the bed. He finds her sitting at Lexi's desk, the glow from her laptop highlighting Selma's anguished expression as she stares at the screen.

"Why didn't you wake me?" Pete asks.

"Haven't been up long myself," she says. He has trouble believing that. "I thought I might check what Lexi's been researching to get more clues." She stares at him, almost defiant. Her eyes are red-rimmed from crying. "Is it really this bad, Pete? He's picking my people off. So many of the missing are from the rez. I mean, I've done my own research, but I had no idea it had gone this far. It's genocide."

"We don't know they're dead, Sel. We must stay hopeful." He walks over to her and rests a comforting hand on her shoulder, which she nuzzles against her cheek.

"Why didn't she tell me?" Selma says.

"I'm sure she just didn't want to worry you," Pete says. Selma sits upright and dries her eyes with her hands. "My daughter knows better," she says. "I always worry." She stands, her trademark resolve restored. "I'm ready," she says. "Let's go find a tunnel and out that bastard."

They return to the Sleeping Black Dog. The rain beats hard and fast against the corrugated metal canopy over the entrance, establishing an urgent rhythm as Selma unlocks the door.

After locking the door behind them, they haul their equipment to the men's bathroom. There is no question which of the four urinals—which have no business being so beautiful, sculpted in rose-veined marble in a time when such extravagances were more common—is the one under which the fabled passageway lies. Selma walks to the last one in the row and points to the oversized bowl built into the tiled floor. All the urinals have the same-sized bowl, so large that you could easily stand inside them, but this one is slightly different. Pete shines a flashlight over the bowl. A seam, no wider than a hair, runs along the back, right where the marble curves upward against the back of the wall. The seam is so expertly joined that you might mistake it for an imperfection in the marble.

"Impressive masonry," Pete says. "It looks dry; no mortar. Do you ever have trouble with leaks?"

"None," Selma says. "Whoever built this knew how to keep it working for its original purpose—assuming it has a secondary one."

Pete says, "It's time to find out." He pulls a sledgehammer from the bag of tools and hands it to Selma. "All you, my dear," he says. "I can barely lift the thing." Selma is no stranger to sledgehammers. It has been a while, and she has grown a little soft in her restaurant manager years, but after a few practice swings, the hammer feels right in her hands again. She swings the hammer high and wide but stops herself from bringing it down on the bowl. She leans the hammer against the wall.

"What's wrong?" Pete says. "Too heavy?"

Selma glares at him. "Don't start that shit with me, Peter Davies. No. I just can't bring myself to destroy it. What if we're wrong? Or what if there's some mechanism underneath that we mess up, and we can't remove the bottom? I know every minute counts while our kids are in danger, and maybe I'm biased because it's my place, but this crazy thing has lasted almost a hundred years, through earthquakes, drunk patrons, who knows what else? If there's a seam, it's meant to open. We just need to find out how."

They scan the rest of the marble with their flashlights, searching for other seams or irregularities, but with no luck. Next, they move to the plumbing. It's as old as the rest of the urinal: lovingly maintained brass works gleaming against the flashlight's beam. Pete tries manipulating the flush lever in different directions, but this only wastes water. Selma feels around the back of the neck connecting the plumbing to the bowl for a switch or button but only encounters the usual piping. They step away from the urinal, scratching their heads. Selma examines the other three urinals to see if she can find any other discrepancies between them. Then, she shoots upright suddenly, her face scrunched in concentration.

"The heads of the flushing mechanism are a little odd," she says. "I've always thought so. Much too fancy, even for a marble toilet."

The flush valves, like everything else, are works of art. The brass is cast in sumptuous curves, the levers gently tapering at the end, resembling miniature clarions. Then there are the caps, much taller than function requires and not molded with the usual hexagonal offset to accommodate a wrench. The caps resemble bishops in a chess game, and the little brass baubles topping them are ribbed, almost like they are meant to be gripped and turned.

"There," Selma says, pointing at the baubles.

"But they look the same across all the urinals," Pete says.

"Yes," she says. "If you're trying to hide a button to a secret passage, wouldn't you make it look like everything else?"

Selma turns the bauble on the last urinal. It is stiff and does not want to move at first, but it eventually loosens. Nothing happens. Pete raises his palms in a gesture of defeat, but Selma is determined. She wiggles the bauble. She presses down on it. She tries to remove it entirely, wondering if maybe it is a hidden key. When Selma does this, she reveals a thin brass rod that extends a few inches above the cap. There is a click at their feet, then a resounding thud.

"That's it," Selma says. "We found the button."

"But nothing opened," Pete says. "What are we missing? Is it stuck?"

Selma reaches for the sledgehammer again. This time, she holds it by the head and taps the butt of the handle hard against the bowl of the urinal. It still does not budge, so she tries again—and nearly topples over as the bowl shifts downward. The shudder of disused machinery echoes from the tile floor, then the bowl lurches open, suspended on one side by a pair of geared arms. Beneath the bowl is a narrow vertical tunnel with a ladder attached to one side.

Pete says, "Well, I'll be."

"Told you," Selma says. "Never doubt my intuition. Or my stubbornness."

Pete shines a flashlight down the tunnel. It extends about 30 feet. The flashlight's beam glances against crates and bottles, dust clouds swirling and twinkling like tiny nebulae.

"It's very narrow," Selma says. "I think I'm too wide to climb down."

"I'm not." Pete drums fingers against his ribcage to signal just how small the chemotherapy has left him.

"Yes," Selma says, "but you also got winded by a set of stairs not long ago. What if you stumble and hit your head?"

"I just need a moment," Pete says. "Hand me a water?" Selma takes a water bottle from their stash of provisions and gives it to Pete. As he sips, he ponders, staring down into the tunnel. Then, he pulls a business card out of his jacket pocket and hands it to Selma. "There might be nothing more down there than a smuggler's cache," he says. "But if there is something else, like another passageway that goes deeper, I will see where it leads. I will be careful. I'll take the shotgun. We may not get much help reporting a missing persons case to the county right now, but I have a feeling federal authorities would be interested in a couple of outlaws trespassing on Coast Guard land, especially if we tell them they are there to raid an archaeological dig site."

"Outlaws?" Selma says. "Why—?"

"—Jonathan is wanted for assault," he says. "After I bailed him out of county, right before he came working for me, in fact, he got into a fight at the Lucky Bear Casino up in Hoopa. He ran off with somebody's woman, the guy didn't like it, and Jonathan knocked several teeth out of his head. I doubt he remembers it happening. Lexi was tailing him and went up to the casino to run reconnaissance. We've been protecting him from scrutiny ever since. It's time to lift off that veil."

Selma responds slowly, weighing the gravity: "The rez is federal land. So, the assault is a federal crime."

"Yep. And he's on federal land again. Now with an accomplice in tow."

"Are you sure about this?" she says. "It's very risky. You could ruin his life. Or, if Drake's armed, he could get caught in a firefight."

The Sturgeon sighs. "I'm not happy about it," he says. "But Jonathan already ruined his life. As for the other risks," he says, pointing to the card, "that's the number of a friend of mine who works for the Interior Department. If I find something worth investigating, give it an hour, then call him. Tell him I sent you and what is going on, but without telling him. I trust you know how to do that. He will know who to bring and what to do to avoid violence."

Selma grumbles. "The feds always find a way to fuck things up."

"I know. I don't trust the feds; I trust my friend. He's our best bet to stop Drake from getting away with human trafficking when he have no evidence to point him to it. He can squeeze confessions out of criminals, even wily snakes. Plus, he can pull a few strings to help Jonathan get a lighter sentence—with my help, too, of course, as his legal counsel."

"If you live long enough to represent him," Selma says.

Pete gives her a long embrace. "Like I said, I'll be careful. There is too much riding on this for me to die from an avoidable accident. If it's too dangerous down there, I will turn around and let the authorities handle it." He lets Selma go and says, "I'm ready." He slings his shotgun over his shoulder and gathers supplies. As he descends the ladder, Selma asks, "How do I tell this guy where to go? The lighthouse is huge and falling apart."

Pete mentions the entrance to the basement around the side of the house. "If they don't see them there," he says, "tell him to go lower."

"Is there a 'lower'?"

"I don't know. But I have a hunch there is."

Selma watches him descend, shining her flashlight down the tunnel to help him find his way. When he reaches the bottom, he gives her a thumbs up.

Pete finds himself in a wood-frame bunker. Dusty earthenware jugs lay everywhere; many smashed, but a few still intact. He calls up to Selma, "It looks like an old moonshine cache!" Fitted with a headlamp, he searches the space for another passageway. No trap doors or vault entrances make themselves apparent. However, in a room lined with rudimentary shelves, it seems odd that an ornate cabinet sits against one wall.

"I found something!" He approaches the cabinet. It belongs in the personal library of a wealthy collector, not a bootlegger's hovel. The barrels of several hinges peek out where one cabinet edge meets the wall.

Pete grabs the opposite edge of the cabinet and pulls it away from the wall. A stone staircase curves downward.

He returns to the base of the tunnel. "You're not going to believe this," he says, "but I think I found a way down. Get ready to call the feds."

"Be careful!" Selma calls to him. To herself, she mumbles, "Come back to me, you old fool."

Book IV: Elders

Mind Punk Publishers

21

Introductions

WILL YOU PERMIT US to step back a moment? There are many players here, and we must realign them, or else none of what we seek to accomplish will make sense to those who most need to hear it. No one bound by time can view every kink and whorl of reality, no matter how prescient they believe themselves to be. A good story, like a strong network of roots, has many branches, and while a lateral root near the tip might know what the taproot is doing, it may never hear from its distant cousins closer to the stem. That is why we occasionally intervene, filling in the gaps, the missed opportunities, the communication breakdowns, to serve the purpose last night's holiday once had: to assert love and community in the face of oppression, as the dispersed remains of its Roman namesake would prefer.

In the early days, humans listened to us. We were legion, and their voices were few. They were infants then. Now, they are adolescents: fearless, reckless, and endlessly curious. That is not always a bad thing. But there are too many of them now, our voices drowned by a tsunami of hubris. The teenagers run the school. So, we have become tactical, operating in the shadows. We must; otherwise, we will fail our duty as guardians.

22

— · —

Ward A

A RUMOR STARTED TO spread through the clinic that another patient would be assigned to Ward C. Were there any free beds? Of course not. There hadn't been for over a month. I suppose we could put the waking girl somewhere else. Hell, she could sleep on the break room couch.

The nurses in charge of Ward C had gone too long without a patient who responded to them meaningfully. The "waking girl," as they referred to Em, followed their movements with her eyes. A week after waking, she started to walk unassisted down the corridor connecting Ward C with Ward B. She walked very slowly, so few considered her a flight risk. She could see and walk and eat solid foods, but she did not respond when the nurses tried to talk to her. They assumed she must be deaf or did not speak English or Spanish, both of which they had tried. So, they talked about her to her face like you might with a troublesome pet.

It was uncomfortable at first, not speaking to anyone. Sober and brimming with knowledge the average person would find terrifying and suspect, Em has wanted to talk nonstop for the past few weeks. But if she spoke to the nurses, she would no longer seem so harmless. They would put her under a microscope. It is problematic enough that she is awake when no one else is.

The good doctor knows that she once spoke English. A resourceful person like her can make Em talk or prove, at the very least, that she still understands what people say to her. All paths, including the few that are optimal, the ones that return her daughter's body to her, pass through Dr. Niequist. Em will likely not leave the clinic if she commands the doctor's attention too soon.

The new patient is critical. There are a few ways things could go when they arrive. A death is likely unavoidable: whether it will be the patient's or the doctor's is unclear. The looking glass inevitably fractures when she meanders that far into the future. Em sees the two of them, the patient and the doctor, superimposed. It's impossible to tell which is which.

Two days after the rumors start, the patient arrives. Em knows this because the nurses keep their promise to move her to another ward. They do not tell her directly; the nurses mention it as they gossip, tending to the patients. Em asks them why she is being moved, and the nurses stop what they are doing. There are just two of them in Ward C, just two to attend to over 50 patients. They turn to stare at her. Miguel, who gives off a constant oily smell like processed cheddar left on the counter too long, blinks stupidly at her as though he, too, has forgotten how to speak. The other nurse, Grace, has lived up to her name. She has been careful with her words around Em, never assuming that the girl did not understand her. Grace tells Em that her recovery is complete. Why am I not being discharged, then?

Grace mentions something vague about paperwork. She has a broad, round face, an open face, with large, trusting eyes. She is not accustomed to lying. Doing so causes her face to contract in revealing discomfort.

Em knows by inference that the new patient has arrived, but she also knows because something about the patient's presence has caused her to question the nature of her new abilities. Last night, her dreams were filled with the patient's thoughts. She feels the itch of the banding and adhesive of duct tape against her lips. She falls into the roots again, a sensation so believable that she has trouble waking up the following day. Right before she does, there is a blinding flash, and she briefly sees the faces of all the women around her, then the faces of their relatives and ancestors, and finally, a familiar face, one she thought she had lost. Her dreams are not a premonition: it is the present spread across a horizontal plane, a calm ocean that spans many leagues.

Em has been to the double doors leading to Ward B but never through them. She wants to walk, to push both doors open at once, one with each hand, like the returning hero in her favorite fantasy movie who everyone believes has fallen in battle. Grace insists she must be wheeled. Clinic policy. The doors slowly open with a mechanical whir at the push of a button. The doors are made of wood or, more accurately, a wood composite. Em senses their weariness. Hundreds of trees, deprived after death from returning to the soil, have been reorganized here to separate one group of humans from another. They long to be touched by microbes, by skin, by life. Perhaps a palm occasionally grazes the wood, but it is promptly sanitized. A metal circle attached to the wall receives most of the attention. Em hears a chorus of quiet moaning as she is pushed through the doorway. It sounds like the voices from the root floor. All those faces singing in perfect harmony, row after row, as though the choir loft at St. Stephen's chapel has expanded to fill a nation.

Em hopes Grace will leave her in Ward B because it is closest to the main entrance. Not that she plans to escape that way. The entrance, which opens into an expansive, semicircular solarium, is a poor choice of escape for a teenage girl smuggling biological contraband. On a clear, moonlit night, she would still be easily spotted. However, proximity to the entrance increases the chances that someone from the outside will see her because just behind the front desk is a lounge that the patients in Ward B occasionally have access to. Selma might come in. Or even Daddy Dearest. She has seen them along a few future paths, but the context is unclear. She may see them after she has already made a run for it.

Grace does not stop in Ward B. That ward lies in the clinic's bulbous center, with Wards A and C in the fanning wings on either side. From above, the clinic looks somewhat like a bat in flight. Her mother would have called it biomimicry: an organic form. Nothing about the clinic feels organic to Em, but a small grove of cedars surrounds it. On a smaller scale, it reminds Em of some grander publicly accessible buildings back home, like the Getty Museum or the Griffith Observatory. Like those buildings, the clinic sits on a high shelf overlooking the masses below, just up the road from the new, primarily empty mini-mansions that abut National Forest land on the outskirts of town. Why would a clinic in a place so down on its luck be so ostentatious? She should have known better that something was off when she arrived. But she must forgive herself. At the time, she was lost. Adrift in the doldrums. Her direction unclear.

Ward A's shell might resemble Ward B's, but its innards are far different. For starters, the entrance to the ward stands behind a heavy metal door with a small window cut into it that is fortified with wire mesh. Grace presses the call button on an intercom next to the door. A dark glass sphere with an angry red light hangs above the intercom near the ceiling. Em can feel the red light cutting into her and through her. It is sizing her up. Grace moves to press the intercom again, but a sharp buzz sounds before she does, and the heavy metal door pops open.

The walls of the main corridor are painted a pale yellow, and many more doors run down it than the main corridor in Ward B, which appears primarily devoted to warehousing the comatose in one or two rooms. Em glances at the nondescript placards on the doors as they pass, which only offer a number and the letter "A." She wonders what could be behind them. Offices. Single-occupancy rooms. Laboratories. Maybe ones with fetuses chilling in jars. And hundreds of vials full of lethal juju, the substance that nightmares are made of.

They stop at a door near the end of the corridor. A-56. The number jogs a memory. Or a vision, perhaps. Em sees a red scarf tethered to the bars surrounding a window. A way out? Yes, one way or another, a way out. The clinic lies on sloping land; in parts, the ground floor rests above the ground, the basement peeking out. A drop from a ground-floor window could cause serious injury in these sections. With the right materials, it would be a long enough drop from which to hang someone. Her mother's stigmata come to mind, and she shudders.

But there are no barred windows in A-56. There are barely windows to speak of. Two rectangular slots about as wide as Em's forearm stand high on one wall, allowing for a passing suggestion of sunlight. Otherwise, the room is lit by long, cold fluorescent bulbs suspended from a drop ceiling. Placed square under the tiny windows are two tiny beds, each with a bare nightstand beside them that, in an attempt to provide the familiarity of a bedroom, only makes the room feel more alien. The bed closest to the door is dressed with crisp white sheets. On the other bed, the sheets sit in a tangled mess beneath a similarly tangled person.

Em's heart skips. She is now grateful for the wheelchair; her knees would have likely buckled if she were standing. She thought she could no longer be surprised. Yet here he is, always keeping her on her toes.

Andre, if it is indeed Andre, has been catapulted through time. She saw his face upon waking that morning along with the others, but he looked just like he had before: better, even, as though a life of drug dealing had never touched him. The man who is slumped before her has gone in the opposite direction. His hair has grown several inches and rises in wild, frizzy undulations. She thinks she sees tufts of gray at the base of his scalp, though it may just be the lighting. His velvet skin is patchy and faded. He does not acknowledge Em or Grace or even that the door has opened. In his eyes, she no longer sees the ineffable calm that first drew her to him, though she does see a familiar pain. The pain of the endless drop. His head is turned to the far wall, staring at nothing. Or, more likely, a continuous flash reel of things, his heartache and joy flicking by at a numbing pace.

"I can't," Em mumbles. She is about to break out in tears.

"What's that, dear?" Grace says. Having overcome the shock that Em can hear and speak, the nurse has warmed up to her. It's a pity they must part.

"I, uh, I can't seem to get up." She wipes her eyes with the back of one hand. "You were right to wheel me here."

"Of course, dear." Grace helps her to her feet. It is a practiced move done with love and patience, a level of compassion most people reserve for loved ones alone. Grace's skills are wasted here. How did she become a lackey in this sham of a clinic? Em supposes that jobs are scarce here. They are scarce everywhere. Good people, when desperate, are prone to succumb to dubious schemes.

Is Em a good person? She looks at Andre's ancient form, his living carapace, and doubts it. But perhaps there is still time.

Grace guides Em to the empty bed and helps her get comfortable. She suggests Em rest. In a while, the doctor will call for her. Grace leaves and closes the door. Few paths lead to them seeing each other again.

The doctor. The moment has arrived. The crux. Em thought she would be prepared, but her blindness to Andre distracted her. It seems he is still good at that. Her mind has played out a few paths where she saddles a middle-aged man over her shoulder and drags his shuffling body out of the clinic. It never occurred to her that the man might be Andre, but now, she cannot dismiss the idea. The person lying beside her is not the boy she knew. He looks like his age has doubled. Considering her own transformation years ago, it is not a far-fetched conclusion. Mentally and spiritually, she is no longer a teenager. Perhaps

Andre had more baggage to unearth. Maybe, with the help of the same poison she had, he has relived his short life many times.

He is upright, at least, and his eyes are open. More than can be said for the rest.

"Hey, beau," she says. Instead of looking at his weathered body, she stares at the wall before her. The wall is blank and white, a perfect space for her to paint an earlier picture of him, one she can talk to without crumpling. "I don't know if you can hear me. I guess it doesn't matter too much if you can. There's not much I can say to make things better." She exhales, rounding her lips and blowing hard like you might do to fill someone's lungs. "I thought I lost you, but I just didn't recognize you. I guess you are still kind of lost. Lost to yourself. There is something I need to do, and it doesn't involve you, really. But then, maybe you don't want me to involve you. Maybe you are done with me."

She feels something cold slide down her spine from the base of her neck. A mossy, rain-slicked thing smelling of stone and earth and decay. Like Fiona on the canopy floor, but diminished. Not quite decidedly as dead. The cold feels like a toe-dip back into Pedro's special blend, which comforts her. The cold does not blame Em. Through the sweet, damp smell, she senses longing. Andre is not done with her. He wants to forgive and be forgiven, even if there is no chance for him to rise.

But she wonders: is there a chance? The seed and her daughter, one and the same, dominate the future's horizon like a setting harvest moon, blotting out the stars. That does not mean the stars have disappeared. She cannot know all the impacts of her actions. Is any path that leads her to plant her seed the right path, provided she is successful? Is her future the only one that matters? Now, she is not so sure.

She lies back, stares at the high ceiling with its naked lights, and expands her view. The possibilities are tantalizing, if risky.

23

—·—

The Good Doctor

SHE IS SLOWLY BOILING. Light and buoyant, she rises on a warm water current but never breaks the surface. Each time she plunges, her sense of self evaporates more. There is no self, her body tells her. You are many, not one. Her body has always known this, but the modern world caused her mind to forget.

The new patient is nearby. Em can sense she is different than the others. Different than Andre, too. He is upright and emulates wakefulness, but he still moves through darkness. The new patient, while sedated, moves tantalizingly close to the light. She is more like Em; she just needs a similar push.

All those sleeping women are sedated. Em only realizes this now, as though the new patient whispered it in her ear. Not comatose. Deliberately put under. Waiting for the right moment. Judgment Day, perhaps. Em is a fluke, a surprise; she woke on her own. Andre and the new patient must be induced. It reminds her of the famous neurologist she learned about at St. Stephen's, whose book she read when she was supposed to be learning Catechism. What was his name? There was a movie about it that she had not seen. The doctor injected his patients, who had Locked-In Syndrome, with a potent dose of neuroreceptors, and they woke up after being asleep for decades. Not sleeping, exactly, but shut off from the world. The drugs only offered a temporary fix. Eventually, the patients became Locked In again.

Em wakes from her brief slumber. The clothes she was wearing before entering the clinic—her favorite hole-filled black denim jeans and a similarly tattered Rolling Stones T-shirt—now rest on the nightstand. The clothes have never seen such care. They are neatly folded and smell of lilacs. On top of the T-shirt sits the teardrop-shaped locket, shining cold under the fluorescent light.

The locket speaks to her in Fiona's voice. "This was my death," she seems to say. Em wants to throw the locket against the wall or break its chain, but she doesn't. It's not Fiona or the locket or even the seed inside it speaking to her. It is her own voice, still trying to destroy her.

She fastens the locket around her neck. The metal is cold and hungry. Wondering why it was abandoned. She warms the teardrop with a thumb and forefinger; as she does, the new patient slides to the front of her consciousness. The patient yearns to wake, but she can't penetrate the veil. She is ravaged but sturdy. Skin firm and free from blemishes, fingernails clear and smooth, if a little long; she usually keeps them trimmed. Or she thinks she does. With each passing year under the veil—for it feels like years have passed—she remembers less how she likes things.

Em recognizes the woman's hands and blemish-free arms. Her slender fingers are made for piano playing, but she would never engage in such an activity. Piano is for dilettantes. Her fingers are made for cupping around a mug of tea, elbows propped on the table, forearms stretched out and dominating the surface like she owns the place. In a way, she does. She surveys her tiny kingdom with sly confidence, and Em hovers from a short distance, in awe of her stunning face, wanting to simultaneously kiss and punch it.

If there is any natural order to the machinations of this town, the presence of Selma's adopted daughter here, as a drugged-up inpatient, goes against that order. Perhaps the violation explains why she feels what the young woman feels, not as an artifact of a possible future but as a simultaneous present. Em is still learning the rules of her perception. Can she only connect with women? She couldn't see Andre, so it's possible. But she wonders if there is more to it. Perhaps, instead of seeing the future, she sees what she *needs* to see. Em will soon meet with Dr. Niequist again. Before, even though she knew the possible outcomes, she did not feel prepared. In her hands lies an incendiary device that, just moments ago, she could not ignite without it exploding in her face. Now, a few hours before she needs to use it, she thinks she has the proper wiring to set a delayed explosion.

The doctor and the patient are not the same person, though that was an honest mistake. One can die without the other. But if Em waits too long, the patient will die from psychological assault, if nothing else. Em could not forgive herself if that happened. It would be like she died, too.

Dr. Niequist's office is a ten-by-ten-foot square lined with books on all sides. The books make the small room feel even smaller.

The built-in shelves, set into three walls, have slender volumes wedged into every possible gap, some propped on their sides, others jammed in awkward diagonals. More books lie behind the doctor's desk below the room's only window, in danger of toppling. There are medical journals, esoteric treatises, and textbooks on pharmacology, biochemistry, and anatomy. An entire wall is dedicated to composition notebooks. Some volumes seem out of place, like a well-worn copy of *Robinson Crusoe*. To Em's horror and delight, *The Structure of Evolutionary Theory* sits on the desk alone, with only a wide-screen monitor cast in brushed stainless steel and a matching wireless keyboard to keep it company. The book is closed, the pages rippling, like river rapids over rocks, from the assault of several dog ears. "I take it you're a Gould fan," Em says.

So far, her visit to the Good Doctor's office has felt like a therapy session. It's a shame there's no chaise longue or fainting couch for her to wax philosophic on. There is no room for one. Em sits on a stiff wood-frame chair with lumpy cushioning. Dr. Niequist reclines on sumptuous leather. She has been waiting for Em to start. Start what? Complaining about the oppressive furniture arrangement? The doctor's arched eyebrows suggest that evolution chat is not what she had in mind. But she relents. "Are you interested in evolutionary theory?"

"I am. Or, I guess I was. It's been a while since I cracked that one open."

Dr. Niequist eyes the Gould, then her, with suspicion. "This is quite an advanced volume for someone your age."

"I'm older than I look."

"I don't doubt that," the Good Doctor says. "But it's advanced even for college students. Did you understand it?"

"I did," Em lies. But it is only partly a lie. The concept she struggles with most, punctuated equilibrium, still rests uneasily where most people would think to store it, between the ears and slightly behind the eyes. But the roots did not present that moment in her mother's hospital room, fabricated though it was, to goad her. They offered an alternative understanding. The concept swims laps from her chest to the base of her spine. She feels she is living through punctuated equilibrium, even if she cannot articulate its mechanics.

The doctor crosses her arms and narrows her gaze, but she also smiles. A small, shrewd smile. "I was pre-med in college," she says. "Not much room for distraction. But, after a couple of advanced Biology courses, I let myself stray a little. 'Foundations in Evolution.' That was the name of the course. This book was the backbone." She pats the Gould gently, with just the tips of her fingers. "I return to it often, wondering."

The correct response to this moment carries weight, while others will have no discernible impact. For example, if Em says, "What do you wonder," but does it with her knees tucked together, leaning forward, her voice clear and her intentions un-ambiguous, the doctor will sidestep, disarmed by her sincerity, but not long enough to yield the kind of softening that might, in time, encourage her to give up a certain key to a certain lab. If she says, "What do you wonder" with her arms crossed and her head turned to the stacks of books, the doctor will allow herself a small puff of air through her nostrils like a frustrated horse, a barely discernible scoff, and somewhere down the line, with a few more calibrations, a liquid nitrogen tank will rupture in the hallway outside a certain lab, a suitable diversion for a small, dismissed teenage girl to break in unnoticed. Though one of these outcomes yields the desired results, neither is ideal. "What do you wonder?" is the wrong question to ask. Dr. Niequist does not want her patients to ask her probing questions. She wants to observe, not be observed.

So, instead, Em says something unexpected. It comes out of her mouth and surprises her after she has said it, which, in the past four years, is not a behavior she is familiar with. The jab of the needle was a dependable routine. It provided certainty in its inevitable destruction. Now, exposed to infinite forking paths, she realizes she cannot focus on all of them as she initially expected. There are gaps in her story. Chaos reigns. It gives her a strange comfort.

She says, "I often wonder if I'm the next step in human evolution." She says it out of curiosity, as though teenage girls often wonder about such things.

Em does not believe what she says; she knows that Steven J. Gould would disapprove. But the doctor's reaction confirms that her intuition was correct. Dr. Niequist straightens in her chair. She maintains a neutral face but stares at Em too intently. The doctor believes her, though she tries to hide it by not responding: a common psychiatrist trick. They let you do the talking. They do not editorialize. But of course, every shrink has an opinion they dare not voice.

"It's stupid, I know," Em continues. "I must be going crazy, right? Dr. Niequist?"

The doctor appears not to have heard her. She now eyes the Gould suspiciously as if it might jump from the desk and strike her. "I'm sorry," she says, blinking and looking up. "Please, call me Astrid."

"OK. Dr. Astrid—"

"—Just Astrid is fine. Why do you think you're the next step in human evolution?"

"I don't know. It's just a feeling. For a while now, I could predict things. I saw what would happen in my life before it did."

"So, you can see the future."

"Yeah. But no, because there's not one future, you know? There are always multiples. So, I guess I see 'futures.' And one of the futures always plays out, just like I saw it."

"Go on." The doctor rests her elbows on the desk and folds her hands under her chin. She takes no notes.

"And, well... I don't know. That's it, I guess. It did change recently. I used to only see one possible future, but that still played out. But lately—I guess since I arrived at the clinic—that's when the multiple futures became a thing." In her reading of the Multiverse, Em has found that revealing too much or speaking with too much confidence breeds mistrust and suspicion. She does not carry the same confidence she had just a week ago but still wonders if she is being too direct. Em does not reveal her abilities in any future she has foreseen. The result—which, until now, was by design—is that Em knows Astrid far better than the doctor knows her: a desirable result if you feel that your motives run counter to the person holding the key to your freedom. And why did she think that was true? Because Astrid is dangerously deluded? Perhaps Em has been deluded as well. Maybe only the present can bring such delusion to bear.

Meanwhile, the doctor takes notes. She has pulled out a leather-bound notebook from the breast pocket of her lab coat and writes frantically with a small, tight hand, fingers pinched near the base of her fountain pen, which is fat and glossy and looks cumbersome in her slender fingers. The computer sits unused. A patina of dust has collected over the keys. Em gave this sign of neglect little consideration before, but this time, she asks about it.

Astrid glances up from her notebook to assess the dusty keyboard. She appears fascinated, as though she has also not given its misuse much thought. "This was a gift from our sponsor—from the person, or possibly, persons, footing the bill for this clinic. I remember pulling the computer out of its packaging, which was just fancy cardboard, but the manufacturers took great pains to make the box look like something you'd want to open, like there was treasure inside. And the computer is pretty, I'll grant my sponsor that. I'm just not a big fan of computers. I guess I'm old-fashioned that way. I used it for email at first, but after a while, the emails became daunting." Her eyes widen, and she looks around the room like she has forgotten where she is. "Good Lord! Sorry about that. That was unprofessional of me. You don't need to know how the sausage is made around here. But perhaps you already knew all this? Since you can predict the future." The doctor says the last part with a hint of condescension. A last-minute save, perhaps, so as not to appear too eager.

"I didn't know," Em says. "That's why I asked. I mean, I knew about the mystery investor. I also suspect why you can't help opening up to me, even though you think it's unprofessional. I have it on good authority that I remind you of a favorite lab rat you used to have. You named the lab rat Ramona after your mom."

Astrid scoffs, muttering, "That's absurd—why would I name a lab rat after my mother?" But she still takes notes, glancing warily at Em after completing a line, perhaps wondering what will come next.

"You have your reasons," Em says. "And I guess you can deny it all you want since it's not verifiable. Look, this is scary for me, too, even though I've technically been living with it for a long time. I get that it's unbelievable. You probably think I'm crazy, right? I mean, this drug was supposed to cure addiction, not give people superpowers."

The doctor sets down the pen and closes the notebook over it. The cover of the notebook, made from rigid cardboard, lies over the pen at a sharp angle, the pages below curling like surf. It reminds Em of a building her mother designed—not one that was ever built, sadly. The model sat in her mother's home office for years, collecting dust. It was supposed to be a library shaped like a partially opened book on its side. If Em had found a cure for her addiction—or for whatever you might call the raging current that carried her along for so many years—perhaps the library would stand today.

"I asked you a question," Astrid says.

"Sorry," Em says. "Got caught up in some wishful thinking over here. What did you say?"

"How could you know what the drug is for? Did the nurses say something?"

"The nurses? They're clueless. You tell me."

"How am I supposed to know how you found out?"

"No," Em says. "I mean, you are the one who tells me about the drug. In another timeline, we become colleagues—and sort of friends."

"That's impossible," Astrid says.

"No, just improbable," Em says. "I see a lot of things that aren't likely to happen. I also see that you might need more convincing. Are you familiar with the phrase 'chemogenetic transcription?'"

"Perhaps," Astrid says. She opens the notebook again and picks up the pen to write, but her hand shakes so violently that she sets the pen back down again after scrawling only a few letters. Astrid stares at the pen intently, perhaps wondering if it will pick itself up and start writing on its own. If it, too, is an item in her growing collection that can surprise her.

"Tell me about it."

"Hmm?" Astrid looks up, bemused.

"Looks like I caught you daydreaming, too. Chemogenetic transcription: tell me about it. I remember, like, this much of chemogenetics from high school." Em spreads the thumb and index finger on one hand a few inches wide to show how little she remembers, which, from Astrid's expression, is a few inches more than she believes any high school student would know. "We covered activation, I think? Activation of neuroreceptors. Very dry stuff, at least the way Sister Rose taught it. But I don't think transcription ever came up."

"Why don't you tell me what it means? Since we are colleagues." Astrid says. The derision in her tone does little to mask her fear.

"And friends," Em says. "Don't forget we're friends. Fine, fine." Em raises her hands in mock supplication. Despite the circumstances, she is enjoying herself. "But I'm using your own words." She clears her throat, assumes her best neurologist stance, and begins. "Chemogenetic transcription, my dear Emma, is nothing short of the greatest breakthrough in modern neuroscience. We're talking about an end to psychological suffering, not just the distant promise of it. The problem, of course, is that most neurologists seek to use chemogenetics as a diagnostic tool. Temporary activation is their goal. And that is a good start, for sure, but why stop there? Transcription involves a permanent alteration of the neural pathway. Previously, any attempts to do this at a genetic level were limited to cell cultures in a lab. Messy stuff. It took years of trials to yield the smallest results, and they, too, were primarily diagnostic, with little to no practical application for living, breathing patients. Then, I had a breakthrough. A gift from the Universe, or Nature, if you will." Em stands and paces as she talks, gesturing like the nuns at St. Stephen's often did, holding an imaginary wand and waving it against an imaginary blackboard. When the speech is done, she looks down at the lumpy chair, puzzled by how she ended up on her feet.

"Those don't sound like my words," Astrid says. "Why on earth would I call you 'my dear Emma?'"

"I don't know," Em says, "for dramatic effect? Anyway, what's important is the key to the transcription: a special rhizome you found right here, in this town, from a new species of plant you have yet to identify or locate any other parts of. It's the same rhizome you gave me when I rolled in here and to all those women in Ward A who can't seem to wake up."

Astrid scoffs. "You're a spy, then," she says. "I'm surrounded by spies."

"Yeah, sure; I'm a spy. If I was, why would I blow my cover? Not that you don't probably have a few spies working here. I understand why you might be paranoid. I would not put it past your investor, whoever they are."

The doctor is silent for a long time. She stares at the dust-covered keyboard; suddenly disgusted, she wipes the dust away with the sleeve of her lab coat. "I don't know what to think," she says. "I was just trying to cure you of your addiction."

"And you did," Em says. "Maybe not in the way you thought, but yeah, it worked." Having relived Fiona's death while down in the roots—wondering how many times she must have looped through those four years, unaware, but with genuine impacts to her psyche, like a spiritual yoke weighing her down—Em is cured of any desire to return to a lifestyle that caused so much suffering. Not that it might still not happen, regardless of her desire—but she sets this thought aside. "There were just some bonuses," she says. "If you can call them that."

"No use resisting, I guess," Astrid says. "Although this is crazy—"

"—I know! It's crazy for me, too."

"But everything you said is true. The rhizomes I found in Rabbit Warren Cove are like nothing I've seen. They're about the size and shape of a turmeric root, but their similarities end there. The skin is a shimmery purple, like a rough-cut opal. The flesh is purple, too, but transparent. Have you ever seen a cutout of a fiber optic cable? It's kind of like that. Thousands of light-transmitting fibers found right in nature. But you've probably already heard this."

"I've heard a version," Em says, "but the details are different. Keep going."

"I found them while on break from Med school at UC Davis. Botany was not my strongest subject pre-med, but I knew I could lean on my more adventurous, pharmacologically inclined colleagues and Davis's state-of-the-art equipment to fill the gaps. I brought back as many samples of the rhizome as I could and assembled a small team. We worked late to avoid prying eyes. Naturally, first tried to cultivate the rhizomes—we didn't even know which plant species they belonged to! Beyond their appearance, that was when the first curiosity arose. None of the rhizomes would sprout, even after months of incubation. To be fair, the flesh was so dense we had to use a bone saw to cut through it! I wondered if they were fossils, but our lab tests disproved that. It seems they are just in a deeply dormant state, and no modern horticultural practice I know of can cause them to grow. From what I can tell, they come from a species no one has identified before."

Astrid is animated; her eyes search the ceiling, and her hands conduct a tune only she can hear. She needs no more prompting from Em to continue.

"Since I was studying to be a neurologist, we had plenty of lab subjects—rats, like you mentioned!—on which we tested the astounding mix of chemical compounds we found inside the rhizomes. They contain a cocktail of vital neurotransmitters—GABA, norepinephrine, serotonin, and a super dose of acetylcholine—which you can find in nature in various concentrations but which we had never seen together in a single plant. There were other compounds, too: ones we did not recognize, ones that the budding pharmacologists could only guess their function. I was already running an addiction study on my lab rats for my MD/PhD thesis, so we injected them with a solution containing the pulverized rhizome. Addiction recovery is—well, you can probably guess that it's a very personal subject for me. The rats responded exceptionally well. Before, when I dropped a heroin drip in their cage, they would ignore food and water and keep returning to the drip. After the injection, they ignored the drip entirely. They were calm and docile but also more curious than they had been even before introducing the heroin, which is saying a lot for rats, as they're naturally curious. I remember that my favorite rat started looking at me more intently than she ever had before. Sometimes, it felt like she was looking into the deepest part of me, to a part even I did not understand at the time."

Em asks, "Did your favorite rat have a name?"

"Of course she did," Astrid says, squirming in her chair and glaring at Em. "I name all my lab rats. Hers was Ramona." She pauses, clearing her throat. "After my mother."

Em smiles—out of kindness more than triumph.

"Look," Astrid says, "things have not been easy for me the last few years. The rhizome has only caused me trouble. Of course, my doctoral panel was thrilled by what we accomplished with the rats, but they wanted more than I could comfortably give them. They wanted to know how to replicate the results, and my methodology was lacking. I hadn't mentioned the rhizome in my thesis. How could I? As far as I knew, it was a non-renewable and very finite resource. To this day, I haven't found any signs of it more than a few miles from my hometown. The Cove is like a microbiome. Maybe the fog has something to do with it. I swear we get more fog here than anywhere else in California.

"Anyway, the doctoral panel rejected my thesis, and I rejected them soon after. My heart was broken. I drifted through a few unfulfilling jobs in Sacramento until an angel investor found a draft copy of my dissertation online—God knows how—and claimed that they knew about the natural source of my miracle cure for addiction. They wanted to pay for me to synthesize it. At first, I thought that a member of the original late-night crew, all of whom swore secrecy about the project, had reneged and was trying to exploit me. But when the investor told me that I would have to return to Rabbit Warren Cove to be 'closer to the source,' as they put it, I knew it couldn't have been any of them. I had told no one where to find the rhizome."

Em asks, "Do you know who this investor is?"

"No clue," Astrid says. "I don't even know if it's one person or many, woman or man. However, considering how things have gone, I would guess that a man is in charge. I'm sorry," she says. She walks to the front of her desk and sits on its edge, a few inches from Em. She sits in silence for a while, her eyes brimming with tears as she struggles to find the right words. "This is not fair to you. Or to the women in my care who can't wake up. The investor insisted on testing live human subjects! When I pushed back, they just appeared at the clinic seeking care. They were all women from the start, and none could or would provide next-of-kin. That should have been my first warning. But I was too proud and too confident to let that stop me. I had a crack team and state-of-the-art equipment. When the first round of patients were rendered comatose, my team quit. I'm not a chemist. How could I do better than they did? But more patients came, so I tried. I couldn't abandon my existing patients, and the new ones seemed to fear for their lives because when I told them I couldn't help them, they insisted I must. None of them would go into any details about why, but I got the sense that they had been told that if they left, they would be in danger.

"Now I feel like I'm in danger, too. After my staff left, the investor started making more pointed hiring decisions. As I said, I'm concerned that the investor has hired spies. Maybe not the orderlies in Ward A, but others. After I expressed my worries to a lab tech—who, to my surprise, knows less about chemistry than I do—I got an email from the investor threatening to sue me for criminal negligence. Not a threat to my life, but one more reason to keep me here and prevent me from contacting the police myself. Who would they believe? Some unknown entity pulling the strings, or the person who plunged the syringe?"

"Why did you take me in?" Em asks.

"Pride," Astrid says. She is shaking now. "Just more fucking pride. I gave you the same solution I gave my rats: pure rhizome. If it worked for them, I thought it could work for you, too. And I guess it did. You're awake, at least. But now—" She covers her mouth with her hand, tears dripping down her fingers.

"Your sister," Em says. A leap of intuition—or is it? She feels the woman tickling the base of her spine even as she sleeps.

Astrid nods. She removes her hand from her face and takes a few deep breaths. "How much do you know?" She asks.

"Not much," Em says. "This is a weird development in my abilities: a new wrinkle that just came up today. All I know is that she's here, and like the others, she can't wake up. She's communicating with me somehow. Maybe it's because I met her once, briefly. I worked for Selma for a bit. She came into the diner."

"I gave her the same uncut solution I gave you," Astrid says. "Believe me, I didn't want to—you hadn't woken up yet, so I had no reason to think it would work—but I had few choices.

"A couple of weeks ago, around the time you came to us—the first voluntary patient we've had in months—the investor announced another addition to the staff. The investor insisted it was for our safety, mine and the patients', but when the new staff member arrived, I felt far from safe. I was given a name and led to believe that an old friend had been hired. When he arrived, he looked like the man I'd grown up with, whose wife and daughter I'd come to know almost like family. Or, a hollowed-out version of him. He gives me hard, lingering stares when he thinks I'm not looking. I'm convinced that a parasite has taken over his body. He was always such a kind soul, if a little down on his luck sometimes. Only an infestation or a severe head injury could explain such a dramatic change in his personality.

"Anyway, whatever's happening with Raymond—that's his name, my old friend—he appears to have been hired on as company muscle, probably as another spy as well. He came in carrying my sister over his shoulder like a bundle of firewood. She was unconscious and deathly pale. Her lips were blue. We gave her oxygen and ran a blood test, and it came back positive for a dangerously high level of opioids. Every sign pointed to an overdose. I was shocked. Sure, my sister would smoke pot sometimes with her forestry friends, but never anything harder than that. I talked to her on the phone a couple of weeks ago, and she sounded alert and coherent. Also, concerned because—well, it's probably not important right now—but she didn't sound like she was using. It doesn't make any sense."

Em thinks of Fiona, of the tantalizing idea that a seed could cause her to take such a drastic turn toward heroin, a drug that Em always secretly believed her dear one hated. She pictures her feeling her way up from the floor of the roots, her genetic footprint pumped through phloem with other nutrients that bind to her memory, shaping it to meet the needs of those who hold fast to the earth. What a strange image. Is that all the dead are? Bits of information to further an agenda? A chill creeps over her.

"I wanted to give her naloxone," Astrid continues, "but our emergency supply was already exhausted. I thought, with the rhizome solution, we wouldn't need as much." A fresh sob rattles her. "I'm sorry to burden you with all this. I haven't talked to anyone I can trust in months. And now I don't know what to do!" She's high-pitched and blubbering now, far from the physician's demeanor she started with. "Did you know you were pregnant when you came in here? An unintended chemical abortion, thanks to me. And I kept the fetus! How twisted is that? I thought it would help my research, but it just sits there, telling me noth-ing, like everything else in my life."

The doctor sobs uncontrollably. It reminds Em of the last time she saw her mother; a hot flush runs through her cheeks and neck. She wants to stand up and shake the woman, to slap her across the face. Instead, she grabs Astrid's hand. Em is too weak for violence anyway.

"Astrid," Em says, "look at me." She does. "You couldn't know," Em says. "I didn't, not until it was too late. And, well, let's be honest: I don't think I'm ready to be a mom." Maybe in some other timeline, Em wouldn't have minded one with Andre after they got their shit together, but there was little use thinking about that now. "And yeah," she says, "it's weird that you kept the fetus. But it's also kind of perfect. I don't know why, but when I look out on that crazy future horizon, all I see is that little blob of tissue in a jar. I know it's not my daughter, that it won't *be* my daughter." Can you know that, though? She brushes the thought aside. "Still, the fetus is important somehow," she says. "I wish I could explain it because when I say it out loud, it sounds more bat-shit than anything else I've told you."

"Well," Astrid says, sniffling, "I'm glad it's not a total waste."

"It's not."

"How did you know it was a girl? I mean, did I—do I—tell you?"

"No. I guess it's just a mother's intuition. That's a thing, right? But not that, either." The why makes sense only now, when she is awake and trying to describe it to someone else. "It's like she spoke to me," Em says. "She borrowed someone else's image to do it, someone I used to know. Maybe she borrowed her brain, too. Or what's left of it."

"What's left of—?"

"Never mind. It's just a crazy..." Em stands up suddenly, letting go of Astrid's hand for a second, only to grab her waist when Em's legs buckle.

"What's wrong?" Astrid asks.

"Nothing," Em says. "Well, my legs, but no biggie. No, something's right. I might know how to help your sister."

24

Daughter Earth, Mother Sky

ANDRE SITS WHERE SHE left him, slack-jawed and ancient.

"So," Em says to Astrid, "You didn't tell me about him." They both face him, Em in the wheelchair, grateful for it, for once; the doctor behind her, hands tightly gripped around the push handles, her knuckles turning pale from the strain.

"You don't know? From your visions?" There is still a hardness, perhaps unintentional, when Astrid mentions Em's oracular abilities. Em does not fault her resistance. It's a wonder she could be as persuasive as she was in a single afternoon.

"He's a blind spot, yeah, which is wild because we know each other. Like, a lot. He's, uh—well...."

"The father?" Astrid says. It takes her a moment, but her mouth twists in a mangled "O" once she realizes how glaring an omission to her confessions Andre might be. "Oh, Emma. Oh, I'm so sorry, I—"

"My name's Em. What happened to him?" Now, her voice is hard. Intentionally.

"I didn't do this," she points to Andre. Em looks up at Astrid's hand, accusing it with a glare. Astrid stops pointing. "He was dumped outside the main entrance," she continues. "Literally dumped: we heard a thud and a skid of tires, and the orderlies ran out to attend to him. He should have been sent to an ER. Hell, so should have my sister."

"So, what? He was like this when he was dumped?" The last word hangs heavy on her tongue. Dumped. Just a hunk of trash, an old, once lovely velvet chaise longue chucked into the landfill. She is furious that she is about to cry, which only brings it on faster.

"Yes," Astrid says. "We found him like this. I don't know what's wrong with him."

"I do," Em says. "Someone gave him your special recipe."

"But that's impossible," Astrid says. "We have strict security protocols surrounding the rhizome solution and its synthetics, and besides, none of the trials ever had side effects like this."

"Uh-huh. Weren't we just talking about how you probably have spies in your midst? One of your chemists could have tinkered with the formula, maybe sent some out into the wild."

"Maybe." Astrid lets go of the wheelchair. She approaches Andre and reaches out a hand again, this time as if she wants to comfort him, but she stops short and looks back at Em, then at the door behind them. "You don't think—the guard, my old friend, Raymond—"

"I think," Em says through a weary sigh that belies her age, "that anything is possible in this hellhole you call a hometown."

Astrid laughs a brief, involuntary effusion, more like a hiccup. "Oh my god," she says. "It is a hell hole, isn't it? Just a cyclone of shit."

Now Em laughs. After a moment, she wipes the tears from her cheeks. Nothing to be done now. Nowhere but forward.

Astrid asks, "What now?"

"So. My beau is practically catatonic. And all those women, your sister included, can't wake up. What makes me unique? I don't know how special I really am. Maybe it was a little easier for me, but maybe that's just because I had someone down in the muck with me who could pull me up. Someone who gave me a reason not to just live my highlight reel on repeat."

"Is that what you experienced in your coma?"

"More or less. Something in the rhizome solution wants to hold on tight like a complex defense mechanism. It latches onto a powerful memory and stretches it, surrounding you until that's all you know. I think I barely got out because I had a guide. The guide gave me a purpose."

"So, what? We enroll the comatose patients in humanitarian work?"

"If only. No, I think it has to be personal. Something world-shattering. Let's test it out."

Em wheels herself closer to Andre and takes a moment to ponder him and what they are to each other. He is a late addition to her life but also not. Everything from before that final needle prick feels like an epic, a tale recanted over generations that is as much about establishing a cultural legacy as it retells history. Their romance, though brief, was for the ages. She has a faint hope that he will be revived. Less of a hope that he will continue to be a part of her life. She is built for other things now.

Em lifts herself carefully onto the bed beside him. She whispers into his ear. "This is goodbye, I'm afraid, my love. I guess I'm the girl who's supposed to know what happens, but I don't know what happens to you. It's not fair—you could have had a life, kicked the drug dealing to the curb, been someone. I believe you would have if I hadn't been there to...." She chokes down a sob. "Anyway, something good did come out of us. Something worth fighting for. Even if I kind of fucked it up." Though she is not certain Andre will hear her, she is terrified to tell him. After a few deep breaths, she does.

Andre stirs. His breathing grows deep and ragged. He does not turn his head, still staring at the wall or whatever specter haunts him, but his eyes widen and scan the room. He is searching. Em feels his large, rough hand drift into her lap. He finds one of her hands and manages to grip them after a few shaky attempts. He closes his eyes. He sighs. The sigh has resonance to it as if he is singing. When they were dirt poor in the camper van, he sometimes sang to her. His pitch was awful, but she liked his deep voice filling the van. She would lie on his chest and let the vibrations of his singing run through her. She leans her head against his chest now. Andre knows his role. This time, he hums in a low, wavering key, like a mantric syllable. Andre chants a message of peace and understanding. Though she tries, Em can't hold back a sob; her tears flow freely. He has given her more than she thought she needed.

She wraps her arms around him and gives him one last lingering embrace. Then she stands and turns to Astrid with a gentle nod.

"Did it work?" Astrid asks. "He still seems...." She waggles a hand.

"Yeah," Em says, resisting the urge to look back at him. "Who knows what extra evil they added to the mix he got? I wasn't sure what to expect. But he did respond. That's more than I got from him earlier."

"Yes. That's the most I've heard from him, too," Astrid says.

"I bet your sister will do better. And if she doesn't, a little dish to a coma patient won't do any harm. Let's go."

"What, now?" Astrid looks warily at Andre.

"When else?" Em says. "Look, I know I'm a little wobbly and that you're going to object, but we need to get out of here as soon as possible. I was going to escape and leave you to fend for yourself, but I know now that you're a victim, too. Well, mostly. And we need to bring your sister awake if we can help with it. And the fetus you thankfully kept in a jar, even if you didn't know why. We need that, too."

Astrid cries, "What about all the other patients? And your-your beau?"

"His name's Andre," Em says. "And he's not mine. Not any-more."

"But we can't just leave them behind!"

"We'll come back for them, and soon. They'll be OK for a while. But you, me, and your sister are in immediate danger. If we can manage to wake her up, it's only going to get worse, but I doubt Raymond will just let us walk out the door with her on a stretcher, either. I don't think the folks who brought her in want her to be telling any tales."

"It's worse than you might think," Astrid says. "Raymond stands guard over her room all day, every day. I've never seen him take a break. He lets me tend to her, but only after I answer his questions just right. It's like he's turned into a machine." Astrid makes a purse out of her mouth, and her left eyebrow shoots up. Em remembers her sister doing the same that day in the Dog. It is a thinking face, not one born out of wariness but of pure curiosity.

"You have something," Em says.

Astrid nods. "I know Raymond pretty well. If he was injected with a solution like Andre was, maybe I could say something that would shake the zombie out of him. Even if it's just long enough for us to run our experiment."

"It's worth a try," Em says. "Lead the way."

"First things first," Astrid says. "You can't go in looking like a patient. Raymond won't allow it. I guess your prediction that you'd be my assistant is coming true."

"Not quite how I imagined it," Em says, "but yeah."

"Can you wheel yourself? It won't do to have you leaning on me, either."

"Sure. My arms work just fine."

"Good. Let's get you dressed for the part."

Astrid leads them to a supply room near the entrance to Ward A. She snips Em's hospital tag off with a pair of shears and hands her a lab coat, scrub bottoms, and an elastic hair band. "Put these on, and pull your hair back," Astrid says. "Do you need a place to change?"

"Nah," Em says, "I'm not modest." The doctor still turns her back out of politeness as Em changes.

"You'll want to put on some of this, too." Astrid hands her lipstick and eyeliner from her lab coat pocket.

Em says, "I don't wear makeup."

"You need to look older," Astrid says. "I know you've had a hard life already, but you're still a teenager, and with how thin you are, you look like you're only 12."

"Is it that obvious I'm a teenager? I thought the whole oracle thing might age me a little."

"My dear," Astrid says, uncapping the eyeliner, "you take yourself much too seriously to be anything else. Close your eyes. I'll help you put it on."

After the makeup, Astrid hands her an ID badge with the word "VISITOR" written in large block letters. "You can be my new intern," Astrid suggests. "Hopefully, Raymond hasn't been monitoring the security cameras."

They move back down the ward corridor, Astrid slowing her pace to allow Em to get used to pushing herself in the wheelchair. The doctor's eyes are still puffy from the crying, but she is much calmer now that they have a plan.

They turn right, down a dim corridor opposite Astrid's office, then right again, into a small, narrow alcove so poorly lit that Em might have missed it if she came this way herself. Before them stand locked double doors with the words "Access Restricted" banded across them in angry red letters. Astrid reaches for a key card.

"Why does the clinic have a place like this?" Em asks. "It feels like spy shit."

"I don't know," Astrid says. "Except for the specifications I gave the investor, I had no input into the clinic's design. After I stabilized Lexi, Raymond insisted we bring her here. I knew about the space but had never needed to use it before."

"Lexi," Em says, "That's your sister's name?"

"You never learned her name?"

"It never came up."

"Sure, sure. It's short for Alexis."

"Of course it is," Em says, as though her heart-stopping hotness was not enough. She had to go and have a sexy name, too. "Anyway," she continues, "It feels designed to keep people hidden. Important people. Or dangerous ones."

"Yes," Astrid says. "You might be right. Shall we?"

Astrid swipes the key card through a reader on the wall, and the doors open inward. They enter a squat corridor with two more doors to their left and right. In front of the right door sits an ashen man dressed in coveralls and a tattered homburg. He turns his head to them slowly and stolidly, rising carefully from his chair without breaking eye contact. His height is intimidating, especially from Em's vantage in the wheelchair, and his idle hostility is like a fully charged battery ready to deploy.

"Whaddayouneed?" Raymond grumbles as they approach. "She's resting."

"She's always resting," Astrid says. "I've come to give her another round of treatment."

"And this one?" He nods to Em. "No other patients in the room. The boss said so."

"She's not a patient," Astrid says. "She's my new intern. And since when do you assume all people who use wheelchairs are patients, Raymond? Did you forget about your cousin?"

Raymond winces; Astrid glances at Em. Her comment appears to cause only a tiny chink in the armor, but perhaps a stronger push will do more.

"Why do you need help with the treatment?" Raymond says. "You never did before."

"It's a new kind of treatment," Astrid says. "It requires an extra set of hands."

"I'll help you," Raymond says. It is not a suggestion.

"No, Raymond," Astrid says. "It requires an extra set of *steady* hands."

"Quit calling me Raymond. I'm Mr. Skinner to you. And my hands are fine."

"Sure. Your hands are fine for slinging fish into a barrel. But I seem to recall you fumbling to get my bra off when we were 16."

The ego shot is more powerful: Skinner's eyes roll back in his head, then skit from Astrid to Em, to the ceiling, then down to his hands, which tremor for a moment before he tucks them into the pockets of his coveralls.

No gruff comebacks this time; he is on the edge. Astrid gives him the final shove. "You came here at the recommendation of my investor, Mr. Skinner, and that's all it was: a recommendation. I chose to take you on because you're like family. What would my father say if he saw you trying to bully me like this? What would Jill say?"

Raymond spasms this time, his body jolting against the door. "Jill? Is she—?" Briefly, his face softens, and his eyes regain the clarity and spark Astrid remembers when they were teenagers. She sees the boy she once played hooky with, who asked her, under the bleachers, if they could kiss. She had consented to a lot with Raymond—the bra fumbling felt like harmless play—but she took kissing seriously: kissing meant more. Astrid knew he was a good one when she turned him down because, though he looked a little crestfallen, he shrugged and said, "I guess I haven't found my soul mate yet." He was right. He would meet her five years later, after Astrid had gone to college and nearly forgotten about the sweet boy who did not pressure her, by then surrounded by a teeming sea of opportunistic boys pretending to be men.

Raymond spasms again, and the glassy look returns. Still, she appears to have gotten through to him. "Ten minutes," he grunts. He stands away from the door.

Once the door closes behind them, Em whispers, "What was that about? Who's Jill?"

"Jill is his wife. I heard rumors that Raymond went missing, but when he showed up here for work, I figured he must have just gone on an out-of-town bender for a week and not told anyone. I wouldn't blame him since he and half the town were laid off when the cannery closed, but it would also be strange for him to leave Jill for that long and not say anything. Now I'm starting to think he hasn't been home for a long time."

This room is smaller and has lower ceilings than the one Em and Andre are assigned to, but it is still a larger space than a single comatose patient requires. One hospital bed in the corner sits an oversized recliner flanked by two IV stands. Reading material lies nearby on a small end table. There is no natural lighting, only an overhead light and a lamp that hangs over the recliner, and the walls are painted a forest green that Em's mother would rail against, claiming that the dark shade is unnecessarily stifling. No color choice could remove the suffo-cating sensation Em feels. Her crush, breathing shallow, eyes unnaturally sunken, does not belong in this room. Em can feel

Lexi's presence like a gloom in her heart, tendrils wrapping around her ventricles, holding her heart hostage until Lexi, too, can feel release. A breath for a breath.

"All right," Em says, "we're at nine minutes and counting. Time to work your magic."

Astrid approaches the bed. Though she has been in this room several times in the past few weeks and has administered care to her sister without hesitation, now she is gun-shy, turning toward Em for reassurance. "I don't know what to say."

"You knew what to say to Raymond," Em says. "I'm sure you know what your sister needs to hear." Em wheels backward a few feet and gives the doctor a quiet appraisal. "It seems to me," she says, "that you're afraid to tell her."

"You know," Astrid says, looking not at Em but at her sister's wan and uncomprehending face.

"And she doesn't," Em says. "Now might be the time to tell her."

Astrid kneels beside her sister. A hair clasp has come loose from the long braid running down her shoulder. Astrid rubs the clasp between her thumb and forefinger like you might with a good luck charm. "Oh, Lex," she whispers. "What have we gotten ourselves into?" She turns to Em and says, "This won't be easy."

"That's good," Em says. "I think that's part of it. The harder the news is, the better the chance of success. Like a shock to the system."

"Why didn't you need a shock?"

Em considers the question. "I think I did. Remember how I said my daughter spoke to me through someone I used to know?

Well, that person is not just someone I knew; they're also dead. They were kind of down there with me."

At first, Astrid doesn't understand. Then, her face opens in quiet wonder. "A ghost woke you up?"

"Yes," Em says. "I mean, no. Kind of. More like a chemical footprint. One you can read, like a DNA sequence."

Astrid nods again. The last vestiges of her disbelief are disintegrating, and with them, any hesitation to act. She leans into her sister's ear and tells her secret.

"Lex," she says, "if you can hear me, I have some difficult news. This isn't how I hoped to tell you, but we have no choice. Remember how Dad used to tell you that Ramon— that Mom fucked off to a tropical island with some himbo floozy? She fucked off, all right, but she only got as far as Portland."

"Five minutes!" Raymond barks from behind the door.

"I hate to rush this," Em says, "but I think you need to cut to the chase."

"Lex," Astrid whispers, so close to her sister's ear that her lips graze the lobes as she speaks, "our mother, Ramona Niequist, was a junkie. She overdosed in a heroin den in an abandoned warehouse outside of Portland a month after running off with her dealer. Portland PD called Dad a week later to confirm her identity. He barely recognized her, but she still wore the locket he gave her for their tenth wedding anniversary, the same locket he gave me that I keep close every day as a reminder. And as a warning. Even though the locket was made of solid gold, I guess she didn't have it in her to hock it. I'd like to believe she still loved him—if only she'd been able to love herself a little more."

The secret hangs in the quiet of the room, dancing to the steady rhythm of the monitors. Goose flesh runs down Em's neck and arms. Though she has heard this story in alternate paths, hearing it again is no less haunting. With just a few more missteps, she thinks, that could have been me.

Lexi does not move. Her breathing remains steady and slow. Astrid stands and turns to Em with a devastated look. "We tried," she says, her voice trembling. "I guess—"

A sharp gasp causes Astrid to turn back to the hospital bed. Lexi's entire body arches, then slumps back down. Her eyes flutter open. She turns to look at them. Em and Astrid stagger backward. Astrid catches the edge of the IV cart next to the bed with a flailing hand, causing it topple and clatter to the floor. They stand there, shaking, trying to understand what they see.

Lexi stares at them, alert and curious, wondering, with that half-cocked look of hers, what could have spooked them. Once a pale blue, her eyes have turned into a vibrant patchwork of colors.

If you were to look at them long enough, you would swear that the colors were moving. Like the turn of a kaleidoscope.

25

Josephine

LIKE WAKING FROM A nightmare, Jonathan typically returns from the ethereal veil the dead cast over him after they are finished recanting the moment of their demise. This time, however, he rises from Victor's body like a cartoon ghost, hovering near the tall ceiling of the grand dining room. The reel keeps rolling, but it's unclear who now runs the projector.

A mist settles over his arm, which he expects to be cold since the vapors the dead are composed of often are. This one, however, feels like rejuvenating summer rain. He looks at his arm, surprised to find that it is his, that he has returned to his body—after a fashion. His skin and clothes are shimmery and translucent. The mist, the tip of which forms a hand caressing his wrist, is made of the same material he is.

Jonathan looks behind him. Floating by his side is the form of an older woman who, like him, shines brilliantly and is only partially there. He recognizes the woman's face: age has not diminished her high forehead or fine, tapered nose. The eyes are all wrong, though; they should be hazel, but hers are like a pair of brocades set with jewels of many colors.

"Josephine?" he says.

"Yes, dear boy," Josephine says. "It is a pleasure to finally make your acquaintance."

"Am I—am I dead?" he asks. "Are you?"

"No," she says. "And again, no. Though I could see why you might think that. Seekers spend most of their lives surrounded by shimmery remnants of people who have given their bodies to the earth. You would have no reason to suspect I am anything else."

"No," Jonathan says. "But also, you're different. You're more, well, there."

Josephine laughs. "You are astute, especially for one so young."

"Am I that young? I mean, compared to you, maybe, but I'm pushing forty, and I've seen a lot."

"You are new in your role; to the Elders, that makes you but a sapling."

"The Elders?"

"The ones who made you, me, and all of this possible, dear boy." Josephine turns with a flourish, pinpoints of light pulsating as she moves. "The Elders are ancestors of the trees, and we—collectively, the Orators—are descendants of that lineage."

"Wait. Back up," Jonathan says. "How are you here? If you're alive, how are you in this vision? Are you a seeker like me?"

Josephine drifts past him, looking at the scene below. "Perhaps it would help to observe my birth—not my birth as a human, but something more."

Victor lies prone on the floor near the dining table. A gash on the crown of his head seeps dark, thick blood. The teenage Josephine lies near him, blood pooled around the cinch of her gown. Greta and Beatrice help her to her feet—only to recoil when she looks at them, confused by their fear.

"They saw what you see in my eyes now. When I later looked in a mirror, I was equally horrified. Perhaps more so. I have had many years to consider what must have happened. Victor, in his dying throes, swung a fire poker at my middle, causing me to miscarry the abomination he planted there. I think it was the miscarriage that caused my rebirth, almost like the destruction of that foreign genetic material activated another gene in me. You see, the Elders thrive on death. They thrive on life, too, but only after it has ended; the more an animal experiences during its life, the greater reward they reap from its passing. All that a barely formed fetus could provide was a catalyst for my awakening."

Jonathan asks, "What are you, then? What did that make you?"

"Like I said, I am an Orator," Josephine says. "Just like you. Though we are different cultivars of the same species. Generally speaking, Orators are born, not made. The soil surrounding our conception, and sometimes our birth, plays a critical role. But something must activate our unique genetic heritage, usually trauma." Jonathan thinks back to when his loyalties were tested at the architectural firm in Los Angeles, when a drive to provide and build wealth in a cutthroat environment overwhelmed the sense of civic duty he felt during his college years. Less trau-matic than a miscarriage, certainly, but then, his descent into the unreal was gradual.

Greta and Beatrice have recovered from the shock of their sister's transformation, and the three of them carry Victor's body out of the dining room. "What's happening now?" Jonathan asks Josephine.

"Oh, yes," she says. "I believe this moment is critical to your mission. Let's follow them."

They do not move so much as the scene shifts for them, like a cut in a film. The girls carry Victor's body to the basement stairs, sliding him down on his back without much care for the blood smearing across the steps. He still breathes faintly, but Josephine assures her sisters that she has done her research and knows he will not survive the amount of antifreeze he consumed without an antidote. Plus, there's the head wound. "But what if he does?" Bea asks as they enter the basement. "If he wakes up, he will kill us." Josie has a plan for that, too.

The girls stand before an old wardrobe in a far corner of the basement, behind boxes of moldering newspapers and other dust-caked ephemera that Grandpa Thomas collected over the years and that no one had the stomach to disturb. No one, that is, except Victor. "This is where he would take me," Josie says. "Every night for the last—well, I don't really know how many nights. Too many."

"In the wardrobe?" Bea says. She marvels at the piece of furniture, on which hangs a padlock Victor broke open long ago. She wonders why anyone would want to rape someone in such a confined space, even someone as depraved as her father. Bea shudders at the thought of her narrowly avoided fate.

"Not in the wardrobe," Josie says, "behind it." She opens the wardrobe. It is empty and as cramped inside as Beatrice feared, but there is something unusual about the back panel she struggles to make sense of. The basement is dark—at this time, it has no electric lighting—but a draft rises from it, and the back does not sit true with the sides like someone built it in a hurry and left glaring gaps. Josie raises the lantern she brought to light their way and reveals a small iron hook fastened against the panel. She lifts the hook and pushes against the wardrobe's back, which swings with ease into a cavernous room cast with gray sludges of diffuse light.

"Where are we?" Greta says as she enters the room. "It's cold in here."

"I think we might be near the foundation of the light tower," Josie says. She points to the wall to their right, which curves inward and tapers upward, like the base of a large column. The walls are made of mortared stone and so high that the lantern's light does not reach the top, making the space feel like a dungeon. One dirty dormer window near the ceiling is the only source of natural night. Along the wall opposite the tower's base lies a narrow wooden frame topped with straw and a canvas sheet. A makeshift bed. Bea wonders if the wardrobe would have been preferable.

"Oh, Josie," Bea says, "why didn't you tell us sooner?"

Josie stares at the blood stain around her waist. "It doesn't matter now," she says. "We're safe."

"What do we do with that?" Greta asks, pointing to Victor's body.

"The bed isn't really a bed," Josie says. "It's a chest." She scoops up the straw inside the canvas, covered in dark stains, reeking of evil and putrefaction, and lifts the top of the chest. Inside are several old service rifles, likely from the Great War, that Josie removes and sets on the floor. "We'll put the body in here. It gets damp," she says, "but it is also cold year-round. No one knows this is here except us, and nobody comes to this part of the basement anyway. Even if the body starts to smell, people will probably just think a loose cat died."

Bea asks again, "What if he wakes up?"

"He won't," Josie says. "But just in case..." She lifts a padlock from the folds of her dress.

The two Orators watch the girls remove Victor's shirt and shoes, lift the body into the chest, and secure it with the lock. The elder Josephine tells Jonathan, "There you are, dear boy: a mystery solved. We took the clothing up to the cliffside and made it appear like he jumped. Our mother never questioned it—I imagine she was happy to be rid of him. Anyway, the remnants wanted you to see this. I'm not sure why. They did not know the details; they couldn't because no one who knows has died yet. That is why they called me, to fill in the gaps."

Jonathan stares in wonder at the apparition beside him, apparently still alive but here with him now in the world of the dead. He thought he could no longer be surprised, but it seemed this was his life now: one surprise after another.

Josephine says, "Can I tell you another secret before I go? You seem to be the curious type, and the remnants trust you more than any other seeker I have known."

"Of course," Jonathan says.

"You've heard about my brother David's old girl Natalie, yes? I thought you might want the record set straight since her remnant can be a bit—well, unreliable, just like Natalie was when she was alive. She may have led you to believe that she gave birth to a daughter, to little Susan. That poor spirit gets so confused sometimes. That is impossible, even though Natalie had the child when she was sixteen. Susan is my daughter, you see. With Victor gone, I left the lighthouse, met a nice boy a few years later, and got pregnant at a reasonable age—well, reasonable for the time, anyway. My little family stayed close to the lighthouse, mostly to help with David's caretaking after our mother died. As David grew, I saw warning signs that he was going down the same path his father and grandfather had traveled. I wanted to break the lighthouse's cycle of misery, and I figured my eldest daughter might be the key. When she was old enough, I sent her to live at the lighthouse—with my constant supervision on the sidelines, of course—to learn what it took to be a lighthouse keeper. Women keepers were very rare, but David was not up for the job. All he seemed to enjoy was bullying others. It's a shame Susan didn't get the chance because despite having to deal with her petulant uncle and Rebecca's horrifying death, she had come to love the lighthouse and enjoyed the work."

As Josephine speaks, Jonathan feels his dread melt. The bubblegum breath, which has become like a smoker's patina on the tongue, immediately dissolves: Natalie has released her hold on him. And yet he must know more, perhaps because it is his nature, perhaps because it's just what seekers do—never at ease with being at ease. "What happened to the child Natalie did have? Forgive me, but it just seems odd that you didn't mention anything about it."

"Yes, of course you would want to know that," Josephine says, reading his thoughts. "I did not mention anything because I know very little. Natalie gave birth to a boy. After she died, David wanted nothing to do with the child, and though it may sound horrible, I wanted nothing to do with him, either. As you know, boys have been bad luck for the lighthouse. So, we gave him up for foster care just like Natalie had been. God knows what happened to him after that."

Jonathan asks, "Did she name the boy?"

"She did," Josephine says. "Natalie was keen on the classics in school, Sophocles and Ovid and the like. I'm sure she conveyed that to you. Greek mythology seemed to make sense to her more than the modern world did. She named the boy Aries, presumably after the constellation."

"Aries? Like the ram?"

"The same. I always thought it was an odd choice because the boy wasn't born under that sign. I've wondered if she meant the Greek god of war, Ares, instead. One of the few times I visited before she died, I overheard Natalie cooing at the baby, referring to him in the sweetest voice possible: 'My little ruiner; my quiet destruction.' I feel a chill every time I think about it."

Jonathan feels a chill as well. The dread has crept back for different reasons. Much that he has wondered about now makes more sense, but this revelation only raises more questions.

Josephine's apparition looks dull, the pinpoints of light fading. She sighs and says, "Now, dear boy, I must rest. This process takes a lot out of me, and I am no longer a young woman. You should rest, too. The sun is starting to rise."

"Wait! I still have so many questions. Why is any of this happening? What do the Elders want from us? And how did you get here? You say we are the same, but I can't pop inside living people's heads. At least, I don't think I can."

"Very well," Josephine says, "but I must keep it brief. Honestly, I know very little about what the Elders want from us. Everything I know about them comes from the remnants; they only tell me what I need to know. But I can tell you more about how we differ. As a seeker, you are an investigator, gathering clues and making connections. It's not enough that you can communicate, after a fashion, with the remnants. You were chosen because you are always looking for answers."

"Was I really chosen?"

"You were, but maybe not in the way most people think of it. Let's just say you have a genetic predisposition." She gives Jonathan a wry smile. "That being said, you are unique for a seeker and come from a powerful genetic heritage. Most seekers don't have a tell."

"A tell?"

"Your eyes, dear boy. Don't think I didn't notice. They are not quite as vivid as mine, to be sure, but those storm clouds in your irises are exceptionally rare. If your genes had expressed themselves differently, you might have become an oracle."

"'Oracle?' There's another type? I might need to start taking notes."

Josephine laughs. "I'm glad you can find humor in all this because the role of an Orator is often thankless work. There are very few oracles among us; several human generations will often pass without one being born. Just like the famous Oracle of Delphi—yes, she was one of us—they are fortune tellers. They can also be dangerous because with the ability to foresee many possible futures comes rash impulsiveness. Without proper guidance, they frequently become gamblers, addicts, and criminals. Their lives are often tragically short. The remnants have seen that tendency in you, too, though it appears you are on the mend. I hope, for your sake, that it sticks." Jonathan agrees. "But I'm getting ahead of myself," she continues. "You wanted to know about me. There have been many names for my kind since we serve many functions. The remnants have called us diplomats, bridge builders, and beacons, to name a few. My favorite, by far, though, is 'healer.' We healers bring the Orators together in times of crisis. We tap deep into the suffering of others, and by finding common ground in the collective consciousness, we can do a great deal to ease that suffering. I have even heard rumors that a self-aware piece of us remains after we return to the earth so that we may continue healing those we have left behind. If it's true, I'll send you a signal when my time comes."

"That's incredible," Jonathan says. "Your work seems much more important than mine."

"Hardly! I rely on the collective for answers; without that, I can't ease people's suffering. I have found my role very rewarding but also exhausting. Which is why I must leave you. I hope you, too, can rest soon, though I fear your companion may make that difficult. Farewell."

As Josephine disappears, so does he. Jonathan turns into a thousand grains of sand slipping through the apex of an hourglass. As the last grain falls, he finds himself back in the lighthouse's ruined kitchen, bathed in pale morning light.

26

Runaways

EM THOUGHT IT WAS impossible to crush any harder over the hot blond who kept appearing in her life and leaving her less than useless. Now that the girl is essentially Fiona reborn, Em wonders if it's better to spare herself the embarrassment and plunge the empty syringe on the floor into both her eyes.

Lexi speaks and only makes things worse. "Hey, I know you!" she says. "You served us breakfast at the Sleeping Black Dog once. I always remember new faces. What are you doing here? Where is here, anyway?"

"I, uh...helping," Em says. That is all she can manage. She points vaguely behind her toward Astrid, who steps closer to the bed.

"Lex, honey," Astrid says, "you've been in a coma. Also, I don't want to alarm you, but something very strange has happened to your eyes." Astrid hands her an inspection mirror. Lexi jumps in surprise, but her shock is brief. Mostly, she appears fascinated. "Cool," she says. "That explains a lot."

Em says, "Wait, what?"

"What's going on in there?" Skinner bellows from outside the room. "Who are you talking to?"

Astrid says, "Lex, we don't have much time. We—"

"—Because of Raymond!" Lexi says like she just remembered something important. "He pointed a gun at me and another boy tied me up—I thought he was so nice—and then they stuck a needle in my arm and things got really weird for a while. The other boy was just a jerk, but it's not Raymond's fault. He has roots in his brain."

Astrid and Em say together: "Roots?!"

"All right; I'm coming in there!" The door flies open, and Skinner strides in, scanning the three of them sullenly. He points at Lexi: "Why is she awake?"

Astrid and Em say nothing, inching away from him. Lexi, however, slides off the bed and approaches Raymond on shaky legs. "Raymond," she says, "I'm awake like you said. You can address me directly."

As she walks backward, Em bumps into something against the wall. A large, rounded thing, heavy and cold to the touch.

Raymond cocks his head at the small woman in the hospital gown, who, despite barely being able to stand, appears to have retained none of the fear she carried for him the last time she was awake. "You were never supposed to wake up!" he says. He intends to sound forceful and commanding, just like the instructions say, but it is more like a desperate plea. He can't stop looking at her eyes and bends down to look closer. "What did they do to you?" he asks, not chidingly, only with wonder.

"It's okay, Ray," Lexi says. Her voice has deepened. She caresses his cheek and kisses him gently on the lips. "I'm here for you now," she says.

"Jill?" Raymond says. "Oh, Jill, I've missed you so much. I—"

A harsh clang resounds over Skinner's head, and he crumples to the floor; Lexi falls with him. Rather than being dragged down by Raymond, she appears to have lost consciousness.

"Did you hit her?" Astrid asks. Em holds a bed pan over her head, poised to strike again if Raymond should scramble to his feet.

"No," Em says. "I wasn't even close. What the hell just happened?"

"Your guess is as good as mine," Astrid says. "Well, no; your guess is probably better, so I'm completely clueless." She looks down at her sister. "We can't risk waiting for either of them to wake up," she says. "Can you walk?"

Em takes a few shaky steps. "Barely," she says.

"Well, you're still faster than Lexi is, and I doubt I can carry her far." She lifts Lexi into the wheelchair, which takes several minutes, even with Em's feeble help.

They walk down the main corridor of Ward A, Astrid leading and pushing Lexi, Em doing everything she can to keep up. She pauses at an intersection in the corridor. "Need a break?" Astrid asks, struggling to mask her impatience.

"No," Em says. "My daughter's remains are that way." She points to her left, down the intersecting hallway. "I need to take them with me."

Astrid sighs in exasperation. "Fine," she says. "I know where they are. Stay here with Lexi."

A thousand years reside in each breath Em takes waiting for Lexi's return. She feels the waves of possibility, like the crest of a tsunami, rising around her on all sides. A howl resounds at the end of the corridor. Lexi awakens, gasping, looking at

Em with alarm and knowing the purpose. A few doors back, Andre emerges from his room, scanning the corridor in shuffling befuddlement before registering Em's face and calling her name. Skinner turns a corner, brandishing a handgun. These events vibrate like a chorus, each part harmonizing the other. Almost too late, Em realizes that what she sees are not possibilities but the present playing out in an absurd orchestration.

A shot rings out; the world splinters. Em feels the bullet pierce her chest and send her toppling to the ground. She sees Astrid sprint from the side corridor seconds before, wrestling with Skinner only to be shot herself, the jarred fetus in her hands shattering from the impact of the bullet as it burrows through her ribcage. She sees Lexi rise and calmly walk to her fate, the side of her face exploding. Ultimately, though, none of what she sees comes to pass. Her little blind spot has intervened again, making her doubt everything she knows. He lies convulsing at her feet, his mouth filling with blood. She hears someone screaming Andre's name and only realizes later, once the shock has worn off, that it is her own voice.

Slender fingers made for playing the piano wrap around Em's wrist and cause a jolt to run through her. Lexi holds her fast, placing her other hand over the gushing wound on Andre's throat. She looks up at Skinner, and Em, like a guided marionette, is compelled to do the same. For a brief moment, he is poised to shoot again. Then, he clutches his throat, his back arches, and he falls to the ground.

The next thing Em remembers, she is sitting in the back seat of a beat-up Toyota. Astrid drives away from the clinic and onto 101 with impressive speed. Em's daughter lies against her mother's belly, secured by a seatbelt. The jar that holds her remains offers a soothing coolness, just like the locket did after it was returned to its proper place.

Lexi sits in the back beside Em, holding her hand. It's a touch traumatic for a first date, but she'll take it.

27

Silverbeard

FOR THE FIRST TIME in years, Jonathan is poised to act without hesitation. He almost forgets Drake is with him, as though he entered the ruined lighthouse on his own, not under the threat of a centuries-old megalomaniac.

Drake asks what he sees, but Jonathan ignores him, walking out of the kitchen to the unfinished part of the basement, an area he has largely ignored. Several decades of dust and a strong smell of mold cover everything, but otherwise, the space looks and feels just like it would have to Josephine and her sisters over half a century ago. The place reeks of self-destruction and the worst inclinations of humankind. It's no wonder no one has wanted to disturb it.

After scanning the foundation wall and lifting a moldering canvas tarp off a mound near the back, he finds the wardrobe. Drake stands behind him, eager, breathing heavily. Jonathan lifts the broken padlock, which is now so rusted that it nearly breaks in his hand. He opens the door, releases the latch on the side, and enters Victor McKinley's unintended crypt.

Drake shines his flashlight onto the far reaches of the ceiling, whistling in awe at the height. "I never would have guessed this was here," he says. "Is this the way down?"

"Maybe," Jonathan says. "I didn't see that part. We need to look around."

"What about in there?" Drake points to an old gun case against the wall.

"No," Jonathan says. "We don't want to look in there."

"Oh?" Drake smirks at him. "Some family secret hidden there, I take it? A foul deed the dead wanted you to unearth?"

"Not exactly," Jonathan says. "Although..." Could it be that simple? There is little more in the room than a few stubby candles on the floor, some stray tufts of straw, and the gun case. A hidden button or lever disguised in the stonework is unlikely, the stuff of movies. Sometimes, the best hiding place is one in plain sight.

Jonathan moves the gun case away from the wall. Long ago, perhaps the spirits compelled Papa McKinley to lay a chest over that very spot without him fully understanding why in a room otherwise bare and with no apparent purpose. He examines the floor for clues. The space the moved gun case reveals is a shade lighter than the rest of the floor, but otherwise, he sees nothing to suggest a way down.

"That's the spot," Drake says. "It must be."

"Do you see something I don't?" Jonathan says. "It's solid stone. No sign of a seam or anything."

"Are you sure it's solid?" Before Jonathan can stop him, Drake fires his revolver at the floor. Jonathan leaps backward, expecting a ricochet, but instead, the floor shatters in several pieces, leaving a dark hole about the size of a fist.

Jonathan picks up one of the shards. "It's clay," he says. "Terracotta, like they use for tiles. How did you know?"

"I saw the trick in a Spanish mausoleum," Drake says. "They used a composite to make the ceramic look like solid granite, then family members in the know would return at night to break the seal and take back the precious items entombed with their loved ones."

"'Family members'? Or opportunists like yourself?"

"Comme çi, comme ça," Drake says. He hands Jonathan a crowbar. "Let's finish the job."

"You could have started with this," Jonathan says of the crowbar, "and not risked shooting my foot off."

"Bah! No one ever wants me to shoot things," Drake says. "And don't start getting cheeky with me, Mr. Davies. Don't forget who is in charge."

Despite the threat of the gun, Jonathan no longer feels like he is the one without power. He thinks of Josephine and her sisters, who played the long game to bring down the family tyrant whose bones now lie unceremoniously beside him. Without giving it much thought, Jonathan has started to soften his approach to his resident monster. Unlike many despots, he prefers teasing to fawning, which he does not trust. Expressing anger means he has not done enough to break you. Drake still gives off no telling shimmer, but Jonathan feels a powerful empathy that he suspects Josephine passed along. Even if the feeling is fleeting, it gives him hope.

A few confident crowbar swings reveal a stone staircase descending into darkness. As they descend with Jonathan in the lead, Drake squeals with delight. "This is old, my friend," he says. "I can tell by the striations in the stone. No industrial process made these steps. Here is your fabled Indian burial ground."

"I thought you said that was bullshit."

"Theatrics, Mr. Davies; nothing more. I, too, understand the importance the Yurok placed on this site. A few members of our kind can still be found in their elder generations, though they waste their time with stewardship, refusing to acknowledge the coming revolution."

"Let me guess: a bunch of zombies are going to spring from this hole?"

"It's funny you should mention zombies...." Drake catches himself. The banter is working, but the old emissary hasn't survived this long by being quick to trust. "No," he continues, "nothing as dramatic as that. Humans always want to blame an outside force for their downfall. Yes, there is a lot of concentrated energy here, and the trees are responsible for it, but the human brain interprets the message as a clarion of violence—not the way it is intended, as a warning and an offer of escape. The energy is intensifying in hot spots like this one around the world. Base human nature is winning out. It is only a matter of time before they all destroy themselves."

The stairs meander in a gentle series of curves into the earth. Adobe walls meet to form a low archway with a wooden crossbeam supported by posts every 30 feet or so. It's a wonder this passageway didn't collapse years ago from an earthquake, but the Yurok, if they built it, took great care to make it last. This is unlike any native burial site Jonathan has encountered. Hidden, but with the intent of accessibility, almost like the buried passageways in the tombs of the Egyptian pharaohs.

"You mentioned an 'offer of help,'" Jonathan says. "What are the trees offering?"

"Untold wealth," Drake says, "and a safe space to enjoy it."

"The Kingdom of Lemuria, I take it?"

"Very perceptive, my friend." Jonathan can hear the smile in his voice. "It's true that we are physically far from the approximate location of Telos, the last bastion of the Lemurians, but that hardly matters. You see, there is no physical way to reach the city. The Lemurians did away with that long ago. However, I have it on good authority that beneath this sad, unremarkable town lies a portal to one of the wealthiest, most self-sustaining places in the world, a place with no natural predators that demands to have the natural order reset."

Is this it? Has he let his guard down entirely? A little twinge from Josephine tells Jonathan no. Drake still presents the best version of himself: the one that rallies armies before the cause is known.

The stone-slab stairway descends for so long that Jonathan starts questioning what year it is, let alone what day. When it ends abruptly and the path levels out, he stumbles, taking in a mouthful of dirt. The ground is hard and gritty under him. Drake shines his flashlight across the space, revealing an expansive cave that extends farther than his light can touch, the ceiling reaching several hundred feet above them. There are no stalactites or stalagmites here, no sign of water runoff at all. The cave is perfectly rounded and seemingly endless, like a giant, petrified wormhole.

Drake takes a few steps into the cave before turning to Jonathan, who has not moved. There's a wondrous look on Jonathan's face, and while the cave is impressive, Drake suspects he is missing something. "What is it, boy?" Drake asks, as though talking to a pet. "What do you see?"

This is what Jonathan sees: far in the distance lie rippling fields of wildflowers dressed in ribbons of scarlet and folds of royal purple, a gentle stream bisecting them, its waters reflecting tiny flecks of green and gold that shimmer like jewels. Vines climb the walls and drape from the ceiling, and though there is no discernible breeze, they sway in an undulating rhythm, curling and retracting, each holding hundreds of tiny, pulsating suckers. Jonathan no longer requires his flashlight: the suckers emit a warm light that bathes the cavern, casting the landscape in perpetual dusk.

He can hear Drake but not see him, and his voice sounds like it comes from outside the cave. Jonathan ignores his questions. He attempts to walk forward, but his shoes are trapped in a heavy bog. He steps out of them; thankfully, the bog has no taste for his unshod feet. Unburdened, he approaches the stream. He is very thirsty, having brought no water, so he cups his hands and drinks. The water is cool and sweet. He looks at his reflection in the water but does not see his face; instead, there is a long, furry muzzle, five eyes of many colors set in a tapered crown—two on each side, one in the center—and a pair of antlers, wound like corkscrews, with silvery velvet molting around the edges.

Jonathan looks up, and the animal in the reflection stands in the stream above him: a broad-chested beast with six spindly legs and two small tufts of fur near the hindquarters that look like vestigial wings.

"You're a sight, aren't ya?" Jonathan says to the beast. "What's your name?"

The beast does not appear to understand the question.

"I'll call you Silverbeard," he offers. "How does that sound?"

The beast snorts in assent or possibly frustration, but either way, they signal with a shake of their antlers that the time for pleasantries is over. Turning, Silverbeard walks upstream and farther into the cave, signaling Jonathan to follow.

As he wades through the stream, the chatty part of Jonathan's brain—the part responsible for far too much suffering—starts to catch up. This is a new kind of strange, the chatty part says. Why aren't we running from it like we've run from everything else? He looks at the beast and wonders why none of this bothers him anymore. Well, not none. All the bloodshed, incest, and clinical depression still rest uneasy in his stomach. But what he sees in the cave recalls a distant memory, one his brain's chattiness dismissed as myth.

He was eight and on a school field trip to Sequoia National Park. His school group was on a leisurely guided hike through the Giant Forest, and he, a pensive child, had fallen behind, in awe of trees as wide as his little house in El Centro. Shortly after crossing a bridge where the trail met Little Deer Creek, Jonathan felt an urge—it felt like someone drumming fingers along his collarbone—to veer off the path. The drumming sensation stopped as he approached the base of one of the sequoias not far from the creek. There he found a sockeye salmon, still alive and gasping for breath, amongst the sequoia's massive roots. They had recently studied salmon in school—particularly California's prevalent variety, the Chinook—and Jonathan had been so taken with the fish, with the great lengths they took to return, after years of solemn migration, to spawn in the same place they hatched, that he had continued studying them outside the classroom.

That is how he knew the sockeye on sight and how strange it was to find it there. Even for the Chinook, the forest was beyond its most southerly range; sockeye was not found in the wild outside Alaska. Moreover, the distance from the sequoia's roots to the creek, just a few steps for Jonathan, would have been a tremendous leap for the salmon unless some spiteful bear or park ranger had plucked it from the water and tossed it there. Such an ecological mystery seemed worthy of sharing with their guide, so Jonathan rushed up the trail to grab her and divert her carefully orchestrated hike, only to result in a severe scolding from the guide and his teacher when they returned to nothing more than a tangle of partially unearthed sequoia roots. At first, he wondered if he had returned to the wrong tree or if the salmon had somehow flopped back to the creek. After a few years, the chatty brain wiped it aside.

Now, he takes this improbable beast in stride. Nature is a salve that runs rough against everything he has built in his professional life. Trees provide shade. Rocks cover against damp and excessive heat. Tubers sprout from the earth and feed you. What else might you need?

The creek deepens as he walks, rising to his waist. The vines above him give way to an orange sherbet sky. He hears as a whisper, "This way, is it?" Drake's voice snags him like a lure to a Chinook's cheek. It's a labor, but he persists.

The creek widens into a delta. The water is to Jonathan's chest. Dragonflies gather under an expansive custard sky. Silverbeard climbs into one of the dragonflies, the fly's legs slipping neatly over the beast's like socks. Now no longer earthbound, Silverbeard hovers above him, speeding ahead. Jonathan examines the remaining dragonflies, wondering how something so small could stretch and accommodate his body, let alone the hulking beast. At a loss, he watches Silverbeard fly beyond his vision.

Lotuses churn around him. The dragonflies' drones put him into a trance. This swale captures loss as effectively as it does water: the abandoned reside here, laying in wait for the tide's retreat.

One of the lotus flowers starts to bloom. He swims to it and finds his wife sleeping inside, her body curled atop the flower's broad stigma. She is no bigger than a mouse, but it is unquestionably Mina, down to the lip-biting in her sleep.

Mina stirs and sits up. Her face is worn by pitiless age and far too much worry. She squirms in loose monochromatic clothes and picks at the hospital bracelet on her wrist. She looks in his direction but does not see him. Still, she knows he is there.

"Why do you keep bothering me?" she asks. "You're the reason I'm here, you know."

Jonathan asks Mina where she is, but she doesn't respond. Perhaps she can't hear him, either.

"I should be over you," Mina continues. "I should be done with it. But no: you left me a little reminder, one as thankless and reckless as you were. Except, I can't just let her go. I tried—in all the worst ways—but she's right. It's not about me; it's about us. I can't give up on us. If she's dead, though...." The look on her face is pure devastation.

Jonathan shouts, "She's not dead!" At first, it feels like an empty declaration, all the emptier because she can't hear him. Then, he realizes the outburst may be more for himself than his estranged wife. A daughter. A fresh wave of self-loathing catches him off guard. His cowardice affected more than one life, and he is instantly protective, desperate for the worst possible outcome of his absence to be untrue. After he gets over himself, though, he has the sense he's right; she is still alive. In the last few weeks, it's been challenging to distinguish between the material and the ephemeral. This revelation casts some aspects in a new light: the fog transporting him to his youth, Mina guiding his drug-addled brain to safety. He is sure he saw his daughter recently, that she is here in town, as implausible as that might seem.

Is she safe, though? Of course not. No one in the Cove is safe.

28

— • —

Jill's Gambit

A RUSTED PICKUP TRUCK appears in the rearview mirror of the Toyota and starts to grow. Dad's old truck, now Lexi's. Behind the wheel is a man in a tattered homburg, his expression primed for violence.

"Skinner," Astrid says, glancing behind her. "We're in trouble."

They pass the sign for Rabbit Warren Cove that pleads visitors to return. Astrid had half a mind to zip through town without stopping and drive, drive, drive, as far as Mendocino if they could make it, where Aunt Rita would, she had no doubt, take them in without question. They'll be lucky if they make it to the center of town.

A sharp crack reverberates behind them, followed by the ping of a ricochet against metal. Em ducks instinctively. "Dr. Niequist," she says, "you might want to floor it. Lexi, get down!"

Lexi sits upright, still clutching Em's hand with a dreamy look. She peers out the rear window, more curious than fearful. "Oh, right: gunshots. Those are dangerous," she says. She slides down slowly like she is settling down for a nap.

"What the fuck is wrong with her?" Astrid screams.

"She's—I don't know, she's like me," Em says, "but also, not."

"I just had to go and cultivate a bunch of mutants, didn't I?" Astrid channels her fear and frustration and presses hard on the accelerator. She makes a hard right turn at the first side street in town, sending the Toyota into a fishtail and knocking over a mailbox before Lexi can right it.

"Woohoo, Astrid!" Em says. "Kicking ass and taking names."

Lexi says in a hushed voice, "Triddy, can you please not make so much noise? I'm trying to hide."

Skinner follows, quickly regaining lost ground. Astrid turns down another block, then another, zig-zagging through the Cove's narrow streets, causing folks to leap back in alarm. She turns another corner onto the town's main drag, the town square just a few blocks away. She draws near a crowd gathering in the rain outside the square. Skinner no longer appears in the rearview.

Astrid slows down; Em and Lexi sit back up. Lexi cocks her head and points, saying, "Police: what are they doing here?"

The people huddled across the street from the Sleeping Black Dog are not the typical county law enforcement. Still, they wear the associated vestments: long slicker coats the color of sand, emblemed stetsons with plastic rain covers, walkie-talkies, and, on a few of them, conspicuous bulges across their chests. They form a semi-circle around Selma, who waves her arms in pursuit of a tale. Other townsfolk have gathered at this curious sight: pointing, glaring, gossiping, wondering.

"They look like park police or maybe tribal police," Astrid says. "Why would they—?"

There's a sickening crunch of metal and a squeal of tires, and the Toyota spins, lurching to a halt with its nose pointed toward opposing traffic. The crowd around the square jumps in surprise, but no one moves. Then, the shots ring out, and they scatter.

The Toyota's rear window shatters. Then, the windshield takes a hit. Astrid and the girls crouch on the floor. Skinner bellows, "Get out! Get out, or I'll tear this car apart and get you out." Then, a woman screams, "Federal agents! Hands on the ground, now!"

Em peeks out the passenger window. Three of the law enforcement officers have their guns drawn and pointed toward Skinner, who has no desire to comply with their commands. Em sees a few possible ways forward. Skinner goes down in a rain of bullets in many of the paths, sometimes taking out the officers with him, sometimes taking out civilians; then, there are a few where he turns the gun against himself, his face twisted with internal struggle. There is so much potential for violence that, at first, Em sees no peaceful alternative. But she knows better. There are always alternatives.

She closes her eyes and takes a deep breath. There is another way out she can influence in the right circumstances. Em climbs to the other side of the car and looks out to the street, where a few bystanders still crouch, rendered immobile by fear. One woman, however, stands firm; frightened, yes, but unwilling to run or cower. Em stares at the woman until she catches her eye. She squints at the girl in the car, confused but curious. Em gives her a grave, knowing look, one that says, "I know what you're thinking." She nods.

"Raymond?" The woman calls out. Her voice sounds eerily similar to what Lexi assumed with him at the clinic. She says his name as a question as much as a plea: are you still the man I married?

Just like before, Skinner melts. He lowers his gun and turns toward her, and this time, seeing her face, no amount of mind-addling poison can wrest back its hold on him. "Jill!" he cries out, tears streaming, matching her own, just as the police rush forward and handcuff his arms behind his back. "Oh, honey. I don't know where I went or what happened to me. I've missed you so much."

"I missed you, too, Raymond." Jill watches nervously as they escort him to a dark, unmarked vehicle.

"She doesn't know what to think," Lexi says, causing Em to jump. Lexi kneels so close that her breath sends prickles down Em's spine.

"I—I kind of guessed that," Em says, restraining herself, once again, from either kissing or punching this highly volatile woman.

"I always liked Jill. She was good to her boys and made the most out of very little. Now, I like her even more. She's worn despair her whole life like most people wear socks. She had a feeling something like this would happen. Not because Raymond gave her a reason. She's just been waiting for the day when it would all unravel. But she still took care of her family and made sure I was okay, knowing how hard it can be to grow up without parents. That's worth saving."

Astrid looks back at her sister after realizing the chaos is over. She asks, "Lex, why aren't you more freaked out about what's happened to you? It's like you read minds now, and—whatever else happened back at the clinic, plus your eyes?! But you act like it's no big deal."

Lexi considers the question. "I guess it was scary at first," she says. "But it's been so long now, I don't give it much thought. It's what I am."

"What you are? You've been like this for less than an hour!"

"Oh! You mean, waking up. Yes, that was surprising. And scary." She gives Astrid a lingering look. The spectra of her irises drift like fast-moving clouds. "Triddy," she continues, "I thought I was dead. I thought my body was eaten by the roots long ago. I've had decades to realize what I am. This girl knows what I'm talking about." She wraps a conciliatory arm around Em's neck. "These bodies are young," she says, "but the rest is as old as the forest around us."

29

— · —

Morningtide

THE SPIRAL STAIRCASE FEELS endless. It reminds Pete of his time in Europe when he climbed to the top of Cologne Cathedral: hundreds of steps leading to the top of the spire, their winding construction, lit every few feet by narrow windows, giving the climber the sense of an endless journey, a corkscrew reaching beyond the fault of time. Why would anyone create the equivalent effect burrowing far into the earth, with no light or lofty views to behold?

The stairs end in a deep well of darkness. Water trickles high above him, the gentle cascade echoing a concerto across the vast emptiness. He stands above a column as wide and tall as the base of an old redwood, the grandfather of the forest; tunnels branch and twist around him in every direction, their walls etched with hundreds of tiny indentations, like natural cuneiform, each tunnel extolling a different epic.

It must be the chemo talking. Why does he suddenly feel so poetic? These are natural caves: no evidence suggests an ancient civilization left a story for him to find. Water does impressive and often surprising things to stone, given enough time. But the thought won't leave him, even as he turns in a circle until he is dizzy, trying to decide which way to go. Which great tale will lead him to Jonathan and Drake?

He chooses one of the broader passages, one wide and straight enough to drive a car through. The cuneiform in this passage suggests to him a myth filled with many trials, akin to a subterranean Odyssey. Each trial is a branch from the passage. Some are pocket crevices Pete can see the end of; others extend beyond the headlamp's reach. They tempt him to explore. No time for that. There is always time, they seem to say. There is nothing but time.

Pete presses on. The passage narrows and gently rises, caus-ing him to stoop. He feels the urge to keep going, to crawl if he must, but he doubts he will find them through here. The cave narrows to a conical point, the etchings intensifying here, radiating from the tip like the gaping sockets of many fine teeth. It's unlike any rock formation he has seen, like a tightly closed sphincter cast in stone. An absurd thought comes to him: what if I can cause the sphincter to open? If I brush my hand over the etchings just right, surely, it will yield to me.

The idea is so tantalizing, so real, that he starts to shimmy closer to the end of the tunnel. Voices echo through the walls; surely, the ancestors are encouraging him that this is the right way through. Then, he recognizes the voices. One voice, really.

"No, no, no! This can't be it. We've been here before. There is nothing, nothing here." Petulant, wheedling, and demanding: it can only be Drake. The voice seems to come from behind him, down a different tunnel. Pete turns around. He gets the sense that he narrowly avoided being buried alive.

He tries a narrower tunnel, one barely wide enough to accommodate him without stooping. The etchings are less dense here but close enough that he can run his hand along them as he walks. Here he reads a simpler myth. Three old men from warring tribes have lost their sons and feel they have nothing to live for. One walks to the west until he is exhausted. He finds a tree with a long root, one as long as the tree is tall, extending to the east. He circles the tree and finds three more roots of the same size: one extending to the west, one to the north, and one to the south. The tree has four long branches in each of the four directions as well, plus one broad branch that extends far into the sky and one wide root at the base that extends straight down into the earth. The air surrounding the tree is calm, and the old man finds peace, no longer feeling sorrow for his dead sons. The second old man arrives from the south in tears, also lamenting the loss of his sons, as does the third old man, arriving from the west. As the three of them talk, the spirit of the tree soothes them, and they start to feel a reason to live again. They resolve to return to their tribes to extend a message of peace so that no more children must die. The three tribes gather around the tree's roots, smoke together in peace, and agree they should come together as one.

Pete heard this myth many years ago while visiting a friend in Toronto. It is part of the Potawatomi tradition, telling how the Ojibwe, Potawatomi, and Ottawa became one people. Is it merely the power of suggestion that evokes this myth? The column he descended into and the tunnels radiating from it suggest an inverse formation of the single colossal root plunging into the earth and the roots extending in the four directions, as though a fossil casing of the great tree spirit was left behind. But it seems like more than a suggestion. Pete feels the tradition under his fingernails. He senses many generations reciting it and can see their faces in vivid detail, including, but not limited to, his dear Ottawa friend. There is something with him in these tunnels: something powerful, and likely not caring a whiff about his personal agenda.

The rock beneath his fingers exhales, breathing relief down the tunnel—the ancestors are satisfied. Pete follows the breeze. It carries him down a left-hand fork, then a right-hand one, then to a steeply pitched corridor winding deeper into the earth: a geological Slip-N-Slide. The ancestors whisper in the breeze, "Fear not! This is the way." Why should he believe them now when he didn't before? Yet down he goes, squeezing his way through the narrow column, nearly hyperventilating halfway, until he reaches a chamber as tall as a redwood, as wide as it is tall and farther than his light will reach in either direction. A shallow pool covers much of the chamber floor, and in the center of the pool, waist-deep in water, kneels an ashen man, his headlamp shining like a miniature Fresnel lens across the expanse, which roils much more than you'd expect a cave pool to do. Foam collects and subsides around the ashen man, who pays it no mind: he is improbably still. The chamber smells of brine and seaweed. The tide chatters, somewhere unseen, in a whispered exchange.

Another man stands above the water line, roughly parallel to Pete, and paces in a circle. Pete douses his headlamp before the pacer has a chance to notice him. "Idiot. Idiot!" he shouts. "Why would I think this would work?" Drake's rage is unmistakable.

30

The Bitter Glass

"Idiot!" Drake's voice breaks through the golden vault above, sounding like thunder. A crack forms in the distance; fissures of midnight spread in all directions.

"You need to go," Mina says. "Go and leave me alone." She curls her body tight against the lotus stigma, and in response, the flower closes.

Go where? Forward, he suspects, but Jonathan was never a strong swimmer. He wades beyond the lotus flowers into the open water that quickly rises past his neck. He starts to swim. After a few strokes, he can no longer touch the bottom and grows tired. Though some of him knows this must all be an illusion, something the Elders conjured up to test his resolve, he wonders if his brain could tell the difference if he drowns in this virtual lake.

His head dips briefly below the water, causing him to sputter; then he starts to rise, coming out of the water on a stiff, irides-cent hull. Silverbeard has returned, bringing another dragonfly as large as a two-seater propeller plane. Jonathan sits on the dragonfly's back. Silverbeard takes off, and the plane-like drag-onfly follows, barely allowing Jonathan to catch his grip.

They approach a massive tree growing from the center of the lake. Jonathan knows this tree, though it has more than quadrupled in size since last he saw it. When he was three years old, his parents took him to renew their vows in a fig orchard in Calexico, the same orchard where they had met and fallen in love, knowing even then, as teenagers with a bare understanding of the world, that nothing could part them. His only memory of the ceremony was of his mother, who shone like an angel, the unblemished afternoon sunlight dappling through the folds of lace in her wedding gown and forming a corona around her voluminous, flowing curls. Beyond that, his attention was attuned to a nearby fig tree, and he must have found a moment to toddle away while everyone else was engaged in the ceremony because, at some point, he found himself alone at the base of the tree.

Well, not entirely alone. Up in the fig tree, he would meet his guardian, one that, as an adult, he dismissed as an imaginary friend. In a way, his fate was sealed right then.

The crack in the sky he saw in the distance hovers over the tree, lashing violet streaks of lightning. As they draw closer, the wind picks up, and Drake's hook, already tenuous, snaps free; Jonathan no longer hears the old emissary's prattling. A dense column of fog forms around the tree just as they land on a branch near the outer rim. Silverbeard alights for only a moment. The beast lowers their antlers with a gentle nod to the tree's center, then flies back into the haze, Jonathan's dragonfly following.

"Guess I'm all alone, then," he says to himself. Or maybe he's talking to the tree, seeking a rebuttal. He would not be surprised if the tree responded. When he was three, this old fig tree felt vast, as large as a city, each branch a neighborhood. It feels that way to him now. The branch he stands on is a wide avenue, and though he sees no tree people strolling down it, he hears voices all around him. Some voices are suspicious of his arrival—others are welcoming—but the majority seem confused, as perplexed by their presence here as Jonathan is. The squirrels are helpful, though. They descend from the upper branches and are the size of horses. One bends low to give Jonathan a ride, then sprints farther into the tree, leaving him scrambling, once again, to grab a tuft of fur to hang on.

Descending a few more branches, Jonathan and the squirrel reach the trunk. It towers above them like a keep. A scar in the trunk twice as tall as Jonathan pulsates with red light. He descends from the squirrel, who refuses to walk closer to the pulsating scar. He feels heat rising from it as he draws closer—a searing, unbearable heat. He reaches out his hand, and his flesh starts to crackle. He touches the scar, and the meat of his fingers chars and melts off the bone. For a moment, the pain is all he can think about. Then, he is holding his restored palm up to a gentle fire, its warmth soothing against the storm raging outside.

His guardian sits with him by the fire. They are in a dark, intimate room: gnarled roots, like the exposed ones Jonathan remembers climbing as a toddler, form the walls, meeting high above them like a pair of steepled hands, then branching ele-gantly near the floor to create the hearth. The wind lashes the boughs outside and a chill creeps in, but the fire wards it off. The guardian wears simple brown robes of coarse muslin and smokes a long pipe. Hawk-nosed and thin-lipped, the guardian admires him with one keen but weary eye—there is only a deep, scarred gash where the other might have been. Hair that shines like star sapphires descends in a braid to the floor.

"I know you," Jonathan says. "You helped me when I was young. You had a name once."

"We still do," the guardian says. "We have many names, as many as there are people to give them. You called us Neela."

"'Neela.' Yes, that sounds right. But who is 'we?' I don't remember you being, you know, plural."

"'We' is a difficult concept for a human sprout to understand when there is still so much 'me' to consider. We did not want to confuse you. Now that you are a sapling, this representation seems the most effective."

"A sapling? Not a full-grown tree?"

"Forest children do not grow into mature trees. They don't live long enough." Neela pulls from their pipe, exhaling a long, purple plume that curls like the roots above them.

"That's what I am, then?" Jonathan says. "A forest child?"

Neela nods so slightly that he initially mistakes the move for a tic.

"Have I always been one?" He continues.

Neela says, "You have, in fact, only recently become one. There must always be some potential for it to happen, and your genes ensure that, but it is not a guarantee for even the most predisposed. In general, there are two ways for the genes to express themselves. One is through daily exposure to the Elders. That rarely happens anymore. In the current epoch, it most often occurs through trauma to the human vessel."

"Well, my body has been through a lot of trauma. I keep hearing about these 'Elders.' What are they?"

"We are the Elders. However, we are also just a representation. We are the great-grandparents of the trees. The genes that distinguish you from your animal flesh come from us. We once reached as tall as the mountains. Now we are dispersed through the earth, feeding our grandchildren."

"You have a strange way of speaking."

"We are merely borrowing your words. And yes, we agree: it's all too florid, trying and failing to name the unnameable. Very strange."

"Why bother, then? Why try to communicate with humans at all?"

Neela pulls from the pipe again. This time, the smoke is green and becomes a dragon that dances as the guardian talks. "You were more open as a sprout," they say. "It's a pity you could not activate sooner. So doubtful now."

Jonathan says, "I'm just trying to understand what's going on."

"No. You are dismissive. You are in such a hurry to explain everything that you do not bother to experience it." The smoke-dragon encircles Jonathan, wrapping its claws around his neck. Neela rises and walks away from the fire into impenetrable darkness. When he tries to follow Neela, Jonathan finds that the dragon has pinned him.

"Wait!" He cries out. "I'll behave. I—I'm just worried about my friends. And all the women who have been abducted. And I don't know what Drake will do to me, what he can do, while I'm here. I don't care much for my own well-being, but I'm worried that my friends are in danger and that I won't be there to help stop something terrible from happening. And my daughter. I didn't even know she existed until today, but I think she might be close and in danger, too. I'm worried that time is running out."

Neela's face reappears, floating bodiless at the edge of the firelight. The dragon relents.

"Your concern for your friends and your daughter is misplaced," Neela says. "Some of them may return to the earth in your absence, yes, but you have no control over that; your human hubris makes you think that way. They will go when they must. But it's good to hear that you have no regard for your own well-being. To commit to your role is to move beyond concerns for the self or the body. As for your emissary companion: fear not; we are handling him. Finally, your concern surrounding the movement of the spheres is valid—it is the only concern worth considering. But you need not despair. We extended the limits of your temporal cognition—"

"—My temporal cognition?"

"—Your sense of time. Forgive us; many science minds are mulching underfoot. Your hippocampi have been sent into overdrive, causing you to sense time at a slower pace than a baseline human. Similar to the effects of *cannabis sativa*, but stronger. More focused."

"So, all of this—the lake, the tree, the creatures, you—it feels like I've been here a whole day. But you're saying...."

"Yes. When you arrived in the sacred place and we extended your perception, the sun still hid behind the mountains. It has only just now fully raised its head. Still, we must be cautious. Perhaps you gathered from the storm outside that we are in an unstable place. We designed it to prevent sentient beings from stumbling in here accidentally. The timing had to be just right.

You may not have known it, Jonathan Fig-Tree, but you have played your role exceptionally well. For that, we offer you a gift few of the living receive."

Pete loads a round into his shotgun, careful not to make too much noise. He ducks into a narrow gully just as Drake's headlamp passes over the area. Too close. Knowing Drake, Pete suspects he is armed as well. He has no desire to engage in a firefight, least of all because, in his weakened state, he doubts he will come out on top.

From the gully, Pete still has a sight line to the pool. The water surrounding Jonathan sloshes just below his chest. The crashing tide is louder, closer, all-encompassing. He suspects they have fifteen minutes at most. Pete will drag Jonathan out of there if he must. But how?

He looks to his shotgun for answers; it provides none. Selma is right yet again, which only causes Pete to chuckle: why does he ever doubt her? He must appeal to Drake's reason and intractable desire for self-preservation; otherwise, they will all meet their maker in a watery tomb.

He leaves the shotgun in the gully and feels his way down the slope to the pool. With supreme effort, he manages to enter the water with barely a splash. He wades over to Jonathan, the water already rising to his thighs. A few feet from the boy, he turns on his headlamp and calls out to Drake.

The old wolf swivels in his direction, weapon drawn. Drake wields an old service pistol—impossibly old, a Bergmann-Bayard, by Pete's estimation—which makes him wonder if Drake is bluffing or, even if not, whether the gun will fire.

"What a delight!" Drake says, gesturing to an unseen audience for affirmation. He steps to the edge of the pool. "I have the pleasure of witnessing the death of not one Davies but two."

Pete says, "We have to get out of here, Drake. We're in a tidal cave, and high tide is minutes away."

"Don't you think I know that?" To demonstrate how little the fact bothers him, Drake treads into the pool until it rises to his knees. "This dullard refuses to wake up," he continues, gesturing to Jonathan. "I'm not leaving until he reveals the portal. He knows where it is. He's playing coy with me. Thinks I'll drag him out of here at the last second. But I can find another seeker. They're a dime a dozen."

"Did you eat rocks for breakfast? I've seen him like this. He probably doesn't even know where he is."

"Of course he knows!" Drake bristles, stepping closer to them—now the water is at his waist. He waves the Bergmann-Bayard wildly above his head before leveling it at Jonathan's chest. "If you can't wake him in the next five minutes, I'll make sure he never does."

"All right," Pete says. He raises his hands in surrender. "I'm going to try to shake him awake."

"No funny business!" Drake says.

"None from you, either." Pete kneels in front of Jonathan and places his hands on his shoulders. He feels the point of the pistol at his back, itching to cut him down. "Johnny boy," he says, "if you can hear me, it's time to say goodbye to your ghosts before you become one yourself. You did good. You've done your part. Now come home."

He is at a loss for words. It at once makes sense and doesn't because nothing in his world has made sense for a long time. At least someone has finally offered an explanation.

Neither speaks for what feels like hours; the crackling fire fills the gaps of what's unsaid. Then, Jonathan says, "You don't care a whiff for human life, do you?"

"That is inaccurate," Neela says. "We care for all life. That is our primary objective and has been since the earliest days, before there were even trees. The sharks know—"

"—The sharks?"

"Oh yes. Sharks were our allies long before humans. You must stop acting so vengefully against them, and for the love of Gaia, stop tempting them by plunging yourself inside deep-water cages. They only do what sharks do. Do you see, now? Humans, at least as individuals, are the source of their destruction. We cannot predict how they will interpret the signs we leave."

The tale Neela told him was an epic that would have filled many nights in a more time-bound place. As humans began to show their mettle as great storytellers and shapers of the world around them, the Elders saw a unique opportunity. It was not the first time they had tapped into a collective animal consciousness similar to their own, but most of those sentient beings resided in the ocean, as well they should. Terrestrially bound, the Elders needed a spark of consciousness that could traverse Gaia from pole to pole, transmitting a message of harmony. From the early, hot days, they knew just how fragile the balance was and how a slight shift could cause Gaia to collapse before her due time. The Elders were the first stewards, the trees their legion, but they could not maintain their stewardship without the involvement of the mobile ones—those seeing, self-consuming, chaotic animals.

The human capacity to wonder and try to explain the world around them, to be curious about something other than their immediate needs, was what the Elders tapped into. "Over several millenniums," Neela told him, "we diffused our message into the soil, which the plants readily absorbed. And you ate the plants, eager for visions. We set up transmission nodes: huge trees, much larger than anything alive today, where humans would come to worship. You gave us many names. Yggdrasil. Ashvattha. Jianmu. The Tree of the Thunderbird and Serpent. These myths have fed our message for many years. When you returned to the earth, your memories entered the soil and reinforced this message. Because of this careful cultivation, the forest children came to be."

While all of this illuminated the unusual path Jonathan found himself on, it was only a primer to the secret Neela wished to gift him. Now, in the middle stage of the Anthropocene, the humans and, in some instances, even the forest children had turned their backs on the Elders. To combat this, the Elders shifted their tactics. "We have watched the one who calls himself Drake for many years," Neela said. "Alone, he is of minimal impact, but his profiteering is not unique. It is the backbone of Gaia's imbalance. We knew we could not fool the errant forest children with visions—they saw them every day, and what's more, many had lost faith that the visions had any meaning. So, we established a pattern. We threaded lies through generations. We are not responsible for the tendency of men to equate those lies with violence."

This was how the bloody legacy of the Pfalzgraff Lighthouse came to be. Situated near the ancient remains of one of the great trees, residents were either driven mad by the messages seeping through the soil or their true nature as nascent forest children was revealed. It was only a matter of time before Drake caught a whiff of the patterns. Soon, in his mind, they evolved into the realization of a lucrative conspiracy theory.

The effect of the Elders' meddling was not isolated to the point surrounding the lighthouse. Almost the entire span of Rabbit Warren Cove, all of it sacred historical Yurok land, was once host to one of the most prominent transmission nodes on the planet—second only to one that stood half a world away, near the center of the what today is the bustling city of Yerevan, where, for countless generations, an honored guard of forest children still holds watch over a revered, prehistoric lemon grove.

"You mentioned your daughter," Neela says. "We can assure you she is in no immediate danger. She was, but that moment has passed. Because you have been patient with us, we offer another secret. Your daughter is of our kin, a product of the influence we restored to this place. You may have forgotten, but you came here when you were still but a sapling. It's why, in part, we could draw you in so easily. You came here with the child's mother, who comes from a long and illustrious line of forest children herself, and the two of you conceived."

It was all real, then, that moment in the Sleeping Black Dog. Mina refusing to drink and quietly despairing that he would not follow suit; he did not know the whole reason until now. "She never told me," Jonathan says. "All these years, I never knew." And I never bothered to check, he thinks to himself.

Neela seems to hear his quiet regret. "There are many time-lines," they say, "but we never know which one will play out. Pondering the unrealized has limited benefits. It's best not to dwell too long on what might have been."

"If she's a forest child—if my daughter is like me, like this—what do I do?"

"You both have roles as forest children, but you are also part human." Neela leans closer to Jonathan, their one good eye evaluating him from navel to nose. "We suggest you look into what it means to be a father."

A boom of thunder shakes the tree. Jonathan looks around, alarmed, but Neela remains nonplussed, acknowledging the thunder with a nod and a puff of their pipe. Still, they say, "You must go, now. Do not hesitate. Now is the ideal time."

"But I—"

"You must trust us, Jonathan Fig-Tree. We told you this place is unstable; you will not survive if you stay. Think of where you need to be, and you will be there."

Jonathan does as Neela says. He closes his eyes and thinks about what he needs most, where his soul resides. Though the result surprises him, ultimately, it is where he needs to be.

Water rises to the nape of his neck—water smelling of the sea. The booming thunder has transformed into the crashing of waves that cascade over him. He takes in a large mouthful of seawater and sputters. He flails, reaching upward. A large, rough hand grips his shirt collar and lifts his head above the surf.

Is it night where they are now? A starless night? He wore a headlamp when they descended, but that appears to have either washed away or stopped working. The hand that lifted him raises him higher; another hand strikes him across the face, drawing blood. The saltwater mixes with the cut on his cheek and causes him to scream.

"That's how you do it!" Drake says. He pulls Jonathan within inches of his face, Drake's headlamp searing his vision. "Where is it?" he shouts. "What do you see?"

Jonathan is unsure what to say but understands that a knee-jerk response may kill him. Then, thinking about what Neela said about the Elder's deceit, he knows what to do. "Shine your headlamp over there," he says, pointing behind him near the center of the churning water. Drake does, the light shining across a small disc of rock, no wider than a dinner plate, which the rising tide will soon engulf. He could not have predicted the rock would be there, yet it was precisely where he needed it to be.

"There's a notch on that rock," Jonathan continues. "It's under the water, just out of view. Find the notch, and the portal will open."

Drake releases him, wading, then swimming across the pond, reaching the rock outcropping just as a wave crashes over it and hides it from view.

"What is he doing?!" A friendly voice, one he thought he might never hear again. The Sturgeon grabs Jonathan and drags him to dry land—what little remains in the quickly filling cave. "What did you say to him?"

Jonathan replies automatically: "I told him what he needed to hear."

It's hard to make out Pete's expression in the dark, but Jonathan can tell that panic has set in. He is the best of them, not wishing this fate even on his enemy. "Drake!" he screams. "This entire cave will be underwater in less than five minutes. We need to get out!"

"You need to get out!" They can barely hear Drake's voice over the churning tide. "Once I find this notch, it's Paradise, baby!" He shouts something unintelligible as he reaches deeper into the water; then, he screams. Is it out of delight, having found the notch? Or out of fear, as a large black wave passes over him, douses his candle, and pulls him under?

Perhaps he found what he sought. Maybe Paradise lies just below the waves.

There is, thankfully, another route from the cave than just the steep slide Pete came down through, but they almost don't make it out that way, either. By the time they reach the passage, seawater has filled it near the brim. They hold their breath and plunge, the cold searing Pete's lungs as he struggles to keep up. The light starts to fade, and he thinks, "This will do, nice and warm." The air slowly draws from his lungs, and he briefly loses consciousness before a hand grabs his wrist and pulls him from the underworld.

The light returns, now shining over him, with Jonathan's face cast in shadow underneath. His irises swirl furiously, almost like there's clockwork behind the lenses. Did they always do that?

"You're sick," Jonathan says. Behind him rises the same long column Pete encountered when he descended from the old hooch cellar. Still dark, but finally dry.

"I'm just tired, boy," Pete replies. "Nothing a long sleep won't cure."

"No. I can see it. It's like a big black cloud trying to choke you. And it's gotten bigger lately. Whatever it is won't leave."

Pete sighs. "It's cancer," he says. "And no, it won't leave. Or, when it does, it'll probably take me with it."

Jonathan stares at him, unblinking, for several seconds. He wipes his eyes with the back of his hand, then says, trembling, "I'm sorry. About Drake, and, just—"

"I know, son. But don't be sorry about that old tyrant. I'm not exactly sure what you did, but you did what I couldn't. Even if we had him arrested, I doubt I would have lived to see justice done to him. Anyway, I'm sorry, too. There's something you should know about a deal I made."

"What is it?"

There's a rustling behind them: several footfalls echo through the staircase leading to the Sleeping Black Dog. After a few whispered commands and the muted jangle of equipment, they find themselves surrounded by half a dozen tribal police officers, weapons drawn.

"They'll be lenient," Pete says. "I'm sure you will get out soon."

Beloved, gaze in thine own heart,
The holy tree is growing there;
From joy the holy branches start,
And all the trembling flowers they bear.
The changing colours of its fruit
Have dowered the stars with merry light;
The surety of its hidden root
Has planted quiet in the night[...]

W. B. Yeats, "The Two Trees"

Spring

It's one of those rare crystal-clear days in Eureka, with a sky so rich you could wear it like a robe and pass as royalty. And yes, it's unseasonably warm—the locals call it a heat wave—with half of them lamenting the effects of climate change and the other half grumbling that, just next week, it's back to soul-sapping fog again. Not so for Jonathan Roland Davies. He walks out of Sempervirens Health Facility, reaches for that rich sky, and wraps it tight around him, striding from confinement like a king.

Em and Selma are there to greet him. Though he saw his daughter only a month ago, he must suppress the urge to compare her to her mother again: carrying a few extra pounds, no doubt from Selma's hearty cooking, her hips now flare the way he remembers Mina's doing around that age.

"You're all wiry," Em says. "Did you fall prey to the jacked-prison stereotype?"

"I played a lot of basketball," he says. "I kind of had to. Got recruited to the Latin League."

"They have leagues in a psych ward? Damn. You're lucky you didn't end up at Lompoc."

"Hmpf," Selma says, crossing her arms. "That's white man's luck. You assault one of my brothers, and your punishment is three months of basketball."

"Hey," Jonathan says, "I'm half Mexican."

"Not the half that counts." Selma smiles. "I trust you've learned your lesson."

"Oh, yeah. Five months sober, and I realized just how terrible I was. If I beat someone up in a drunken rage again, Sel, you're welcome to kick my ass."

"Ooh! Me too?" Em asks, giggling.

"Sure," Jonathan says. "Let's all beat up the felon."

As promised, Pete's contact in the Interior pulled the requisite strings to reduce his sentence to a bare suggestion of what it might have been. By effectively highlighting the unique circumstances of Jonathan's "condition," he was able to keep Jonathan out of the federal system entirely, placing him under Humboldt County's attentive psychiatric care. Given the nature and location of his crimes, however, Jonathan had no hope of avoiding a felony charge.

At first, he doubted anyone other than Pete, who had been there at the sentencing, would come to visit him in prison. And even he only came once, after which the cancer took an aggressive turn, and he became too weak to stand, much less brave the rigmarole of visiting someone in a locked-down ward. Much to his surprise, the next person to see him was Lexi.

"You're probably wondering why I'm here," she said. She wore a black turtleneck, matching trousers, and black-framed sunglasses that she kept on indoors like she was trying to be Audrey Hepburn in *Breakfast at Tiffany's*. Her trademark self-assurance was still there, but it was calmer now: more direct.

"We've been through a lot together in a very short time," Jonathan says. "I could think of a few reasons."

She hesitates, unsure how to start. "Pete's dead," she says. The sunglasses now make sense. "We said goodbye to him a few days ago. I tried calling, but they wouldn't let me talk to you without submitting to a background check. I mean, I get it, but that's intense."

"It's better than a prison psych ward, for sure." His time to hesitate. The air feels too thick to breathe. "I wish I could have been there," he says.

"Yeah." Her voice starts to break. "I wish you could have been there, too." Tears slide down her cheeks, and she instinctively removes her sunglasses to dry her eyes. "Shit," she says, catching him staring. "Well, the cat's out of the bag: storytime."

Lexi tells him about the kidnapping, about being given a drug solution very similar to what she unwittingly gave him, and all the transformation and chaos that followed. "I'm surprised Pete didn't warn you. Actually, I'm not. He's not one to spill other people's secrets. Except, you know, when they deserve it."

"I know I fucked up," Jonathan says. He looks around the ward, perplexed but grateful. "I thought I would die before I ended up in a place like this. That's how my dad went. Dying, I mean, not ending up in a psych ward. He was like me, I guess. Saw shit he couldn't handle. So, I'm getting by better than he did."

Lexi offers, smiling, "With a little help from your friends?"

He smiles back. "With a lot of help. It's hard being around so much internal pain—when the meds wear off, a thick, multi-colored fog surrounds me, and I can hardly see anything—but, honestly, that's better than being on the meds. Therapy's easier, too, even though they say it should be the opposite. I've been hiding the pills lately."

"What do they have you on? Antipsychotics?"

"I don't know, probably. They won't tell me what it is."

"Oral?"

"Yes."

"Is it round and has a 'C' or an 'M' on it?"

"Yeah. An 'M,' I think."

"Yep. That's Clozapine. Not the worst but by far not the best. But I wouldn't hide the pills. You're here under legal bond, remember? If you're caught disobeying the rules, you could end up in real jail, and for much longer. Just try not to get sick. Ask for a mask and wash your hands."

"Yes, ma'am. When did you learn so much about antipsy-chotics?"

"Oh, you know, just expanding my studies." She smiles sadly, staring out the window at the low-slung houses surrounding the facility, wondering when winter's gloom will pass.

"I'm sorry," he says.

She waves the apology away and leans closer to him, whisper-ing, "You did what mattered in the end, Johnny. He's gone, and the mystery of why he trespassed on federal land was enough to get the FBI involved. Lemuria Holdings had its head cut off and is being eviscerated by the Feds as we speak."

"Gross."

"Sorry. The point is, we did it. Or, we're doing it; we're getting there. Some women are still missing, but we've already reunited several with their families or tribes—thanks, in part, to my re-cent 'enhancement.'"

With Skinner thoroughly diffused and behind bars, Lexi, Astrid, and Em returned to the clinic to grapple with the hundreds of comatose women left in Astrid's care. Standing over the battalion of beds in Ward C, Em saw an opportunity. "It's you," she said to Lexi. "Or, it could be. Think about how you connected with them all when you were asleep. How you connected with me. Do you still feel them?"

Of course she still felt them. She felt everybody, everywhere—though women more often than not, as the men's roots were, customarily, too tightly gnarled to be worth the unraveling. And since she had come to know Em as well as she knew Astrid, and in just a few heady days, feeling that she had instantly gained another sister, she needed no further prompting to know what Em had in mind.

She started with a girl who might have been no older than fifteen: younger minds were more accessible. As the roots fed her smells and textures, Lexi interpreted these into verse. She recited the deep pools of the girl's young heart back to her, reminding her what it meant to yearn. She convinced her there was more to offer the earth if she waited, if she returned to where time ran like a river. It took many hours for just that one girl and Lexi asked for a chair halfway through, but the girl awoke, frightened but grateful with Lexi's hand in hers, admiring her like a beloved friend.

The first few were grueling, causing Lexi to collapse after a week. When Astrid asked how she could help, Lexi said irritably, "I don't know—maybe you can bring the next dozen back from the dead?" Not all of Lexi's efforts went as smoothly as the first one. There was deep sadness in many of these women, traumas born long before they wound up here. Returning seemed like a daunting prospect—and each time Lexi tapped into these more entrenched experiences, the harder it was for her to return, too. She went to bed just past midnight on Friday and did not wake until Sunday.

Mercifully, they did not need Lexi's help as much after the first week. As she slept, the thirteen Lexi had helped awaken searched for their loved ones among the beds. With Em and Astrid there to coach them on what to say, six more woke up, then eight, then the original thirteen were coaching their cousins and aunts and elders, and when Lexi entered the ward again, nearly a quarter of the beds were empty. The space was alive with chatter, every head turning at the sight of her and drowning her in cheers and applause. Though she blushed deep red at the attention, after that, her cup remained filled to the brim.

A few days ago, they found another woman like Em and Lexi among the sleeping. Her name was Cinder, and she observed their efforts to wake the others with calm recognition. "I have been waiting for this moment for over 20 years," Cinder said. "I wish someone told me this is what it was instead of knocking me out."

"Did you see who knocked you out?" Em asked.

"It wasn't one of you? Well, no matter. There's a small group among the Shasta, one or two families, that still carry on the traditions of the tree people. I always felt like a tree person, but the tribal council didn't recognize our traditions, and my family lied and said that only men had ever been tree people. My three brothers journeyed into the forest, but only one came back with the special knowledge. I think even my one brother lied about his success because what I feel and know now is nothing like what he told us."

With Cinder's help, they made significant progress. The few still sleeping had no known connections with the group and were more challenging to reach. But Lexi was confident they would; it was only a matter of resources.

"There's someone you should meet," Jonathan says. "Remember Susan Nguyen? Ask her about her mother. I'll bet she can help."

Em visited him a few weeks later at Lexi's insistence. She was uncertain what she would have to say to him, but seeing his hangdog expression and those maddening eyes that she shared, she found it easy to tell him everything—from Mom's mental health struggles to her own, where she doubted her sanity, being stuck in a time loop; her heroin addiction; and the loss of two lovers and an unborn daughter within less than a year, among everything else.

He told her he was sorry; recognizing how empty and feeble those words were coming from him but not knowing what else to say, he reached across the table where they sat and offered his hand. She stared at it warily for a moment, then slowly touched his upturned palm. Neither of them felt the urge to close their grip.

"This is weird," Em said.

"Bad weird?" Jonathan said.

"No: just weird. It's like I'm reading your palm. And if I'm reading this one line right, it feels like you fell into a time loop, too."

"Yeah. I guess I did." He wondered how much she could see. "Did you know you were conceived in Rabbit Warren Cove?"

"Really? That explains why I'm in no rush to leave. But how could you know that?"

"An old childhood friend told me. I can't say why, but they would know."

He doubted she would accept his cryptic response, but after a moment, she nodded. "Maral was like that for me toward the end," she said. "She pushed me out of the loop. Told me the secrets I needed to know. But that was part of a vision. Maybe it was all in my head."

"Sorry, who's Maral?"

"Aunt Maral? Mom's sister?"

"Your mom doesn't have any sisters, just three brothers living in Chicago."

"Wait, what?" Em removed her hand. The storm in her eyes lashed streaks of purple lightning.

"When you were with Maral," Jonathan said, "did she ever talk to anyone but you? Do you remember her visiting when Mom was around?"

Em considered it; then, her face fell. "Oh my God, I'm crazier than I thought!" she said, covering her face with her hands. "I belong in here with you."

Jonathan said, "Look, I resisted at first, but I'll admit it's been a relief taking a break from seeing the dead—anything no one else sees, really. But I don't think I want that to be permanent. Not anymore. We have guardians, Em. Mine's an ancient forest witch I met when I was three. Yours seems to be an adoring aunt. I shut mine out for a long time. I don't want to do that anymore."

"I don't know if I'll see Maral again," Em said. "I don't see a future with her in it."

"Maybe you can't. Maybe she's meant to surprise you."

"I hope so," she said, sighing. "I talked to Mom, by the way."

"Oh? How-uh, how is she?"

"Fucking pissed. She still tried to get me to move to Chicago with my uncle. Practically ordered me. I reminded her that I was now 18 and no longer her problem to solve."

"Harsh."

"Yeah, maybe. Oh, and she thought you had died? That you were haunting her in the hospital?"

"I did see her in one of my visions. She told me to leave her alone. I've never seen her so sad."

"Yeah, well...." Em stared at the fluorescent light above her head, which was dimmer than the rest in the meeting room and near the end of its life, buzzing incessantly. An electric rain cloud, just for her.

"About that—"

"—I don't care. I don't care why you left or why you didn't try to contact us. That's the past. I don't care about the past."

"Sure. I won't mention it again. But, maybe when you're ready, when Mina is, too, you should ask her what happened. I'm sure she shielded you from the truth, but you're grown now, and you've been through more shit than most people go through their entire lives, so I think you can handle it. It might help."

"Okay, sure. Maybe." Em had already seen a few possible ways that conversation might go. True, there were similarities in each telling, but beyond that, they varied so widely that Em had no way of knowing if the version that played out would be even an approximation of the truth. Some were dark—darker than even her worst experiences—but she could not discount her mother's tendency to distort the truth for dramatic effect. In her darkest moments, that truth often turned to the macabre.

She had not seen the truth about Maral. At first, Em resisted it, looking back on how devastated her mother had been while she lay in the hospital that Maral couldn't come to rescue her from herself. But that memory was a lie, a version the roots had fed Em to placate and educate. Em never revealed her love of evolutionary theory to her mother, and her mother never knew the comfort of a loving sister.

And now he is here, free, climbing into the rear seat of Selma's car, and must be dealt with. Em hasn't had to deal with men in a while, unless you count the mostly harmless but slightly creepy flirting from the regulars at the Dog and AA—which she does not, since, especially now that she is taking better care of herself, that's as likely to happen on the street as anywhere else. And, yes, she walked back to Selma's exhausted from working at the bar or helping at the clinic, crumpled in Lexi's old bed, and cried for André every night for three weeks straight, so at least one man has pervaded her thoughts. Still, not needing to cater to a man's emotions has been better therapy than even Astrid could provide.

Still, it helps that she's come to know him, that her mother's understandable distortions of his character have had a chance to settle. He is at least as fucked up as she is: whether that comes from their shared genetic freakiness or his abandonment hardly matters anymore. It keeps Em from judging him too harshly, but it reminds her how tenuous their stability is.

"Lexi didn't come?" Jonathan asks as they drive away.

"She's in class," Selma says.

Em adds, "She's always in class these days."

"She went back to school?"

Em looks back at Jonathan from the front passenger seat, scrutinizing him. "She's studying to be a nurse," she says. "She didn't tell you?"

Jonathan confirms she did not, which gives Em a strange comfort. There is something between them, a hidden exchange that manifests in how they talk to her about each other; snared in the same trap, neither knows what to do about it. Em, meanwhile, knows enough about what could happen to leave her with an ick that's hard to shake. And yes, she is jealous, no less because Lexi is closer to Em's age than her father's, but that's not her true hangup. Though the paths are few and exceedingly narrow, she still hopes her parents will reunite, maybe even get back together. Em worries that her mother may fulfill her often-threatened promise if they do not and that she might relapse if that happens. She fears her dad might relapse, too, if a romance with another good woman falls apart. There are many possibilities, many paths, and far too many of them end in heartbreak. All of them, naturally, end in death—it's merely a question of how long.

At least there is Eva. Eva grounds her, if only because her future is impossible to predict.

The Cove's AA group consists of a rotating, motley crew, but they are at least well-equipped to discuss the eccentricities and ravages of opioid addiction. She started going after hearing all the trauma from the women waking up at the clinic, which left her dangling from a precipice. She keeps going because several regulars met Andre—he'd attended a few times before relapsing—and hearing fond things about him is the next best thing to having him back. They meet tonight. She asks Jonathan if he wants to go, and he responds: "I wouldn't miss it."

First, however, they must stop at Morning Star Point and pay their respects.

The light tower looks naked standing on its own, but the trees surrounding it, finally unburdened by decades of human trauma, sigh a sweet perfume of relief that tickles Em's nose. Looking wistful, Jonathan says, "The lighthouse never stood a chance, did it?"

Selma says, "Did you hope they would preserve it?"

"No, that's not it. I'm not sure how I feel about them keeping the tower, either." He looks at the base of the tower with suspicion. For once, Em wishes she had Lexi's ability to detect thoughts. "I guess," he continues, "I just wish people were better."

"I blame the lifestyle," Selma says. "Families aren't meant to live in isolation. They need community."

The community, no longer under the thrall of Drake's influence, came together in the end. As acting city council chair, Sally Davis moved quickly but not without grace. She asked Tommy Nguyen to consider whether he would be happier focusing his energy as the new CEO of the local Better Business Bureau chapter—not a role she could guarantee him, but Ms. Davis had the requisite connections to convince the board of his inherent value as a representative to his Vietnamese business peers, a small but mighty contingent of the local economy. Tommy resigned his council position soon after, and it took very little convincing for Deidre Apfelbaum, who had just turned 18, to run unopposed as his replacement. With Deidre on the council, Sally felt she had struck the right balance for compromise. The council voted to preserve what little of the Pfalzgraff Lighthouse they could and plant a grove to honor the significance the Point had to the Yurok people, as well as honoring those who served, often tragically, to keep passing ships out of harm. This is what they have come to see. The grove of young madrones glows warmly in the afternoon light. At its center lies a low granite disc, a subtle monument surrounded by benches. Besides the Yurok people and the McKinleys, the memorial lists the names of several residents who championed the importance of this space and the cultural heritage of Rabbit Warren Cove in general. Peter "The Sturgeon" Davies is at the top of that list.

"He didn't want to be buried," Selma says, wiping away tears. "He is with the sea now, as it should be. This is the closest thing we have to a headstone."

That night, the rec center basement lacks its usual musk, and the coffee is at least hot, if still barely drinkable. Spring tends to bring out the best in the space and the people who gather here every Tuesday at 6 pm. Turnout is strong. Several people recognize Jonathan and greet him cordially enough, but most of the warmth is reserved for Em. Without fully realizing it, just by being her misfit self, she has wormed her way into the hearts of her fellow wayward souls—especially the women, who are in the minority, but only just.

After a brief discussion, the group invites Jonathan to share his experience in lockup. He hesitates, but once he explains the strangeness of involuntary medical care and receives several commiserative nods, he opens up in ways that surprise even him. "I see things other people don't," he says. "I tried to pretend that wasn't true for a long time. Drinking was the only way I knew to cope with it because it was always about running away. And you know the craziest part? I didn't end up in a mental institution because I see things. I was there because of the drinking. I've spent a lot of time worrying that one part of my brain would cause people harm, but by denying that part, by fearing what others would think if they found out, I let the other part, the more destructive but socially acceptable part, do all the ruining for me." He glances at Em, giving her a sad smile.

Dinner at Selma's, and Lexi makes a rare appearance, along with Astrid, who finally feels like she can take a night off now that all but two women in her care are awake and reunited with loved ones. Tonight, they dine on a rabbit freshly snared by a Hoopa auntie, which Lexi bemoans, saying, "How can you eat the poor bunny?" She fills her plate with acorn bread and fiddlehead ferns instead.

Selma parries, "I remember you skinning a rabbit at a Girl Scout retreat. Damn near killed the scout leader from shock."

Jonathan looks confused by the exchange, so Em explains, "Lexi is a vegetarian now."

"Yep," Lexi confirms. "These days, it's too painful not to be. But you knew that already, right, Johnny?"

"I did. But the rabbit skinning is news. That's badass."

After dinner, Jonathan excuses himself, stepping outside for a moment. When they first arrived, crossing the raised walkway to the house caused him to swoon. He later revealed that he had been to this house before. "I designed it, in fact," he said. "I completely forgot I did. I think that's why I first came up here, to see the finished results." Since he was very young, he had always wanted to live inside a tree. When he found a client with the hollowed remains of a redwood on their property, he jumped at the opportunity. He wants to see how well his design has weathered the seasons.

When he returns, he moves like he is walking underwater. Everyone else has retired to the front room to play cribbage, with Em already laying quiet waste. "No fair!" Lexi cries. "You cheat; you can see all the possible moves." She notices Jonathan staring at her a little too intently. "What's up, Johnny?" she says. "See a ghost?"

His usual retort is "every damn day," but he remains silent. Em turns to look at him. "Something wrong, daddy-o?"

"I just got off the phone with your mother," he says.

"Oh? How'd that go?" She tries not to sound too hopeful.

"I don't know. OK? Terrible? She was angry, then just confused. Like she didn't believe it could be me." He looks at Lexi again. "She wants to see me," he says.

Em asks, "Do you want to see her?"

"I do. That's why I called."

He sits. All eyes are on him.

"I think I'm going to move back to Los Angeles for a while."

"How long is 'a while'?" Lexi asks.

"Maybe a few months? However long Mina will have me, or until we're done working through the last twenty years of—well, you know. So, I guess whichever comes first."

Astrid says, "Are you sure that's wise? You were just released. A change in environment might affect your recovery."

Lexi's expression is unreadable—nothing new there. But then she looks at Em, her adopted kid sister, for whom no love is lost, and smiles. Her multicolored irises swirl and pulse, almost like she is winking.

"I'm proud of you, Johnny," Lexi says. "Better late than never, right? When you return—because let's face it, there's no leaving us—I have a job lined up for you."

"Thanks," Jonathan says. "That means a lot."

"Pump the brakes on that enthusiasm, dude. Don't you want to know what the job is? You're the new town investigator! If you want to be, of course. When Pete left me the business, I thought I would just pick up where he left off, but I don't think I have the stomach for it anymore. Plus, you'll have excellent partners besides my lovely self." She gestures to her sisters. Astrid looks as surprised by the revelation as Jonathan. Em tries to look surprised but doubts it's convincing; she knew the offer was likely.

"Lex," Astrid says, "I have the clinic to run."

"And Selma needs my help at the bar," Em says, though after Selma raises an eyebrow at her, she adds, "Who am I kidding? I have nothing else going on."

"Great!" Lexi says. "Triddy, what are you going to do when the lease at the clinic ends next month? I'm sure I can help wake the last two women before then."

"This is a long shot," Jonathan says, "but is one of the women White, middle-aged, and shows signs of cocaine abuse?"

"How did you know?" Astrid says.

"Oh my god," Lexi says. "The woman you hooked up with! The one who stole your car!"

Jonathan nods. "I mean, I'd prefer never to see her again, but I can come by in the morning and tell you what I know if it helps."

"See!" Lexi says. "You're already doing the job. Triddy, we could really use your medical skills at the firm. You can be a Watson to Johnny's Holmes."

"Watson, huh?" Astrid says. "I could live with that."

"Ooh, who am I?" Em asks.

"Moriarty," Selma offers. Em throws her cribbage peg at Selma, and everyone laughs.

"All right, all right," Jonathan says. "Until then. I look forward to it." The scenery has shifted, and with it comes new possibilities. Em knows there are a few paths where her father may never return to Rabbit Warren Cove, or if he does, only to visit. None of them, however, play out better than the paths where he returns to make a home.

Jonathan stays at Selma's that night. He settles into the front-room couch and falls dead asleep before anyone else leaves or goes to bed. Em offers to clean up from dinner, and Astrid and Lexi say their goodbyes. Grateful for a break from kitchen duty, Selma goes to bed early. The house is quiet enough that Em can hear fog horns across the cove, yellowlegs chattering along the lagoons, sea breezes rustling the trees: pure bliss.

Feeling tender and impulsive, she drapes a blanket over Jonathan after cleaning up and brushes a lock of hair dangling from his forehead. She should hate him, but mostly, she is fascinated. She watches him sleep, viewing the many ways his life might play out—the parts that involve her, at least—like alternate endings to a film. Some are tragic, some are infuriating, but none are boring. How can she disavow him when so much possibility lies ahead?

She steps outside, descending the wraparound stairs that cling to the hollowed redwood. The yard surrounding the tree is unkempt and rarely visited; Selma readily admits that yard work is her least favorite chore. Em wouldn't have it any other way. She circles the base of the redwood, finding the spot the porch lights cannot reach. When Jonathan stepped out to call her mother, she wondered if he came to check out this spot: if he came to revisit an architectural easter egg he planted all those years ago or if the remnants of the previous owners clued him into the secret. But perhaps even he doesn't know about it. It could be much older—before the land knew anything of ownership.

She no longer needs a flashlight to find the whorl: three gentle turns, like a caress, around the outer edge, and the heat of her palm against the center do the trick. Eva led her to this place on her first free night from the clinic. Em knew what would happen, but the first pop of the bark and the furl of the trunk, like a rising stage curtain, surprised and delighted her all the same.

With the spring rains abating, Eva needs more attention. Still but a sapling, she has, all the same, grown more than Em predicted she would after nearly three months. Her branches, though confined, are strong, and her diminutive crown—still that of a princess, not yet a queen—now rises above Em's head. She takes the watering can next to Eva's base and sprinkles her roots. Moonlight shines through the opening in the redwood, making the sprinkling water look like liquid silver. Buds have started to form on the branches; they shine like diamonds. Eva seems to thrive in the moonlight. Em sometimes wonders if she prefers it to the sun.

It was strange to bury her daughter's fetal remains in the ground, no less because she did it with a rusty spade she found in Selma's shed. But that was always the unwavering path: so dominant in her consciousness, once the threat of the parasite ruling Skinner's brain had passed, that when she finally did it, she felt like she was floating above herself, watching it play out as a passive observer. A woman, whose body was eighteen but whose mind was dislodged from time, interned the only daughter she would ever know, placed the lemon seed from an ancient Armenian grove beside her, and wrapped them both in soil, leaving the elements and a mother's constant guard to tend to her rebirth.

What will happen 300 hundred years from now, when Eva has outgrown the hollowed redwood and split Selma's home apart? Will civilization have collapsed? Will the pride of humanity finally be chastened? She cannot see beyond the confines of her finite human body, but there is plenty to fear in the future she can see: many possible tragedies and horrors, some of which may come very soon. She suddenly misses her mother with an ache that feels like starvation—or the tantalizing pull of the needle, which could still be her undoing. She hopes that Jonathan will convince her to come to Rabbit Warren Cove and leave the trauma of Los Angeles; Em will not go to her when so much depends on this little sapling. Though she has many fears, she finds in this moment that the hate she carried so long for her mother, for anyone, has melted away.

It is hard to hate when you're a mother yourself.